To my friend, Jesse Wood

Published by The Head & The Hand Press, 2014

Printed in the United States of America

PUBLISHER'S NOTE
This is a work of fiction. Names, characters, places, and incidents are either the product of the author's imagination or are used fictitiously, and any resemblance to actual persons living or dead, business establishments, events, or locales, is entirely coincidental.

Original cover design by Claire Margheim

Cover photograph by Amanda Ritter

ISBN: 978-0-9893125-6-1

Library of Congress Control Number: 2014945526

The Head & The Hand Press
Philadelphia, Pennsylvania
www.theheadandthehand.com

10 9 8 7 6 5 4 3 2 1

BLOWIN' IT

a novel by
winifred
ausley

1

The figures were huddled together, ten or so, looking shadowy in front of the long, low building made of sandy bricks. This is a quiet, older neighborhood. People gathered together at dusk in these numbers exuded menace here. Peeking from behind a kitchen curtain, the scene appeared quite conspiratorial (hushed talk, hoods up, the glowing tip of a cigarette and someone hunkered on haunches). There was silent nodding, spitting on the ground. One of the hooded indiscriminately kicked at small, kickable things near his feet. And that crouching man, what was he up to? No doubt diagramming a sinister plan in the dirt. But then altogether they burst into good-natured laughter. They dispersed, chuckling amongst themselves.

"Alright, y'all," one man announced, peeling away from the crew. He leaned back on his left leg and arced his tall, half-full can of sweet tea towards a blue recycling bin some yards away. "Kobe," he said, calling his fadeaway shot.

Silence. Wide eyes watched the glossy cylinder twirl through the dusk. Centrifugal force kept the drink contained as it spun round. He gave it enough oomph to reach the target. It was going to be close. Not a few of the onlookers held their breath and imagined digital numbers racing fast to zero, the sound of a buzzer. The aluminum clanged off the lip and jarred some unseen glass. Tea shot up as the can kinked into the shape of a '7' and landed on the sidewalk. Before anyone could jeer, a burly marmalade tom spirited out from behind the bin and into the street. An old diesel Benz slammed on its brakes. It rocked like a small pleasure boat docked at the marina while the shocks squeaked like motel mattress springs. The car turned its headlights on and crept forward.

The asphalt was unstained. The cat was nowhere in sight. Nobody picked up the can.

On the calendar (and in the hearts and minds of many), it was an important day—Election Day. A big decision was being made right then all over the country, across all the time zones. But in Philadelphia, where the polls were preparing to close, it had also been a *weird* day. Everything had been in-between since day broke. Nothing was fixed. The boisterous city was unusually quiet, perhaps because nobody wanted to jinx it and you never knew: maybe Romney would win. For many, nothing was as it seemed this Tuesday. Up until lunchtime, for instance, it had been blandly colorless and cold outside like a pot of leftover oatmeal. But by evening it felt way too warm for November. So here people were, heading home, over-dressed and grumpily unlayering, tossing burdensome coats and scarves into their cars.

Only minutes before sessions had ended at the Philadelphia Leadership and Business Technology Charter Academy, the sunset had been a blaze of color. Now there was only a periwinkle touch to the day's last light. The low, fading light was blotted out by tall buildings. No clues of the dramatic and vivid palette clung to the clouds overhead.

The soft-hued sky mingled with the drowsy street lamps flickering right as Duane was dismissed from a work-mandated training at 5:30. Duane took a deep and gratifying breath. Whoever set the heat at P.L.B.T.C.A. had not fiddled with the thermostat since the chilly morning aberrance. The rooms were reminiscent of a malarial jungle outpost—stifling heat, torpid bodies drowsing off in every corner. That was behind him, however. Duane thought himself quite the optimist: the extra thirty minutes it would take to get home were looked forward to; it was pleasant outside and you could do so much worse for November.

"Nice to meet you, man," Duane called to the new guy he sat through the 'Terms and Conditions' session with.

"Yeah, ditto," he said.

He was in no rush to get home. The new guy confided to Duane that his apartment was being fumigated that day. He did not want to be the first roommate on the scene to sweep up hundreds and hundreds of dead roaches.

Duane wished his acquaintance well. "Good luck with the, uh, *thing*," he mindfully sayonara-ed. The new guy nodded and moped away, dragging his dirty white sneakers along the pavement splotched with blackened gum and fresh '*I Voted*' stickers.

The bike was locked up to the right of the P.L.B.T.C.A.'s front doors. Duane got his keys out of his pants' pocket and began working the U-Lock. He stopped to notice a few bright, early stars, or maybe just slow airplanes.

"Damn, man, ridin' that shit all the way up here!"

Mr. Walt gave Duane a friendly clap on the shoulder, surprising him from behind as he was about to separate the bike from some hastily-added-on ADA ramp railing.

"See you tomorrow, playa."

"Yeah, have a good one, Mr. Walt." He watched his co-worker bounce off towards the mass transit. Duane carefully removed the U-Lock from his front wheel (half of a recently-purchased $400 set) and dropped it into his backpack. The heavy piece of metal crumpled the hand-outs and obsolete schedules inside.

Those wheels (and the premium tubes and Kevlar-reinforced tires) had been a prudent investment. *The ride home won't be too bad*, he thought. Not like when he rode that clunky, ponderous old Varsity that someone mercifully stole the year before off some fencing around Temple. Duane patted his caramel-colored English leather saddle appreciatively, as one might the head of a loyal dog. He drifted an index finger along the matching handlebar tape almost sensually before he put his gloves on. His Gitane (burgundy-colored and French) was *class*: a four-star steakhouse of a bicycle.

His helmet was special too—if you were in on the joke. It was a gold punter's helmet. Like the one worn by Jack Nicholson's character in *Easy Rider*. It had taken an entire evening of online research to find one like it because nobody seemed to be manufacturing the old-time helmets (certainly not for purposes of cranial safety). Perhaps you *thought* that was the kind of thing thrift stores always had, but they didn't. Not in an adult size, at least. And when the helmet finally arrived, it was not the right hue and it needed a navy stripe down the middle, too, and the face-mask had to be removed and Duane had to additionally buy and attach an older-styled chin-strap—the kind Jack had—and even then the fittings didn't quite jibe. So much work went into that homage and he smiled and admired himself every time he wore it.

It was not going to be a cold night. Duane's breath was invisible still. He considered stuffing his white bubble jacket into his backpack, too, as he would certainly heat up once he started cooking homeward. But the white coat made him more visible for drivers who seemed to need all the help they could get. Duane zipped up.

He rolled up the fashionably-tapered right cuff of his robin's egg blue trousers (recently purchased on a trip to Manhattan and (in Duane's proud estimation) heretofore unseen in Philadelphia).

The mauve hint of a new pair of silk long underwear peaked out above an old and unexciting wool sock. The long johns were luxuriant, warm, and worn for the first time today: just in case things stayed cold.

Duane got on the Gitane, slipping his new

Sebago Kettle Boots (Luggage Tan, $79) into the toe clips one at a time, and, quickly discovering his balance, shot off towards home.

What a difference that extra $2.50-per-hour had made in Duane's life since he became a Group Leader/Elementary Programming Co-coordinator at James Buchanan 21st Century Cyber-Achievement Charter Campus! This was no mean raise or minor titular bump. An extra $200 on every paycheck was the difference between hand-to-mouth and a free hand. Duane was twenty-nine years old and his birthday was coming early next year. He hadn't made this much money since he did landscaping work under the table between semesters six summers ago, when he slept soundly every weeknight.

Those savings went away slowly like the muscles he'd built up laying sod and carrying mulch. He then spent the better part of eight years forgetting piecemeal what he learned in school, working part-time, dating some, and visiting family when he could. For one of those years he was employed at a Center City parking garage, sitting on a barstool and listening to a beat-up radio; these were early mornings for thirty hours each week. The précis of this period of his life was 1,560 hours spent in a small booth, reading tickets, making change, letting the orange arm up, and watching people drive away.

The barstool was upholstered with duct tape, sticky in the summer and extra cold in the winter.

The radio got horrible reception inside the garage.

This year, his third in the schools, was a

$12.50-an-hour revolution. A personal renaissance was underway in earnest as Duane finally felt adequately compensated for the work he was putting in. And if the wardrobe upgrades were bougie (albeit *petit* bougie), at least the bike and its dapper accoutrement were functional, justifiable, and made life noticeably better.

The potholes were filled with pale street light like bowls of milk bereft of breakfast cereal. Traffic was on the light side for this time of evening. Although: *not as many people driving home from work today*, Duane speculated. *It's a holiday, sort of.* The bike sailed smoothly along the sea-level-city flatness.

It had been a good day, the kind rappers used to rap about when he was growing up. It was practically a day off (he didn't have to work with the kids, who were all starting to get runny noses). He was sharp-dressed and told so. People at work liked him and work gave him more money. In turn, he could soon buy more new clothes and repeat the cycle afresh.

On Election night, Duane discovered himself settled into a contented version of adulthood where he earned enough and was free enough (on evenings and weekends) to re-live the idyllic and unrivaled life of the average middle-class child. It was back to video games and cable television and *we eat what we like* all over again—but with better graphics, more channels, and organic 2%.

Even the weather was on his side: it was a mild November night.

His bike was cruising with the flow right down

Broad Street, crankset and chain in buttery-smooth concert. Earlier that morning he'd voted (again) for a black president at a neighborhood mosque and received a sticker that read 'Yo he votado'…

Even today's roundabout cynic would have to admit it was a funny, wondrous, and generally unbelievable time and place to live in.

Duane certainly had to laugh at it all.

In fact, he never even saw it coming. It was a block away from Norris, where he always turned off the ever-busy Broad Street thoroughfare. Duane was eagerly anticipating the bottom-shelf champagne chilling in his fridge when a driver's-side door opened. First there was just a somehow audible *click* when the door met the right front hub of that sensational new wheel, a sound so delicate that Duane thought maybe it was going to be another close call. But the terrible physics of the scene had yet to play out and the door had another fifteen degrees left on its trajectory. He sensed (and soon knew for sure) that he would not regain balance. The door swung out with no more force than usual. Duane turned slightly and caught its edge in his chops. The bike's usual elegant motion became as clumsy and unsure as a foal still slick with the goo of birth. He was toppling right over into what he knew was a heavily-trafficked street and it was true: he became a leaf, a slow-floating thing miraculously endowed with time enough to breathe deep and think, *Well… this is it*. Duane might have stretched the thought into perpetuity had a car not been right behind him.

So life was not flashing before his eyes when the sedan smashed into him.

The Gitane, whose lightness had been a major selling point months ago, launched forward some twenty feet closer to the Rite Aid on the corner. Duane, meanwhile, being a heavier and more complex mass, only went about five feet through the air before landing, bouncing a couple times, and sliding belly-down into an unoccupied bus-loading zone, where he promptly began to wail in a motionless and agonizing freak-out.

"Fuck! This hurts so bad!" he eventually heard himself crying to the entire listening world, which had undoubtedly stopped to gawk. "This hurts *so fucking bad*." The last four syllables were without a doubt the loudest sounds he could ever produce without some sort of a public address system.

He began grinding the forehead of his golden helmet into the ground like a pestle while muttering quietly. From a distance it looked like an ancient and forgotten ritual being performed on north Broad Street. "Fuck," he said with each fast breath in and out, sounding like he had a thick echo effect on his voice. "Ow," he added, many times, over and over.

When he first came tumbling down, time was in suspense sweet and slow, like rich maple syrup drizzling onto steaming, Sunday morning hotcakes. He was gifted a few dear instants to prepare for and appreciate the perilousness of his situation. He held his breath and in a mad way reflected upon what was happening *as it was happening*. Those were the last moments, probably ever, when Duane wasn't going to be in some degree of pain. So it was nice that the fall seemed to have lasted longer than normal. Because now there was this unheralded sensory input … signals jammed and wires crossed … a wild, unruly chaos of injuries all over the place, both specific and sheer … so many visceral, animal instincts and sounds … neverbeforefelt chemicals coursing through him like uncoordinated and ill-prepared evacuees, too dumb to realize that they're in the middle of a raid and the only thing to do is stay down.

Now it was the last thing he wanted: time moving slowly.

Duane apostrophically pleaded with no higher power in particular and asked repeatedly *what in the hell, why am I still awake?* There was no reply. And there was no battlefield epiphany nor unveiling of an infinite and lofty sky. Duane could not rebuke life's vanity and the delusion of it all and embrace stillness and peace—not while he was face down in Philadelphia, badly broken, things turning darker and colder outside. Perhaps thirty seconds passed since car met ass on Election Day, 2012, at Broad and Norris, right by the Nubian Hair Braiding Salon and Lucky Emperor #3 Chinese and American Take-Out, but it was a lonely and imponderable eternity for poor Duane (and also for the other parties directly involved who remained quietly shaken inside their automobiles).

"You'll never know how bad this hurts right now," he was saying matter-of-factly, between groans. He had stopped howling, like a baby that's cried itself into an air-hungry stupor. His throat was dry and he gulped cold air like water. Instead of breathing out, Duane steadily intoned a breathy, profane mantra towards the Orange Line train rumbling below.

Onlookers figured he was tag-on-the-toe dead when his constant, clamorous bellowing abruptly ended. It took a few seconds longer for the voices to begin closing in.

"You alright?" someone ventured.

"Yo, what the fuck you mean *he alright*?" a husky talker countered, lampooning the good samaritan's bumpkinish naïveté. "Muthafucker laying there hit by a car and shit. You fuckin' see he fucked up. Bull need a ambu-lance, man."

Vehicles moved south past the scene, though bottlenecked, while the traffic lights dutifully changed in cold and colorful disregard. The Route 16 bus crawled past Duane and dropped a passenger off half a block further down the line. Its diesel fumes made Duane pause his whimpers and cough pathetically.

"You alright, baby," said a sweet and tranquil voice. "Shhh … you alright."

And then Duane felt alright, considering. Such was the sweetness and tranquility of this voice.

She held his gloved left hand.

"But it *hurts*," he said in an excusably whiny rise. "This hurts *so bad*."

"I know … shit, that's just *got to*." She gave his limp hand a little pump and a wiggle. "They're coming to get you right now, though, okay? I know it hurts, but they're on they way."

Duane nodded.

"Don't move your head, baby, okay?" said another equally-sweet and tranquil woman's voice.

Next came a sensible pain in Duane's heart. His body still hurt right then as well, but he smiled slightly and there understood inwardly the broadest possible meaning of 'suffer.' He was happy and thankful that his hand was being held right then and he was being called baby. And suddenly he wished to die, while being held and loved and cared for by perfect strangers. There would be no better moment than this for credits to roll. It had been a good day, after all. He didn't especially want the days ahead and the life ahead and all the grim announcements doctors were going to give him about it.

While Rachel and Bernice piteously watched over him, talked to him about how *alright* things were going to be (all the while nervously clicking their teeth in disapproval of the slow-moving ambulance), Duane just tried not to think about whether or not he was going to *walk* or *move* ever again. Duane's only response to whatever was said was to tell both the girls that he loved them. He hadn't meant it that badly in a long time. It was a little uncomfortable for the two kind women, even though they knew not to take literally what someone so distressed was saying, but Rachel still wrote her phone number down and put it in Duane's wallet while he was gurneyed into the ambulance.

"Call when you get a chance, honey, let us know

you're okay," she said, as if Duane was going off to summer camp.

The hospital wasn't too far away and things suddenly moved along at a relatively swift clip. He could move his left toes when he tried to (no sense in even *thinking* about that other foot and leg right then...) and could bend that left leg a little, too. This was a great relief. He also still knew his name, phone number, date of birth, and address. The lack of dire medical dialogue in the back of the vehicle signaled nothing imminently mortal was afoot. Still, nothing actually *felt* good.

Duane was wheeled into the waiting area of the Emergency Room to the sound of the staff's whistles and breaths sucked in through closed teeth. He could hear the grimacing faces. He must be in a bad sort of way to earn that kind of reaction at the ER in North Philly. Folks with horrific earaches and seriously mashed digits groaned, knowing that they'd have to continue waiting their turn so much the longer.

"Thanks," Duane said dizzily, "for bringing me here."

"Um, sure thing," said the paramedic, caught off guard and un-expectant of ER civility. "Take care," he said on his way out.

At this point everything began happening at a fast-forward pace. People in teal smocks moved around the patient with pit-crew efficiency and an air of routine (not in the lax sense but simply work-ing their way down a checklist that compelled calamity itself to bow down before it). It was hard to tell when they were asking each other questions and when they were asking Duane questions.

"Whoops," said the member of the hospital staff that cut open the bubble coat. There were feathers floating all around now, thousands of slow, tiny feathers drifting like soft snow. Duane weakly raised a hand to try and shoo some away, but that was promptly brought to a halt.

Duane decided to try and make the best of it and imagine he was abducted by aliens. The chemicals that roiled through his system, that not long ago unleashed a heightened and keen bewilderment, had lately settled into an eerily groovy calm. Things were in the hands of others.

And now they're scanning me … analyzing me with their sensors … processing my data … they are stripping me of my clothes, too … I have nothing to fear, Duane told himself, *what they're doing is beyond my understanding … Just let them run their experiments and they will take you home, un-remembering, when they're through.*

Everything he told himself was true enough and the ruse worked pretty well, even when Duane had to slip out of character and answer questions about what had happened and where the hurt was. That is until they began cutting off his trousers and shearing those silk long underwear into snakey purple streamers.

"Oh man! Not my gaberdine shirt!" he sobbed, which pained the cutter who said "Yeah, sorry, buddy," in earnest response. Duane announced that he'd had that shirt since he was in high school. So much of the job was tougher when the patients were awake.

And then Duane was naked save his golden punter's helmet. They wouldn't take that off until some more advanced evaluations could take place. His sex was now such a small, unimportant thing for anyone to look at and all the more ridiculous with the helmet taken into consideration. Once again, though, the chemicals were taking much of the sting off an otherwise embarrassing and dehumanizing experience.

God bless those chemicals.

The thin, oblong face of an African man, unmistakably from that continent, popped up right over Duane and talked with him over all the medical chatter and mechanical beeping. "Ay, buddy," he said. He had a gravelly, well-seasoned voice but looked no older than twenty. "Whad habben'd to *you*?!"

"I got hit by a car," the patient wheezed and winced.

"Ah, no-oo," the man said with a wistful head shake. "Whad, you were jus' crossin' da street?"

"No, I was on my bike."

"Ah, no-oo … you were onna *motuh* cycle?"

"No just, a bike."

He brushed it all off and got right to business. "Tell me some-ting: you were drinking beers, no? A couple beers tonight?"

"What?" Duane asked, legitimately baffled.

"You gan dell me da drooth. You'd been ad a pardy?"

"No, no, no, I was, I was …" *How long ago was it, what time was it*? "I was coming home from work, from a training and—"

A pair of hidden hands delicately swooped in under Duane's shoulders and his knees and rotated him ninety degrees. Before he could inquire as to why this was happening, someone else's latexed middle and index fingers swiftly slipped right on inside of him and felt around. It was a lot like having the wind knocked out of you. Nobody took note of Duane's groan. It was over soon enough. He was rolled back to his original position gently and then was covered with a papery gown.

Duane tried to tell himself that the penetration wasn't the worst part of his day, but the words offered little cheer.

"Just be still, okay?" a medical professional told him as he was being slowly inserted into a large beige cylinder. Duane didn't think he could move much then, anyways, but breathed something positive in assent. A door clicked shut. The chemistry experiment inside of him was winding down. While trying to stay motionless inside the whirring and busy tube his body started giving him grief again. There were no aliens, not even to be imagined behind all this space-age equipment. There were other people, strangers, safely behind layers and layers of protective materials while the x-rays busily blasted away at his groin and back and head and chest.

Couldn't they knock him out for all of this

or something? Again and again, again and again, Duane asked the same question: *why am I still awake*?

He knew his right foot was smashed and tendons and ligaments were probably the only things keeping it attached to his leg. His pelvic area had taken a direct hit and he cried from inside the big diagnostic pipe, imagining his important lynchpin of a bone cracked up and possibly separated.

"Don't move," said a drive-thru intercom voice.

"Get me a pillow." His puny demand echoed briefly and the machine hummed some more before clicking, pausing, and humming again.

His back. Duane wanted a pillow for his back. He didn't remember anything in particular happening to it. But, still ... it hurt bad ... which meant *something* ... not something he wanted to feel or think about, though, so he instead tried to raise morale by making his good leg twitch and move some.

"Don't move."

Removed from the pod and awaiting the results, Duane was handled over to a room. By all accounts it was a very *plain* room that possessed few inherently hospital-like qualities. No aseptic jar of swabs, no CDC scare-posters or government-issued BMI charts. No scale, even ... It was the first time he'd had been alone and unmonitored since he first got plowed into. A clock ticked and tocked steadily with predictably unnerving results.

He heard footsteps that sounded destined for

him. A large man with a buzzed head and long pharaohic goatee ambled into the room. He began whistling a Stephen Foster-esque ditty while forcing his big hands into latex gloves. He gave the gloves the ubiquitous (though maybe necessary) *sssnap!* along the wrists. He stopped whistling.

"Hey there, Aikman. Doctors say we can lose the helmet. Sound good?" He grinned, revealing a chipped front tooth.

"Uh-huh."

"That's more like a Terry Bradshaw helmet, really," he said under his breath, correcting himself.

The man had on large seafoam-standard scrubs that might have been special-order. The nurse was that big. On his inner right forearm the letters "A-OK" were tattooed in bold outline. "It's a real cool helmet, dude," he said while carefully removing it and revealing Duane's full head of matted, reddish-brown hair. "Where'd you get ahold of it?"

"Internet," he answered.

"Sure, sure. Everything's on there these days." He held the helmet in his hands and furrowed his chin with the thoughtful frown of a connoisseur before placing it beneath the stretcher. "Hey, man: anything I can get for you?" he asked.

Duane moaned.

"Yeah, buddy—I'm gonna go get that business right now. I see you're a *straight-talker*. You need me to call anyone and let 'em know you're all right and here at the hospital?"

Duane began making a low blubbering sound, trying to remember (on his own) a single phone number from his fairly short list of contacts. He couldn't do it anymore, though, and, if he did, didn't know who to call, what to say, or how to explain.

"Can you turn the TV on?" he finally ventured. America's decision might distract him, maybe? Soon enough he listened to political insiders and polling wonks, none of whom he could really keep up with or pay attention to for too long. He only recently got hit by a car, after all; and still no, he could not have a pillow—they weren't budging an inch on that one.

"This is gonna be a lot better than a pillow, dude," the burly nurse soon explained, poking him with a needle. He stood back a few inches and watched. "Am I right?" He flashed his chipper grin again.

Foot specialists came in the room, introduced themselves perfunctorily, and pronounced his foot broken. All kinds of tiny bones were smashed into smaller-yet pieces.

"More would be good," Duane meanwhile said. The nurse gave him more.

The podiatrists were still going over and breezily itemizing all the little bones that needed fixing. Every bit they said was as incomprehensible as the sounds coming from television. Duane nodded with the docile, trying-to-please-you-all countenance of a black lab that keeps putting its paw out for a shake until a treat is given. None of this much mattered now, as Duane was finally feeling alright, just now getting a taste of whatever it was that made things less excruciating. The injections turned his mind pleasantly soupy. He wondered to himself what they'd do with the shards of bone, if they just threw them away like bits of a broken plate.

There was another back-and-forth going on in the room, another team of physicians in the mix now.

Someone paused and then quietly mentioned 'severe deformity.'

"Okay, Duane," a small, nervous-looking doctor, a man Duane's age and size, stepped forward. "We're going to *sedate* you for the next hour or so and try to *re*-set the foot as best we can, somewhat close to its natural form … Then we'll be placing a temporary cast on you." The doctor paused. "Sound good?" He seemed to be asking everyone in the room.

"Sounds *great*," Duane said, able to grin wide at the word "sedate."

"Alright, man," said Duane's big friend, "I'm gonna give you some *keh. tuh. mean.* Okay?" He inspected the syringe closely in the bright hospital fluorescence like an Antwerp diamond merchant eyeing his wares. "That's ketamine, buddy. It'll help put you right out. It should get weird," he said, giving the vial a couple cautious flicks, "and then you'll be zonked out a while. Eventually you'll wake up; you might even start saying some loopy stuff, okay?" Duane smiled feebly, having heard this same lecture from a similar-looking guy a few years back, a wasted Saturday afternoon with less touch-and-go circumstances. "You might wake up and feel a little woozy. A little nauseous."

"That's fine," Duane interjected, not really needing to.

"Yessir, it's gonna be fine, slick." A little dribble of weird, woozy stuff spurted out from the tip of the needle. "And here. We. Go."

"I couldn't, I—" Duane said *sometime* later, just as was promised, feeling like he had awoken and at the same time surged up to the surface from the floor of a swimming pool's deep end. The principal podiatrist, who, it turns out, was a very pretty woman with dark, parted hair, looked over towards the patient with a slight tinge of confusion and worry on her face. She was removing a blue latex glove from her slender, ringless hand.

"I tried to save...*half*...for you, but then...why, I couldn't..."

She left the room without saying anything.

"Oh..."

What was that word, he wondered...

"Sorry!"

That was what he was looking for!

The television was still on and seemed to have begun using a more approachable vocabulary. Or maybe there were just less words and names to read. He squinted his eyes and tried to make out what was going on, but there were *two* scrolling tickers with microscopic text at the bottom of the screen and a column on the right with percentages and check-marks and headshots that changed every few seconds. There were periodic bar graphs and pie charts, too, that would swipe in and out without warning. It was a lot to take in, especially on a nineteen-inch set mounted in a not-too-close corner.

"If these numbers continue in Florida *and* Ohio, though—like we are now predicting they will—based on the early returns … And especially knowing that there's *still* California—which is a *mega* slam dunk— then it looks as if we will, indeed … witness … the re-election … of Barack Obama … as president of the United States of America."

"Whatheysay?" asked a middle-aged woman, an administrative type, passing by.

"We did it, baby … *we did it*," Duane said with a big smirk and a silver-dollar-sized scrape scabbing up on his chin.

Her head popped back out of the room, shaking in bemused disapproval all the way back to her desk.

Finally, after hours unbound by minutes, Duane was ferried up to Intensive Care, still feeling and sounding completely out-there. He had a big, $9,000-a-night, top-floor room all to himself. Not quite the sort of high-priced spread that lends itself to a brassy, Robin Leach voice-over, but … it was a good place for him to find himself after a long day. The skyline view was partial, not that he could sit up or look towards the window. He lay flat under a thin blanket and said, "What a fuckin' day." The night nurse poked a catheter into him like a meat thermometer and then made up for it by demonstrating how to use his personal morphine drip. It was as simple and handy as a garage door opener. He could press the button every nine minutes. Duane stayed up a little longer, until eleven or so, until Mitt called it quits, and wondered before falling asleep about that champagne in the fridge.

An intern with dull blond hair both very curly and very thin (like ramen) woke Duane up sometime before the sun was out. It was presumably Wednesday. He explained that the following bones were broken: the sacrum, two lumbar vertebrae, and, generally speaking, his right foot. That's what yesterday evening boiled down to.

"There didn't seem to be any neural damage," the intern said casually, as if informing a driver, post oil change, that his timing belt still looked alright. "Sometime today Dr. Wu—he'll be here to meet with you shortly—and the pelvis people are going to get some screws in there for stability." He kept his head down, not looking up from the printout, scanning and condensing, translating for the patient. "Aaa-and podiatry might try and operate while you're anesthetized, too, before the swelling takes off and makes the foot inoperable for a while … let's see …" *More text, more words he'd need explained to him,* his face appeared to say, and then, "oh, and, any questions for me?"

"Um, yeah," Duane said, trying to rub the strange taste on his tongue off against the roof of his mouth. "Is there a, uh, *phone* in this room?"

An artlessly affectionate, born-to-help nurse named Arielle wheeled in a cart with an old rotary phone, the taupe kind with a curly plastic cord and a heavy receiver. He couldn't dial this sort of phone in his present condition (having to stay absolutely prone) and had her do it for him while he read Rachel's number to her. Duane was cleared to hold the receiver to his ear while the tone pulsed five and then six times. It was 6:15 a.m. and he was still heavily-drugged. One beep meant he had to wait longer to self-administer more morphine while another beep signaled that his message had gone on too long. Since he was on a rotary phone Duane couldn't press '1' to re-record something more lucid.

Podiatry, it turned out, could not work on Duane at the same time as Dr. Wu because one operation required the patient to be on his back, while the other one was better-suited for him to be flat on his stomach, where you can actually get at the posterior. He woke up later that day in his ICU penthouse, not *feeling* like he had screws holding his sacrum together, which is mostly what the next twenty days marching on towards Thanksgiving were like: everything happening, most definitely and certainly happening, but … the *dreaminess* of it all (and no, not nightmarish—it was all too mundane and plausible for that word); it was the surreality of every day that made things difficult to accept and believe. Granted, having one's finger on a private morphine button could do that. It's just that there were *so many X-rays*. And there were so many people working on you—so many different individuals and machines keeping you alive—even the ever-astute and polite Duane could not name a single recurring character in his hospital drama. Neither could he explain what tube went where and for what purpose. There were countless doctors, nurses, and visitors he'd never remember; all the plastic piping, pills, and transparent sacks of intravenous liquids; the wires, beeps, bloops, buzzes. Every day demarcated by three meals he didn't want to eat… And "they made the mold of your torso based on the measurements taken from yesterday and the clam-shell wrap is being shipped from Boston *right now*, but that leg component… that one that orthopedic says you're going to need? Says you need so they can keep that natural hip-swivel we discussed from happening? It's on it's way from the Miami facility, so …"

… Had somebody actually said these words to Duane? *In regards to Duane*?

They obviously had, as he was soon in a hospital bed, snug and able to sit up of late thanks to his customized white plasticine wrap-around torso spinal-support-cast (something that looked like post-apocalyptic guerrilla space-war combat armor)… *that* was real, all right. He *had* to wear it in order to sit up!

It was real, too, when he had to call his roommate, Grady (a pudgy, pale man who came into his life only out of a panicked need for half of the rent to be abruptly covered since last May, a man with a gee-whiz haircut and the social life of a recent widower, whom Duane had shared less than a paragraph of even the tersest interpersonal prose with) and summon him away from his weeknight warmed-over chicken dinner routine to come to the hospital and go over, well, *everything*.

"I guess you're gonna have to call Mike," he said to Duane, referring to their landlord, "and then, uh, just let me know what he says."

Then Grady made that uncomfortable laugh that served as punctuation signaling the end of one of his ineffectual and awkward thoughts and gave a weak shrug.

On the other side of a thin curtain, a machine hooked up to Mr. Hotlunch, Duane's *new* hospital roommate (having been moved down to a less-desirable wing of the hospital after a week of steady improvement), began noisily beeping. The monitor concluded that the patient's heart had stopped. Really, though, everybody (Grady included) knew that the wires had just gotten loose after Mr. Hotlunch adjusted himself in bed.

"Sorry, boys," he said. "Damned thing."

"Oh, it's cool," Grady assured Mr. Hotlunch before letting fly another one of those unsettling chuckles of his. "No sweat."

"Keeps on fussin' over nothin.'"

This was not one of those "*nothing is as it seems*" stories where a character wakes up at home with a bandage wrapped around his head. Duane hadn't merely *dreamt* of having to take a dump while lying completely flat on his back. And yet, kind of like that lucid hour before the alarm clock goes off, there was a very definite sense that this would all be ending soon and there was no telling what you'd remember and mull over after you got some coffee in you and listened to the traffic report. Strange and disturbing, yes: having to later share a room for a week with a sixty-six-year-old Cuban man with two broken arms who suffers from *regular* panic attacks and speaks no English … being woken up three times each night to have blood samples drawn by a large and surly Jamaican woman … working one's way up to the rehab wing and spending an afternoon playing tennis on a Nintendo Wii, clobbering stroke victims trying to regain their motor skills … but the hospital was a city block squared and ten stories high and Philadelphia had always been a strange and disturbing place when you got right down to it.

She gave it some thought. "We'd *prefer* it if you were on *Flovador*, given the severity of your trauma—in addition to the prolonged time during which you've been laid out. We'll have to get somebody in here to show you how to properly administer it—"

"Well, I've been getting it for the past two-and-a-half weeks, so—"

The doctor laughed softly to herself and explained that "injecting yourself is really quite different." She had the tiniest scar on the right side of her thin upper lip and it really showed up when she flashed Duane her alluring and incongruent smile. "I understand your concerns, really. *Flovador*'s definitely a little on the expensive side, but, really, again, taking into account—"

"What's expensive?"

She hesitated. *He's not going to like this one, but* … "I believe it's around two-to-three-hundred-dollars-per-dosage." The scar turned a little whiter, as it did whenever she frowned. "We'll get one of our social workers in here tomorrow to discuss prescription options before you're discharged, though, okay?" She immediately read his thoughts, felt the ensuing bad vibes launch like porcupine quills. The sting of pessimism was palpable. "Oh, shoot ... but tomorrow's Thanksgiving, right?" She let out a genuine sigh.

"It is."

"So they won't be around until *maybe* Friday, but ..." and she let the patient fill in the blank.

He was ready to melt once the doctor left. Suddenly Duane was powerless, seven or eight years old again, all the way at the final level before the secondhand Sega overheated and the screen froze.

"Nah, nah ... Dey *do* got me on da mef-a-doon, do'h, da sunzabitches," Road Dog whispered into his cell phone, as best as he could whisper. "But, b-b-b-but, but check dis out, do'h, right? I been here *four days* wit dis in-*feck*shun and dey, dey, d-d-d-dey say dey gon opuhrate yestiday, but den dey go 'n' say that dey '*mis-skeddul'd*' 'n' gotta make me wait to tomorrow."

The person on the other end of the line had something to say about that.

It was hard to share a small room with Road Dog. He made a lot of phone calls and paid the $6 daily to keep his television tuned (full-volume) to a sports-news cycle that rotated in thirty-minute in-

tervals. Duane soon learned that this station's pro-
gramming was updated at 3, 6, and 9 o'clock. Road
Dog was a fiend and only the *crème de la crème* of
the 6th floor could draw blood from his worn, spent
veins (which hurt him like hell, getting pointlessly
stuck so much; and he let them know it). Road Dog
was there because he had a big, festering lesion that
made it appear as if his right calf was caving in. He
complained profusely through an inch-and-a-half
gap in his upper palate where four teeth used to be.

"You gon bring me a plate, do'h, right? … haw
haw haw! … Nah, nah, man … yeah-huh … yessir! … I know dat's right!"

Every night for nearly three straight weeks
had a certain "dark night of the soul" quality for
Duane before meeting each sickly-sticky-oatmeal-
and-weak-coffee-breakfast with the enthusiasm of
a child going through an Advent calendar (so eager was he to be out of there). But the last two days
and nights next to Road Dog proved be the toughest
since his admittance and all the hubbub that came
along with it. The worst came when Road Dog got
wheeled back into the room with his leg in the same
grotesque condition and Dwayne had to pass by
his bed a little later to have his foot fixed by the esteemed *wunderkind* surgeon Dr. Piranha. Road Dog
said something, not to Dwayne or anybody in particular. Maybe he just made a sound. Nobody but
Road Dog could say for certain. But it was clear that
he was not amused with the cards he kept getting
dealt.

It was another unseasonably-upper-forties-and-partly-sunny-day, a Monday in early December and Duane was hanging out on the futon downstairs. A quarter-to-eleven and *Easy Rider* was remarkably on channel 17.3 this morning. And channel 17.3 even came in clear today. Duane went through his light physical therapy routines during the commercial breaks. He rallied himself, thinking about how Dr. Piranha said "you'll be walking in six weeks."

"With crutches?" Duane had asked him.

"No—with *shoes*, dude," Dr. Piranha replied.

Up and down, up and down, Duane kept his right thigh perpendicular to the futon and brought his foot up far enough to where he could see the toe of the black air cast before easing it back. He did so again, ten times, 'til the movie was back on.

He'd be wearing a pair of shoes by ... January 10th!

They managed to save those Sebagos. The right one had tire treads on it.

Duane felt a warm rush. He grew flushed. He took a deep breath, thinking he must've done too many of those leg exercises. He was light-headed and really warm, from his insides on out.

"Here's to ol' D.H. Lawrence," ACLU lawyer George Hanson toasted from channel 17.3 before taking a generous swig from the pint of Jim Beam and doing his inimitable wing flap.

Grady came home at 5:30, like he did every day he wasn't at his parents' in the suburbs, and the TV was on. Duane looked asleep. *Best to let him rest*, he thought. He even *thought* one of his trademark laughs. Grady hoped that this nap would be over before the Eagles game tonight. But Duane was dead and cold from a small blood clot and of course did not move by 7 o'clock. So Grady ended up listening to the game upstairs, on the radio, dining on ruffled potato chips and French Onion dip in his bed.

2

Billy George was moving to Philadelphia with his girlfriend of some months, a New York emigre named Lucy. Things were going okay between the two of them. Well enough that they decided to make a bold cross-country relocation to a place neither of them had ever been. But within two hours of the forty-two-hour drive from outside Seattle, sharing a single radio and repeatedly compromising on when and where bathroom breaks could take place, it became clear that it was not going to work.

They were both twenty-three years old. He was working on becoming more serious-minded (having just graduated from The Experimental Liberal Arts College) and she was a free spirit revivalist who did free-spirited things like call cats *elmos* and cut her own hair. This used to be fine: his highbrowery private, her quirks nymphy, all of which was tempered by a mutual jigginess that more than compensated for the differences. But Billy soon struggled to envision how it would all fit together in a post-baccalaureate world. They were headed in different directions trapped together in the same import truck for nearly one week. Nothing was ever said outright, but somewhere approaching Harrisburg, PA he politely asked if he ought to maybe take her home, as in her mom's house.

"Yeah, *I think so*," she said quickly, without malice.

And it was the best part of the long journey, maybe even of their whole seven months together: the detour into Queens. Everyone was relieved. It was like hearing of a painfully old relative who finally succumbed peacefully to a common cold.

Mom was taken aback, of course, as neither of the two freewheelin' kids thought to call ahead. Would it have killed them to call? Mrs. Muraski's initial hostility towards her daughter's latest boyfriend was offset by Lucy's bubbliness and confident posture, which then made the whole scene very baffling. *Might they be on drugs?* she wondered. She settled on making some sandwiches while they brought in bags of clothes and small pieces of bedroom furniture.

"Welp … I better get going," Billy said, finishing off the last of his lemonade and getting up from the table. He put his arms akimbo and squinted out the window at the brownstones across the street, like a stout conquistador surveying the Pacific.

"Okay," said Lucy.

"Will you *please* call and tell those people at the apartment that you're not coming?"

"Sure."

"They're your friends, after all."

"Well." She turned herself pigeon-toed and bent her knees a little. Lucy liked to appear antsy, awkward and at the same time adorable when there was something she didn't want to do. "They're friends of friends, really."

She wasn't going to call anybody.

"Either way, can you please try'n' call 'em?"

Billy pleaded. "Try 'n' let 'em know?"

"Yes, Billy, I'll *ca-all* them," she said with an eye-roll. She corrected her posture rather disdainfully, clearing her throat and crossing her arms. That West Coast free-spiritedness took a sassy turn the instant they drove on to the Queensboro Bridge. Billy went in for a kiss but saw Mrs. Muraski out of the corner of his eye and so backed off a bit, giving Lucy a soft, playful punch on the arm in the style of a folksy uncle.

"What the hell was that?" he heard her mom ask while the screen door eased shut, "what the hell's going on here?"

It seemed like driving would never end, but when he approached his address in Philadelphia he began to hope in earnest that he might have to drive a little longer—to a nicer part of town. This was it, however: *north* North Fifth, a stone's throw from the Big Pun mural. He parked the truck by a lot full of angry dogs, running and barking amid tall, tilting turrets of rotting pallets. A twenty-foot-high barbed-wire perimeter was not deterrent enough for this operation. *Somebody* tried to get in there and got repulsed: a frayed clump of weave was tangled in a coil of barbed-wire, flapping like a tattered flag in the wind.

Billy crossed the street. A semi-truck did a California stop at the four-way and sent a black plastic bag gliding over the sidewalk like a manta ray. A plastic juice bottle, shaped like a wooden barrel, rested next to a spent pint of Mad Dog 20/20. Each had a squirt of Windex-blue liquid left ringing the base. Nearest the entrance, somebody's trash bag of clothes was smooshed and spilling out into the street, getting run over and over and over again like yesterday's unfortunate opossum.

Billy stood by the door to his building for minutes; nobody in apartment 609 answered the buzzer. He called a number belonging to one of his new roommates and waited. '*Sponge Mill Luxury Lofts,*' he read on the maroon awning. The phone rang. It was hot and rancid-smelling in the old factory's shade. He toed at a thick hunk of glass and repeatedly debated the merits of leaving a message.

A blond, mustached man came bursting out of the building, leading a raspberry bike with one hand and frantically trying to answer his phone with the other. "What the fuck," he said to himself, "Hello? Hello?"

"Hey, hello, over here," Billy said.

"Yeah, hey, what's up," the man with the bicycle automatically replied without making eye contact. He kept his attention focused on the phone. "Hello?" In one surprisingly supple, gymnastic motion he was getting on his bike, still trying to talk into the phone. "Hel-*lo*? I'm hanging up now ... hanging up. Bye."

"Hey!" Billy shouted at him and into his phone. "Hey, you! Kurt!"

The handlebars wobbled as he looked back, one foot in a toe clip, one on top of a pedal upside down and dragging along the sidewalk. He pressed on the front break, causing the rear of the bike to comically pull up off the ground in a screeching halt. His phone hit the pavement and the battery popped out. "God. Dammit," he said matter-of-factly to himself as he got off the bike and gathered up a few scattered parts. Billy nervously walked toward him, ending the call. *Duration: 41.*

"Hey, I'm the new roommate," Billy said. "Sorry. Hi. I was calling you."

"No, it's cool." Kurt brushed his frustration easily aside. "I was all, like, *who the hell's calling me*? and then I was, like, who's *this guy* talking to me on the street. But it turned out to be the same person. Weird. I'm Kurt."

"Yeah, Billy George; a pleasure."

They shook hands, exactly like their fathers before them would have.

"Billy George?" His head pulled back a few inches. "… I thought you were from Or-uh-gone or something."

"Yeah, I'm from Washington. I drove four days to—"

"Sounds more like you're from the *Oh*-zarks with that name. *Billy George.*"

"Oh, no—William Henry George is my *full* name."

"Ah! I get it. Three first names—how about that? That's funny. Anyways, sorry! I didn't mean to call you a hillbilly."

They stood there for a beat saying nothing, both having presently forgotten why exactly they were there meeting one another for the first time on north North Fifth Street.

"Well, hey, man, sorry, but I'm fucking super-*late for work ... again ... so*—"

"Oh, I won't keep you waiting then, I just need to get this stuff out of the truck."

"Sure thing ... go right on up. 609. Sixth floor. Apartment Nine. Take the elevator. Right from the elevator, right again, all the way at the end of the hall." Kurt was saddled up, out of the factory's shadow, and ready to go again. "Apartment 6-0-9."

"Um, okay." Billy found a new chunk of glass, the bottom of a malt liquor bottle, to poke at with his sneaker. "Do you think I could borrow a key? Or keys? You know, to get inside?" He motioned back towards the building with his head.

"Oh, you didn't get a key. Shit. Well," he dug into his faded black cutoffs, "you'll be around tonight?" Billy thought so. Kurt busily pinched at and tried to slide two particular keys from off the ring, but gave up and handed over his whole set, souvenir keychains and all. "Here, just take 'em. Fuck it. I'll see you later, man. Sorry I can't help you unpack and everything—"

"Do you need one of these for your bike lock?" But he was already off, a good ninety seconds tardier than he was to begin with.

Billy was a fairly anxious driver (though not debilitatingly so) and refused to parallel park on principal. He eased the truck into a spot marginally closer than where it was initially parked and pulled two boxes out from under the mottled grey blanket covering the lumpy bed. The lock to the building's entrance took some finesse: push in hard, pull up soft, *then* twist counterclockwise. The elevator was slow and worrisome. The sixth floor hallway was poorly-lit and decorated with motivational posters. It felt like a long, skinny break room in any number of chain stores. Billy followed Kurt's directions precisely, jumping a bit at the sound of angry dogs behind the door to 608, and ended up in front of 609.

There were five keys left to choose from and two locks on the door. He nervously worked his way through possible combinations. He hoped people weren't staring at the door when he walked in.

Nudging the door open, the first thing he saw was a great A-frame of unfinished two-by-fours, seven feet high and fifteen feet long, with big screw-in hooks along the ridge beam. Two mutilated, incomplete racing bikes were lumped together at one end and a nicer-looking operational one hung from a hook further off. A pile of tubes and tires huddled in the corner like a nest of black snakes in knotted pursuit of mutual warmth. Jackets, several of them, were aggregated on the wall to his immediate left and made a dusty abscess. Billy slid his stack of two boxes across the hardwood a little further and cagily walked deeper into the space.

The wall, the one swollen with coats, was part of a freestanding, unfinished Sheetrock-and-stud structure built entirely within the apartment. From here on out, it was where he'd be sleeping at night.

Having seen his complete new address (huge brick building, spacious loft, two-story interior slum-hut, and *then* a small cell to call his own), Billy didn't know what to think. He was glad that Lucy had opted out, space-wise. But he was also quite disappointed at himself for allowing a free spirit to select his apartment. Finally, he reassured himself, noting that he was still on the top floor of the building, with penthouse views and twenty-five-foot high ceilings. Hardwood floors. Luxury lofts.

Down on the street below, the truck bed was noticeably less lumpy. Billy knew he should've gone back to the truck sooner and cursed the elevator for good measure. He began piling his boxes into the grimy foyer of the building, under the wall of gray, uniform mailboxes. By his last go-around some cunning crook had brazenly burgled from the truck a hockey stick, the final box, and the moving blanket. They may well have formed a clever bindle to simplify their delinquency. Spinning around and around and scrutinizing an empty 720°, Billy stopped and shook his fist like an old codger.

Making the circuit between the lobby and the sixth floor got tiresome after two go-rounds. He did that three more times and doggishly stuck his tongue out with fatigue when it was all finished. He made himself at home in the kitchen and selected an over-sized frosted-green cup. Roaches in the cupboard scattered in every direction. It was too hot to care about the roaches.

It was also too hot for a shirt, and he began to

move boxes naked from the waist up like an old-time stevedore. Nobody was visible nor making any noise from behind any of the seven doors. Billy wiped the sweat off his brow. He rather enjoyed toiling bare-chested.

The entrance to a room near the kitchen was cracked open. Billy nudged it with his foot. Inside was dark and empty and probably his. He pulled a flashlight out of a box marked 'STUFF' and felt like an Egyptologist exploring a tomb, right down to the threat of vector-born fever and disease. The light was weak and the batteries were about to die, but he saw that a previous tenant had inscribed some kind of a mural on the wall.

He'd have to tack a sheet up.

Actually, he'd have to buy some sheets because the ones he'd been using were Lucy's.

The room was ten feet deep. If he stretched his furthest like Vitruvian Man, Billy could *almost* touch his other two walls. The ceiling was low and grey like a summer sky over Puget Sound. A rag-tag collection of white epoxy-coated wire shelves stuck out of the left side of the room with a one-half-inch wood-dowel-and-bracket job that appeared loath to handle his shirts, to say nothing of his many irreverent sweaters. The floor was hardwood three-quarters of the way across until the strip of cheap linoleum where the kitchen started. That was the whole of the space.

The room was dusty, so he swept it out before unloading anything. The Sheetrock seemed to be the culprit, coating things with a chalky, industrial dandruff. After feeling the walls over like an enormous Braille book, he located a dubious outlet and plugged in a small lamp. He stowed the few soft goods he could on his shelves and kept the rest boxed up as a furniture of sorts. Having too large an A/C adapter to fit in the outlet alongside the lamp, Billy inflated his air mattress in the dark before fixing up his pallet in the lamplight.

Billy felt satisfied for the day. Everything was close enough to where it needed to be. He felt relieved, too, when it turned out that along with the hockey stick and moving blanket, the purloined items were limited to various kitchenwares and photo albums. Billy naively hoped that the thief would be ratcheted with pangs of guilt, having stolen baby pictures, and might go clean from then on.

While his own room was dankly underlit, the rest of the loft was filled with magnificent late afternoon light. It was illuminated like a cathedral, but without all that showy stained glass. Billy roamed through the space while talking on the phone with Lucy and narrated everything he picked up or saw. A tumbleweed hung down like a chandelier and a swing was suspended by ropes that went up to the rafters. She'd have to see it for herself, really. He asked if they were still dating and she said, "Sure, why not?" and he listed a few reasons, and that was pretty much the end of that conversation. He sat on the swing and went back and forth torpidly, looking melancholy. He got over his moroseness quick and headed to the dartboard where he played a game of cricket against himself. Standing at a wide row of east-facing windows, he watched cars going into and out of New Jersey with the aid of a telescope.

Three roaches were on the coffee table. Two were brown, scuttley insects and one was the remaining inch of a marijuana cigarette. "What the hell," Billy figured out loud. He stretched out on sofa that was molting white-to-gray, speckled with filth like a seagull. It was itchy. He wasn't ready to slip back into a shirt. He moved around like a house cat in search of its proper spot. The French doors led to no balcony but were open and caught an excellent evening breeze. He smoked and watched the sun dip behind the jagged skyline of Temple's dorms, blazing red like an electric burner left on high.

Muffled sounds came from the upstairs of the sheetrock shanty. A body's distinct rustling. For a moment he considered dashing into his room and finding a shirt, but it was too late. The door opened. It was a young woman in a daringly-threadbare heather gray tee shirt with a black brassiere underneath. She had on small, black shorts, the kind sported by volleyball players. She smudged her Sallie Jessy Raphael glasses with her thumb and forefinger swaddled in her thin shirt and stopped to wince at Billy from the middle of the staircase. She had an expressive, dark brow and hair dyed auburn. She put her glasses on without altering her scrunched face.

"Oh, hey," she said, "I *thought* I heard somebody."

Billy nodded and stood dumbfounded that someone was here all along.

They introduced themselves and she was Jenna, a photographer.

"What brings you to Philadelphia?"

"My girlfriend wanted to move here."

"Uh-huh."

"She's back in New York. We broke up earlier today."

"Uh-huh," she said, busy making some coffee.

"Yeah, it's probably for the best. Did Lucy call you? Do you know her?" Billy ventured.

Jenna volleyed her eyes back-and-forth a few times like Kit-Cat Clock. "No-oo, I don't think so. Wait! ... *Laura*?"

"No, Lucy."

"No. I'm not friends with any Lucys."

Billy went into his room and found a shirt to put on.

When he came back into the kitchen, Jenna slammed a drawer violently. She stared at Billy with her eyebrows at an angry and obtuse angle.

"These roaches are dis-*gust*-ing." She did an about-face and snatched a dry-erase marker from the counter. "If *some*body would *do the dishes*," she said huffily while scrawling an aqua green missive on the kitchen cabinet whiteboard, "we would *not* have this problem." Her memo was crude and to-the-point.

"Yeah, I saw some bugs."

"Uh, *yeah. I'm sure ya did*. More like a billion."

Billy said that he was not pro-roach, but, when living in the city, what are you going to do? *Start with the dishes*, Jenna reiterated. That much was incontestable. And even though he just practically drove across a continent and broke up with his girlfriend who was supposed to be there too and got his stuff nabbed outside, Billy didn't have much to say.

Jenna gave a half-assed audio tour from the kitchen while the new roommate strolled along the perimeter.

"Huh, *oh yeah*…that's the swing. Lance put that in. You don't know Lance. He moved out, like, four months ago…"

"*That* is a giant stuffed unicorn that our friend rode in the Mummers Parade. You *do* know about the Mummers Parade, don't you?…

"*Jesus*…ha. Some of Jeremy Bonaventure's *art*. I mean, some of his 'art,'" Jenna said, adding the statutory air quotes to show her disapproval of the enormous canvas near the washer and dryer.

"Alright," she said, pulling her hair back tight until it was a dark-red swim cap with a small ponytail. She poured the press of coffee down the sink. "I'm going to an opening in Center City. That's what downtown is called: Center City. It was nice to meet you." Jenna took her bike off the rack and left. Watching her leave, it didn't seem like she had enough shorts on.

The night wasn't over and Kurt came home wanting to go to the bar, the Sidecar, even though it *used to be* much cooler. The only other option was buying a thin plastic bag of heavy loose cans at the Puerto Rican place down the street where a door man would pat you down and hassle your privates but never ask for an ID. Each option cost about the same amount of money.

They went to the Sidecar and you could see right away what Kurt was talking about: the joint was a dim dump full of young, confident people. The bar bustled with loud declarations of good times, with rowdy table-smacking and knocked over drinks— and that was without surveying the back patio, even. A tall can of beer and a snort of well whiskey was $3. The shot glasses were too full to clink together and their faces creased and wizened in pained reaction to the brown liquor. Suddenly that familiar tall domestic tasted great.

They'd found a seat near the pinball machine and had to shout over its flashing clamor as well as the drunk protestations of its players. The lay of the Loft-land proved to be colorful, amusing, and at times salacious. For instance, Jenna had not put enough time in and paid enough dues to earn a top-floor room but simply squirreled her stuff in there the instant it was vacant (a blatant violation of the unwritten Code of the Loft).

"That says all you need to know. She can be a real see-ya-next-Tuesday."

The joke wasn't immediately clear, but it was right away apparent that Kurt was solid and simpatico with Billy. He was from the nice part of New Jersey that didn't receive much notoriety. Taken on faith, Billy would like Julian, too, who was currently at a mass drug-binge-*cum*-music-arts-festival-gathering out in the middle of nowhere.

"But not *that* one; I forget what the one he's at is called. It has a made-up name. It's pretty new."

No, Kurt didn't know Lucy. They shared a laugh over that.

"Nobody seems to end up here on purpose," Kurt said, which was funny in its own strange, sad way.

Dylan was weird and to be avoided. The same was twice as true about Mike, but he didn't loiter around the apartment as much. Yes, Billy's room *was* sandwiched between those two... But, hey, Olivia ("Maybe *she* knew Laura?"—"Lucy"—"Maybe *she* knew Lucy?"), *she* was fun. She was in Baltimore doing a clinical study about sleep cycles.

"So she's, like, a doctor *and* she lives at the loft?"

"No-no-no," Kurt replied sternly, even wagging his finger, "she's getting paid to take part in some research investigation about sleep cycles. She has to, like, stay in bed all day and get monitored and—this is all *literally* in the dark, mind you—no lights whatsoever—and I don't know, I *think* they might give her a pill or pills or something (which, you know, *could* just be a placebo), and then at some point they barge in and wake her up at random times. Just make noise and turn on all these lights at once and write down the results."

"Jesus," Billy said from behind his beer can.

"I know! I know! Like, everyday; that's the routine (if you can call it a routine), for three weeks or something." Kurt laughed to himself. "She and her boyfriend both do it. Lab rats, but nothing *too* gnarly. And they do okay at it, too. I think this one pays two grand."

"Jesus," Billy said from behind his beer can again.

"Right?!" Kurt took the last drink from his can. "Right!" he answered himself. "She pretty much uses the loft to store her shit in between these trials. Waitresses in-between some, too, over at this Mexican place. Do you know Don Rodriguez?"

"No."

"It's good. We'll have to go there sometime. You know: when she's working. But, yeah, basically she comes out $1800 ahead after twenty days or however long it goes for ... I'd do it, too, but you need to have clean piss, drug-free and all that."

Ah, so that's *the catch*.

"Apparently," said Kurt, pausing and giving Billy a devilish eyebrow raise, mid-sip from his empty can, "apparently, there's a big NASA-funded study coming up, looking into humans going to Mars and shit, where you just have to stay in bed, hooked up to an IV for, like, a year, but that's it: you just hang out in a bed, bring all those books you've been meaning to read, and they hand you a big, fat check."

"How big?" Billy asked.

"*NASA* big," which was enough said.

Not long after, they clumsily went back to the loft and took some hacks with the vaporizer, which was a healthier way for one to do recreational drugs. The machine was new to Billy, who prudishly shied away from marijuana while studiously working towards his degree from a college commended yearly by *High Times*. To get stoned while enrolled at the Experimental Liberal Arts College was to prove every priggish twig in the family tree right. But tonight they inhaled under the guise of science, as Billy had some rust-veined pot that Lucy forgot to snag. Kurt wanted to compare it to the local I-95 fare.

"What's this called again?" Kurt asked, slouched low on the ratty "the-stories-this-thing-could-tell" couch.

"*Spiderwoman*," Billy said, the word a veritable plume of pungent vapor.

The name tickled Kurt. He crumpled down onto the floor and lay there cracking up for a full minute, helpless as a flipped-over tortoise. Billy caught on, too, as often happens under these sorts of circumstances, and the two stayed up late marveling at the television's highlights of the previous year in ski-jumping. Billy shuffled off to bed eventually and noticed that his mattress was pancake-flat on the floor. His senses were as dull as an old butter knife and he was in no condition to try and remedy the problem, so he slept on a pile of loose blankets and deflated rubber.

3

The two most important things to do that first week in Philadelphia were: a) sell the truck before it got stolen or the insurance expired (whichever came first), and b) go to his upcoming job interview. Billy would have to get his bearings along the way.

A prospective buyer wrote Billy highly enthusiastic and strangely punctuated emails concerning the truck, and an interview with an educational non-profit had been lined up for weeks now. Billy was on his way out the door to show the truck. His interview was the next day.

"Alright, Dylan, I need to go see this guy about selling my truck."

"Cool," Dylan said over a mixing bowl of confetti-colored cereal.

"But I'm expecting a very important letter. FedEx."

Dylan munched away and nodded. Could he even hear what was being said over all that chewing?

"It's a copy of my birth certificate. I need it to get hired for this job. Are you going to be around to sign for it, if it comes while I'm gone?"

"Yeah, sure, sure, no problem," Dylan said, with milk in the corners of his mouth. "I'll sign that thing—if it comes." He'd poured too much milk in the bowl and had to now square things by adding more cereal. He tilted the box at too steep an incline, though, and the last of the cereal avalanched in. After a few insipid attempts to scoop it back in the box, Dylan decided to pour another half-cup of milk in the bowl to re-balance things.

'*If it comes*' … that hardly sounded reassuring. And watching him mishandle the fixing of breakfast cereal at 3 p.m., Billy saw that this wasn't the sort of task that you'd like to depend on Dylan for. It required concurrent spatial and temporal awareness. But there was no other present option.

Billy was ready to go get *at least* $850 for his truck that day—he was *not* walking away without getting at least $850.

Out the elevator and down on the street, walking towards the truck, Billy knew he didn't leave his window rolled down. That would've been stupid in this neighborhood. Then he realized he *was* being stupid because someone had busted out the driver's side window.

"You sell the truck?" Dylan asked with his mouth loutishly full and *crunch-crunch-crunch*ing away.

Billy sullenly rummaged through the utility room, causing enough racket to disregard Dylan's jackassery. He came out with an orange contractor's bucket and a dust pan. "Window's broke," he said on his way back out the door. He heard the hounds of 608 howl and bark menacingly until the elevator doors closed.

Billy didn't know any better and agreed to the meeting place not far from home on Front Street, under the El. It turned out to be an open-air drug market currently in an afternoon lull, taking an Iberian siesta and sleeping off the day's score.

"Well, that window's broke, for one thing," said the prospective buyer.

"I know. I know. It just happened. I'm asking $800 now: that's the asking price minus the cost of a new window."

He sucked his teeth in skeptical riposte. "Who quoted you that?"

"That's just a ballpark figure."

"So you're saying you made it up. Right off the top of the dome."

Billy was poised to tell this guy off—who in the hell does he think he is and such—but he was three inches and fifty pounds larger than Billy (who'd never been in a fistfight) could conceivably manage.

"Atchually," the man said abruptly, almost shouting, before soundlessly staring down between his boots for a full five seconds. Bringing his head back up, the man's gaze unsettled Billy. "You know, I got some ins over at a dump, so nobody's giving nobody $200 for a window on some Jap truck. Not unless you want to throw your money away for one of those hot-shot, mobile repair wetbacks that'll come and do it." He spat something brown from the side of his mouth. "Shit, they'll rip you off, plain as day. That's their game. And they'll steal your woman, too." He winked at Billy and a chill ran through him.

Baby-blanket-blue-colored steel I-beams stretched on in a ribbon of shadow and sketch. Billy gulped like a nervous character in a comic strip.

He realized that he was meeting with a man he'd exchanged one email with, a man he only knew as need2rideher@bizz.com. The two of them were alone and near a vacant lot where they were to exchange cash for truck.

The man was a muscular blond with colorless, close-cropped hair and eyebrows. He sported a tight-fitting shirt with a rhinestoned Celtic cross. He had ass-kicking boots and a digital watch with a face the size of a tea saucer. Every movement he made made Billy increasingly tense and disoriented to the point that he now merely wanted *out*. This was simply not a good place to dicker. There were hypodermics on the pavement.

The man crouched down and looked up around the wheel well, playing the part of border guard with methodical zeal.

"Drove it from Washington?"

"Um, yeah, that's right. Week straight, plenty of miles, ran like a champ. Never had to—"

"I see," he said, unimpressed, thumbing his nose. "So you drove it from the state, then. Not, uh … you know. The *other* one." There was something vindictive about the way he said "other." "Lots of Indians in your Washington, though."

"Well, I wouldn't say '*lots*,' but—"

"You know what's the difference between an Indian and a buffalo?"

"Uh … I think so."

The man didn't follow up on it, fortunately.

"Friend of mine once had one of these trucks. Thing started smelling completely out of nowhere.

Just stinking of its own accord. Smelled like…"
Billy didn't want to hear what this mind was going to
come up with and zoned out for a second, if only for
his own wellbeing. "Yup. He had to flat-out *abandon*
it outside of Saginaw, Michigan. Shit, nobody in their
right mind woulda paid money for that thing… Turd
on wheels." The man slid his thick fingers, sans
thumb, into the door handle's hollow. Billy watched
as he friskily wiggled the middle digit about as if performing an intimate and secret tickle. "No sir, me-
chanics couldn't say what it was. I know what you're
thinking and, yes: they checked the engine block for
various dead animals. Cats, as you well know, will
climb into an engine for a rest. Dumbasses. Think it's
a cozy place to nap in. Killed my share of cats that
way. A ferret once, too. Course, a ferret is much more
intelligent than your average goldbrickin' piece-a-shit
house cat." The man nodded pensively. "Then again,
you got to take into account that some ferrets are
naturally *dumb*." He stopped nodding and indeed all
movement. "They could not get rid of that smell." He
stared up at Billy with his green, ocean-colored eyes
and wasn't going to break his gaze until his opponent
deferred.

No sense in asking this guy if he'd seen the
Seinfeld where the valet has such potent B.O. that
Jerry has to get rid of his Saab.

"This one never did that, no cats in the engine,"
Billy answered, his attention focused down at his
own dirty white sneakers. "Smells fine, usually. Gets
good mileage. It's a good truck."

The man raised an eyebrow but didn't alter

his flinty expression. He walked to the back of the truck and stood erect at the tailgate. Quite out of nowhere, while still ogling Billy, the man began jostling the bed up and down for some seconds. He then stopped, satisfied, or perhaps just done with, whatever he saw, heard, or felt.

I shouldn't have added that "usually," Billy reprimanded himself.

"No, I don't suppose that's a fault or problem with this particular make and model. You don't want to throw the baby out with the bath water … and that's coming from a man that was thrown out from the tub a time or two growing up." He laughed brusquely; it sounded like he was clearing his throat. "Yeah, I bet that stink was just a freak thing." He hustled his balls openly and spat down near Billy's shoes, close enough to make him take a step back. "Transmission going out ain't a freak though, is it? New break pads, new break *drum*. No sir, those ain't *freak* things. No, sir." He began prattling off car parts under his breath while slowly circumscribing an oval around the vehicle in shamanistic motor rite, stopping only to measure personally consequential parts of the truck with his thumb and index finger serving as a caliper. "It'll get me to Colorado Springs, though, won't it?"

"Yes, it certainly will," agreed Billy, placated by the thought of distance.

The man "smiled," showing Billy as many of his teeth as he could at once.

"Tell you what: I'll give ya six hunnert."

"Okay," Billy said, screaming at himself, running through imaginatively reprehensible and bitter pronouncements concerning his own manhood. But whichever gland was in charge of safety told him to take the money and run.

They signed papers on the hood (Billy not wanting to get in the cab and use the dashboard) and the buyer persuaded him to put the agreed price of sale down on the title as 'GIFT' so "that slick jellybean Obama can't get in on the action." Then, sounding as if through no fault other than the dreaded hand of fate, the man (his name he scrawled on the title revealing him as one "Dish McAlister") announced that he had only $500 cash on him and would have to write a post-dated check for the balance—*MEMO: not to be cashed until I call recipient with the "O.K."*.

A sticker from FedEx was on the door. They would try and deliver again tomorrow.

Inside, Dylan was sprawled out on the couch like an effete potentate with a Wii remote in his hand. He was bowling in palatial repose.

"Hey," Kurt whispered, focused on the screen. "We were about to go toss the frisbee, but Dylan's bowling a perfect game." Billy was none-too-glad at the news and hoped that the jinx was on. "He's got this new form."

Minutes later (everyone in agreement that 291 was a very, very good score) Dylan explained (spread out in the same position on the couch that every day looked more like a dog bed) that he hadn't heard any knock.

"Dude, that's weird," he said, "because you saw

it, I was really in the zone for the past, what, hour and a half?"

This alibi satisfied some and seemed quite damning to others. Billy signed and re-attached the sticker-waiver. Erring on the side of caution, he used a strip of packing tape to further affix it to the door.

Billy couldn't stay mad, though—it was Labor Day. This wasn't just a holiday: it was *his* holiday. He was a laborer because there was no pile of cushiony family money to fall safely into like a stuntman should he choose to make daring leaps with his life. Billy was a prole, even if he didn't have a job yet (and hadn't had one in ages aside from a twelve-hour-a-week work-study job at the college Language Lab (a forgotten room in the Com II building with three computers and a shelf of assorted dictionaries)). At his heart, Billy was industrious. Sure, he'd spent much of his first week in Philly loafing and getting toasted, but he was still capable of industry. Unpacking, selling his truck, cleaning the loft and watering its various flora. He was a worker. He would always have to earn his way and was proud of it.

In observance of the American worker, Billy, Kurt, and Dylan (who tagged along), took their show on the road. They scarfed down pepperoni slices and watched baseball on a pizzeria patio's mounted big screen. The gang enjoyed a holiday happy-hour at a *tap room* serviced by an attractive wait staff. On his receipt beside the word 'TIP,' Billy boldly wrote 'CASH' and left a ten. Hamilton's smirk reassured Billy and had him feeling magnanimous. Camden's sallow skyline shimmied on the waters of the Delaware while the three young men shared a joint and wafted a frisbee back and forth in the Penn Treaty Park sunshine. The statue of William Penn smiled benevolently on the boys' merriment and mirth. Afterwards, the trio ambled and perused along a trendy, boutique-lined route home. Billy paid $4 for an iced coffee, conspicuously dropped his dollars' worth of change in the big glass jar for the cute freckled girl that poured it, and then spent more than he wanted to at a sidewalk flea market while riding a caffeine high.

Back at the Lofts, the growling and woofing started as soon as the elevator opened to the sixth floor. Six heavy, slowly-sobering legs tromped towards the furthest door, the one with the FedEx sticker stuck to it. Seeing his own signature taped up on the door reminded Billy that he had had more than enough of Dylan for one day. Kurt was late for a date and only stepped inside the loft long enough to grab his bike and say goodbye. Billy felt sunburnt and on the edge of a 6 o'clock hangover.

Inside his room, Billy glared at the purchases heaped on top of his flaccid air mattress. A soft, old yellow tee shirt read 'New Mexico—the Land of Enchantment' and featured a faded hot air balloon. On the sidewalk it looked light and fun; here it looked like a size-too-small souvenir from a place he'd never visited. 'Horn Broken—Watch For Finger!' read the bumper sticker he decided to get a few hours after selling his vehicle. The handsomely-antiqued wooden crate he bought with winter hat-and scarf-storage in mind seemed particularly stu-

pid in the small, stiflingly hot room. Billy counted
the cash in his wallet. The tap room receipt was
folded in amongst the remaining bills.

He undressed and laid down. An image of a
lovely-but-fleeting waitress, the disquieting face
of Dish McAlister, and countless numbers floated
through his head like a grim and boring mobile.
Billy closed his eyes and waited to fall asleep.

Miraculously, forty-five minutes before his job
interview the next day, a loud knock announced the
arrival of Billy's belated birth certificate. Inside the
big, tamper-proof envelope was his document, officially stamped with the state's holographic seal of
approval.

Part of the logic behind moving to Philadelphia,
a subject upon which he was grilled and made to account for at every opportunity, was to find *meaningful*
work. A job where you could come home not smelling like whatever food you served, preferably. Not
many were citing economic opportunity as the mo-
tivation behind relocating to this place, lately of 1.5
million residents, but in Billy's mind it would all work
out. The city seemed to have more needs than willing helpers. Phone interviews with one organization
went well enough to earn him an invite to the second
round once he got into town. Getting involved with
a non-profit serving the city's tumbledown schools
probably wasn't going to become a "career" and it certainly wouldn't pay well. But people might even come
to respect him, which would be a first.

Billy sat down on a folding chair in a small, windowless room, horseshoed by seven old computers, the kinds with deep monitors and screens that bulged out like beach balls. Wishing to exude aplomb, he sat as planned in a "Rock of Gibraltar" stance: legs spread wide, confident and Lincolnesque. Without the necessary arm-rests, however, Billy felt crude if not downright raunchy. He scrambled into a figure-four (ankle-over-knee), but found the nervous bobbing of his foot a distraction. In desperation, he settled on a full-fledged Continental pose with his hands contemplatively clasped, his knees together and thighs squeezed. His grimy white sneaker dangled coolly.

"William, what *is* service to you?" asked a very dark-skinned woman who spoke in a raspy, island patois.

It felt like a word association test and Billy wasn't sure of what worked better: short, decisive, sanguine answers or a thoughtful pause, a deep, sincere locking of the eyes and something beginning with a baritone "Well…"

"Service, to me, is… doing things for others… you know, kind of like Christmas. *True* Christmas, that is. Not that I'm religious, really. Oh, and being a difference-maker. That as well." Somehow he managed to fail at both options simultaneously and nervously waited for the next question. "Sorry."

"Uh-huh, very good," said the other examiner, an older woman with a sort of bee-hive of skinny braids wrapped up and held together by an unseen force. "William: what's an example of a difficult situation you encountered and how did you deal with it?" She looked up from her packet at Billy and smiled good-naturedly for a moment.

"Shoot, just moving here." Billy knew how bad this might backfire, giving his would-be employer a glimpse of his true, off-the-clock self, but he also knew that his canned answers were ringing hollow and tinny. Billy laid into it: Lucy, the bindle bandit, his small room, the birth certificate episode, the lunatic he sold his truck to for *half* of what he wanted—

"But you're liking living in Philadelphia?" the hoarse-voiced questioner interrupted.

"Oh, yes, definitely!"

"Okay. That's good."

Billy had anxiously squashed his legs together *too* tightly during his antic rant. He undid his legs and took a deep breath before switching into an upright and rigid posture. He sat like a monolithic statue of an Egyptian pharaoh while the two ladies excused themselves from the room. He watched the screen-savers. Busy and colorful pipes popped out from blackness and cluttered things up, only to vanish and start over again, forever waiting for a mouse to jiggle. The women walked back in the room.

"We know you applied for the mentorship program, but, looking at your credentials and qualifications, we think there's a unique opportunity for you with, well, ha, the *Opportunity* Career and Educational Advancement Network—O.C.E.A.N. It's at their new charter, the Academic Vision Institute. We'd like to offer you a position there. How does that sound?"

"Great," Billy said, "sensational!" Nobody had ever cited his credentials before! "What does that mean?"

O.C.E.A.N. was a nationwide social welfare improvement organization with roots in '60s anti-poverty programs from the other side of America. They had only recently spread out into the burgeoning world of charter schools after decades of varying community involvements. The Academic Vision Institute was O.C.E.A.N.'s mid-Atlantic flagship. Baltimore was said to be watching it closely.

The AVI was a regionally-accredited accelerated charter school designed for sixteen- to twenty-one-year-old out-of-school and under-credited students. The term "drop-out" was strongly frowned upon, though AVI was colloquially known as "the school for drop-outs." Often enrolled in school by court-order but too old and altogether *grown* to attend classes with other appropriately-aged freshmen and sophomores, the students at AVI had the chance to play catch up and graduate in two years or less if they stuck with it. Daily four-hour sessions, AM or PM, to fit the students' work/childcare schedule, a state-of-the-art computer lab with cyber-courses in everything from Art History to Zoology… All told, a pretty sweet deal if you were willing to play the game, wear your cranberry polo and black or khaki pants (no exceptions), and sign in on time (8:30 or 12:30, depending).

For all the talk about flagships and Baltimore, though, the AVI was a rented corridor in one of the city's half-full historic high schools. Similar to the movie *Speed*, the school had to maintain equilibrium by enrolling between one and 225 regularly-attending students or a malevolent, unseen force would blow the whole thing up. The staff was a patchwork of PA emergency-certified educators, substitutes grown weary of that particular grind, and some young "difference-makers" like Billy, who became a case worker for sixty or so of the students.

The dignity and respectability of being a serious person with a serious job wore off as soon as it became apparent that nobody, Billy included, took the Academic Vision Institute seriously. The "kids" Billy was accountable for were mostly two to four years his junior and, despite having not having much in the way of scholarly success, were still far beyond needing the guidance of a strange and shabby white man from somewhere out West.

For the first month, everything that occurred between the hours of 8:30 a.m. and 4:30 p.m. frustrated Billy. He knew his wisdom was being was being squandered daily. He couldn't get the simplest message across: that all you needed to do was come to school for half as long and you'd get your diploma twice as fast. This failure to communicate couldn't possibly be his fault. For some reason the students struggled to see how the math worked out so plainly in their favor.

He told them so all the time.

He exclaimed and pleaded and even studded his sentences with "yo" and "chill," but the words came out dry and dead like loud autumn leaves whose color quickly turned brown. His voice was just another thing for the students to tune out … By October he was cool and passive like the weather outside and mostly concerned with finding a clever Halloween costume.

Only a few Cambodian and Laotian girls seemed to be noiselessly making something out of this grand opportunity. Attendance was highest on Friday when trans-passes were handed out. Nobody sought suggestions or help. Everyone had an attitude, a chip on their shoulder, and often times both. Billy's most important responsibilities were holding onto his students' cell phones during school hours and going to the cafeteria to get breakfast and lunch for the Institute.

4

There were many disappointments that were plain to see just by looking at Billy (who always did a very poor job of masking expressions of displeasure, disgust, or despair), but his biggest grief was kept secret and had to do with his diet.

The first thing Billy did every morning at work was to swing by the main school's cafeteria in the basement two floors below and pick up breakfast for the Academic Vision Institute: a plastic crate of thirty assorted milks (chocolate, obviously, being the only one anybody ever drank), twenty foil-topped orange juices ("contains less than 6% juice/product of Brazil, Honduras, El Salvador, and the United States"), around ten individually-sealed plastic cereal bowls (plus ten spork-napkin-straw kits), various fruits (almost always mealy, thick-skinned Red Deliciouses and rock-hard pears), and motley breakfast pastries. On a good day there'd be an assortment of aluminum-wrapped breakfast sandwiches (usually crumbling biscuits with white government-issue cheese and institutional scrambled eggs that were, up until recently, yellow powder in a large carton). There was no hot stuff today, though, and Billy topped off his crate with Frosted French Toast Cereal Munch Bars and Nutri-Taste Flapjax 'Sploders.

The kids liked those 'Sploders and the sticky

pretext it gave them to wander out of class and use the bathroom for minutes on end.

Give the people what they want, he thought to himself, snatching up a few extra squishy syrup logs from the warming compartment.

No small part of the embarrassment incurred during the most important meal of the day was the shameful march back from the cafeteria to that strange school in the separated hallway. The food would be stacked high like luggage trunks on the *Beverly Hillbillies'* jalopy. Students wandering the main school's hallways before advisory would stop and stare, no doubt timing and envisioning the ideal moment for stick to meet spoke. Billy always made certain to walk this route most heedfully, like a drunk utilizing every bit of his wavering focus to make it to the bathroom and take care of business without incident.

Once safely at the Institute, Billy would carefully (and some mornings delicately) present the day's bounty on a hallway conference table in full-fledged continental splendor. This morning, for instance, he fanned out the Munch Bars in a manner inviting to the eye and lined up the milk cartons like an elite North Korean Army parade unit.

"Now *that's* what I'm talkin' 'bout," a student said in response to the 'Sploders, "them jawns be *on point*."

The truly humiliating part of the day's routine took place inside of Billy's "office."

You had to punch in a simple code on the tacky, round buttons below the heavy door's handle to gain entry inside the windowless, cinder block space. Eight-foot-high racks of servers blinked, hummed, and kept the temperature sweltering. Running the length of the opposite wall was a row of several beige filing cabinets. Only one of them contained files on AVI students: the rest were locked and mysteriously "there when we got here." A large, dusty clock hung on the wall and remained forever at 10:17, telling the correct time twice a day. The lights, naturally, were fluorescent.

Billy's bunkerish office was the sort of place that dictators, generalissimos, and lesser military strong men had recurring nightmares about, visions of their last days. It was also where the faux-wood-grained mini-fridge was—the only safe spot for the remainder milk and any other perishables.

And it was while behind the cover of the thick, dented steel door, at around 8:40 a.m., that he would *actually eat* what he knew to be horrible, gunky junk, gorging himself on whatever he could. He consumed fast and made gross sounds that were grosser because of their softness and secrecy. He was a hungry person not wanting to get caught. You could casually sit with a container of Multi-grain Breakfast O's there beside you, (a smart, healthy snack), but you couldn't expect to get caught cramming 'Sploders in your face and not be viewed ... *differently*.

Sometimes students, especially the pregnant ones who had *carte blanche* when it came to eating food on their own terms during the school day, would come in and look around for something they'd seen that morning.

"Yo, where the banana bread go?" a girl would ask, confusedly looking into the orange plastic crate.

"Oh, they ate 'em," Billy would explain. "Dehquan and, uh, Kamir."

"Dag, they *greedy*."

"There's some actual bananas left," Billy would try and placate, maybe feel like he'd done something positive, turning a kid onto fruit. "They're over there by that stack of folders."

"Nah, I like that *bread*."

Lunch was the same, just later in the day with different sorts of sandwiches and sometimes pizza.

Today happened to be pizza: a plump, doughy wedge covered with a thick quilt of sweating, yellow cheese. The only thing hot was the red sauce in between.

5

The gang was all at the bar one night hearing Billy's side of things and drinking from their signature tall cans of beer.

"Koran-with-a-K called me *old-head* today. Champagne and Khadijah got sent home because they altered their uniforms to the point of distraction. Derek Murray said he was gonna have his uncle 'talk to me' because I told his P.O. what his attendance was. I mean: shit, I didn't call the guy. He called *me*." Billy took a sip. "Like I get up every morning so I can sit around and narc on Derek Murray."

"What's that mean? What's he gonna do?" Alex asked. He was an ambivalent type with watery eyes made waterier after a shot of well whiskey.

"Nothing. I told him, 'Dude, your uncle is *not* going to come down here and fight me because you haven't been coming to school. *I'll* talk to *him*. *I'll call* if you really want me to.'" Billy poked himself too hard in the sternum in an act of demonstrative toughness. "Not that I was trying to be a wiseguy or anything, but... it's just... c'mon, Derek Murray. Get it together."

The table nodded in consensus.

"I mean, isn't my advice good, worth something?" Billy asked rhetorically, subconsciously stopping short of *Look where it got me.* "I'm the one that got the degree, that went through *college*," he said earnestly.

No one was sure how to assuage their friend properly or if that's what he was after, even.

"Martinez pops up a *towering* can of corn," the TV's play-by-play blurted.

Somehow Billy thought this to be a good segue: "Then I saw a woman throw a cup of coffee on her kid today coming home. Stormed off the bus, yelling at him—he must've been, like, twelve—'this ain't the right bus, you lil' dickhead!' and just threw her Dunkin' Donuts cup right at him."

Alex looked all the more ready to cry.

"Where'd you see that?" Ray asked dumbfounded, lazily. He never paid much attention and yet always looked dumbfounded.

"Cecil B. Moore, down by those water or gas buildings or whatever. I mean, the coffee had a lot of cream in it. It didn't scald him."

"That's good," someone at the table added.

"Yeah, but still: what the hell." Billy finished the can and gave it a swirl to be sure.

If there was one of those time-honored silver linings to the great gripe that was his life Monday-thru-Friday, 6 a.m.-5:30 p.m., it was that all the heaviness at work gave Billy exciting new social personae: he could let himself get loosey-goosey amongst his peers or be thoughtfully taciturn or something in-between. His grievances were no longer esoteric things. Nowadays he blew steam daily about *life*. He earned every cheap ounce he drank after work. And on weekends he danced and drank and sang.

Lucy would not recognize him these days.

So Billy changed things up, opting to shrug and stop talking about work, to go get another can of beer, and to use his change to tip Hector and use the jukebox.

He *Super-Search*ed a popular rap song from the year 2000 and for the next four-and-a-half minutes the bar was a wild, festive place for the four guys drinking beer at a table and for the bartender casually munching a personal-sized bag of BBQ Chips. Then the song gracefully faded out and the bar was quiet save the ball game.

"Hey folks—it's that time again. That's right: Second Commonwealth Bank's *Caught In A Pickle Fan Trivia Challenge* question of the game, sponsored by … Second Commonwealth Bank. Did you know that if you saved *three dollars* a day, you'd have over *a thousand dollars* towards that dream vacation next year? First Commonwealth Bank reminds you that saving *small* … can mean big things! Alright, now, Chief, which third-baseman led the league …"

"Oh, thanks for the math lesson."

"Yeah, jeez, wow. Three dollars a day, times three-sixty-five, equals … over a thousand. Great."

"I believe I'd rather buy myself a beer every day," Billy said to the resounding approval of the table and Hector the bartender even. Billy was obliged to raise his can in humble recognition of this *bon mot*.

Later in the evening the same two girls that were

at the bar most nights came in. Their faces were dolled up but they were dressed like lumberjacks with boots and dirty jeans and plenty of plaid. Straight blonde hair hung from beneath their wool caps. Not long after he first moved here, Billy bought them each a can of beer. He tried to small talk with them, but they didn't have much to say and he walked away feeling like he'd bought five dollars' worth of bread to feed to park ducks.

And before too long, what definitely felt like *too soon*, Billy was awake and getting dressed for work amid the damnable quiet of other people softly snoozing in their sheetrock suites. He waited for the train with the same group of anonymous, recognizable people, like he did every weekday morning. Aboard the El, Billy held a book like a shield covering his face. This did not stop a hustler in highwaters and buttery Timberlands from shuffling up before him and offering his bootleg wares.

"Check it out, man, I got that *Argo*," he said, flashing a jewel case. "Ben Af-lack, man. I seen it myself and give it two thumbs up." He paused and moved on. "I got *Paranormal Activity 4* and I got *Taken II*. Five bucks each, three for ten."

A small bomb had gone off elsewhere in America earlier that week. Nobody got seriously hurt but there were still police with assault rifles monitoring City Hall station. Two of them were shooting the shit with one another early in the a.m.. One of the officers demonstrated the outrageous length of something by holding his open hands about ten inches apart and shaking them for effect. His partner seemed incredulous, but they both laughed about it. Before making his free interchange to the Broad Street Line, a dark and withered homeless man shook a coffee cup full of something that was not spare change at Billy. The man begged for help in a gruff whisper. Billy mouthed the word "I," shrugged, and pretended to be in a great hurry.

Then a pigeon got on board a southbound train and caused much confusion and hysteria before it got off at Tasker-Morris. A sleepy mother got her stroller and infant passenger jammed in one of the rotating turnstile exits at Billy's stop.

"Yo!... a baby stuck in that jawn!" said one of the AVI students on his way to class.

By November, when it becomes most apparent in this hemisphere that things are going to get dark and cold for a while, Billy was locked in to the demoralizing and undeviating cycle commonly referred to as the work week. For five consecutive days he would have the same 5:59 a.m. wake up time (so he could say that he got up before 6 a.m. for his job every day), the predictable thirty-nine-minute commute to work, the slow, changeless nine hours *at* work, the mirrored thirty-nine minutes it took to get back home, just in time for *Jeopardy* and *Wheel*—all this only to crap out by 10).

Mandatory trainings were even scheduled on days when schools were closed. He'd arranged for the fumigators to come spray the roaches on Election Day and left a key under the doormat while he sat through a whole day of terms and conditions. Hadn't he been over most of this in September? The only amendment Billy noticed was a lone piece of paperwork concerning life insurance.

Of all the things in the world: life insurance!

The dull gyre of employment earned him a biweekly stipend of $393.76 direct-deposited into his bank account. But rent and phone bill were due ($250), and a grocery trip to Hermano's was needed to buy, among other essentials, a sack of potatoes, two bricks of coffee, and plenty of dried pink beans (stocking up Oregon Trail-style in the Goya aisle) ($36.50); he had to get two weeks of transit tokens ($31); then Billy had thirteen days left to stretch $76.26. It would be a fortnight of leftover steam-cooked cafeteria burgers brought home for dinner (and eating those un-microwaved and in bitter silence and dour drywall solitude).

Eventually came another biweekly stipend of $393.76 direct-deposited into his bank account, with only utilities due ($84 (even split seven ways, the Loft was expensive to heat, illuminate, and connect to the Internet)). These special weekends were spent living like the playboy of the western world to the tune of $30 (?!) at the bar, $55 for an eighth of *Green Goo*, a very generous $10 towards a case of Boxer Beer ("*The Beer of Champions*") to be split amongst friends, and an $8 contribution for a stake in a G-town Pizza "family special"; $15 got spent on a clean copy of *Station to Station* on vinyl (because even if he had it on his MP3 player, "you see *Diamond Dogs* sometimes, but you rarely find *Station to Station*"); groceries were bought at the new shopping plaza near Temple ($63.87) where young coeds shopped in their jammies, and, how could he forget?, *tokens again* ($31), with $96.89 left to show for it.

Sometimes he cursed David Bowie and sometimes he felt lucky to have that much.

Finally, like the inner mechanisms of a watch that click together and bring about the visible movements on its face, you could track whichever mood-altering chemicals were within Billy's price range and maintaining his system just by glancing at his expression. He never binged so hard or spent so recklessly that he was forced to dry out longer than a couple of days, but one could easily tell when he was furthest between paychecks, practically sweating Cafe La Llave and seldom making direct eye contact…

6

Billy figured out that his air-mattress couldn't hold air because the mice had chewed holes in it.

He concurrently furnished his room with useable objects picked up the night before the trash was collected and made some shelves out of an old ladder and some perfectly good pine slats someone was throwing out.

Trash day in Fishtown was not as bad as it sounded.

Billy's scrappy decor looked like garbage a few days later when Jenna sold some of her photography to the airport. Suddenly the girl living nine feet away from him was flush with jet-set cash. Her pictures were framed up along the moving walkway in the D Concourse. Billy hadn't seen her photographs but knew them to be black and white and mostly of nice things and ugly things near one another (*i.e.*, children hop-scotching in the shadows of a defunct factory, a tramp fishing on an empty and serene pier). Jenna surely considered doing a self-portrait somewhere in her downmarket dwelling.

If she ever did, Billy would know. The young woman was rightfully proud and the walls were thin. She talked about her photos often, conversing inside her room or freely rambling through the loft with a slender, squarish phone held to the side of her head. She would speak thusly: "It's weird to think all these people are seeing my *photography*, so randomly, you know, before they zoom off all over the world … It's like … they're taking my art *with* them—which is *exactly* what I've always tried to do, as a photographer …"

Meanwhile, packages arrived for Jenna nearly every day. Spontaneous online purchases patiently awaited her in yellow bubble mailers and plain brown boxes, piled up on the kitchen table two or three times each week.

"Ohmygawd, it's *here!*" she one day squealed before prancing over to the parcel on the table and ripping things apart like it was Christmas morning. "Oh. Wait." She made a glum face. "This isn't what I *thought* it was." Jenna looked around the room with a baffled expression and pulled out a small glass pyramid. "I totally, completely forgot about this—that's how long it took them to ship it." And then *it*, whatever it was that she was actually excited for, would arrive the next day.

The mail brought with it a much more personal misfortune for Billy later that week. One chilly Tuesday there was a single item in box the box marked 609: an envelope addressed to William George with the heading "URGENT" on it. He scrutinized it on the way upstairs. It almost didn't appear official because it was peppered with exclamation points and italicized words and other typographical features typically pooh-poohed by legal and governmental writing manuals. When he got inside the apartment,

Billy plopped down on the moldering sectional next to Kurt and Julian. All three of them were slouched low and wearing their coats inside. The high that day was thirty-nine degrees (and that had happened some hours ago). Billy leaned forward with no small amount of effort and flipped on the vaporizer, readying himself for problems. The machine's neon undercarriage glowed like the underside of a souped-up Honda.

"Well, hi, honey, how was *your* day?" Julian said before laughing in his warm signature tenor. "Go ahead and take a load off."

Kurt smiled and his mustache went along for the ride.

Billy exhaled and twisted the grinder back and forth frantically. "Hey guys. My day was fine," he replied automatically. "How are you boys?"

"Oh, it looks like we're about ten minutes away from being alright," Kurt said, chuckling, then coughing, then sneezing twice.

"Yeah right! More like twenty minutes since we *were* alright," Julian added.

More laughter, high fives, wheezing, and hacking.

"So tell me, then: is it true?" Billy paused while loading the glass apparatus. "Is Doctor Phil better ... *on drugs*?"

They thought about it. "Pretty much," they agreed, "*much* better."

Before joining in with his friends, Billy opened his mail and tried to make sense of what it told. *1998 Mazda Truck ... I-80 toll plaza ... Illinois ... October 16, 2012 ... $28*. What was the meaning of this? He drove here in *August*. On I-90, mostly. He stroked his chin and furrowed his brow until the name "Dish McAlister" urgently popped into his head. Dish must not have handled the title paperwork and left the vehicle under the heretofore good name of William Henry George, XXX-XX-2233. $28 was only the tip of the iceberg, as Billy nervously imagined the speed trap cameras he surely blew past, the unabashed illegal rights taken on red lights across America ...

"Hey, you *do* know you turned this thing on, right?" Julian reminded Billy as he walked towards his room, busily dialing an 800 number.

"Yeah, yeah, g'head, I'll be out in a minute."

He pressed many buttons on his keypad before opting for '0' and a personal care representative. Very quickly, Billy learned that the number he was calling and the mail he had received was from a third-party billing and collection agency with a call center located in Iowa. They were subcontracted by the state and toll plaza authority, utterly powerless to handle an issue concerning transfer-of-ownership. Billy needed to call the department of licensing when they opened tomorrow.

"I *can* assist you with paying the citation notice you received, however," the polite Midwestern woman on the other end offered.

He thanked the representative for her service and said he was far too busy to do so presently. Then Billy rejoined his friends at the vaporizer before hitting up the indoor swing in hopes of some light spirit-lifting.

"Can we put a record on or something?" Billy asked an indistinct half-hour later.

"Sure," Kurt said, "that sounds cool."

Billy fetched the Bowie record and brought it out to the living room.

Kurt cooed while examining the sleeve. "I see *Let's Dance* and *Lodger* and stuff all the time, but I don't usually see *Station to Station*."

Billy smiled.

"Are you putting a record on?" Julian asked from his 2' by 4' balcony of 2x4s.

"Yeah," Billy called to him. "Why? Are you trying to transcendentally meditate?"

"No, but that receiver doesn't work."

So Billy got the receiver out from his room (which was the only bit of audio equipment that wasn't Lucy's) and swapped it with the fritzed-out rig. This task took both brawn and finesse: the cumbersome piece of trash was intricately tangled with many important cables and cords behind the ramshackle fake-oak entertainment center. Kurt lent a hand. This was not light work. The equipment was heavy and oblong. The unit was finally in place and plugged in to a worrisomely overburdened powerstrip. The red and white ends of the RCA cables were correctly inserted into the appropriate PHONO IN jacks. Kurt took the record out and ceremoniously placed it on the platter.

"Ha, *duh*," Billy smacked his palm into his forehead with a wet *thwack*. "We forgot to hook up the speakers."

"Gosh, that was dumb," Kurt agreed.

"We don't *have* any speakers," Julian shouted through his wall. "Those were Laura Beth's. She took them when she moved out."

Before going to bed, Billy secretly stared at the check for $100 and prepared himself to deposit it tomorrow, repercussions be damned. But then he thought vaguely of repercussions and he changed his mind.

Absolving his ties to the truck was fairly straightforward, although not paying the tolls incurred under his name could cause his license to be revoked if whatever state(s) the charges were left unattended to had a reciprocal motor vehicle agreement. The DMV worker did not know offhand which states were in league with the Commonwealth of Pennsylvania.

"Don't you have a list of states that PA works with or something?" Billy asked.

The icy silence of the DMV worker shamed Billy.

Eventually he called the 800 number again and paid $28 out of the $100 or so that was left in checking. The $3 fee for paying over the phone actually stung. The next afternoon a similar notice arrived in the mail from Colorado and he immediately took care of the $12 in fees Dish McAlister had welshed high in the Rockies.

At least the truck made it to Colorado.

"Look. *This* isn't what's important," Billy said, tapping the blue-gray flip-phone on his desk. "You're here for four hours a day. In school. *Learning*, right? You shouldn't even need this right now."

"*Yes I do*," said Quran-with-a-Q in a rising tone, "I want my phone back, yo! Look: I didn't have it out. *She always gotta make things deep*," he whined, "she the one makin' it deep! She the one actin' all joe 'n' shit!"

Billy watched Quran-with-a-Q shaking his head in frustrated disbelief.

"She drawlin', yo," he said, barely audible. "Shit's corny."

He was a good student and, besides some common attitude issues for a seventeen-year-old, he could foreseeably test into Community next year and go on from there. Billy desperately (and sincerely) wanted to keep him on the right track.

"Señora Schumann is not acting joe, Quran. She's being fair. It's her class. It's her room. Those're her rules." Somewhere along the way Billy had picked up the habit of speaking in short, declarative sentences with elongated lulls. "There's nothing corny about following the rules, Quran."

Somewhere a clock ticked. They paused at the impasse. Quran-with-a-Q was clearly too smart for the little Dick-and-Jane lecture, so Billy organized what he thought was a very helpful and lucid comparison to make things obvious for his bright-but-tempestuous understudy. "Look, man, let me *be real* with you. If it was, like, twenty years ago, right?, and this school had a rule against you having a *beeper* in class, you know—a pager? And then you got caught with it…" Billy's hands moved frantically when he couldn't find the words he was looking for. "Whatever, let's say you get caught being paged by your, uh, by your *boo* or something, 'cuz you forgot to put the thing on vibrate, say; and *then* you decide to make a big deal out of it, instead of just handing it over—we're talkin' about *a beeper* here, mind you—and then, *boom*, next thing you know: *you* end up *not* graduating because you didn't pass this class that you need to get your diploma, right? All over some gadget that's not going to matter in another year or two…"

Billy felt like he was on a roll with this one, but looking directly at Quran-with-a-Q, he could see that the story problem backfired.

I figured you'd know what a pager is… Biggie Smalls always rapped about his.

"All I can say, man, is that it's an easy rule: you're supposed to turn your phone over to your case manager [pointing at himself] at the beginning of the day and get it back (from me) before you leave. You don't need to make a big deal out of it when the teacher asks you to follow that rule."

The student thought about it. "*But she always the one who make it deeper than it need to be,*" Quran-with-a-Q shot back, gently pounding on the desk, "she put me on blast in front of the class, man. That's *dis-respec'ful.*"

He reached for his phone.

Billy nudged it back out of reach and then remembered the teacher somewhere north who got badly knocked around after confiscating an MP3 player "until school's out or your parent comes and gets it." He performed a pathetic audible and tried to flip the situation into a heartfelt moment with a captive audience.

"Just keep it on silent." He moved his hand away from the phone. "Don't have it out. If you *need* to check it, 911 *need* to check it, go to the bathroom." The cool cop routine didn't register much with Quran-with-a-Q, who greedily took the phone back from his case manager and stood up. "Don't make me look dumb, Quran," Billy pleaded. Quran-with-a-Q mumbled something tacitly insulting on his way out, something about a beeper.

Knowing that he probably would not be seeing the young man for at least another day or two (these flare-ups happened pretty often at the Institute), Billy settled into what was most consoling when he failed and blamed the student, the school system, the parents, and whatever else was in bad shape and close at hand. By next week he'd be sending letters (if they ever got some more stamps at the AVI—he'd been asking for *weeks* now) to the address on file for Quran-with-a-Q.

The letters would probably be returned to sender, anyways. They generally ended up right back in his bunker. Scanning his spreadsheet of names and streets, Billy hummed a doleful song of Springsteen's. He imagined the dingy homes, the untold relations huddled together in squalor. He could vividly picture the towering dishes in the sink, the roaches and mice scurrying from the corners of his sight. Unknown dogs barking constantly, somewhere. He shook his head ruefully at the thought of soft flickering butane flames and the distant sound of a pipe being pulled. Graphic as they would often be, Billy never saw a mailbox in his visions, though.

Billy clicked keys and muttered a mantra about the futility of his work, his days spent writing, addressing, and mailing threatening but ultimately toothless letters. The toner was forever low and the words were poetically ghostly. The dismal heft and overly-smooth texture of the economy paper inspired ridicule and scorn, if it elicited response at all. Theirs was a letterhead which struck fear in no one. Upon opening an AVI envelope, one might mistakenly believe they'd received an old fax, complete with cover sheet. But he had nothing else to do then, so he began to fill in the form letter for the parent/guardian(s) of Quran Christmas. He pasted Section III, Article i, [ATTENDANCE], of the Academic Vision Institute's Parent-Student Handbook into the body of the letter. Eventually there would be more dire mail sent out, shorter and intended to be more intimidating.

Nobody ever came back to AVI because of the letters. You had to send notices out, at least three of them before removing a student from roll, as per district policy.

There was a long waiting list to get into the Academic Vision Institute.

Billy clicked the small printer icon and heard the enormous copy machine in the nearby office warm up and hum. He staggered out stiffly from his office *à la* Boris Karloff's mummy. There were more fluorescent lights in the office, and windows, too. Billy grabbed the meaningless sheet of paper, wincing from the brightness and the sound of a student banging on one of the vending machines.

"Yo-oo. This shit took my dollar."

The young man had a teardrop tattooed beside his right eye and looked all the more dejected while staring at the bag of M&Ms dangling on the edge of the spring. He gazed helplessly before violently striking once with the butt of his palm against the glass face of the appliance.

"Yo, you got a quarter?" he asked.

"Why d'you want to put *more* money in there? That's not my problem," Case Manager Billy George replied, "I don't handle the candy bar refunds."

The student was already ignoring Billy, though, and put an outstretched hand on each side of the vending machine. He clearly intended to rock it until his demands were met or the object was adequately destroyed, like when a police car gets tipped over after a local sports team comes up short in the big game.

"Hey now," Billy cautioned. "Enough of that."

The student sucked his teeth.

"Get back to class, Steffan." The command sounded more like a recommendation.

"*Ma-an*," the young man fussed. "Shit's *corny*."

Once he was out of sight, Billy pressed the refund button. Nothing came out. He caught his reflection amid the orderly rows and columns of candy and nuts. Billy saw that he looked *disheveled*, like he belonged at a dog track, not a school.

"Not that this place is a school," he said bitterly to himself. He lurched back into his bunker, feeling churlish and hung-over.

Señora Schumann walked into the office while Billy was scouring the Internet for nothing in particular. He did so all the more assiduously once she entered the room. She was a tallish, unfussy woman in her mid-twenties who wore little barrettes in her choppy chestnut hair. Her dress tended to be lively in a comfortable sort of way. Today she wore a new merino wool sweater colored like pine needles. She had a short navy skirt with cozy hand-knit ski-lodge leggings and floppy cowl-looking things adorably rumpled around each ankle. Her boots were tan suede and elfish. There were no rings on her fingers nor garish colors on her nails. Señora Schumann smiled at Billy. Her soft grey eyes had sleepy lavender bags beneath that made Billy feel very funny inside.

She came into the office to retrieve a container of left-overs from the brown minifridge. They smelled Thai. Her lunch required the microwave and Billy swiveled and adjusted his chair while it hummed. He looked with deep interest at sports scores until he heard a "ding."

"Hey," Señora Schumann said, a thought coming to her while she stirred pungent noodles around in a clear plastic container, "you didn't by chance grab something off the copy machine a minute ago did you?"

Billy tried to clear his dry throat while watching the Señora put her lips together and gently blow the rising steam off the fork she held before her mouth.

"Um, let me check," he whispered. His small crypt was flooded with a bouquet of fish oil, purple basil, and exotic dried peppers. He looked around his scattered surroundings, behind his monitor, and even under his mouse pad.

"It's okay, I thought maybe you accidentally—"

"Hold the phone," Billy said. He snatched up the envelope addressed to Quran-with-a-Q and tore it open. He carefully unfolded the paper inside and playfully allowed the tension to rise for a moment, not unlike a game show host. "Whoops," he said coyly, folding the sheet back up. He held the paper in front of the bottom of his face like a geisha hiding behind a fan before extending it out towards his Señora Schumann. "Es su prueba. Lo siento, Señora." He raised each eyebrow suggestively, as if to say *that's right—I was once in Spanish III.*

"Muy bien!" Señora Schumann said radiantly, gracefully taking the paper from him, "y muchas gracias!"

She lingered and polished off her lunch in the bunker. A bell rang loudly and for a long time, interrupting their conversation and signifying nothing within the AVI corridor. The students changing classes in the main building could be heard, though, even through all that thick concrete. Before the Señora left they shared a brief laugh over the thought of sending a Spanish test to the parent(s)/guardian(s) of Quran Christmas.

"That's okay," Billy said, "there wasn't a stamp on it, anyways."

7

For all the talk surrounding the decline and eventual end of traditional postage, Billy George's life continued to be impacted by it. And not just because of his trifling routine at the Institute either: his personal life continued to take strange turns when mail showed up for him at home. Besides the sordid serializations concerning his old truck there also came some unintentionally unnerving postcards sent by Lucy from her mother's house in Queens. She wrote cryptic verse with a calligraphy pen (possibly even a quill) and also weirdly-collaged together scenes on the obverse. Why couldn't she just call and say that stuff over the phone? Didn't she realize anyone could read a postcard?

One Saturday, in a fit of ennui, Billy opened a letter from an insurance company that was addressed to him.

What he read was a lot of adult jargon he had never picked up. The message was not at-once clear. He ran his eyes over the words and stopped where it said '$50,000.' Instinctively, it seemed like maybe he *owed* $50,000. Was this another thing about the truck? Maybe Dish McAlister ran somebody over before the title got switched over.

Panicky and not thinking clearly, Billy asked Dylan to explain the meaning of this letter. Dylan, it should be noted, was studying to be a lawyer. He seemed at peace with the prospect of a career in law, but was presently more interested in smoking weed and going to the climbing gym five times a week. His mellow mood vanished once he began inspecting Billy's document, though. He had his serious eyes on. Maybe he would wind up being a lawyer, after all.

"Huh. So who's Duane Richardson?"

"I don't know." Billy had read right past the name and gave it thought now. "I don't...know a...Duane Richardson. Beats me."

"Well, it looks like he had a life insurance policy and died and you're the beneficiary."

Billy grabbed the letter but did not look at it. "So I don't *owe* that money?"

Dylan took it back with a cool restraint and eyed it up and down again. "No-oo, you *get* $50,000 because this guy died."

They looked at one another for a very long three seconds.

"Weird," Dylan said and offered his hand up high.

They halfheartedly high-fived.

"Wait," Billy said with his hand distractedly on Dylan's for a moment too long, "*Duane*. I work with that guy. I mean, I know him *from* work. We did this dumb training together on President's Day or Election Day and..."

It suddenly became clear. They had happened to sit together and lightheartedly put each other down as beneficiaries for their organization's free life insurance policy. It was hearing the man going over the packet full of forms explain that "you might as well put *some*one down—God forbid" that sealed it for Billy (who didn't yet know Kurt or Julian's last names for sure).

Billy didn't hear anything about someone at work dying. Even if Duane was at another site, in another part of the city, wouldn't he have heard something? He didn't get so much as an email. And now this!

"*That guy's dead?*"

Dylan nodded solemnly. "He was a friend of yours?"

"No. Well. I mean. Yeah, I guess he was. I didn't know him, really. We just wrote each others names down."

"That fucking *sucks*, man, dying... But, I mean, also: cool for you, dude."

Re-reading the letter multiple times, Billy could not contain himself. Here was some of that Jenna money he'd been hearing so much about—*and then some*. There wasn't much guilt along with it besides the fact that he didn't feel all that guilty. The pangs of conscience were just... *muted*. So much more so than if Billy had benefitted from the passing of, say, a dear family member or a close friend. And he did feel bad for Duane whenever his mind would wander. He decided to make it a point to find out how he died and donate some of the money in his honor, get Duane's name on a plaque or a brick in a public space.

Hundreds of decisions were made during that

first night alone. There was a lot to do. So much was going to happen. Understanding $50,000 was hard to do, though. He imagined all the ways it would go wrong: his name subtly misspelled on the check, his bank not accepting deposits from this insurance company, a *different* Duane Richardson passing away and Billy having to return the full amount (part of which he'd, of course, foolishly blown).

This sort of mistake happened once before, when he was nine years old. Between the time he checked the mail after-school and his mother walking in the door from work, young Billy had dreamed of a million things thought he would do with that Clearinghouse Sweepstakes Jackpot cash. He called friends and bragged. He threw away his rattier action figures and gleefully tossed old comic books into the trash. He did not want to get burned like that again.

For a single moment, supposing it all went off without a hitch, the young man suddenly saw that he had no clue how much $50,000 really was, how much time it bought you, and what you did with it.

After a Sunday filled with static anxiety and cautious elation, Billy called out sick for the rest of the week with Hay Fever.

"I went to Amish country this weekend," he explained over the phone, "I must've contracted it out there."

He then used his initial bit of free time to double-check with the insurance company and establish that everything was in order. Following that, he decided to do a load of laundry, benevolently tossing the kitchen towels thick with grime in among his own private things.

Somebody hadn't taken their stiff and now-musty clothes out of the washer, though.

And somebody hadn't taken their wrinkly things from the dryer, either, (much less emptied out the lint trap).

Presented with no other options, Billy begrudgingly moved all the items down the line. The articles in the dryer were Jenna's. In an attempt to pull them out *en masse* and avoid an unintentional glimpse into his housemate's underwear proclivities, he wound up dropping the majority of her things on the dusty floor, including a pair of panties that fell in the forbidding crevasse between the two units. Billy retrieved them using a nearby paint-stirring stick and then tried to remove the fuzzy debris off the clean clothes. He slapped her socks against his thigh and briskly whipped her shirts back and forth. He had originally wanted to place the shameful wad of Jenna's lint atop her basket of dry clothes, but at this point such an act would feel counter-productive.

The extra Springtime Mountain fabric softener sheets tossed in with the moldy clothes did little to mask the warm, fusty odor emanating from the dryer.

"Sorry about the smell," Billy said to Julian as he sat by him on the decrepit couch. "I think Matt's gonna have to re-wash those guys."

"Yeah right," said Julian, digging his hand into a bulk-foods-section bag of dried mango, "like Matt's gonna notice the smell. He eats pork and beans right out of a can like a hobo. He'll wear that shit around just fine."

They each chuckled at the sad and strange ways of the man that lived under the same leaky roof as them.

"Hey, I'm getting $50,000," he mentioned during a commercial break.

"Cool," Julian said, busy working on a hunk of dried mango like a puppy in a rawhide daze. He was either unimpressed or not paying attention.

That night Billy couldn't sleep. He dozed right off during the weekend, engorged and quickly relieved by fantasies of stealing away someplace warm with Señora Schumann. He wanted badly to share his newly-minted whimsy with her. But on Monday he revisited the fantasy and then felt restless. Instead of drifting off into sleep on some faraway beach, Billy saw numbers. He pulled the blankets up to his chin and worried about account statements and tax forms. The money would surely change things. On the surface it was a good change and one that removed needless anxiety and stress. But everything he did, every opinion and habit and friend and indeed every*thing* that made him who he was heading into that night, was now in question and up for debate. There was no saying where it would take him and leave him. Most joyrides end up far from home with no clear way back.

Meanwhile, on the other side of the sheetrock, roommate Mike hacked up something resistant from the back of his throat. Billy squeezed his eyes tightly like a child trying to make it through a windy night. Then came a regular flatulent rumble next door and commensurate chuckling and guffaws, disgusted and at the same time revelatory.

It took a week of waiting for the check before things started feeling dicey and the decision to call in his resignation seemed hasty and dumb. Billy saw $393.76 appear in checking one morning and could expect another $196.88 two weeks after that. And that would be it (excepting a $50,000 deposit sometime soon).

Like a castaway hanging on the beach while a cargo plane thousands of feet above only inches nearer, it was maddening to wait on so much money while also utterly broke for the time being. Billy could now leisurely window shop online (which he could have done at work, too); his "wish lists" grew longer and more detailed while his cart stayed forever empty. He could not yet *buy* anything, of course. By lunchtime he'd despondently lie down on the dirty sectional with his particular case of consumer blue balls.

At 12 p.m., 2 p.m., 2:45 p.m., 3:30 p.m., 4:15 p.m., and 5:00 p.m., he went downstairs and checked 609's mailbox. When the mail wasn't there by 5 he would use his computer and research what holiday might be happening.

Some days, it turned out, there was just no mail. Not even junk mail. Not even for seven people.

Dylan (his counsel), Julian, and Kurt were the

only people aware of Billy's curiously awkward position. Julian and Kurt tried to buoy spirits by coming up with outlandish things for Billy to soon spend his time doing as an eccentric.

"Buy a car," Kurt would offer. "Or some art."

"Get a girlfriend," Julian advised. "You're always saying how you're too poor to have a girlfriend. Well, now," and he'd make a sort of shrugging gesture.

Billy was inconsolable, however, and suggestions that seemed perfectly good to him (like switching over his entire wardrobe to identical British-cut suits of a yet-to-be-determined signature color) were starting to add up. Just how much would be left of the miraculous money pile after all the peacockery and good-timing?

So that Thursday, a day before his last full stipend came in, Billy budgeted rent and his phone bill, leaving him with around $100 to his name. Planning for the worst, he made a grim trip to Hermano's and cashed out his savings at the coin-counting machine. He used the ensuing profit to buy two #5 bags of white potatoes, a Styrofoam container of twenty-four medium 'Grade-A' eggs, four oval tins of a fish cheaper, per ounce, than tuna, five pounds of flour and three packets of yeast, and a stamped metal canister of smooth peanut spread (which was less expensive than a similarly-sized jar of creamy peanut butter). This would get him through the proverbial winter, he hoped.

That night was to be his first attempt at full-fledged paesano living. He planned on eating a loaf of homemade bread for dinner with a can of fish, soaking up the packaging oil for added nutrients. It did not go well. The cold spell outside had been partway snapped, but the loft was still fairly drafty. So the tacky solid of flour and water rose only marginally. Also, the yeast might have been dead. And, distracted by Julian's high jinks earlier, Billy did not adequately wipe off the counter before kneading and the bread had an array of unintended spices, crumbs, and hairs worked into it. There was no olive oil to coat the loaf like the recipe called for so he slathered some long-unclaimed vegetable shortening all over the damp lump. It looked to be glazed in Vaseline once he put it in the oven. Eventually it came out ashy and crude. Commonly-used baking genera like "rustic" and "farm-style" were inapplicable, even.

He cut into the bread too soon, while it was steamy, and whatever life was in it quickly escaped. Billy saved the fish and instead tried to slather peanut spread onto a piece. This only managed to pull the bread apart and make it stick to the butter knife. He ate that like a corn dog and washed it all down with a beer.

"Well, there's nowhere to go but up, right?" Kurt offered hopefully.

"Or this is going to suck until it doesn't," Billy said as he cleaned up his mess. "I shouldn't've quit my job."

"Yeah, well, okay, maybe," Kurt said in earnest support of his friend. He concentrated on the rolling papers in front of him, a new kind with a thin aluminum rod built-in to help smokers get at that troublesome final half-inch of drugs. The little pink tip of his tongue was fixedly poking out the side of his mouth. "Maybe you could do some funny side-work just to keep things afloat."

A thought bubble wherein Billy wore a sand-wich board and passed out menus for a Jamaican restaurant popped up over his head. "I don't know, man. I really don't want to do food stuff anymore. That'd feel like a big step backwards," he said as he put the gravity bong pitcher back up where it be-longed. "I moved here to do something with my life." He opened up the dishwasher to load his plate and butter knife. "Ugh, Kurt: another baby mouse drowned in here."

Kurt got off his stool and cased the scene. "Were those dirty or clean?"

"Well, they're all dirty now, right?" Billy guessed.

"Yeah, I suppose so."

Over at the couch, Kurt nodded and pensively narrowed his eyes, working his lips around a spliff. "Yeah, I know what you mean." He choked a bit and unleashed a billowing cloud of smoke from his nose and mouth, as if he'd just eaten an especially fiery pepper. "Whew," he said with red eyes and great re-lief. "About the wanting to do something with your life. I know what you mean, dude, cloud and ear." Kurt didn't catch his own stoner malaprop and bliss-fully stared towards the dormant television. Then his red eyes flashed brilliant and gayly as he handed the cigarette over to Billy. "Dude, I know what."

"What?" *cough cough cough*-ing.

It was plain to see that Kurt needed a second to get this straight. "This guy I work with," he set in, "Jacob—he's kind of a twat, but, anyways—this guy Jacob needs some shit moved, driven somewhere and delivered."

Kurt worked for the art museum, cleaning the art. He buzzed into work on his bike four times a week and used tiny handheld vacuums to suck the dirt out of medieval tapestries or dust off the replica Shaker dwellings with small, specialized brushes. Nearly all the tools of his trade were petite and the work was always delicate. He excelled at his job (though, like the pastry chef that craves nothing more than a pickle when he gets home, Kurt was not especially fond of cleaning the loft).

"Yeah, man: Jacob Jeffries," Kurt said reassuringly. "He works in the Asian department. A bit of a hot-shot, but he seemed like he was *really* looking for someone *not from the Internet* to do this for him, you know? He asked me if I knew anybody, and I was, like, 'Uh, let me think about it.' Good thing I did, too!"

Kurt was naturally an agreeable sort and Billy suddenly felt rightfully lucky to be sitting where he was (and on the indoor swing, too).

"I bet you could start, like, Thursday or something."

"Today's Thursday."

"Then Friday or Saturday or something."

"Okay, so," Billy said in his *let's get down to*

brass tacks here tone, "I'd just, like, *drive*. Drive what again?"

"Some stuff." Kurt contemplated the possible goods. "Some art stuff."

"Where to?"

"I don't remember. I don't think he even said *where* when he brought it up to me. He just asked if I knew anyone."

"Hell yeah you know someone," Billy said ecstatically. "*Me!*"

"I'll have a...beer and some more water, please."

It was the dark-haired bartender's third check-in with Billy and his "I'm waiting for someone" routine was wearing thin.

"What would you like?"

Billy paused long enough for her to begin listing the available brands of beer, on draught, on cask, in bottles—

"I'll have that one," he said as she reached the bottom of the list, believing that's where the cost-efficient stuff tends to settle.

As per Jacob's instructions, sent via Kurt, Billy was at Barcelona by Byzantium: Tapas ...Y Mas the next day by 4:30. It was 5:15 now. He made sure to eat the rest of his rat-colored bread before the rendezvous, but was getting peckish while surrounded by so many olives. Barcelona by Byzantium was the kind of place where they wrote out the prices on the menu, though:

ANGULA CON ALCAPARRAS ESTOFADOS
(YOUNG ELVER EEL WITH BRAISED CAPERS)
❖ TWENTY-THREE

and that was always too expensive.

The bartender came back with a dark, lava-lamp shaped bottle and a dainty glass goblet to drink it out of. He felt serious buyer's remorse while watching her pour it out at the recommended angle. The kicker came when she pulled out the mahogany and pearl-handled beer scraper and planed the drink for Billy.

"Thanks," he said. "Can I just keep a tab open?" hoping that this guy Jacob would show up and take care of this new problem, too.

Then it was 5:30 and 5:45. Billy nursed his beer enough to hold the woman behind the bar at bay. Things had taken a turn for the warm, drink-wise, and it was hard to not drink when getting edgier and more tense as a languid Friday happy hour ticked on towards a bustling weekend suppertime. Beautiful people trickled in to grab a bite before their evening's gala, fete, or event.

"Do you have anything … *lighter*?" Billy eventually inquired.

She pursed her red lips contemplatively. "Let's see. There's the Chevrier Herbes de Provence-infused Belgian farmhouse ale, Hobgoblin Creek Cato the Censor Imperial Hefeweizen (ecru-colored with a snappy bouquet—a distinctly Californian beer), um, what else … Bartok-Saaz Bohemian Pilsner (pretty self-explanatory), Fat Rascal Alsatian Gruit…on cask, of course, we have the Landstriecher Bock—that's kinda light."

"What about *waterier*? Do you have anything *waterier*?"

"Hey, bro, you Billy?" He felt the unmistakable clasp of a self-assured man on his left shoulder. "Sorry, man. Whole fucking set of Imperial erotic porcelain. Comes in at 4 o'clock *on a Friday*. Of course. It's like: *fucking* of course, man. Complete pain in the dick. I'm Jacob, by the way."

They shook hands. Jacob squeezed Billy's past a point of manly assurance that verged on bullying. Jacob clearly relished playing older brother to every other man he met, regardless of their respective ages.

He looked as fresh, crisp, and all-American as an ATM $20 in his blue polo and red seersucker slacks. The *coup de grâce* had to be the braided white leather belt, though. He might have been a grandson to an actual Brooks Brother. He sported a freshly-cropped shock of wheat-colored hair and had a neatly-cleft chin. His TGIF cow eyes slowly scanned the room for poon before focusing back on Billy.

"Yeah, man, again: sorry. Friday, though, knowwhatimsayin. Killer week. It's been *the* week from fucking *hell*. Besides this whole moving stuff shit that we'll get to in a minute. That's a whole other thing. But, Jesus, it's just been," Jacob puffed his cheeks out and made a soft exploding sound as he pushed out some air and softly shook his head, "like *that*, basically. Sorry to go on about work. It's just got me stressin' hard, dawg. It does. You have to admit it when it gets to you: otherwise." He waited for words or, failing that, expressive noises or gestures, but none came. "But, hey, enough of that." Jacob closed his eyes and spoke, mantra-like: "I'm outta there, freakin' weekend, let's just fucking *do it*, forget all the bullshit for the next forty-eight hours, fifty-four hours, whatever, not at work, so it's cool. It's cool." He opened his eyes and smiled. His teeth were incredibly white. "What are you drinking, dude? I fucking *owe you*. What is it, 6 o'clock?"

Billy felt a wave of immense relief. "I don't know for sure, I just ordered one of—"

"Paola!" Jacob shouted. "Two saffron martinis! So, you know Kurt, huh? Yeah, Kurt's cool," he said before Billy even nodded. The whole time Jacob watched himself carefully in the mirror behind the top shelf liquor. He still hadn't taken a seat and leaned with his elbows on the well-polished dark wood bar. "He's a bit of a *whatever* sort of dude," rolling his eyes as if that completely summed up who he was talking about. "You know, totally art school. But he's basically cool, too. Which I can trust, you know?" His eyes darted quickly from left to right and back again. "He said you're cool."

"Great. Thanks."

The bartender placed two martini glasses brimming with light ochre liquid between the pair. Once she walked away Billy wondered out loud why there weren't more olives in the drinks.

"Yo! Hook my man up with some more olives, wuddya, Paola?"

Jacob couldn't have been much older than Billy but his skin was so much better taken care of. He appeared groomed in numerous ways Billy was not.

"She's hot. And nice, too." Smiling smugly, Jacob shook himself back into focus. "So, basically, while she's off doing *that*: I have some things I need delivered to clients. But first off: hello and thanks."

"You're welcome." Billy took a drink of his yellow martini. "Hi."

Jacob now intently looked at Billy. "Yeah, man ... Kurt said you were cool." He popped an olive into his mouth like a mafia heavy. "You think you're cool?" he asked with his mouth full.

"I mean ..." Billy felt confused, flustered. "Doesn't *everybody* think they're cool?"

Jacob bobbed his head. "See: only a cool guy would say that. Good." He put a cocktail napkin up to his mouth and spat out a garlic clove. "So, I need somebody to move some junk for me. Not junk, though, actually. I'm talkin' rugs. Prints. Some snuff bottles. All of it Chinese and all of it priceless. In the old sense. *Plenty* valuable, as you may well assume. Nothing too outta control, though. I'd go and do it myself, but we got this huge-ass fucking *event* coming up with the Kleinmanns, they're big-time benefactors of ours, and I am a complete *no-go* when it comes to more vacation time after Venice."

Jacob was visibly transported back there for a moment.

"Dude: have you been? Fucking ... wow. You should go. Just go. I'm serious: it's *that* fucking amazing. Don't put it off, I mean it … anyways, what was I saying?, right, it's just driving out to drop this stuff off. Nothing heavy. I mean, you gotta be careful with it, duh: it's Chinese. It's old. But it's mostly pretty small stuff, about a quarter-van-full. Two drop-offs, even you can handle it on your own, and that's it."

Even you *could handle it* … Billy was still ruffled after being told to go to Venice. A white ramekin with six fat green olives appeared on the bar between them and eased the tension. Billy selected one and sipped his pale dandelion-colored drink, still unsure of how to properly hold his glass. It took the savvy and grace of a plate-spinner to get a nip in without any splash-back or dribble.

"So you want me to drive *your* van with these lightweight Chinese antiques to …"

"Correct," Jacob said, adding "drive a van to some dealers in New Mexico and down south. And that's pretty much it." He untucked his polo with matador panache.

"Down south li-ike Old Mexico?"

Jacob laughed heartily at this, like Hercules might. "Dude: you're funny. *Old Mexico*," he mused. "No, like, as in Mississippi. This dude Andy. A *private* collector, a friend of mine. He's also a very cool dude. You should check out his pool. And then you come back and drop the van off."

"Okay. And where in New Mexico?"

"Santa Fe."

"Oh, okay … I have a friend in Albuquerque."

"Uh-huh. Look, I know what you're thinking:

I don't want to ship it because I've had bad experiences shipping this sort of stuff. They just toss shit around, willy nilly, who gives a fuck. You can insure it, but people are still pissed when their shit shows up fucked up. Pain in *their* ass, pain in *my* ass, *ex* cetruh. I need someone I can trust to do this, someone that's gonna give me and everybody involved minimal ass pain. It'll cost *a little bit more*, yeah, so what, big deal. There's always more money where that came from. Didn't fucking Ben Franklin say that or something? Anyways, the people buying don't seem to care if I tack on a couple extra hundred to git-r-dun the first time. At least I know it gets where it needs to go." He gulped down the rest of his martini and signaled Paola for a refill. "So, I can pay five-hundred for driving and three-hundred for gas and expenses. If you can finish up and have the van back here by … *Saturday*? A week from tomorrow, I'll make it an even thousand."

There were no suspicions when Kurt first made the suggestion and got things rolling, muddling the details along the way. Last night a solution to a problem was put forth. But hearing the words "I know what you're thinking" made Billy think, and made him a little skittish about why he and not a moving company stood to make one thousand dollars moving art.

Hot art?

Listening to Jacob, yes, of course it was stolen or illegal or in some way crooked. And to wit: who, indeed, cared so deeply about whether a potential business partner was 'cool' besides the shifty-eyed, small-time traffickers of '70s cop films?

He seemed far too dumb to be any sort of mastermind, though. And it was equally likely that Jacob was incredibly shallow and didn't want to pay an uncool person to do his bidding.

Plenty was going through Billy's mind, but pressing the issue here at Barcelona by Byzantium would kill the deal. And the price was right. So Billy sipped his free martini and resigned himself to becoming an accessory to the impudent manboy's grift, whatever it was.

Beneath the bar stools, the sound of Jacob's docksiders busily (impatiently?) slapping against the soles of his feet distracted Billy enough that he couldn't even come up with cursory, obvious questions. He noticed Jacob studying the bar closely.

"What kinda wood you think this is?" He looked to Billy. "You think this is that Kona wood from Hawaii?" He knocked on the bar.

"Isn't that a type of coffee?"

Jacob hedged. He tilted his head. *Doesn't coffee grow on a tree?* his expression asked. "Who fucking knows. Anyways, sound good?" he asked. "Do I have my driver?"

"Sure," Billy said.

They agreed to meet early tomorrow morning at Jacob's storage unit.

"Rise and shine early," Jacob clarified.

Billy deferentially declined to stay for dinner, citing the need to go pack and make certain unmentioned accommodations at home before departure. They volleyed "thank you's" and "no, seriously: *thank you*'s" back and forth a few times before some of Jacob's contemporaries spotted him.

"Marco Bocanegro: *What. The. Fuck*, dude! What up?" Billy heard shouted behind him as he left Barcelona by Byzantium.

Kurt was staring into his laptop, not looking particularly entertained, when Billy got back to the Loft. The video he was watching cast a strange, eerie glow over his face until he decisively folded the computer in half and turned to his roommate.

"So ... how'd it go?" he asked with the same cadence and pitch of a teenage girl inquiring about a blind date.

"It was *all right*," he said, hinting at the tolerable trespasses not worth elaborating upon. "I'll be gone for a week it looks like."

"Well, I'd say that went pretty awesomely." Kurt did a raspberry with his tongue. "Just *all right*. How much is he paying you?"

"Eight-hundred. A thousand if I get it all done by Saturday."

"*Plus* gas?"

"Uh ... no, part of that is for 'expenses.' Such as gas."

"Dude," he said flipping his computer back open and X'ing out of whatever Billy walked in on earlier. "Let's see ..." typing ... results popping up, results skimmed, a click and Kurt offered up his research, condensed: "as of today, national average is at three-sixty-two a gallon." He looked up at Billy. "Where are you driving to?"

"New Mexico and back through Mississippi."

Without saying anything, they each noted to themselves how strange that combination was.

"Okay, so, Phil-uh-del-phee-uh," he said phonetically while clicking and clacking, "to New Mex-i-co … is: 1,906 miles."

"Okay."

"That's going to be a lot of gas, dude."

Billy looked to his left. He could almost hear his dad. *Why didn't you dicker? Didn't I teach you better'n that?*

"He's giving me a lot of money for gas."

"Yeah, but that leaves you …" Kurt cut himself off. "Let's get the facts on our side."

The two of them sat together on the beat-up couch and tried to figure out how to calculate "expenses," chiefly gasoline. It was harder than they thought. For starters, you had to know your vehicle's fuel economy, which would make a noticeable difference. Supposing that Billy would drive something like his old truck, though, something that got twenty-four miles to the gallon, freeway; they were looking at eighty gallons of fuel.

"Two-hundred eighty-eight and eighty cents," Kurt revealed. "And that's just to New Mexico!"

Billy wrote what seemed pertinent down on the clean side of a nearby envelope that somebody had been doodling on while Kurt continued his cracked research:

PHI —> NM = 1906   *gas $3.61*   *80 gal*
                    $280   24
          NM —> ~~MI~~ MS = 1070   *45 g*
                              $162
m-i-s-s-i-s-s-i-p-p-i
          MS —> PHI = 1070 too!
                    ——————> *the Same*
IMPORTANCE?

Neither could believe it, that Mississippi was exactly in between New Mexico and Philadelphia. Kurt suggested something consequential might happen there and Billy quietly ran with the thought for a few moments. In his mind he parted a curtain of Spanish moss to reveal a southern belle. The air was laden, *thick*, with honeysuckle ... the suggestive draping of soft magnolia petals ... What did those sexy flowers even smell and look like?

Between Billy's reveries and Kurt's boredom, interest in all the figures faded and—quite suddenly—it was 12:53 a.m. and the credits to *The Running Man* were rolling.

"Dammit," Billy said, disgusted and confused by the taste of his own mouth. It was like someone snuck an old dollar in his there while he was sleeping. "Dude," he said, but Kurt didn't want to wake up right then. *So be it*, Billy thought, *his stiff, achey funeral*. Billy pulled himself out from the couch and creakily shuffled towards his room. After a few moments of idle looking about, jumbled picking up and subsequent setting down, the only thing Billy had decided to pack was a rainstick that he planned on taking to his friend in Albuquerque. It was an inside joke, the rainstick. Finally, Billy settled on bringing three of every necessary garment and changing every other day. He felt as wise and judicious as Solomon. Then he selected an additional oxford dress shirt, his "go-to" shirt, just in case.

He gathered the mail about the toll charges and the personal check for the remainder of his old truck, also just in case. Colorado Springs couldn't be *too far* from Santa Fe.

8

The phone rattled on the floor and woke Billy up. For the past ten minutes it had been buzzing like a fly helplessly caught between a window and some aluminum blinds. So Billy left fifteen minutes later than he'd planned on but was able to hustle to the self-storage building, rainstick in hand, by the agreed-upon 7:30.

The sun hadn't been up for long and it was still cold and grey outside, especially in front of the U-Store-It facilities near a knot of interstates. Standing out amid the drabness, the first thing Billy noticed in the parking lot was a big, red, early-'90s Dodge cargo van covered in a crisscross of black and white stripes like Eddie Van Halen's guitar. It was visually arresting, just like the guitar. Billy shrugged it off and walked by but, quite startlingly, the van honked at him. He turned around and noticed Jacob in the driver's seat.

"Whaddaya think, bro?" Jacob asked with a crooked arm hanging out of the window. He wore a sincerely proud grin. "Pretty dank, right?" He gave the horn another lusty blast.

"Yeah…" Billy searched for the right reaction. "Good morning."

"Yup: check out the new work van, dawg." He stroked the dashboard suggestively. "You ready to pop this baby's cherry or what?"

Billy didn't mean to say "What." It was an involuntary response. He'd only been awake some forty coffee-less minutes and now this.

"I mean, yeah, that's pretty, um. Pretty cool," he gamely backtracked.

"Thanks." Jacob turned the ignition off and got out of the Van Halen van. He was wearing tassled burgundy loafers, pleated white shorts, and a gold jacquard rain slicker resplendent with fleurs-de-lis and designer initials. "Is that a rain stick? Suh-weet. So: everything's packed up in the back, labelled with what goes where. Oh, and, I forgot to mention this, but I need some other shit dropped off outside of Marfa. It's on the way. In Texas."

"Really? On the way? Texas?"

"Uh … *shyeah* … check a map-book, holmes. Texas is right between New Mexico and Mississippi. Anyways, I put the addresses down on that sheet of paper for you."

"Alright."

"You got a smartphone for directions?"

"No."

"Hm. You'll figure it out. People used to, I guess." Jacob yawned and showed off his great gleaming chompers. He idly scratched his head. "Okay. You're good to go. Anything else you need to know?"

There were three important questions and the first one Billy blurted out was about the van, naturally.

"So why is the van painted like this?"

"Like what?"

"Like Eddie Van Halen's guitar."

"Oh, it's a guitar thing? What do you mean?"

Shifting to the offensive, he explained, in the briefest terms he could, Eddie Van Halen's distinctive set-up as well as a few of the band's chart-topping tunes.

"Might as well jump!—*Jump!*—Go ahead and jump!—*Jump!*" he sang demonstratively.

"Yeah, I think I know that one from a Six Flags commercial or something," Jacob said, nonplussed. "Either way, it's a totally sick van. Feel free to really … *use it.*"

Billy wanted to ask somewhat more pertinent questions about the van: who was its previous owner; what was his (or *her* (one never knew)) personality like; what line of work did Jacob envision himself in where this was the appropriate image; what was the status of the vehicle's title; what should he do if he got pulled over; what was the gas mileage for the van; were there any nagging issues with it, quirks or special cares to be attentive to? Billy's eyes may as well have been question marks and his mouth an ellipses. This line of overwhelming and unspoken curiosity inched him closer to his main question, though.

"So, that reminds me—"

"What does?"

"Um, nothing, actually … I just wanted to ask about the 'expenses' stuff you mentioned last night—"

"Right, the expenses, okay."

He wasn't going to let Billy string together his whole thought, clearly.

"It's a long drive and gas is, like, *expensive* these days, and I did some research—"

"Uh-huh."

"And," reaching into his pocket, Billy pulled out the scratch paper he and Kurt had tabulated on, "I just kind of estimated what it'd cost for gas and—"

"Can I see?"

"Sure."

Billy handed him the paper. Folded in half, he only now took notice of the cartoons that someone had scribbled on the outside of the envelope. The paper was already in Jacob's hands and his eyes were intently studying the crude figures he and Kurt came up with. The side facing Billy, though, was covered different sorts of crude figures, all engaged in an explicitly vulgar and imaginative underwater scene. Someone at the Loft had illustrated the envelope in heavy, scratchy ballpoint blue. A bearded Neptune figure took noticeable pleasure in a watery harem. Each creature in the drawing possessed very graphic, identifiable bits of human anatomy, most often grossly exaggerated. Billy helplessly looked at the filthy seascape and did not catch what Jacob was saying to him.

"How much did I say I was giving you?"

His focus was still on the envelope.

"Um," *gulp* "three hundred for gas and—"

"Seven hundred for you … right?"

He turned the paper around to see if there was anything else and barely raised his eyebrows before handing it back over to Billy.

"Well, yeah, if I did it in a week, but—"

"How much do you even make in a week, bro?"

"$600, usually," Billy lied.

"Well, okay, and, so, I give you, what, eight hundred now, up front, and you drive for a week, go on a nice little trip (my expense, all of it), head off and see the country, and you make, what, $200 more and—"

"Okay, okay," Billy said, getting it, still embarrassed by the dirty doodle in his back pocket.

"Besides: this thing gets thirty, thirty-five to the gallon. No shit. Gas will *not* be a issue, dude."

There was no way in hell that was true, but they agreed that Billy could save his receipts for gas and if it added up well beyond what Jacob intently believed the "expenses" would amount to, then there could be some additional recompense when the job was successfully completed. Meanwhile, it was five to eight and time to roll.

Billy felt weird having sixteen fifties crisply folded in half in his breast pocket.

Jacob wished him good luck and said "*Arrivederci!*" in boisterous, spaghetti-sauce-commercial Italian before slapping the Van Halen van on the back door.

The van crept forward a few feet before Billy jerked it to a stop. He had one more question.

"Oh, hey, just so we're clear: did these guys already *pay* you for this stuff or do I have to, like, bring back checks or something?"

A great and mysterious sensation tickled Billy as soon as he got on the freeway, still within sight of Center City's skyline. If he played his cards right, this trip could become a bona fide *mystical jour-*

ney. Anything was possible in a van rolling across America.

Road metaphysics aside, simply waking up and driving early had Billy feeling somewhat special, like a go-getter. And having $800 in his shirt pocket felt comfortable after about thirty minutes. In fact, he thought himself invincible, like a rich man. He noticed that his eyes looked happy in the rearview mirror.

An hour outside of Philadelphia, he nervously laughed and realized he never got Jacob's phone number. He could always get it from Kurt, he guessed.

He drove through tunnels and held his breath for over a minute both times. He got light-headed after the second attempt. Back on the road, the cargo kept still in the back. The van ran smoothly and so far had surprisingly good mileage, although he was still hesitant to go so far as thirty-five mpg. No fewer than five cars honked in a show of support for the Van Halen van.

By 1:30 a good deal of driving had already taken place—but Billy was an hour or so from Ohio, still in Pennsylvania, and rethinking the decision to forgo lunch. With so few calories left to burn, he abruptly wondered to himself how much additional jail time he'd face for crossing the imaginary line separating the states (assuming whatever he was transporting was illegal (which seemed probable)).

Had he given himself an actual minute, sixty full seconds, to consider that maybe there was dope rolled up in the rugs? Not nearly. He'd thought about it for ten seconds, tops. For instance, those jade bottles? How else would one deliver opium to your well-educated and high-end fiend, the sort wishing to keep things "authentic"? He had not weighed any of this before now, an hour from the first of many borders. Billy would have to check his freight next time he gassed up and got food, which would be soon, in Pennsylvania yet.

In Washington, PA, twenty-five miles from the Buckeye State, the van stopped at a large fuel plaza. There was an all-reaching fuzzy buzz of bugs outside. It was humid and the enormous travel center was on top of a tall, sloping green hill. All you could see from up there were the freeways and a couple unassuming houses where, presumably, somebody in charge of a different green field lived.

Billy pulled around back, near the buffet entrance. He opened up the glove box and inspected the title. The registered owner of the van was not Jacob Jeffries. Far from it, in fact: the van belonged to one Dac Kien Ngyuen, who lived on the 2100 block of Kensington Avenue in Philadelphia, PA, 19125. Billy was not surprised, though he certainly did not expect the Vietnamese to suddenly be in the mix. He next set about pawing through the boxes and uselessly patting the rugs. They were valuables, and plenty old. Nothing immediately stood out. Billy found a napkin wedged in one of the cup holders and used that to carefully, smudgelessly, inspect. He started rifling through a box marked for Larry in Santa Fe. It checked out and contained an empty vase and a few prints. He pulled out the container marked for Marfa. It was mostly full of jade trinkets. He gently shook the shiny vials like tiny maracas and listened with his head at a subtle angle. Something rattled inside of one vial. The dull sound spooked him. The Chinese ran deep: their pictographic characters and tonal tongue, the strange, medicinal tubers they dried and ingested in tea form: all of their magic bordered on sorcerous.

"Uh oh," he said after jiggling the green jar into two separate bits.

There had been a Pez candy inside of it.

Billy wandered around the inside of the travel plaza, having just inspected about one-third of his load and also putting fifty on pump nineteen. Now he was looking for the fountain drinks and some high-grade adhesive. There were many beverages to choose from and the spigots went on for nearly ten yards. Four icy slushes were being whirled around and around like washing machines doing a load of tie-dyes. The base price for an insultingly small soda was $1.99. The sizes grew exponentially but went up in cost 10¢ at a time. In this economy, one had to go wherever the deals were. The Tanker Tanker! was only $2.59 and could be refilled at any other Flying J for only 89¢.

"This thing's gonna pay for itself," Billy muttered into the cold, fizzing soda mist, quite pleased with himself.

Next, he aimlessly went through the place as if divining for glue. When he did find it there was great consternation, as the small tube was $5.49. The cost was an outrage, to be spurned on principal at such a ludicrous price point, but there were circumstances and constraints to weigh.

While he was in the middle of this rather intense inner debate, vacillating for and against the glue, ten times each, a beautiful young woman materialized from seemingly nowhere and crouched next to Billy, comparing some nearby electrical tape.

She was tall, even while scrunched down, but not taller than Billy. Her hair was peroxided a severe yellow. It was not too clean and in a choppy, boyish cut. The roots were black and persistent. Her nose was well-bred and of an interesting shape; regal. She wasn't looking over at him, but from her profile Billy could see a dark, thick brow and a tired, sleepy hazel eye that began making him tingle inside curiously, uncontrollably. Day-old eyeliner only bolstered this sensation.

She also seemed peeved by the gouging of life's essentials at this travel plaza.

Billy began sighing and snorting. *Me too! Me too!* he was trying desperately to signal, *I'm right there with you!* "Jeez…" he said under his breath, scrutinizing the glue, "I mean … really?"

"Fuck this," she said, grabbing a large roll of duct tape before straightening up and walking off.

Billy grabbed his glue off the pegboard and went in the same direction as her. Then he turned around and grabbed his Tanker! and continued tailing her easily-visible head over the aisles. She snaked her way around the postcards with Billy further behind. He followed the mustard hair directly through the compact discs and cassettes at blow-out prices, before taking a hard right past the glowing Ferris wheel of hot dogs. He stopped there to watch her walk calmly outside. Billy stood dumbly and inhaled the meaty aroma for some seconds before speed-walking over to an open register.

She was sitting by herself at a round, concrete table with a polished pebble terrazzo top. A mossy umbrella spired out from the middle unopened. One of the straps of her backpack was thickly-wrapped in duct-tape like an arm freshly-set in a silver cast. She was busily running her thumb across the surface of her smartphone.

"Hey," Billy said, nearing her, his heart thumping. "You didn't pay for that tape."

She looked up from her phone and then back down.

Her eyes!

"And I thought that was pretty cool, I guess."

"Um, okay … thanks," she said snottily, still using her phone.

"Yeah, I was sittin' there, like, 'This glue costs too much,' and then you came in and just *took* that tape and then I was, like, 'Whoa, she's got it figured out. She's got the right idea.'"

She didn't say anything in response to the feeble attempts at flattery and kept sliding things around on her handheld screen. The top of her arms from wrist to elbow were sumptuously downed. She had on black cutoffs that were a few inches shy of just being a waistband and belt loops. A pair of holey, white nylons stood out underneath. Her long thin legs and knobby knees reminded Billy of two aspen trees growing side-by-side.

Ah, look at me just once more…

"Anyways, take 'er easy," Billy said, turning his heel in the pea gravel and heading towards the raucously-striped van.

"Sorry," she said, looking up from her phone, "what were you saying?"

Angela slunk low in the navigator's seat with her dirty bare feet on the dashboard. She was nestled in an egg shape and explaining how she ended up in a Washington, PA truck stop.

"We were just in Pittsburgh… at the D-11 conference…" She paused between thoughts to stare pontifically into the rushing scenery. "Five… six thousand of us." Her brown suede ballet slips were curled up on the floorboard beneath her like two over-ripe bananas.

"What's that?" Billy asked, eyes on the road, hands at ten and two.

"Pittsburgh?"

"No, I mean the D conference. Is that like a college sports meet or something?"

She took a deep breath. "The D-11 are eleven so-called 'dee-veloped' nations of the world (at least according to bankers, conglomerates, international consortiums, and massive global corporations)… Their representatives get together, *clandestinely*" (a word she obviously reveled in using) "every four years. They pretty much try and decide how to screw over the entire rest of the world. That's why we show up and speak our minds."

"Hmm. Interesting," Billy said not-too-convincingly. "I haven't heard of 'em."

"Oh no, of course not: they try and keep it secret... Try and keep us from showing up... Keep people like you in the dark..." Angela was determined to be ruminative, as if reading a deathly-serious and barely-interesting book in some public place. "You know, I was thinking about it: too many people don't use their *minds* these days. It's all television this and Internet that. But, like, you don't see people using their minds, you know. People don't do *puzzles* anymore. Families used to have *puzzle night*. It's sad..."

Her phone made a chimey tinkle. She stopped in her tracks.

"The D-11. So there's the U.S. of course... Russia? They're still a player." Billy drove with a focused guise of deep thought, of serious mind-usage. "England-slash-Great Britain, France, Germany... that's five, let's see. Six more. Don't tell me. I'm gonna go with... Japan and China. Okay. India, don't want to forget India. Been hearing *a lot* about Brazil lately, too—"

Angela put her phone down to stop Billy's talking. "Yeah, actually, I don't know for sure who all's in it, but that sounds right." She took a short breath. "I mean, they're all a bunch of millionaires, anyway, all the same. So it basically doesn't matter what *cuhn-tree* they claim to be from," she said with disdain.

"They're the ones that invent borders and flags. The ones with money."

"Right, like I said: I've never heard of this group myself, this particular *cabal*." He noticed Angela was looking at him now, paying attention to his words. She had lips the color of ripe peaches. They were probably soft and sweet, too. It was easier to talk with her looking out the window and him focused on the driving. "But, uh, they do sound *evil*. Like, world domination is their game or something."

"Oh ... it's ... *not a game*."

She turned back towards scenic Ohio with the grave and composed look of having delivered the action movie's tag line.

Angela was nice, though.

She was from the Headless Horseman country of New York and had been living all over the place since she was eighteen. Lately she found herself staying in New York City. "Brooklyn," she said disparagingly. She said she was twenty-one. Billy respected her sober outlook, even if it did seem misguided from his point of view. She was as smart as a whip; Billy wished he was that smart at that age, two-and-a-half years ago. And, really, most of her judgements were fine—agreeable, even. It was just the way she'd nonchalantly tack on such intense addenda that Billy tried to overlook.

"I'd like to set every cop in the world on fire," she said casually when they passed by someone being ticketed on the interstate.

And now she was off to California for a while, going the same direction as Billy.

"What's in California?" Billy asked. "I mean, I don't want this to sound like a cheesy pick up line or anything, but: you *are* going into acting, right?"

The comment must've been benign, pleasing even, as she demurely smiled and shook her head. "No, I'm going to work on a farm … up north …"

He was hip to the lingo.

"Are you trimming weed?" he asked enthusiastically. She didn't respond right away. "Dude, that's rad," Billy continued, "*really* rad. How much do they pay you? If you don't mind my askin'." He swerved a little to avoid a chunk of tire. "You know: I've considered that lifestyle myself, being a west-coaster and all. Have you ever tried O.G. Blue Frog? You can't get it on the east coast."

Angela gave Billy a sweet look and closed her eyes before going into detail. "It depends on how long I stay, but …" eyes opening up, diverting the driver's attention from the road, "they pay a certain cut of the crop, plus room and board at this beautiful place in the middle of the redwoods … big, delicious communal meals and—" her phone buzzed against her thigh and she took it out of her shorts to investigate. "Stuff."

"So you get paid in top-shelf reefer and free rent at a retreat with four-star food and all that and then, what, you take off with some and sell it or keep it or what?"

"Yeah, I guess, either one," she said distractedly before putting the phone back into her shorts.

Its screen glowed through the cotton pocket that peeked down an inch or two below the cut-off fringe. It made a rectangular impression above her pubis.

"Well that's *neat*," Billy said after a considerable break in dialogue. "That all just sounds … *neat*."

Things went by quickly with someone else around and, despite the purpose of her own travels, Angela kept Billy's mind off of the potentially felonious nature of his trip. The two of them had a sporting contest to see who could spot the worst bumper sticker. For a while 'Sasquatch Lover: And I Vote!' appeared destined to take the cake (although a plain white oval that plainly read 'Cashews' led to a heated debate over what "worst bumper sticker" really meant).

"Alright. This could be it," she announced. "'Your honor student is just a pawn in my Shih Tzu's plan for world domination.'"

She had a laugh that honored the definition of "lilt." It filled Billy with doofy, boyish joy.

"That's good. But a mouthful." To his right he noticed a Celica that had few miles left in it and he instinctively slowed down to get a good look at the bumper. "Okay. Here we go: 'Read Revelations: Because the Answers are Always in the Back of the Book!'" He grinned. "See how 'Always' is underlined, too?"

The mood had lightened to the point of conviviality. Billy drove and happily let his imagination go too far.

"So where are you from again?" Angela asked for the first time later that afternoon.

"Washington. The state," he predictively added after some months spent living on the eastern seaboard. "I actually just graduated over there. The Experimental Liberal Arts College."

Of course, Angela had friends that went there.

"Did you know Sequoia?"

"*Sequoia*?" He squelched the incredulous look immediately. "Sequoia *who*?"

"Just Sequoia."

Billy huffed. "*Uhhh*, no: they don't let you just put one name on your school ID. Believe me. My friend Tyler lobbied, unsuccessfully, for quite sometime to have his ID just read 'Tyler.' Of course, *everybody* knows him as Tyler, and Tyler alone, but. Try telling that to the admin. I mean —" He cut himself off and turned to her with an apologetic grin. This monologue was turning up-tight. "I mean, no, I never met Sequoia. Sounds like an upstanding guy, though."

"Hmm…did you ever meet Francisco?…*Moody* or something? *Moopy*?"

"Doesn't ring a bell."

"He worked at the Experimental Farm."

"Oh, yeah, well…I didn't hang out with those guys much. I was mostly in, you know, English programs. But I did use to have a partial C.S.A. So, you know…I still *supported* Francisco."

"Maybe his name was Felipe…*or was it Felix*…Oh!" Angela clapped her hands excitedly two times, "you *must* know Aspen Zephyr!"

Billy clutched the wheel. He tried not to instinctively bristle. A forgotten and irascible choler bubbled inside like lava in a seemingly dormant volcano. He saw the ridiculous name written in its compulsory whimsical font. He circumspectly bit his tongue and made rapt humming sounds while secretly venting. It sounded like Angela liked the guy, after all.

Oh, Aspen Zephyr, the bon vivant *with the novelty Coke-bottle lenses? The quirky man that sang off-key a capella sea chanties at house shows? Ah, do you mean* Aspen Zephyr? *The skinny strange fellow who always wore yellow? The guy that bounced between the coffee shop and the record store each weekday like the ball in a slow-moving game of Pong? Why, yes, of course, that Aspen Zephyr, the charming thirty- (or was it forty-?) something Peter Pan that proudly smelled like jicama everywhere he went! The man that wore gawkiness like a bespoke suit! The large and lovable clown fish of the small Pacific Northwest pond!*

Ha! I scoff at the name. Ha! The embodiment of the goof-ass a tough city like Philadelphia would not tolerate...

You mean to ask if I know the weirdest beard of a college-town renowned for its eccentrics and their facial hair?!

Do I know Aspen fucking Zephyr?!

"No, I never heard of him," Billy said flatly, a bit exhausted-sounding.

"Hmm." Angela looked puzzled. "Well, I think you'd like him. He's such a talented, sweet guy." She smiled towards the driver. "Did you ever hang out with Vera Schlessinger?"

"Vera…"

"She does, like, social justice puppets and tons of political street theater stuff?"

"Oh, well, no. No, I don't think I ever met her."

"Yeah, I bet you'd know *of* her if you thought about it. Or, like, *recognize* her, even… she's pretty well-known. One of her puppets got interviewed in *Mother Jones*."

"Rii-iight," Billy droned. "I think I saw that in an Alumni magazine."

After narrowly avoiding gridlock in bigger-than-you-realize Columbus, Ohio, Billy began to fret. He did not know how to deal with the night's sleeping arrangements. Something would have to be decided upon fairly soon.

His plan had been to plunge well into the dusk and sleep at either KOA campsites or, if willing to go a little further during some stretches, park and snooze in an off-ramp hotel parking lot. This was his own compromise between sleeping at a rest stop (dangerous) and staying at a hotel (costly).

But when Angela hopped on board (or was invited on board), it became a thornier situation. It became *their* plan. And whereas, on the one hand, Billy most certainly wanted to sleep with Angela and had to try mightily to not daydream about a simple, sex-filled life on their humble self-sustaining California Drug Hacienda, he also understood that even the slightest whiff of licentiousness could rightly scare her off. She was a hitch-hiker, after all, and he had picked her up at a truck stop in his strange van. Only pornos and slasher movies started that way and you didn't want to increase your passenger's suspicions that you were trying to produce either sort of feature.

They pulled off the freeway for some dinner. The van easily found a spot at a local establishment called the Lucky Duck. It had a sign like a fifty-foot-tall lollipop with a cartoon of a beaming duck set inside a large diamond. It was the sign that lured them in from a great distance.

Stepping out onto the lot and stretching their gummy limbs, they could tell that the Lucky Duck used to be a Mexican restaurant. It still had stucco and arches and a red tile roof. Out of nowhere someone honked encouragingly at the van.

"Yeah!" the passenger rowdily yelled at Angela. "Pan-uh-Ma!!"

She was unshaken, if whatever just transpired even registered with her.

It was somewhere comfortably between "busy" and "dead" inside the Lucky Duck. Angela and Billy were pleased to seat themselves at a cushiony booth. Outside their viewing window, boxwood shrubs grew in a bed of white rocks. Further away was a busy intersection and local business. Silverware clinked all around them. An old man chuckled jovially. After being cramped in that van so long, the pair felt like a couple of Goldilockses prepared to enjoy perfect bowls of porridge together in the coziness of a *just-right* bed.

"So, what are you thinking about getting?" Billy scrutinized the menu quickly for meatless, gluten-free, and dairy-free items. It was stressing him out. He didn't want the Duck to screw this one up. Angela was prettier than anyone he'd dealt with. That would be abundantly clear once her hair came back in like normal.

"I don't know." Angela regarded the laminated page before her. "A cheeseburger's sounding *pret*-ty good right about now."

After hearing her say that, it seemed like anything could happen.

The soda was cold and bottomless and they split a piece of strawberry-rhubarb pie that caught their eyes in the mirrored, rotating display near the entrance. They were over-sated and generously left to groove on a caloric high together while their waitress did the crossword in an unseen corner. Angela began offhandedly explaining practical adjustments one could make to take down the consumerist power structures.

"Like, for instance, I wash my hair with shampoo that my housemate makes from vinegar, honey, vitamin E oil, rosemary, and sage." She'd put up a finger for each ingredient and held her hand splayed out before Billy like a spindly starfish.

"That's amazing," he said, lost in her custardy locks.

Angela leaned forward over the empty pie plate and pair of forks. "Go ahead: smell it."

From his seat he slowly slanted towards her bowed head and almost pressed his nose into her scalp. He gently placed his right hand just above her ear. It didn't matter what it smelled like, really.

"Yeah, wow. Just, wow. Smells *fantastic*. I'd sure love to get my hands on some of that." He drained his Coke. "Maybe I could buy some from your housemate."

Angela tittered knowingly. "Oh, Mose doesn't believe in money. He only *trades* or *barters*."

Billy wanted to know how he bartered rent every month and what Angela traded for her shampoo. But he also didn't want to ask.

"Well, either way: your hair smells sensational."

"Thanks." She smiled and ran her hands through her hair. "And conditioner is the same, just swap coconut milk for vinegar." Her eyes went serious. "See: now I'm not supporting some multinational consumer goods corporation that tests on animals and jacks up prices for normal people just so the assholes at the top can, like, buy another yacht or whatever."

"Talk about a win-win."

Time was money for both travelers, who would plow on for another couple hours, until near dark. Angela even found a camper-friendly park on the way using an atlas she'd packed along. They could probably park somewhere there and stay the night.

Nobody was at the entrance to the site to collect payment or say where to go. There were no other vehicles. It was 8:15. It looked like a drive-in movie without a screen or listening devices or concessions.

"Does this spot seem good?" Billy asked before

stopping and turning on the dome light.

"Sure," Angela said, "this spot seems absolutely lovely."

She reached over and touched Billy on the shoulder. This sent a thousand scattered signals throughout him like a jar of marbles hitting the ground. He patted her hand.

"Thanks."

"For what?"

He slid his hand away from her and moved it under his seat, sliding forward a few ratcheting inches. He pushed the driver's side door open with a lateral leg kick. It was buggy out in the darkness. The air felt thick. The moon was big and shined waxy yellow as cloudy wisps passed by quickly.

"I guess I can take this middle seat out and you can sleep in this section. Just watch out for those boxes and rugs—they're Chinese."

He started pulling the seat out, clumsily clutching and grabbing at pullers and straps until he hit upon the right sequence and popped the seat out. It fell to the ground with a dull thud. Angela was standing behind him with her backpack. Her duct-taped strap reflected the serious moonlight.

"Where are you gonna sleep?" she asked literally.

"Oh, I dunno, I can sleep in the front seat or something, lean it back, tuck myself in there."

If there was anything to adjust or fumble with in the middle of the van, Billy was doing it. He crawled in and pushed the boxes back a little further and lightly slapped the rugs like a masseur.

"Well…" She looked around in the dark. "You

can sleep back here with me if you want."

"Oh, okay."

"I don't feel like having sex tonight, though."

"... Okay."

"I'm kinda wiped."

"Uh-huh."

"Travel sorta drains me."

They laid down together next to one another, each face up.

Billy figured he should say something, surely, but he had no clue what.

So much small talk was exhausted at this point. Besides, Angela was in the driver's seat when it came to the back of the van. Then a movement. She rolled over and faced Billy and then she put her arm across his collarbone. Her eyes were closed. He took a deep breath. The roof seemed far away, the dome light as distant as the moon outside.

Billy sighed. He started the day in Philadelphia and tonight Angela's hand was right there on his shoulder. Not bad for a day's work. It was still Saturday. There were miles to go. He *did* feel kinda wiped and sorta drained. When the name Aspen Zephyr popped up again, Billy idly wondered, for the first time ever in his entire life, if maybe *he* was the asshole. For all he knew, people with tree names might well make good friends. And then for the rest of the night (which was only about five more minutes until he was asleep) he thought about Lucy, the last person he slept beside.

9

The sun crashed through the windows intensified, like light passing through a magnifying glass. The interior was humid and dewy with breath. Last night's shadows were now tall, green trees. Bright morning light illuminated everything in sight.

Angela pretended to be asleep and comfortable on the floor of the backseat. Semi-nestled together, Billy went in for a romantic (but subtle) sniff of her neck and trapezius. He was prepared to play possum as well. This could have gone on for hours, the road ahead be damned. She groaned softly and stirred, rustled around in her sleeping bag and backed up an inch closer to big spoon Billy. Everybody was sufficiently aroused when her phone dramatically shook and buzzed like a scoreboard announcing *time's up, the game has ended and the results will not change; please drive home safely*.

"Ugh, eight already?" Angela groaned.

Rising at such an early hour in the back of a van only heightened that alluring languid look of hers.

"Oh, wait," she checked the phone with one hand while also unabashedly flicking the crud just removed from her eyes with the other. "It's 7:45 …" She slid her index and middle fingers around the phone like a little figure skater and laughed to herself. Her hair was rowdy with cowlicks. She dropped the phone on the floor beside her head. "How'd you sleep?" she asked, lolling her head a few degrees towards Billy.

"Pretty fine." He slept right above where the seat latched in and had a terrific knot in his back, but why bring it up now? "I probably could of laid here fifteen minutes longer."

"I know, right?" Angela rubbed her eyes with her palms for an unusually long time.

Though it was a quarter to eight somewhere in Ohio, the pair of weary travelers felt like they'd woken up in some desolate place between the Tropics, one of those small, rock-beached islands that made for legendary colonial prisons. The van must've been parked in a spot highly-prized by cold-blooded things. The temperature rose incrementally with the morning sun. Hoping to conceal his full-fledged erection (though not quite ready to part ways with it), Billy was halfway out of his sleeping bag. He put a hand on Angela's hip (or where her hip probably was underneath her own black nylon cocoon) and left it there. But soon she sat up, sleep sufficiently banished from her eyes, and turned to Billy, smiling. His hand weakly laid sprawled beside her.

"Ready, spaghetti?"

"Sure," he said before unleashing a leonine yawn.

Billy took his time head-scratching and knuckle-popping. Sliding the door open from the inside was no easy task, particularly with a body of creaky, slept-in-a-van joints. Outside, the sound of his own footsteps seemed deafening in the face of so much gravel-lot silence. The bugs were quiet this morning. He walked a good ways into the brush because he felt certain that he'd be relieving himself for a preposterous duration of time. He was not outside of earshot, however, as a strange, high yawp from over near the van jarred Billy mid-stream. No small amount of piss splashed off a large, smooth rock and sprayed all over his left shoe and pant leg.

"Come on! What the hell!" he breathily lamented to himself before foraging a nearby leaf to towel himself off with. It wasn't too absorbent, though, and mostly spread things around.

Pushing aside pokey twigs and brittle branches, he came upon Angela stretching next to the van. He wished he had a camera or a better memory. Billy watched while she twisted her midsection slightly and made another of the unexpected squeals that had caused his earlier accident. Her stomach was visible and when she brought her arms back down, she gave it an appreciative rub before pulling her worn-out white V-neck back down. She had breasts that would keep poets up at night, scribbling and crossing out unsuitable fruits of comparison. Looking down at his pant leg for a second, all was forgiven.

"Thanks for putting that seat back in," Billy said, coolly moseying closer.

"Did what now?"

"Putting that seat back in. Thanks."

The blank look on Angela's face made Billy flash into action and gallop a full circuit around the van.

"Dude ... that's *disturbing*," Angela said indignantly a minute later, when it was clear that the middle row of seats were missing.

Billy frantically dropped down onto his stomach to look under the van.

There was a small puddle of oil on the rocks below and nothing more. Nobody else was within sight at the campground still. Where had they actually parked? It seemed as if this *used to* be a campsite. How old was that atlas?

"Somebody creeping around while you're asleep and taking your, your fucking *car seat?* ... *Really though? A car seat?*"

There was no escaping the bright morning light and Billy just shook his woozy head in the midst of it all. He was powerless, with no choice besides playing it cool. He could not afford to start the day off with a melt-down.

"It's, like ..." She dropped her arms to her sides and then wrapped him up in a soft, girl-fragrant embrace. "I'm sorry, Billy," speaking into his shoulder, "this fucking *sucks.*"

"Oh, it's not you're fault, don't worry about it."

"I know, but I still feel sorry *for* you ..." They separated and she surveyed the lot. "Taking your car seat." She laughed, but just to herself. Then she spat on the ground.

Ever a sound option to an American in trying circumstances, Billy decided to pack up *tout de suite* and leave his troubles behind. By 8:45 he and Angela were on an open stretch of interstate. There was no rush hour in this part of Indiana save for the truckers who were always charging across the fruited plains. A few them honked in bellowing recognition of the van.

"Why do people keep honking at us?" Angela asked.

How does it take somebody a whole day to ask about the paint job? he wanted to snappily respond.

"Well … I can't say for certain *why* they're honking, but it probably has to do with the *Eddie Van Halen* homage." Then came a ten-minute lecture on Van Halen, focusing primarily on the iconic guitar—its aesthetic and its sound. "So, really, there's two camps," Billy concluded, "Sammy Hagar or David Lee Roth. It's quite divisive, actually. Families torn apart. Blood has been shed."

"Huh," Angela watched Indiana zip by. "So why is it painted this way?"

"Yeah, *that* I don't know."

Another $50 of regular guzzled into the tank. The pumps were shaded beneath a gigantic ceiling pillared by six great, yellow columns. Angela was over near a vacant McPlayplace, sitting on a bench beside a fiberglass clown. She was talking on her phone.

Inside Billy was on his haunches trying to pick out a pleasing bouquet of breakfast bars.

"Whatchadoin'?" Angela asked, sneaking up behind Billy.

"Just pickin' out some granola bars. You like carrot cake?"

"No ... I *love* carrot cake!"

He grabbed two of the most-important-meal-of-the-day-supplements and straightened himself up. Blood rushed to Billy's head. He and Angela walked to the register together and she put her hand in the small of his back. He felt dizzier still. He tried to walk off without his change. Then he left an obscene amount of it in the purple *leave a penny, take a penny* tray—close to a dollar.

Angela's fingernails softly raked between Billy's shoulder blades while he fumbled with the key in the ignition. She leaned over and, grabbing a carrot cake breakfast bar from a cup holder, gave Billy a soft kiss on the cheek. A pair of proud and debonair eyes stared back from the rearview. He peeked over at his passenger. She was vigorously chewing the entire bar. She crumpled up the empty wrapper.

"Leth roll," she said, her mouth spilling over with orange debris.

A few minutes later.

"Billy?" she said while gnawing some purloined, early-morning teriyaki jerky.

"Yeah huh."

"Do [*chewing*] you think [*chewing*] we could pick up [*swallowing*] a friend of mine?"

"Pick up a friend?"

"Yeah, I mean … you can say 'no,' of course, obviously … he's just in Bloomington and … he's going to the same, um … farm as me. And—"

"He's in Bloomington?"

"Yeah, and he's going to—"

"And where is Bloomington?"

"I dunno. Indiana somewhere."

It was quiet for a solid thirty seconds. They entered a tricky on-ramp involving a 270° turn and the need to reach seventy mph quickly. A passing big rig trumpeted its horn during the van's merge, not likely out of support.

"You can say 'no,' it's fine."

"No, no, no, it's cool," Billy recovered, trying to play it off like it *was* cool; really. "Check out on that atlas what we need to do."

"Really? Oh, Billy … are you sure?"

He knew the look she was giving him, like he was being so sweet it pained her a little. And maybe it was genuine. Billy took whatever he could and turned to Angela, smiling.

"Of course I'm sure." He nervously glanced over his shoulder using the driver's side mirror. That semi seemed to be staying close. "I'm positive."

Bloomington was neither on-the-way nor out-of-the-way. It was a relatively short state highway away, close to where they were on I-70 when the detour was first broached. It was a long drive for Billy.

"You'll like A.D.S."

"What's his name?" *What the shit …* Billy's face

was plainly covered with a revolted glaze. "Wait, you mean, like, he goes by his initials?"

"No, we just call him A.D.S." Angela explained rather authoritatively.

"…"

Her phone vibrated. Billy shuddered.

"Hello," she said into the thin device. "Yeah…Yeah! We're on our way…nononono, to Bloomington!…Ha ha, yeah *right*…No…No… *Billy*," she almost whispered. "No, *Billy*…you'll meet—…pshhh. Shut. Up. [*soft laughter*]…Okay, see you soon." She slid her phone back into its pocket. "That was A.D.S."

"The man of the hour," Billy said, getting a head start on the pissing contest that was undoubtedly about to commence. "So, I don't understand. This guy's name is A.D.S. Like American Dental Society, Association of Demonic Sorcerers, Another—"

"His name is Simcha, but we call him Animal*istic* Defender Simcha. It's a nickname. A.D.S."

"A nickname. How'd he pick that up? Animal Defender."

"Animalistic Defender. I don't know. I don't remember, okay? I have *a lot* of friends, all right?" There was pronounced guff in Angela's tone. "Maybe that sounds '*weird*' to *you*," she said with mandatory air quotes, "but it's just what he's called: same as being called *Billy*…or *Dick*…or *Chazz* or whatever."

"Well, I don't think those are all quite the same, but, you know, uh, to each his own. So that's fine by me." There were about twenty-three miles to make up for whatever he'd just done. "Sorry if I came off

condescending or anything. I just haven't met anyone with a name like that. Or even a *nickname* like
that." He cleared his throat. "Sounds interesting, actually," Billy muttered.

There was little talking after that. Billy tried to
drum along to the radio, bouncing his palms on the
steering wheel arrhythmically. Angela kept her eyes
on the countryside. She shook her head in revulsion
at a billboard for an RV dealer with the last name
Raper.

"I don't think they should just be putting that
on a sign, even if it's his name. I mean…" she trailed
off.

Her phone buzzed again—another droll message—she smiled knowingly.

"Okay, pull off on this next exit and make
a right," she said. "Then follow that road for one-
point-six miles."

They slowly crunched to a stop outside of a
cluttering of umber cottages that were a part of the
local campus. The walls were covered with water-
logged shingles. The dormitories might have once
been a nice cedar color, but now they looked like
overlapping brownies with a roof on top. Next to
these bungalows was a fly-clouded dumpster that
someone lazily tagged "today sucks" on. It was
10:39 a.m..

"I'll be right back," Angela said as she thrust
open her door and hopped down onto the pavement.

There wasn't a clever plan being hatched inside the van to solve *what am I going to do?* but, rather, a vapid stare in response to *what am I doing?* The stare, seen from the various angles of each mirror and reflective surface, said it all for two full minutes.

Voices approached the van. The back door was violently pulled and slid to the side—so hard that it actually bounced back shut. Then came a stupid chuckle, a *whoa*. The door was given a second go, not much less forceful, and a large black duffle bag was tossed in. In the rearview appeared a medium-sized man with greasy, curly brown ringlets and a swath of acne that spread from cheek-to-cheek and across an upturned nose. The man was dressed up like a ninja: monochromatic Chuck Taylors (except where the canvas separated from the sole around the big-toe anterior and a dingy grey sock stood out); a pair of black cotton-spandex-blend pants from the juniors/young missus section (all but pasted on him from ankle-to-thigh before abruptly sagging around the crotch); and an itchy-looking dark wool sweater (on this warm and sunny day). The only thing betraying his complete darkness was a purple paisley bandana hanging out from a back pocket like a psychedelic tail.

He was a good distance away from Billy—as the middle row of seats were gone—and looked quite in his own world. He comfortably positioned himself squarely in the back with his elbows reposed near the headrests and his hands and forearms restfully dangling. He put his feet up on the duffle bag as if it were an ottoman.

Nobody spoke and there was no noise for a few

seconds. Billy thought he could smell him, that it smelled like a can of Pringles in the van ever since he climbed in. Angela opened her door and pulled herself up to the navigator's seat.

"So, wait. What'd Horace say?" she asked, immediately twisting around towards the back of the van.

He snorted. "*Horace* said he'd evict me if I went to California and that I'm gone too much and it's not fair to all the people that quote *need a room* close quote." He pushed aside the hair from his forehead. "So, basically: one of his girlfriends is gonna take my room if I'm not there by … uh, yesterday." His voice was reedy, like the unpleasant attack of a third-chair clarinet.

Angela made an indignant, grumbling sound. "That's *so* like Horace. Ugh. *Ugh!* He's so … so … *slea-zy*. He gets all these dumb girls that've never been to New York before and he, like, you know: *charms* them. He basically charms them all and makes them think he's an *intellectual* and that he's, like, the one *in charge of* all these kick-ass things like the feminist bike co-op and the anarchist flea market—"

From the backseat: "He is *not* in charge of the anarchist flea market."

"I know, but he *acts* like he is. He *acts* like the Gleaner Burrito Cart is *his* cart, was his idea." She was using her delicate fingers to keep a running tally. "He *acts* like the entire share library is his, he *acts* like he came up with the idea for the Ned Lud Demolition Derby, he *acts* like he started Subversive Movie Night—"

"Uh, hello, *Puck* and *Scottie* started Subversive Movie Night."

Angela flopped her hands out, loose-wristed, as though tossing all the enumerated examples up in the air like so much obnoxious confetti. "I know that," she said. "*Every*body knows that."

The turn signal clicked metronomically up front.

"Yeah…" A.D.S. added, "I helped them pick out the first movie."

"Really?"

"Yeah—some documentary about the *maquila-doras*." His Spanish accent was very pronounced if not entirely accurate.

"*Oh yeah* … I remember that."

"Well, *actually*, they ended up picking *V for Vendetta* because they thought it would bring out more people."

The van merged with traffic and began cruising back north to the interstate.

"Well, either way, Horace is a douchebag," Angela concluded once the van found its proper lane.

"Right."

"And he just does all that crap so he can sleep with dumb, naïve seventeen-year-olds that don't know any better. That's why he's freeing up your room."

"Wait, hold on—did you ever…" A piquant smile minutely curled his thin lips.

"He's such a asshole," she went on. "Of course he's gonna kick *you* out so one of *them*, one of his little *con-cue-bines*, can have a place to crash (among other things). Sick. And there's more where that came from, too. There's always more with him."

A grave look and tone from the back: "Ange. Do you even know how old he is?"

"No," she said, savoring the scandalousness. "Tell me."

"*Thirty-six.*"

They both made the same Mister Yuck face before laughing.

"Yeah, and, *excuse me*, but when did *Horace* become the one in charge of booking shows at the thirteen-twenty-two space?"

"*I know!*"

"So annoying."

"*So* annoying."

Angela returned fully to the front cabin and pivoted her attention towards Billy. She opened her mouth to speak but was cut short.

"It *used* to be cool and now all he ever wants are these retarded punk bands full of fat, old-dude racists and shit," the sharp voice hastily added from the back of the van.

"Racists?" Angela asked, her face baffled while still watching Billy.

"Yeah, dude! Remember? The guy with the head tattoos and the beard—"

"Clem?"

"No, not Clem. Clem doesn't play music anymore, remember? He's doing the butcher school thing in Vermont." He ceased his explanation to chomp at a troublesome hangnail for some seconds. He spat dryly out of the side of his mouth.

He snapped his fingers. *Eureka!* "It was at the show where, like, a million people showed up because of that rumor that Crystal Bullets got back together and were, like, gonna play or something. It was *that* show. Head-Tats was in some band called like Hammerfuck or something."

Angela nodded sadly.

"No, I didn't go to that one … I think I thought that *Seth* was gonna be there." Angela sighed.

Billy adjusted the dashboard vents. He was about to say something.

"Horace is this guy we know back in New York," Angela said, "who, uh … I guess *owns*? this house that a lot of us live at."

"He doesn't own it," A.D.S. corrected.

"Really?"

"No."

"So why's he in charge of—"

"Nope. He's just the name that's been on the lease the longest." He swept the hair aside again. All the grease made the kinkiness lay flat and lent him an unflattering part. "He's fucking lived there since, like, *the nineties*."

Angela and A.D.S. laughed for ten seconds straight.

She caught her breath. "So, Horace is this guy who I guess *likes to think* he's in charge of this place we live at and is just gross and full of shit." Billy took his attention from the road long enough to nod slightly towards Angela. "This is A.D.S., by the way. A.D.S., this is Billy."

"Hey," they both said flatly at the exact same time.

By noon the van was making good time on the interstate. They might see three states by 3 p.m. if they kept this pace up. A.D.S. and Angela's conversation lost some steam. They were soon engrossed in their phones, not unlike docile kids on a family vacation occupied with tiny Etch-a-Sketches. Billy unconvincingly tried to remain silent without seeming sullen.

This was not a part of the plan, Billy thought, as though the plan all along had been to pick up and abscond with a sexy vagrant.

The mileage had sunk below thirty mpg, no doubt due to the extra weight in the back (which probably was offset by the missing row of seats anyways). A few times Billy made some witty observations about passing signage to Angela. She was rightly blasé about this forced humor. A.D.S. chewed his nails and snickered from time to time about whatever was on his phone, sometimes passing it up for Angela to also see.

"What's this?" A.D.S. asked while bent over his seat and probing the furthest reaches of the van.

"Uh, could you keep out from there, please? Those are priceless antiques that I'm delivering."

"Oh, cool, bro." A.D.S. shook the rainstick. "How much is this one worth?"

"Oh, that. That's an inside joke. It's also priceless. Leave it alone, too, please."

The talk was interrupted as the van got ebulliently honked at. Billy spotted a hard-charging

Subaru Brat on his right. The orange mongrel car swerved alongside the van.

"What the hell's that?" A.D.S. demanded.

"It's this guitar thing," Angela clarified. "The car's painted like a band or something."

Looking across Angela (her surfeit of lips and patrician nose in profile, looking like Roman coinage), Billy saw the driver of the Brat. He was a grizzled man, a hard-liver with scraggly blond-gone-grey hair. He was flashing the Van Halen van some reverent horns. His eyes were closed. He appeared to be screaming. The passenger was a woman either middle-aged or severely-ailing. She had pulled her shirt up and was leaning over trying to flash the van. She was wearing a leopard print sports bra and her skin, too, was sallow and tawny-splotched.

"So … *A.D.S.*," Billy said, shifting his eyes towards the rearview. "You got family back in Bloomington or something?"

He laughed haughtily, like a boy duke.

"No."

"What were you doin' there?"

"The school paid me to teach a Muay Thai Kickboxing seminar and an outdoor survival skills clinic. This friend of mine hooked me up. Adrian." Angela nodded in consent. "I hitched a ride there after the D-11 protests."

"Uh-huh, sure, the D-11s. Pittsburgh. And where *does* your family live?"

"Connecticut and New Jersey. They're divorced."

"Sorry to hear that … Mine, too. But you live in

New York. Right between 'em. You all get to visit. That's nice."

"That orange car is, like, swerving all around," Angela chimed.

"I don't really talk with them too much. I mean, my mom … whatever. Once they got divorced, she wanted to live in Connecticut and just sit around getting money from my dad. So, it's, like: what is there to go visit even?"

"Seriously, like: I think they're drunk in that orange car."

"And my dad …" His voice petered out. "The last time I saw him, he was crying. *Literally in tears.* Just, like, 'I don't know what to do right now,' his head in his hands, crying."

"What happened? What'd he do?" Billy found himself interested, actually. "If it's not too, you know … if it's not too personal, my asking."

"Hey, Billy, you should get over into a different lane or something."

"He works for some bank in Manhattan that got in hot water with the Securities and Exchange people. He's some sort of a lawyer." A.D.S. pushed his hair back to little avail. "*He* didn't do anything, but the dudes he works for are total tools."

"Oh my God; *ew*," Angela said. "That woman's got her shirt off."

They were outside of a fuel plaza in southern Illinois waiting for Angela to finish powdering her nose. It was the biggest such station Billy had ever seen. Every trucker in North America must have made a stop here at some point. And not just to diesel up but as a kind of highway hajj to pay respects.

A homologous steak was offered at the adjoining Wagonwheel Diner. The prize for eating it in less than sixty minutes was that it was free. No hat, no placard: just a free ninety-eight-ounce steak.

An intercom noisily announced shower-stall availability. "Shower Thirteen is open. Shower Thirteen … is now open."

A.D.S. was busily listing some of the vegan foods he swiped from inside that most people didn't even realize were animal- and dairy-free.

"People always say, like: 'Being vegan's hard. I can't do that. How do you *eat*?'" he pleaded rhetorically with a nasal tone he himself used often enough. "But, like, this apple pie," he said, shaking a small, coffin-shaped box with a tiny baked turnover inside, "this apple pie doesn't have any dairy. I checked." He produced a bag of sweet'n'tangy Quesadillas at Dawn-flavored chips from underneath his droopy sweater. "No cheese … just artificial flavors, dude." He gave the bag a few gentle squeezes. "And they're fuckin' *bangin'* too. And these," A.D.S. pulled out five foil-packaged toaster-pastries from the rear of his pants and held them splayed out like a poker hand, "*these* suckers are vegan, too. Just gotta make sure and get the *un*-frosted ones."

"So you're telling me there're a lot of options for the vegan lifestyle?" Billy took a long pull from his silo of diet cola.

"So, like, for example: Oreos are *actually* dairy free."

"You can eat Oreos, huh?"

"Yeah. Most cookies are vegan, actually."

"Not the way I make 'em, they're not."

"Hey boys," Angela spritely wedged herself in between them with her arms playfully yoking the trio together. "Yu-um! Quesadillas at Dawn! My favorite!"

Inside the van A.D.S. and Angela were again chatting away, their spirits buoyed by the last pit stop. They spoke brusquely with their mouths full. Billy wanted nothing more than to impose rules restricting snacks and loud conversing but knew that would make him the always-unpopular driver of the school bus.

Billy was, straightly-said, pissed off. Every time he tried to say something to Angela in a low voice, A.D.S. would yell "what?" or "huh?" from the van's stern.

The strategy of making his adversary's preposterousness apparent through friendly-seeming interrogation was doing little more than rile Billy up. A.D.S. was simply too confident. He was impenetrable, unimpeachable. He even knew some sort of martial art should it ever come to a head.

In the far rear of the van A.D.S. lounged like a pampered star en route to his next engagement. From the third row seats he would anecdotally gloat over an encounter he had with someone he and Angela had hopped trains with ("Guess who's working at the American Apparel by Canal Street"

…), then he'd make a transition into political philosophy, saying many intricate and queer-looking Russian names that Billy had always scanned past in text and never offered to say out loud ("That's *not* what Bakunin meant, though. I mean, just sit down and actually *read Statism* and you'll see" …), and he'd do all that before glossing over some run-in with a mutual acquaintance that hinted at his virility and prowess ("Ugh, *Gina*," he'd groan, looking at his ever-beeping smart phone. "That girl will *not* quit. I keep telling you," chastising the phone, "I'm *not in Bushwick right now*" …). In short: he was a tough and shifty opponent. It was like trying to pin Proteus. Every effort Billy made to attack what he saw as weakness or hypocrisy only made him appear stuffy or dense.

"I think I could've eaten that steak back there," Billy abruptly proclaimed for all to hear. He was going on the offensive.

"What steak?" Angela asked.

"The ninety-eight ounce one. That's probably a pre-cooked weight. So you're really only looking at … let's say *seventy-five*, for the sake of argument." He looked out over the road nobly. "I believe I could've handled that steak."

Billy could not remember the last time he actually ordered or even ate a steak.

A gagging noise issued from the rear of the van.

"Why would you do that? It's just gonna clog up your colon and you'll die, with, like, a hundred ounces of meat in there or whatever."

A.D.S. brushed the apple pie crumbs off his

sweater and then went on to cite a widely-contested urban legend concerning the contents of John Wayne's colon and large intestine, which of course Billy refuted.

"Well, whatever. I saw pictures of the x-rays from John Wayne's ass online and it was disgusting." He began excitedly tapping his fingers on the phone screen.

"I mean, we don't need to see some guy's photoshop of John Wayne's colon," Billy said, voice-of-reason-style.

"Dude: this is *so* not a photoshop," A.D.S. said, shoving the phone towards the driver for a split-second before handing it off to Angela. "That's real. I used to date a girl in medical school. And, *yeah*, and also, think about it: animal foods are not *meant* to be eaten. It's like, we learned how to keep our gag reflex in check, you know? Because, like, honey is just bee vomit. An egg is a chicken's period."

"Gross," Angela said.

"I don't know if that's even true," Billy consoled her.

"Yeah-hunh it is true," A.D.S. said in voice from the schoolyard. "Did you read that article about vegan poop?" He paused to allow adequate time for memory jogging. "They figured out why vegan's poop doesn't float. And do you know why?" Billy's ensuing silence was a mix of perplexity and hostility. "Vegan shit doesn't have all those *animal fats* in it making it float. Because fat floats. It rises in water."

"Well, number one, I'd like to know who '*they*' are, the ones conducting this, uh research, and, also, it seems to me..." Billy stopped himself, not wanting to take such a fruitless detour. "Meat tastes good, it's an excellent source of protein, I—"

"Uh, *hello*: flax seeds, soy, hemp, nut butters—"

"Right, I just—"

"Quinoa, tempeh, lentils...I could go on and on."

Gripping the steering wheel tightly, Billy checked to see where Angela stood on the matter. She was curled up again, daydreaming, with A.D.S.'s phone still balanced on her knees.

"Bulgur. Bulgur has a shit-load of protein," he said conclusively as he grabbed his mobile device and crawled on all fours back to his seat.

Angela woke up and drowsily asked what state they were in.

"Missouri," Billy said in a gentle, romantic caress.

"Oh...so we're halfway there. Cool."

With the steady green backdrop of the endless shady leaves and grassy embankments, Billy saw that she looked bored. She patted her tummy and gave herself a baby's wet belch, then returned to looking bored. It was unsafe and unhealthy to find these sorts of things endearing, even vaguely titillating, and Billy was in the danger zone.

A nasal gurgling bubbled some feet in the back.

"Poor A.D.S." Angela said. "He suffers from sleep apnea, you know."

Billy sensed a private moment. "So you're *really*

going to California?"

"Uh-huh," Angela swiveled her head to the left slowly.

"You know ... you're more than welcome to come with me and check out Santa Fe."

"Oh yeah?" There was polite interest in her voice.

"Of course. It's supposed to be really beautiful. *Breathtaking* even. Then we could maybe go to New Orleans."

"I've been there."

"Well, wherever. We could go wherever you want."

The words hung in the air and Billy felt fully-exposed: romance, desperation, and no clear plan, all mixed together.

"Why don't you just come to California, too, then?"

"Hmm ..."

A.D.S. gnashed his teeth and groaned.

It was not easy to say, but: "I still have to deliver this stuff and then return the van to Philly."

"Yeah ..." she faced the road ahead. "And I said I'd go out to my friend's farm."

The radio got turned on but there was no good listening. Stopping at the least offensive station (the one not playing commercials right then) they listened to some palatable vibraphone jazz. The pair each pinched their lips and affected a close, hushed interest in the scenery. A few minutes later the song ended and nothing was said until the disc jockey made his way back to the microphone.

"... Simply stunning. Alf Mon*toya* on drums.

Pairing … as always … with the imponderable and ex*quisite* bass of Pop Pop Myers. Jimmy "Hot Stuff" LaBianca on alto sax. "Tall" Kenny *Pugh* on guitar and, of course … you just witnessed the inimitable, unmistakable Knox Pepper on vibes. An un*usual* but nonetheless de*light*ful arrangement … *Ha*, those were just the cats in the studio … *Haha*. That's just the way *jazz* is. Absolutely beautiful. [*shuffling papers*] That song, "Astral Search/Love All (Take Three)," was actually the *fifth* take recorded by Mike McHenry at Gamma Epsilon Studios in—"

Billy turned the radio down nearly all the way.

"I'm getting $50,000 this week."

He didn't know why he'd said it then or what he wanted the reaction to be. The DJ murmured on.

"What for?" Angela asked placidly, not showing much surprise.

"My friend died. My best friend. It's insurance money…" Didn't girls like mysterious wayfarers? And dream of someday puzzling out the insinuations of a rugged and solemn loner? One with a secret fortune tied to a personal anguish, no less? It was worth a shot. "I guess I just had to drive. I had to *ramble*. Couldn't stick around. Everything reminded me …" He shook his head. "I needed to leave, okay?" he said with an affected over-sensitivity. "I had to really go find myself. *Out there*," he whispered, sensing that this last bit was a touch too much.

Billy turned the radio back up.

"—originally it was supposed to be Trickle McCoy on sax, but he had got *strep throat* … It was a record-cold winter in New York in 19 … 68, it was.

Thankfully, Knox knew that "Hot Stuff" was in town working on the *Golden Spike* sessions with Spike Powell and the rest, as they say—"

Angela wouldn't let the DJ finish.

"I'm sorry to hear that." There was earnest empathy behind the words. "What happened?—If you feel like talking about it. You don't have to if you don't want."

Billy still hadn't gotten around to finding out what had happened to Duane.

"Cancer," he said faintly, looking for nothing in particular from right to left.

She rubbed his shoulder. "You must be going through a lot right now." She gave his biceps a tender squeeze.

"Yeah…" he said, letting his arched eyebrows and faraway gaze say the rest.

The volume went back up. "—100% *tax*-deductible, so please, consider donating your used vehicle to KCUD to help support and keep this mag-*nif*icent, mag-*nan*imous, mag-*jes*tic thing we call *jazz music* alive for your listening pleasure."

A.D.S. was stirring in the back. Billy began to panic that he'd feigned sleep in order to eavesdrop. He stretched his arms and released a boorish yodel of a yawn.

"Hey, um, *Billy*," he said before smacking his gums a few times, "would you mind if we put something else on?" He sounded refreshed, worrisomely energetic. "This grandpa music is *killing* me."

"After this song." He held back an impish smile when he saw A.D.S.' churlish arm-crossing in the rearview. Like a complete pill, Billy hit the 'SCAN' function nintey seconds later and let the radio roll through every station in the area at obnoxious three-and-a-half second intervals. They were not far past the evangelists when A.D.S. slithered a hand up and put an adapter into the cigarette lighter.

"Here," he announced, "I brought this."

The song he selected from his phone was aggressively pell-mell. Someone played an acoustic guitar as fast, hard, and loudly as they possibly could. It sounded like the guitar was covered with provocative bumper stickers. Somewhere in the hinterlands of the mix, an accordion howled like cats having sex. All the while, the singer threatened Ted Turner and Rupert Murdoch without much in the way of melody or specifics.

"Okay, now Angela gets to pick a song," Billy said when the long two minutes were up. He jerked the adapter out of the dashboard with the same motion and force one uses to start a lawn mower. Serendipitously, the opening tom fill of "Young Americans" perfectly tumbled out from the speakers as the cord whipped back at A.D.S..

"Hey," he shouted. "That could have totally hit me in the eye or something."

"Sorry, " Billy said as he bounced excitedly over the radio miracle. He moved his shoulders fluidly along with the sax blasts.

Angela made a motion towards the radio. Billy seized her hand. They looked at one another, equally surprised by such boldness. Whether she was going to change the station or turn up the volume, it did not matter: they held hands and did small loops with them together. She pressed his right hand tighter. It felt like a hug. From their seats they danced with one another. Ideally, (*i.e.* if A.D.S. weren't back there), this would be the precise moment where reality segued into a fast-moving montage that faded out into gentle laughter and sudden nighttime.

Bowie began singing. They slowed their boogieing but did not separate.

Billy softly sang along: "Gee, my life's a funny thing, am I still too young?"

"Dude," A.D.S. interrupted, "*nobody* knows the words to this song. I tried to do it at karaoke once in Austin: *big mistake*."

"Bowie knows the words," Billy smartly replied.

"Yeah, obviously." He pompously giggled at his opponent's playing into such an obvious gambit. "But you're no Bowie, cuz."

Cuz?!

Billy hadn't been called that since working at A.V. I., when one of those smarmy South Philly kids told him he didn't *need* to spit his gum out.

Billy clenched his jaw. He pretended to need his right hand on the wheel and peeled it away from Angela. She smiled uncomfortably at him. Her look begged Billy to drop it, please, to enjoy the song some more. She faced forward and swayed in the navigator's seat with a strained impression of musical entrancement.

David Bowie meanwhile asked his audience if they remembered the bills they have to pay, or even yesterday.

As the song changed dreamily-phasered keys,

Billy took a deep breath and tried to make direct eye contact with A.D.S. in the rearview. The passenger sat upright, though, and all Billy could see was the bottom of his face—a pimply chin and a cocksure grin. It was a goad, a gesture of double-doggery, a game of low-stakes chicken.

"Ever been a young American, just you and your idle *simple* sense of uh," Billy sang loudly, about a quarter-second behind Bowie, just hoping to grasp context clues about what the genuinely indecipherable words were. "Leather feather everywhere and mama something, from the ghetto …" he trailed off.

"Yeah, I'm pretty sure those aren't the words, man."

Angela rolled her eyes. "You guys," she said with a mother's tired timbre.

"Well," Billy sorrily began, "I know the all words on *Station to Station*. If "Golden Years" came on..."

The idea flashed into Billy's mind as he was putting gas in the van and he promptly followed through without debate.

"Dude," he said urgently once he found A.D.S. busily searching for a shot glass with his name on it in the souvenir section. "Dude, there's, like, a whole entire section back there of, like, holistic foods and stuff."

"Really?" he said, clearly intrigued.

"Yeah, man. I'm pretty sure I saw a T.V.P. wrap over there, some sort of kefir—"

"I don't do kefir."

"Yeah, well, like I said: it's a *holistic* section, not necessarily a A.D.S. section. It's like a little healthy oasis."

A.D.S. went off in the direction Billy indicated posthaste. While he searched in vain for a texturized vegetable protein wrap and while Angela stole some aspirin, Billy furtively fled the interstate shopping center and speed-walked directly towards the parked van. He flipped the ignition and reversed out from the spot.

In the rearview mirror he saw A.D.S.'s duffel bag and put the van in 'P.' Determined not to get out of his seat, Billy stretched himself out, undid his safety belt, and grazed the bag several times with his fingertips. Finally he caught a canvas loop and hooked the whole thing towards him on his index finger alone. He opened his door and, cradling the bag to him, gave it a robust heave out onto the pavement. The van peeled off and a group of young faces in an older white Accord honked repeatedly at him as he approached a stop sign.

"Rock and roll!" they shouted.

Trying to amass a sizable distance between himself and everything he left behind, Billy drove due west at sensibly illegal speeds. Things got eerie, though, when the dark settled in not much later. It was too quiet and too still. Although he didn't much regret the decision made at the service station, Billy was now on his own, 1300 miles from home. And wherever he was, it had no FM radio reception or visible substance beyond the pale reach of the highway lights. He switched over to the AM band and its mix of heartland politics, theology, and conspiracy theory. Their messages were inextricably braided together.

"Yeah, hi there, my name is Horatio and I'm a time-traveler," a caller said with the familiar Alcoholics-Anonymous-introduction cadence.

At least this'll keep me awake, Billy thought.

"Okay, go ahead Horatio," the host said with the heartfelt support of a sponsor. "What've you got for us?"

Before Horatio could reply, however, Billy's eyes widened as he saw several soft-blinking red lights in the distance. He told himself to relax. He briefly assured himself that radio towers and aircraft might explain what he drove towards. But neither of those would be so legion or low to the ground in such a remote place. Was there a city out here he forgot about? His heart pounded. There were no other vehicles on the road. The red blots hovered and disappeared, flashed back in a slightly different spot over the horizon (or what he *assumed* to be the horizon).

It would have been nice to have A.D.S.'s kickboxing and survival skills in the backseat still, just in case.

"Now, this is just what happens in 20-*15*. Of course, [*cough*] that'll all be *before* Obama removes term limits and annexes Mexico," Horatio added. "Like I said, there're plenty of warning signs out there already."

Billy drove slower and slower as he neared the

lights. The Van Halen van was still the only car in sight. He set the cruise control at forty-five. The high-beams suddenly hit a sign in the distance. It was some kind of sheet-metal, though not of the informative, government-stamped variety. It was probably just an advertisement for some disappointing highway attraction 500 miles away. The van prudently approached it at a cagey forty mph anyways.

"Alright, thank you Horatio for your riveting ... *vision*. Our next caller is ... *Matthew*. Matthew, you're from Blue Springs, you're 39, and you've encountered some *lizard men*."

He cranked the volume knob left until it clicked.

The sign came into focus. It leaned back against a small pump house shed. It was a large piece of corrugated, chicken coop scrap tin.

'*Matthew 25:14*' it read in bright, shining gold spray paint.

Billy pulled over and waited for the either the sunrise or the lizard men. Finally, when a semi barreled past him ten minutes later, he followed from a safe distance, like a small fish tailing a large shark. The brave driver in the truck was unperturbed by the glowering phantasms floating in the Kansas night.

At 11:17 p.m., Billy was close enough to see that the red lights were simply reflectors on massive wind turbines. He again decelerated and rolled his window down to hear the strange sonorous *whoop*ing of the great wind farm. It was nothing to be frightened of.

And then came Junction City, Kansas, where

Billy found a suitable interstate hotel to park his vehicle near. At the end of a very long and strange day, the Billy was ready to rest and return to his intended plans.

The lot was nearly full. Billy wondered what all these cars were doing then and there. He guessed that there are simply a lot of people moving all around the place—you just don't think much about them. You don't often consider where everybody sleeps at night. It was a dumb revelation, but it was a revelation nonetheless.

On the verge of passing out under the yellow incubator of a dome light, Billy used Angela's atlas to weigh his options for tomorrow. There was 56 West and there was I-70; a thin, squiggling line between Junction City and Santa Fe or a broad, chisel-tipped warpath that led to Colorado Springs. Billy told himself he was ready to shake down Dish McAlister for toll money and let that freak know that now was the time to give the "okay" on depositing that $100 personal check. It had been a bruising day for his manhood and he needed to atone.

D. McAlister—he looked at the check. The address was right there in the upper left-hand corner. There was a two-inch-by-two-inch inset map of Colorado Springs in the atlas that would hopefully lead him there. And once he took care of that, Santa Fe was four hours south on I-25. He could make the drop-off that next day and move on to Texas or wherever was next.

Either way: a ten-hour drive tomorrow and he could start unloading the Chinese things. The important thing now was to keep moving and not think too much.

10

Free to stretch out in the van's spacious cavern, Billy only tossed and turned. He ground his teeth and gripped the lip of his sleeping bag. He had many dreams. They were all scattered, fast-paced, and short. He woke repeatedly. Things seemed amiss. Billy sat up in the middle of the night and listened for rustling, mumbles. He waited for sounds of something afoot. But there was only an unnerving and cricketless silence. He explained away his foreboding as a normal consequence of sleeping in a cargo van in a hotel parking lot and laid back down. Eventually he checked his phone and it said 3:54 a.m.. Billy conceded that he was awake. He had slept just enough to feel rested.

The van started and made a sound like an emphysemic clearing their throat. It was dark out and the streets were deathly still. The on-ramp was less than a mile away. Driving to it, Billy passed a pharmacy with a scarecrow reclined on a bench out front like a town drunk. He noticed a donut shop, open, illuminated, and empty save a lone paper-hatted employee wiping the counter down with a sudsy rag. He crossed only one other vehicle on the streets of Junction City and that was a slow-rumbling street sweeper. It was green and tortoise-like as it methodically tidied up the gutters before quaint townspeople started their old-fashioned days.

Billy waited for a green left arrow for a comedic amount of time at an intersection. He turned the radio on and SCANned. Every station went by and, still, he waited at the light. The radio played a weird sound collage of news and commercials and country twang and snippets you might recognize but did not want to stop for. Craning forward and waiting for the other light to turn yellow, Billy finally stopped on NPR. The opposing light went red.

"Let's turn our attention now to the latest up-surge of violence along the Mexico border," a reporter segued while the van finally turned.

The early morning, pre-dawn driving had a cinematic feel to it, especially now that it was being done solo again. Billy witnessed the sunrise in his driver's side mirror, poking up over a rich, emerald slope he'd crested some minutes ago. There was nobody else on the interstate. The rock 'n' roll van blazed a path surrounded by endless fields of soybeans and the occasional billboard advertising a distant *Wizard of Oz*-related attraction.

Around 7:45 traffic started to materialize. Billy was surprised at how many cars were honking at him, especially at this hour.

Kansas must love Van Halen, he thought to himself.

Billy could have driven straight to Colorado Springs but soon the gas meter hovered around the ¼ mark. He rolled up to an unassuming station and stopped the van. A dark cup of joe with the word 'Coffee' written in rising steam-letters appeared in his head. He bounced out of the van and walked vigorously towards the facility.

"Yeah, gimme fifty on…" Billy cranked his head over his shoulder to double-check what pump he had pulled into.

The van looked a little off.

"Pump four," he said distractedly.

The old man behind the register punched in the appropriate code and awaited further instructions. For the moment, the small digital screen read 'REG. UNLEADED … $50.' Still looking at whatever it was that he was seeing, the customer, Billy, peeled a crisp $50 off a thin wad of bills and slid it over the plexi-glass counter. He staggered back outside without so much as a "thank you" or a "take 'er easy."

It turned out that somebody had spray-painted swastikas all over the Van Halen van at some point during the night. There was a range of sizes but they were all black and bold—with minimal drip. It was the work of a steady hand—or hands …. Slowly walking around the van, Billy estimated that there were no fewer than twenty, the biggest of which was roughly the size of a manhole cover.

And Billy had actually pulled into pump three and thus had to do a hairpin 180 to get his fuel tank on the same side as pump four.

Billy's heart raced while the gas chugged into the tank. He'd been driving around Kansas in a hate crime on wheels. Thankfully, the unruly crisscross graphics of Eddie Van Halen's "Frankenstein" guitar obfuscated and concealed the damage somewhat. In a vain attempt at optimism, Billy wondered if perhaps the busy design of the van made the entire thing an optical illusion. Maybe he'd be a confusing highway blur, not unlike the Dazzle-Camouflaged battleships that his grandpa said kept Tojo dizzy on the high seas back in WWII. He pumped gas into the van and shook his head in disbelief. No confusing blur got honked at the way he did that morning.

Three days in: he'd lost a seat and got the van smothered in swastikas a thousand miles from home. So long, piddling two-hundred buck bonus. *He* was gonna have to pay *Jacob*, more than likely. Dac Kien Ngyuen was gonna be pissed when he saw his van.

"Hey, man, you got any spray-paint?" Billy asked the cashier.

The closest spray-paint was down the interstate "a ways" since all this exit was was a gas station. Other cars were now on the road. Billy made eye contact with none of them. He kept the radio off and heeded every noise. What if a Jewish Highway Patrolman sat poised on his motorcycle, well-hid behind a speed-trap billboard? Or what if he passed a VFW Pancake Feed? What if the van tore by the recently-dismissed congregation an African-American Baptist church? These things were all unlikely on an early morning somewhere in Kansas along I-70, but Billy worried that just such an incident might as well occur at this point.

Eyes on the road, he swore loudly and inventively at A.D.S., who he knew for a fact to be behind it all. Then he grew sullen and angry at Jacob for making him drive such an identifiable, one-of-a-kind monstrosity, too. This was all proving to be well beyond his pay grade. For a minute or two he seriously toyed with the idea of just leaving the van in Kansas and trying to stretch out the money in his pocket until he could figure something better out. That plan was so stupid, though, that it made everything abundantly clear and Billy began to curse himself. The self-hostility would not abate until he purchased a can each of black, white, and red spray paint.

It ended up being deeply cathartic to cover up all those swastikas. An enormous problem was getting solved right before his eyes. If you looked closely, you could see that there were some incongruous colors and textures (the original paint job was a professional one) but the spray paint didn't stick out *too* much. It was certainly better than it had been.

Enjoying the inimitable sound of a rattling can of spray paint, Billy was now performing some detail work. Even he couldn't even point to where most of the swastikas had been. While he was crouched down low finishing off some fish-stick sized graffiti around the passenger-side front wheel well, Billy heard a car come to a crunchy halt on the other side of the van.

His head appeared over the hood like a prairie dog and tucked right back down when he saw that it was a cop.

Oh shit, Billy thought.

The words came into his head, too acute for grammar, like boulders rolling down the mountain: *stolen—Jesus—Chinese—antiques—I'm from Philadelphia—fuck, in Kansas—PA tags—Washington license still—driving to, meeting with … dealers—oh, shit, shit, shit anarchist hitchhiker—hitchhikers!—D-11 protests—going to a California pot farm, I drove them to—fuck—that's aiding and abetting—but I abandoned them, that's good—ugh, they were probably on the run—probably burnt down Christmas tree farm—probably fucking narc'd me out to the Feds!—freed lab animals and pinned it on me—swung a deal with the D.A.—Je-sus jumped up Christ weeping on the cross, what in the hell—Okay, get it straight: this van? Not mine, sir, I'm just a driver covering swastikas up—act of revenge, hitchhikers—I'm just going to New Mexico to Texas to Mississippi—going back home, officer, I swear!*

The cop stayed in his patrol car for what felt like a long, long while. This maybe lasted thirty seconds. Rather than look suspicious and stop in the middle of what he was doing, Billy decided to spray with even more satisfaction and care than he was moments ago. The squad car's door opened. The scanner spewed out a stream of unintelligible and fuzzy jargon.

"Good morning, sir," the officer loudly greeted Billy. He wore the usual black uniform and was stout and blond with a pair of angular, reflective sunglasses like a center fielder.

"Oh," Billy warmly responded, rising and feigning surprise with the skillfulness of a soap opera actor. "Why, hello there. How are you today, officer?"

"I'm just fine, sir, thank you. My name is Officer Silver. I, uh, I happened to notice your van there and, um—"

"Right, yes, *the* van, of course. She's a beaut." Billy smiled at the officer and put the can of spray *paint* down and capped it. He smoothed down his hair and noticed that his right pointer finger was red.

"Yes, I happened to see the, um, the paint on the van and—"

"Yeah, *I know*," Billy said understandingly, "some no-goodniks painted some *reeeeal* ugly stuff on there, officer, sir. What's this country coming to?" He expressively raised his palms and then smacked them against his jeans. "You must see some things yourself, obviously. But, yeah, so, I guess you may well have already, uh, deduced this, but, you see, I had to pull over and, and, and cover it up quick before... well, before people thought *I* was the one that was advocating, um, *hate*."

"Oh? Well, wait. What's all that now?" He'd clearly only started listening part-way through.

"We-ell..." Billy began, "I woke up this morning, Officer, sir, and... there were... a bunch of. Well. No other way to put it: a bunch of *swastikas* on the van."

"Oh, wow. Goodness." Officer Silver seemed genuinely stunned. He swiftly turned his head to the left as his shoulder radio muffled something of note. "10-85," he finally said, "I got a vandalized van over here at the, uh, the Home Depot over on Mont-gomery…"

Billy cringed and shook his head. "No," he whispered, as if a friend was trying to pick up the check for lunch, "please, it's nothing, *really*."

"Be advised 10-49 at 2100 block of Buxton and Powell. Over," the radio replied.

"10-4," the officer said into his shoulder. "Sorry about that sir. Do you know where this took place?"

"I believe it was in Junction City, Officer, sir."

Officer Silver nodded, perhaps looking at Billy. One couldn't say for certain behind those shades.

"That's truly unfortunate, it really is. I just—"

"Thank you, officer. For your support," Billy butted in.

"Right," he said. "I just wanted to get a picture of this, actually, because a friend of mine, a cop buddy, actually, he's *way* into Van Halen and he'd get a real kick out of this, you know. Like, when I show him this, he's gonna *flip*." He smiled. His teeth were pearly tools of grain mastication. "This guy's, like, world's. Biggest. Fan sort of deal. Wears the tee-shirts, goes to the tours, the whole nine yards."

"Oh. Yeah. Sure." Billy felt ready to collapse with relief. "Go right on ahead."

"Thanks a lot," Officer Silver said with his smartphone out, sideways. He patiently waited for the camera feature to autofocus. "Yeah … you mind stepping out of the shot for a second?" He took three or four pictures of the van. "Cool, man. Thanks."

"Not a problem. Please. Comes with the terri-tory."

The squad car was still running and Officer Silver was back in his seat when he called over to Billy.

"Hey! So, do you want me to report the vandalism that those kids did? I can have Junction City notified right now."

"Oh … no thanks, it's fine. I mean, it's not fine, obviously, but, well, it's probably too late to catch 'em and I got to get to Colorado Springs here soon—I'm traveling, actually … so—"

He cut Billy short. "Alright, sir. Just thought I'd ask. You take care. Have a good 'un."

"Yeah. You too."

He stood still and waited for the squad car to turn back onto the road before he turned back towards the van. He strutted along the pavement.

"I thought that went pretty well," Billy said while inspecting his hair for paint in the driver's side mirror.

As someone who worked a fairly-sedentary nine-hour workday and ate public school cafeteria food, Billy was well-suited to cope with many of the rigors of the road. His was a body that could handle empty hours and calories. But it was still proving to be a taxing journey. Driving long distances brought with it a life not steadily-fueled by the usual cocktail of hippie speedballs (coffee and marijuana) and domestic chasers. There was gas station coffee every morning and plenty of Tanker!s of soda, but that woefully failed to compensate for the other missing elements. Alcohol, he mistakenly assumed, was what he'd be drinking after a long day on the road (this fantasy was set at a cowpoke roadhouse joint where the band played behind chicken wire and bottles were broken over ungovernable heads). And as for pot, Billy wrongly assumed he could easily manage a week without it.

By this point, too, his body began having some (not ha-ha) funny reactions to the absence of its usual chemical humors. Things came crashing to a halt a few miles outside of Colorado Springs. There was no way he could face up to his bête noire McAlister with a stomach this disruptive. There was no way he could drive another five minutes under present conditions. The noises and movement were completely beyond his control. Something tobogganed through his guts and neared the finish. There were intense, palpable fears while he tried to lock the van and rush inside of the travel center. Billy moved as quickly as he could without running.

After pushing his way through the swinging bathroom door, two shirtless men appeared, browned from a life full of direct sun and dust. They were hunched over a single sink, each washing their underarms. Billy hardly paused for them or for the cautionary yellow nylon rope-and-pylon barricade cordoning off the closest series of freshly-cleaned stalls.

Sitting alone enclosed by a tile backsplash and three putty-colored metal dividers, Billy let out a relieved sigh. He shuddered. His skin prickled with goose bumps. Slowly his higher-order cognitive skills returned. He could now notice that the men at the sinks were lustily singing along to an instrumental version of "Hotel California" that was pumped throughout the travel center. He had no need to continue sitting where he was, but the scene by the soap dispensers and hand-dryers was maybe more than he could handle right then. The song was long. So he waited.

"They stab it with their steely knives—" one sang.

And the other jumped in, "But they just can't. Kill the beast!"

After he'd read all the poetry and prose adorning the stall walls, Billy came out to wash his hands during a guitar solo (which they impeccably whistled). It took many abortive chops to signal the infrared faucet to spurt out water. The bathers, meanwhile, knew exactly what they were doing and were as happy as a pair of fat little birds in a tiny porcelain bath. The taller, less-sun-burnt one was primping his hair with a tortoise-shell rat-tail comb. He had his shirt on now. The squatter man was hard at work on the back of his doubtlessly filthy neck. He tugged two more paper towels out of the dispenser and set to scrubbing. There was a USMC bulldog tattooed on his upper arm that had gone blue and disfigured with age and exposure. It looked like a bruise unless you were as close as Billy happened to be.

"All right, guys," said a balding managerial type, partially inside the bathroom. "Finish it up. Folks are complainin.'"

They would not stop their song to grumble, though, and continued singing along while packing up their modest toiletries.

429 East Vanderbilt Drive was in a sprawling subdivision where all the streets (or *Drives*, rather) had collegiate names. These were The Campuses at Park Crest East. The Van Halen van prowled along the freshly-paved residential maze for a quarter of an hour (although, even for the disoriented, it couldn't be considered a maze proper—none of the streets were straight and the intersections were never perpendicular). The Campuses were billed as a "mountaintop promenade." Billy wrongly stalked around from one end to the other. He mistakenly followed an intuitive guess that Sewanee Drive would get him closer to where he needed to be. He started to feel suspect himself, like the white eyes and shadowy trench coat on Neighborhood Watch signs. Eventually he chanced upon East Vanderbilt Drive and made a soft right.

The van popped and clicked as Billy parked along the sloping sidewalk's edge and killed the ignition. It didn't like the altitude. He decided to wait for the noises to stop before getting out but they didn't. He took his time gathering the toll-related mail from the glove box where he'd stashed it. The van's innards continued popping and clicking. He looked to make sure that the check was still in his wallet. He took out his phone and synchronized the dashboard clock. The van popped and clicked. "Fuck it," he said, and took a very deep breath, the kind a doctor asks of a patient with a cold stethoscope on his back. Billy got out of the van.

The house was an over-sized craftsman with fake stone siding all along its base. There was a heavy brass knocker and a doorbell at 429 East Vanderbilt. Billy froze at the door. First he touched the button daintily as though the bell would ring quietly. There was no audible sound from inside, so he pressed it harder and waited. Since doorbells are in no way fail-safe, he finally gave three clear, declarative knuckle-raps on the door to announce *I. AM. HERE.*

When the knob began to stir he was facing the van, surveying The Campuses. Billy turned around and grinned for the peephole.

A sliver of a wrinkled face appeared. A string of gold-plated chain link sagged at her forehead. A yellow eye narrowed and the door slowly shut again. Billy stood mute and immobile. Just when he was about to go back to the van he heard the lock being fumbled with. The door opened up gradually but not much further than before. An old woman stood with hunched shoulders covered in a lightweight fuchsia track jacket. It matched her lipstick. Her hair was crispy, brittle, and off-blue like week-old cotton candy.

"Hi…" Billy began. "I'm looking for Mr. McAlister."

"WHO?" she cocked her head to the side and cupped her ear.

"Mr. McAlister," he repeated.

She brought her other hand over and made a full-on funnel around her right ear.

"MISTER MAC-AL-IS-TER," Billy said with fortissimo.

"No, no," she said, bringing her hands back down to their natural T. Rex position. "That person doesn't live here, I assure you. It's just me and my dog, Pootsie."

"Hmm…" Billy hummed before going into a physical description of the man he was looking for.

"Ohhh. Well then, yes. He *used* to live here. Before I arrived. The young man that was in the Army, yes. My husband was in the Army, too, you know."

"Great. I didn't realize he was in the Army."

"Yes, Lester. He served in Korea. He was a cook."

Billy's eyes roamed the dark living room behind the crone.

"Your husband, you mean."

"Lester died in … 2003."

"I'm sorry to hear that."

"He died in a, um, a, um … what're those hot little rooms called with the steam and rocks where you—"

"A sauna?"

"Yes. He passed in a *sauna* at the Radisson in Flagstaff."

"God, that's terrible."

"We were on a trip visiting my nieces."

A car passing the van gave two short honks. The old woman peered around Billy and watched the car move on.

"Wow, so your nieces…"

"They lived in Tempe at the time."

"Uh-huh."

"It was a nice little vacation … until Lester died. We ate Mexican food beforehand. I think all those spices contributed to it. Over-worked his heart." She suddenly sneezed three times, little old lady sneezes. She took out the square of worn-to-transparency paper towel from her back pocket that every old woman keeps on hand and blew her nose into it with an unexpected zest. She folded the paper back up and returned it to its proper spot. "But, then again, he *was* a smoker. And he used to drink quite heavily, too, before the doctor made him quit. That was in 1994 after his heart operation."

"Ah."

They paused and Billy shifted his weight from one leg to the other. The old woman needed a reminder of why he was standing at the door.

"One moment," she creaked, turning back into the shady house. "I believe I have it written somewhere here …" she trailed off.

Billy didn't want to enter the house. He could faintly hear sounds inside. She was still talking to him. His head crossed the threshold as far as it could with feet planted on the other side. Finally she was shuffling back.

"… we had a very nice time. He said he'd come back and get that cobbler recipe from me someday, but I haven't seen him since. He must have gotten caught up with some of those Army monkeyshines." She looked at Billy proudly and smiled revealing a gold canine tooth. "You know, Lester raced Elvis in a tank once." There was a piece of paper in her shaky skeletal claw.

"Amazing," Billy said. "Racing with the King, that's—"

"Let's see, they live at...21...12...Rush Street...Apartment..." she was having trouble making out the script. "'B,' I believe it says here."

"Thank you so much. I appreciate this so much, ma'am."

"Of course. You tell them that Pootsie and I say 'hi' and, goodness, that's right. Wait here." She vanished again into her shady and unstirred lair and came back with a phone-book-sized pile of mail (mostly fliers and circulars). "This is some more-uh the mail I've been getting."

"Yes, thank you so much," Billy said, receiving the colorful bundle of glossy, thin paper. "That's very considerate of you."

"Pootsie is my dog. She's a Scottie. She's probably hiding under the daveno."

Billy thanked her and said he knew right where Rush Street was.

Why would a hotel in Arizona have a sauna? he wondered.

The Rush Street Arms were on the other side of Colorado Springs. Billy was on the receiving end of some spot-on directions from a helpful clerk at the AM-PM and got there effortlessly. Sometimes you just have to know who to ask.

There were eight large, cadet blue units that were divided into two uniform halves of four. Each side had its own gated pool and every building had a five-foot-tall letter (A-H) hanging on one of its outer walls. 'B' was easy enough to find but the building itself was arrayed in an 8x3 layout of two-bedroom residences. That left Billy with twenty-four doors on which to knock.

After zig-zagging through the complex he saw a sign pointing him to the building manager's office. It was in the rear of a large A-frame where 'D' Unit did their laundry. There was a soda machine next to the manager's office with a defunct citrus drink prominently featured on the front display.

The on-duty manager was a surly, older Australian named Roger.

"We 'on't just *tell* random people off the streets where our residents live."

"I understand and respect that. I just have some mail from Mr. McAlister's former residence that I wanted to forward along."

"Well, I 'on't *see* any mail. That right *there* tells me that *youah* suspicious."

Billy went back to the van and sorted through the coupons. Most of what that old woman had given him was addressed simply to 'Resident.' He found a few credit card offers for Rachel McAlister.

Roger carefully audited everything Billy brought back. A walkie-talkie on a file cabinet behind him bleeped.

"Hey, uh, Roger-Dodger...looks like another kid took a crap over in C pool. Over."

"Bloody 'ell," he breathed discouragingly. "Be right there, over," he replied. "This never 'appens when *Jake* is on duty..."

"So..." Billy made his presence weakly known once more.

"Oh, right. You. 7B."

Roger stood up and grabbed an orange five-gallon bucket from behind the desk.

The McAlisters were the second to last unit on the ground level. They had a concrete landing with a picturesque, spigotted jug of sun tea brewing. There was a small charcoal grill and a half-full bag of briquets slouched beside it. There was a welcome mat. Billy took all this as a sign that The Rush Arms were all right and that neighbors here looked out for one another.

None of this fit in with the guy that had hosed him under the El. Billy had always imagined a decrepit mountain shack where a pull-up bar and a static-y thirteen-inch television set were the man's only companions. He certainly never envisioned a *Mrs.* McAlister. It must've just been a very successful ruse, a personae he used to get the price he was after.

Well played, Dish, Billy thought sportingly, *well played*.

He knocked on the door, no longer quite so nervous. It opened almost right away and revealed a young, curvy woman two inches taller than what's generally considered short. She had lank black hair down to her shoulders (clearly not naturally so raven-colored) and an alluringly beaky nose. Her face was naturally pretty and highlighted by a small stud on her upper left lip and some subtle, discerning make-up around the eyes.

"Hello," she said.

"Hi."

He had pumped himself up to deal with Mr. McAlister. This was the best unexpected turn things had taken in recent memory. He shook himself into focus.

"Is, um ... *Dish* around?"

He'd never actually said that name aloud.

"*Dish?*" She scrunched her face in confusion. Her Monroe piercing almost touched her nostril.

He couldn't say it again.

"Mr. McAlister. Is he..."

"Oh, *Dick*. No, Dick's not here. He shipped off two weeks ago. He's in Afghanistan."

"Ah ... dang. Well, that's right: the person living at your old house mentioned he was in the Army."

She shifted her shoulder onto the jamb and leaned as a cool kid naturally would. She was shoeless and had a tattoo of a fox leaping on the top of her left foot.

"Are you a friend of Dickie's?"

"No. I mean. Not personally. My name's Billy. I sold him a truck in, um. Philadelphia."

"Oh, *right*. That thing fucking *sucked*. I mean, sorry," she did a quick Japanese schoolgirl giggle-mouth-cover combination. "No offense. I'm his wife, by the way. My name's Rachel. I think he mentioned you."

She put her hand out for Billy. She was definitely moisturizing. It was not easy to reconcile how young and kept-up she was with what Billy thought of when he heard the word "wife."

He limply held her hand and started to apologize. "Jeez, I'm sorry to hear that. I drove that thing around pretty far and it never—"

"Whatever." She took her hand back and began playing with her hair, idly wrapping it around her silky index finger. "Dickie likes spending money on things that don't work. Not your fault." She bit her lower lip briefly. "He can't help it." She stood back up straight. "So ...?" She raised her eyebrows and kept her lips in an 'O' even after the vowel ended. "I'll tell him you stopped by?"

"Right, I, um, was in the area and I have some mail for you guys—"

"From Philadelphia?"

"Yeah, well, some of it, you see..." He began producing envelopes out from nowhere, springing mail out towards Rachel. "I got some bills for tolls that I guess, um, *Dickie*, passed through and didn't pay for. Before he transferred the title and all that."

She made no motion towards the mail and gave him another full second to make sure he was finished before responding.

"Seriously?" she asked. "You drove for, like, two days to *come get toll money*?" Rachel's lips parted and slowly bent into a red smile. "Is this, like, an Army prank or something?"

"I'm not in the Army, no."

Her mouth closed and leveled out.

"You actually drove here for twenty bucks?"

"Well, *actually* it was forty bucks..." he laughed nervously. "I mean, I have some other business to tend to not far from here and I just thought..."

"You just thought you'd swing by and ask for money."

"Exactly." Billy produced the bills from his back pocket again. "I mean, I covered these for him. Like a favor, I suppose. I paid the, uh, forty—"

"Let me get this straight: you drove all the way to Colorado to get $40?" She took the papers from Billy but didn't look at them.

It could have gone on longer, Billy could have told her how badly her husband had weirded him out, how he called the president a jellybean, how he sold the truck for half the asking price just to get away, but none of that would get him his money. There was no way.

"Alright, I see your point. Thanks for your time. Tell your husband I say 'hi' and 'thanks for your service.'"

"Uh-huh. Don't mention it," Rachel said before rolling her eyes. Billy didn't see her do it, but he knew she did it right when he turned away.

The encounter would have bummed him out more but on the way to the van he heard the distinct sound of a garage band (or, more accurately, the sound of a carport band as there were no garages at The Rush Street Arms). A distorted guitar crunched and yowled out of a shoebox-sized amplifier and a loose-tempoed drum kit erratically clanged from crash to hi-hat and back again. He followed the music and soon saw Roger, the Aussie manager *pro tem*, trying to shout over two kids. They stopped abruptly and let him finish making his point at a suddenly comical volume.

"Not so loud you can't!" he screamed. Roger

cleared his throat. He began again with a normal voice. "You can't play music—"

"One … two … one … two, screw you!" the guitarist shouted before going into a less-rehearsed number.

Billy ran back to the van and grabbed the rain stick but when he returned, everybody was gone, even the equipment. He'd wanted to jam with the kids some.

Luckily for Billy, Colorado Springs is a military town, so plenty of places were glad to cash a check for a small fee. Surprisingly, the woman behind the bulletproof glass asked if he got the "okay" to cash the check.

"I just did," he told her.

It was 6 o'clock and Billy was ready to head south to New Mexico and finally start doing what he'd come out all this way out West for: delivering Chinese antiques. But there was a file of cars backed up at least a mile from a highly-desired on-ramp. A renegade dirt bike cut to the front of the line.

"The hell with this," Billy said, pulling the van out of the queue.

Down the street was a small, shabby place called Kyle's Kantina where Billy ate the standard-bearer burrito while waiting the traffic out. The Kyle was served on a Styrofoam rectangle (the kind grocery store meat is shrink-wrapped on). The burrito consisted of two tortillas, ground beef, jack cheese, and a fistful of crinkle-cut french fries. The laminated menu on the table said that it was developed to help Kyle Jr. make weight for the wrestling team.

Billy read the menu after he'd ordered. He grumbled as he tottered towards the van. Hindsight being 20/20, he knew he should've ordered Los Supernachos.

There was no telling what was beyond the towering interstate lights, but the dark shapes in the distance were a nice conclusion to a day spent passing through miles of Kansas and Eastern Colorado. The five bonus twenties cashed out inside his wallet were like hard-earned bounty money (even if he hadn't taken down or brought the Outlaw Dish McAlister to justice). Billy felt cavalier. He felt like a rich man once again. At around ten at night he arrived at the outskirts of Santa Fe.

"Why the heck not," he said, turning into the parking lot at the Inn of the Desert Cow Skull.

It did not look particularly modern nor did it advertise anything besides vacancy. No mention made of cable television nor promises of cleanliness and amenities. The Inn of the Desert Cow Skull was a motor-court throw-back, a single story horseshoe with a cement parking stop ten feet in front of every door. The paint was chipping and the roof probably had another season or two before something would have to be done.

The clerk was a round woman with a reddish perm and a lime green blouse. A room was $120 per night, she said.

"Even at 10:30?"

"It doesn't work that way, hon."

The van pulled out of the gravel lot conscientiously, not kicking up a lot of hot-headed gravel and dirt, and went along the well-patched road towards the chain motels. Billy picked the least crowded-looking one and parked far from the entrance. Tourists were still trickling in and boisterously making their way from rental cars to the lobby.

"You really think Jesus built them stairs?" a booming Texas-sized voice asked with a hint of dubiousness.

"You know what, Beau … I wouldn't put it past him," his companion sagaciously countered.

The desert wasn't as hot as people played it up to be, but the nights weren't as cool as advertised, either. The van's windows were rolled up high enough to keep strange hands out. Not much air breezed through. The asphalt retained the day's heat and released it at night, stickier and sharper-smelling. The lot stayed silent long enough to make him restless. Then some noise would arrive and give Billy something to pin his fitfulness on. He laid on his back and sent text messages to friends, inside jokes and quotes from movies and television. He shot off silly song lyrics to people he hadn't spoken to in months. He sent Lucy a rather terse and candid message. It was lonesome in the Van Halen van.

"Mmmm … baby, not now," came a woman's voice outside of a freshly-parked car nearby.

The other door slammed shut.

"Hunh-unh: I can't wait," her man said before the sound of long, loose, sloppy kisses. "You know … I thought about ballin' you 'bout near a thousand times today." This last line was spoken like verse recited and there was a deferential pause as the car alarm was activated with a two short bleeps.

"Well, let's go then," as their soles smacked against the smoothly-paved lot.

By midnight his insomnia became destined and unavoidable. With his guard down, exhausted and delirious from the excitement and travail that the journey had so far presented him with, his brain turned into a bored operator patching calls between random numbers. Disparate and surprised faces stayed on the line. Old lovers and acquaintances had interesting and unexpected conversations about faded and distant things. Billy listened in like a detective up on the wire.

Then his actual phone buzzed and stopped Billy cold. He seized up, believing it might be Lucy. He took a deep, prayerful breath and he checked the contents of the little yellow envelope on his two-inch-square screen. But it was only Kurt, letting him know that he was laughing out loud in response to his friend's *Simpsons* quote. Billy smiled.

And after trying not to all day, Billy let himself think about Angela … She might have been the most beautiful woman he'd ever been physically touched by or had spoken to. She might have painted swastikas on his van. She might have thought he was charming or an uptight asshole or both. She might be in A.D.S.'s kung fu grip that very moment. They might have gotten along—Billy and Angela. He counted the different adventures he could've chosen for himself like sheep.

11

By 8 a.m. the van was hot enough to constitute animal cruelty were there a not-so-beloved pet left waiting inside. The morning sun was low and the parking lot offered no shade. It was a lot, after all. Over five or so hours of trying to sleep, Billy sweated profusely and never once managed to get comfortable. He woke up that morning feeling like he'd strenuously exercised. He was more dehydrated, dirty, and sore than even he was used to. Somehow his hair hurt. He sat up and slid the door open. Sunlight exposed the van as the dank tomb that it was.

"How ya doin'?" Billy said to a clean family of five piling into their minivan in an orderly fashion. He sat on the floor, door gaping open and his legs sticking out. He put on yesterday's socks.

Down from the parking lot was a restaurant called The Larder. Wavy illusions came off the road and made it shimmy and waver in the distance. There was a line of people waiting along the wall in a narrow strip of shade beneath the slight eave. Groups waiting to be seated went all the way around the corner, although goggle-eyed patrons leaving the cafe mingled and took time to crow over how satisfied they were with their breakfasts. They clogged the scene with their reassurances and aggrandized gut-patting.

Billy was able to squeeze right in at the bar,

cheek-by-jowl with what must've been the real clientele, the local money. Nobody spoke to him, offered him a "Good morning" or a "Hot one out there today." He had the look and stink of the homeless about him. Billy had not shaved since a few days before he left and his stubble was cropping up in its natural unflattering pattern: an isolated upturned crescent of a goatee that was only elsewhere sported by country musicians and baseball players (over-the-hill designated hitters and your fatter relief pitchers). And he should've at least put on some fresher clothes before wading out into public life. Over the many wafting aromas he could smell his own stale socks. There was no good reason to give those another go today. Even his hearty, workaday denim was turning a bit marshy.

Not looking too intently at the menu and increasingly self-conscious, he gulped down a tall plastic cup of water and then another. But the old men bookending Billy at the bar figured that that was simply the style these days: being dirty. And busyness mercifully surrounded him. Nobody stopped to notice what a mess he was. Billy listened to the kitchen clatter, the frenzied Spanish coming from the back and the regular dings of the order-up bell. All around him parties made elaborate substitutions, asked for high-chairs, and left tips small enough to disillusion the waitress' jaundiced view of humankind that much more. The paterfamilias of a nearby table planned the day's sightseeing agenda using salt shakers and silverware like a 19th century military strategist clinically outlining an upcoming battle. A weary mom asked for some crayons.

Billy's waitress came and seemed ready for an order. She was older but good-looking. She had a take-no-B.S. sort of toughness with a matronly touch—a steel fist in a velvet glove. Billy smiled and opted for the apposite New Mexico Omelette.

"Red, green, or Christmas?" she asked automatically.

"…Christmas," he replied, no clear idea of what that meant.

"White, wheat, sourdough, English muffin, multigrain, biscuit, sopapilla, or gluten-free scone."

"Sourdough."

He'd stopped listening at "sourdough."

"And a coffee," Billy added before she left.

While waiting for his breakfast, Billy found a nearby paper (the hipper, freer, weekly kind) and tried to get a sense of what living in Santa Fe was like. It was not easy to properly fold out and enjoy while seated at the bar, though. He opened it carefully and began reading. Seconds later a man to his right tapped him on the shoulder and pointed to where the corner of the paper was dipped into some of his pancake syrup. Billy wisely folded it in half and studied it on the counter. All of the usual stuff was there: city council were up to their old tricks again … a local band was exciting and playing a show that week … a new Cambodian restaurant recently opened and promised to shake things up with three and a half forks to their name.

His food arrived on a hot oval platter. He was

given a stern warning not to actually touch the platter or the food until it cooled some. He assented and spent this interlude scanning through the paper more and forming an ad hoc chart of the city based on ads with inset maps designed to direct visitors to certain businesses. The address he needed to deliver to looked to be near the center of town, ("*right near the historic Plaza!*"), between the Bodhi Dog Holistic Pet Health Center/Animal Reiki Clinic and Los Tres Cowgirls Contemporary Sculpture Gallery.

He then ate fast, his great purpose suddenly remembered. The waitress seemed quite admiring of his big appetite and brought him the check with a friendly smile. He reminded himself that servers make their living being friendly; but who doesn't need to make a living? he countered. So he gave her an excessive tip, all the same.

Back outside the sun was intense enough to make seventy-one degrees at 9:15 in the morning unbearable. A towering digital bank sign reminded him of these two facts over and over again while he walked back to the hotel parking lot. Billy squinted against the glare and felt his phone vibrate.

It was Kurt. He had good news. It looked like the insurance check arrived.

"The envelope looks pretty official and has your name on."

"Great!"

There on the sidewalk Billy took the phone away from his ear for a moment to do a curious Little-Teapot jig. He allowed the usually-stiff spout arm to whip around like an unmanned fire hose.

"Whew," he said, the phone back against his sweating face. "That's awesome."

"You also got a postcard."

"From who?"

"Lucy, I think." Kurt coughed. He cleared his throat. "I mean, yeah: definitely Lucy. Says so at the bottom here. 'Lucy.'"

"What's it of?"

"It's a picture of a guy. Let's see … It says 'Marcel Proust.' He looks to be some sort of a serious man with a mustache."

"Oh boy …" He let out a sigh, distorted through the phone into an oceanic white noise. "What's she say?"

"You want me to read it?"

"Yes," Billy said resolutely. "All of it. Spare not a gruesome detail."

Kurt coughed and cleared his throat again and began reading. "'Dearest Billy,'" He stopped, giving his friend an opportunity to renege … He continued. "'I am writing you this puh … puh … *postcard*', yeah, duh, sorry. Her penmanship is weird."

"I know. She must've written this one left-handed. Still trying to teach herself to be ambidextrous. Don't sweat it. Keep going."

"Okay, so, writing you this postcard, right, 'to let you know that I am moving to … *Florida* with friends on a …'" Kurt drifted off, laughing to himself. "Sorry, dude. Okay. Are you ready for this?"

"Yes."

"'Moving to Florida with friends to *pick and collect seashells*,' I shit you not, that is what is says here: pick and collect seashells. Okay. Then it goes: 'My friend *Devin*?'—does that sound right, Devin?"

"Yes."

He'd heard of Devin, the guy back in New York who was always trying to get with Lucy—even though she saw themselves as friends.

"Can't a boy and a girl just have *non-sexual* escapades together?" she used to ask. The answer was evidently "no," because Devin was part of why she had such an extended visit in the Pacific Northwest, to get some space. But now she seemed willing to give this peculiar relationship another kooky go.

"Wow. Okay. Collecting seashells with Devin. Sounds like something on public access television. Go on."

"Ha. Cool. Right. So, then, 'We are probably leaving soon. It might be fun to visit or hang out sometime before I go. I still miss you.' Then she did a little heart with a comma and signed her name."

"A heart with a comma?"

It wasn't so long ago that Billy used to stay up, fatigued from vigorous intercourse, and listen to Lucy explain, among many things, the inter-connectivity of the universe. He acknowledged that she might have been on to something after he too wrote 'I still miss you' from the back of the van last night.

"Alright, well, that's an interesting development. Thanks, Kurt."

"Yeah, man, no problem. A fucking seashell farm though? You were right: she's a strange bird."

"A little bit—everybody kinda is, though. But, anyways, listen: I'mma get back to you about the check and stuff, go to the bank and see if there's a way I can, uh, deposit it. Remotely or something. Or find out if you can wire it to me. Western Union, I think that's still a thing—I'll look into it. I could sort of use that money soon, more'n likely."

"Yeah...we could all definitely could sort of use that type of money. Fiddy jee-eez, duuuude!" Kurt said in a bombastic DJ voice.

"Yup. So I'll get in touch with you again soon."

"Perfect. How's wherever you are?"

"It's good. I just ate a Christmas omelette in New Mexico."

"Yum."

"Some anarchists spray-painted swastikas all over the van. I fell in love with one of them for a day or two."

"Was this before or after they painted the swastikas?"

"Before mostly. I'm getting over it. I left them somewhere near Kansas. I have to run, man. I'll talk to you soon."

"Okay, take care. Drive safe."

For the entire distance from The Larder to the van all he could think of was Lucy. She was further out-of-reach than the money and now it was her that he really wanted. Billy idly imagined Lucy collecting shells, a victim of Devin's tender attrition. In Florida, where nothing good seemed to happen. He probably had a hammock picked out for the two of them to sway together in, hung up between two calm and crooked palms.

"Damn it all," he concluded as he plopped back

into his now custom-molded driver's seat. Billy sounded awfully defeated for a man that came into a lot of money not long ago.

The streets of Santa Fe were unintuitive. Nobody laid down a grid in these parts. And the roads themselves were as patchy as the fourth generation of hand-me-down jeans. The van had to swerve and avoid basin-like potholes. It almost overheated while waiting for a commuter train to pass through a busy intersection. Vehicles backed up for blocks and it took three full changes of the light for Billy to get to the other side.

Driving into town wasn't all bad, though. All along the road, in practically every parking lot, were enormous bingo cages hooked up to propane tanks. Men in leather gardening gloves slowly spun roasted green peppers around and around. The smell it gave off was mesmerizing.

Then came the pedestrians. They were the same people he'd just seen at the Larder: variations on an older woman with a large foam visor and UV-blocking sunglasses and her husband in his socks-and-sandals splendor; the families with plenty of disinterested and fussy children. All moved with equal parts impunity and cluelessness. The closer he got to the address, the more likely it seemed that Billy might run into one of these skinny-legged, sun-dazed pedestrians.

Weary of having to try and park any closer (where spaces were limited and spectators were sure to gather and check out the hulking and garish van),

Billy found a spot blocks away. Hopefully there'd be a driveway at the house.

A worker at The Bronze Bear Tea House and Custom Frame Shop directed him towards his destination. The address was near the can't-miss Plaza. Along the way two men were loafing in the grass on a shady embankment.

"*Odelay*, holmes, check out the movie," one with a dirty Tecate hat said as Billy passed by.

He stopped and looked up. Just a blue sky full of cottony clouds.

"Pretty good one today, no?" he said before he and his friend burst with spirited laughter and happy, grassy lolling.

Everything was stucco-adobe and came in a handful of dusty shades. Unlike where he'd woken up, this part of Santa Fe had trees and old churches tall enough to cast shadows. Puffy lavender bushes buzzed with fat, harmless bees. He saw the Territorial library building that looked like it could make a fine last-stand in a western. At a cafe across the street he was tempted by cool, colorful gelato but settled for some iced tea. A scraggly man asked Billy for some money to buy water. Genuinely wishing to help, he tried to give the beggar his cup of ice.

"Aw, no, man, ya see…the straw is dirty," he protested.

"Throw it away then."

"I can't eat ice. It's too cold on my teeth. They're sensitive."

"Let it melt. I don't know. Or see if you can get a refill."

"Where'd you go?"

"Uhh…" Billy looked around, "Sacred Essence, across from the library."

"Oh no," he said, "they 86'd me a *long* time ago."

Billy left it at that and walked to the Plaza. It was an old-world town square with a nice memorial obelisk in its center. Every bench was full of tourists giving their barking dogs a break. In some cases real dogs were resting with their masters, lapping up bottled water poured into smart little travel dishes. It was a quarter past ten. The aroma of funnel cake clashed with sizzling fajita meat. There was a bandshell, empty save two tow-headed boys with wrists together and palms pressed to their mouths. They took turns making resounding and thunderous flatulent noises before squawking with reverberations of delight. Their mom was torn between stopping them and keeping her space in line to buy them lemonade.

"Quit it," she yelled, trying unsuccessfully to get their attention.

Surrounding the Plaza were three connected strips of shops and restaurants gussied up in theme-park Wild-West pastiche. There were unfinished wood logs and wagon wheels about. Signs for businesses were lettered with branding irons. One place sold only men's dusters, another exclusively featured dried red peppers decoratively strung together.

The final side of the square was a line of American Indians hunched and crouched down with blankets covered with all sorts of jewelry before them. Silver and turquoise things spread out on display along an entire city block. Visitors milled around and inspected the goods from three-to-four feet away. There was little dialogue other than bargaining. Buyers and sellers each pretended to speak a trading-post pidgin English. Billy walked along this row for a few yards, thinking about a gift for Lucy, but a pang of guilt over the zooish feel of it all forced him back to the benches and grass.

Faced with a full wall of postcards to choose from at Kit Carson's Old Santa Fe Trail Outfitters, Billy judiciously selected one with a jackalope and described the scene at the Plaza on its reverse. He addressed the card to Lucy in Queens, hoping she hadn't left her mom's house yet.

Near the municipal blue mailbox an Andean man played pan pipes. He was windswept and leathery. He had a rumpled felt hat with a colorfully-patterned band and, below that, a thick braid of silvery hair. He played along to a lively karaoke track of "My Heart Will Go On," the love theme from *Titanic*. His version had an odd time signature and enough festivity to make it a different listening experience, though. Billy was pleasantly surprised to find his toes tapping. The song wrapped up with a rather long flutey flourish and a succession of synthesizer tom fills. A smattering of people clapped and the Andean man offered an enthusiastic and toothy grin.

"Alright, alright; yes, yes; tank you, tank you; muchas gracias, muchas gracias; si, si, tank you so muh-sh," he rattled off before giving his shoebox a subtle, dissatisfied nudge with his boot.

The small crowd dispersed.

"I have *always* preferred the original," confided an older woman in a fringed buckskin vest and gaucho hat. Her sexless traveling companion had a gauzed-over right eye and nodded in respectful agreement.

A few passers-by tossed change into a brown shoebox in front of the pipe-player. There was a suggestive paper dollar languishing in there surrounded by so many pennies and nickels.

"How much do you make an hour?" Billy asked.

"Wha? I dunno. Eet depen.'"

"On a good day then."

"Twenny, I dunno. Depen.' Today, ear-for-uh-hour … fidteen, twenny. But sohmtime peeble put beeg money in." He lurched an eyebrow up at Billy. "Muy generoso, eh?"

"Yeah, there was a guy like you at my college. He used to make, like, a hundred bucks an hour during School Daze. That was this big festival thing they'd do on McCandles Square every spring. Lots of people got *pret-ty* into that flute music, if you know what I mean."

"Uh-huh," the flautist responded. He was busily looking through his leatherette book of CDs for his next tune.

"You know: college kids. Anyway. He did well. Pedro, his name was."

"I don' know heem."

"Naturally."

"I work atta hotel at night."

"Playing music?"

"No."

"Okay, well," Billy took his wallet out and saw that it was empty. "I'm gonna get some cash and I'll be around later then."

"O-gay, chure," the Andean replied before shooting his breath testily over his reeds. The unmistakable opening congas of Lionel Richie's "All Night Long" came booming out from his mobile PA system, encouraging a passing middle-aged couple to stop and perform a diminutive cha-cha before continuing on.

The numbers on the buildings were rising, getting closer to the address. It did not look like there were residencies in this part of Santa Fe. Many of the small, homey structures turned out to be obscure government offices with mirage-like parking spaces out front reserved for out-for-lunch state workers. Still smaller were some of the galleries he passed, which seemed to contain little more than two or three similarly sparse paintings.

Billy saw the tramp he gave the cup of ice to earlier, stumbling around with a well-creamed iced coffee. He gave him a thumbs up from across the street but the man busily shuffled along. He was on his way somewhere or just possibly moving around in order to avoid a loitering charge.

As he was nearing where he was supposed to be, Billy got nervous. There was no house. A stick-like white woman with a red turban speed-walked in his direction, asking her Bichon Frise if he felt better.

"Are we happy today, Pumpkin? Are we feeling

happy today, my lovely little friend?" she asked the dog with a rising, excited pitch.

Billy saw the sign next door for Los Tres Cowgirls and there in the middle was a barn-shaped building with a red Fender Stratocaster drilled to the front of the place like it was a mailbox. The sign near the guitar said Wise Lizard Art Collective in a comic sans font. Billy was troubled. He was lost. His wanderlust had gotten the best of him and he was already starting to get hungry again. He decided to walk back to the information booth at the plaza, careful to avoid the glare of the Andean.

The young man standing behind the Dutch door looked as unhappy as a bird placed in a cage outside. There were clearly other places he'd rather be then.

Billy was on the west end of the street when he needed to be on the east end.

"Is it far? Walkable?"

"Yeah, you could walk there."

The sun was unmerciful. It was a thirty-five minute walk to the address. There were large dark patches along the underarms and back of Billy's shirt. Wearing a beige button-up seemed like a good foil to the heat and light, but sweat made the fabric stick to him. His whole back was brown as a paper lunch-bag.

On the way, a newer white sedan with Oklahoma plates pulled over. An indeterminably older and recently Botox'd woman rolled down her passenger side window while her husband glowered behind the wheel.

"Pardon, señor," the woman called to Billy, "but donde esta la plaza?"

"Dammit, Brandy, cain't you see he's white?" her husband whispered.

"I know *that*, but people *do* speak Spanish out here."

Billy pointed back in the direction he'd walked from.

"You see," the woman gloated as the car pulled off, "he understood what I asked him."

When he finally made it near his destination, only a few doors away now, it became apparent that he was a sizable distance from the van and its cargo. So the courier was about to show up at the doorstep without the parcels, just sweating and in serious need of water.

Billy turned around and got a bottle of orange sports drink at a gas station. Waiting in line, he gulped the electrolyte-rich elixir and then used a card to pay for the empty bottle. He got $5 cash back in ones in case the piper was still on the Plaza. The Andean was gone, though (possibly covering a swing-shift at the inn). The van was waiting for him where he left it, unmolested. But what had been a shady spot a few hours ago was now under a siege of midday sunshine. You could make an order of Los Supernachos in there.

Since he never actually reached the house while trekking earlier, Billy was taken aback by how big it was when he brought the van to a halt in the driveway. He reconnoitered while letting the A/C run a few minutes longer. The place was a mud fortress—

dark adobe with a thick and turreted wall. You could envision conquistadors laying siege here. Of course, only a child or an abnormally-small person could go man the tower, perhaps tossing water balloons down on the mailman. All told, it was still an impressive and imposing place to call home.

Billy daubed and dried as much of his upper-body and face as he could with the napkins he'd stashed away in the cup holders before finally getting out of the van. He approached the heavy-doored entrance. There was an unusual piece of verdigrised bronze on the door that could have been a knocker or a piece of modern sculpture. He was about to rap the thing when the door pulled back.

The man in the doorway was not what he expected.

"Woah, hey. Uh … Can I help you?"

There was some kind of an accent and, like his face (long, rounded nose, full lips, hollow cheeks), it seemed to be a product of the eastern seaboard. His hair was thin, short, and dark and he wore a blue checkered oxford partially buttoned. His chest hair was visible, wispy, and going a little gray.

"Hey, I'm here to deliver the stuff, the, uh, Chinese stuff from Jacob in Philly."

The man's puzzlement turned into concern.

"I mean, sorry. That sounded sketchy." Billy rubbed his hands dry on the thighs of his pants and extended one out. "I'm delivering some Chinese rugs and I think some vases to, uh, Larry."

The man took Billy's hand. "Yeah, I'm Larry."

"Cool." They continued shaking hands. "I've got

the antiques from Jacob … Jeffries in Philadelphia."

He let go of Billy's hand and smacked his palm against forehead. "*Ah-hh*, right, right. Hey, welcome, come in, come in. Sorry, I forgot that that stuff was on its way." He went back inside to his house. "I get emails. But who reads emails these days? The answer, in short: no one. Good thing I didn't drive up to Taos this morning." He walked off out of sight. "I almost drove to Taos!" he yelled from inside. Larry's head reappeared from behind a corner. He had a phone receiver held to the side of his face. "I'm being rude, though. It's hot out there, come on in, please," he called to Billy, "I was just about to head out and meet with somebody I don't feel like meeting up with."

"Oh, well I can—"

"No, I'm calling him right now. This is perfect. I really don't want to—hey. Yeah, it's Larry. Listen, man, I'm sorry but I got this friend of mine here all the way from Philly. *Just* showed up at my doorstep. Yeah, I completely *spaced it.* Uh-huh. Uh-huh. See, the thing is, he's dropping off some stuff and I need to give him a hand unloading …"

Billy came five feet inside the house. Everything was well-selected and thoughtfully placed. There were many books and framed objects, some on shelves and walls, others piled up or leaning.

"Okay, sure." Larry scratched his neck. "Sounds good. See you at the Biennial or see you in hell … sure. *Haha.* Yup. Okay. Take care." He hung up the phone. It was the old, taupe kind that had a curly cord connecting two parts. "Asshole. Anyways, again, I'm Larry." He put a hand out and gave his guest a few strong pumps once more. Before Billy could respond he was being offered a beer. Larry disappeared again into the kitchen. "Wow. Honestly … I'd love a beer." Billy felt overwhelmed by the decor. "I like your phone, Larry."

There was the sound of glass clinking together as the refrigerator door swung open. "Thanks. I got it a couple years ago at a hospital that was closing down," he said into the refrigerator. Jars and cans were being moved around. "Hm." Larry came back with his keys in his hand. "Let's go get a beer, man. I'm all out."

"Oh, well, really then, no," Billy started. "I don't need a beer *that* bad, I just—"

"Nah, fuck it, c'mon. *You* want a beer, *I* want a beer." He went past Billy who stood motionless inside. "Come on, let's *go*," he said and locked the door behind them. He put on a pair of sunglasses at exactly the right moment and pressed down on the Ray Ban's bridge to leer at Billy's ride. "Alright, now, that's just … *yes.*" He marveled at the striped glory. "*That's* a fuckin' sweet van, man. I dig it."

"Thanks a lot."

"Fuckin', no way, man. Thank *you* a lot for riding that around America. Right on." Larry swung his keys around his pointer finger like a shootist spinning a fancy pistol. "Alright, let's roll."

Larry drove what looked to be a worn (but not quite beat-up) GMC Prospector. The truck was rodent-hued and sat on big, knobby, white-walled Goodyears.

"I got this truck from Gustave Baumann's daughter-in-law," he said as he pulled himself inside. "Name ring a bell?"

"No," Billy admitted.

"Yeah, that's fine." Larry slammed his door shut. "'It's only *Gustave Baumann*,'" he said to himself.

It was strange to watch him climb into the cab wearing his preppy shirt and subtly-pleated linen bottoms. Something seemed askew about his Spinnaker on the worn clutch. But the seats were astonishingly lush and well-upholstered in soft, coppery leather with elaborate cactus-colored filigree stitching.

Was the appearance of the truck a ruse to avoid attention, to keep his ride from being messed with by hoodlums and thieves? Billy didn't ask, but Larry explained that there was no reason *not* to have a good stereo—wherever you were. Also, didn't this kind of truck look better with a haggard exterior?

"Who takes a clean truck seriously?" Larry asked.

"What about the leather?"

"You know about Igor in Tijuana?"

"No."

"Well, Igor in Tijuana is serious. He's an upholstery *legend*. There can be no other word. A legend." He savored the syllables like a $60 steak. "He did this whole get-up for me. It's a name that means something…" Larry sheepishly smiled. "What's your name again, man?"

"I'm William. Or Billy. Whichever."

"Nah, William doesn't drive the van *I* saw. Good to meet you Billy," he said. He took his hand off the gear shift to shake Billy's one more time.

"So, Igor in Tijuana," Billy continued, "who put you in touch with the legend?"

But Larry wanted Billy to listen to a particular song. While the music went on, Larry explained that he'd personally installed a tasteful stereo system and a single disc Alpine CD player ("the same one Easy E had"). No tinny noise smothered in excessive, tailgate-rattling bass here: just an honest, clean, and (if need be) loud sound that'd please even a fastidious prog rock sound engineer. When the song ended, he asked what Philadelphia was like. He'd been there, years ago, and liked its gritty spirit. Billy conceded the grit and mostly shrugged.

"My friends there are the main draw, personally." He went into aimless detail about the Loft, its history (as far back as his understanding of the lore went) and its general layout. He told Larry about Jenna, the Academic Vision Institute, and the best sandwich in the city.

"Last thing they do is they plop a fried egg right on top of everything I just went over," he concluded.

Looking to his right, Billy saw some of the men still lazing by the steep banks of the empty river. They'd found a thin slice of hobo Acadia. While pondering the enormous spiral he'd so far traced around Santa Fe, the truck did a power-slide into the mostly empty gravel lot.

"Sorry. Sometimes I forget how much *torque* this thing's got." Larry took the keys out from the ignition and put them in the visor. "But, yeah, eggs are good."

The restaurant was called The Foundry and had a courtyard with an old, gnarled pinon tree reverentially in its center. All the bricks were the color of dark sand and identically-stamped with the word 'LINGOTTO.' The only patron outside was an old dapper man reading a crisp, non-regional newspaper. There was a small, neglected espresso cup on a saucer before him and a four-legged stroke-victim cane stood next to his seat.

Larry pulled up a chair outside and motioned for Billy to join him. They sat at the wrought-iron set and took the scene in for a quiet moment.

"Whaddaya call that?" Larry asked, jerking his head back towards the old man.

Billy discreetly leaned to the right and squinted his eyes. "Wha'?" he murmured, "The *Washington Post*?"

"No, I mean, is it a walker, is it a cane? Which one is it?"

"Oh," he looked back at Larry. "I'm fairly certain that's a cane."

"Even if it has four legs? If it can stand up on its own? If I say 'Imagine a cane and imagine it's upright but nobody's holding it,' in your mind, the thing falls over, right?" Larry didn't let Billy respond. "Anyways, this place is pretty decent, right?"

"Yeah, way nice. Nicer than I'm used to."

"I mean," Larry took off his shades and rubbed his eyes. He put the glasses down and motioned around with both palms upturned. "You could do worse. Sometimes 'you get what you pay for' is a good thing. Anyways, so, Billy. Billy from Philly. Ha! Betcha heard *that* before. Sorry. But it sounds like you got a pretty good life out there, man. And good friends: *that* is the straw that stirs the drink. How ya like Santa Fe so far?"

"It's, uh, different." He searched for something to back that up with but could not produce any evidence. "I got in last night, kind of late. Had breakfast and—"

"Where'd you go?"

"The Larder."

"Oh yeah," Larry's eyes glazed over. "Hands down, the best potatoes in town."

"Come to think of it, they *were* good. But, yeah, just walked around. Saw some stuff. Went by the square."

"Plaza. Only Texans call it a square. You're not from Texas, are you?"

"No."

"Then it's the Plaza." The waiter showed up with two glasses of ice water. "Let's get a pitcher of G&Ts. Hendricks. Plenty of lime on the side. Thanks, Max."

"Not a problem, Mister Larry, one moment," the waiter said, snappily disappearing back to the bar inside.

"Sorry. Not beer, I know, but it sounded too damn good. So. Santa Fe. Yeah. Not an easy destination to plop into. Unless you happen to like scenic beauty and clean air."

"Well, *I do*, but, yeah, you know." A fly buzzed near Billy's head and reminded him of his B.O. It also made him feel distinctly dunce-like. He shooed the bug. "I've just been driving through Kansas and the flat part of Colorado, so it's taking me a minute to get my sea legs here."

"Oh, I know the feeling. In fact, I know the drive."

The decanter of tall, cold drink arrived with a pair of classy, heavy, glass tumblers. It was perfectly-suited for everything going on right there and then.

"Wow. That's refreshing." Billy squeezed his lime wedge for all it was worth.

"Yeah. It's what one might call a 'perfect drink.' My friend Christopher Woggin—not Christopher *Walken*—this guy's name's *Woggin*—he's a Brit, so he *always* orders a G&T, Hendricks, and he always gets it. Takes a sip." Larry demonstrated. "And goes, '*Ahhh*, blimey! That's *just* what the doctor ordered!'"

Billy made an uncertain noise almost like a laugh.

"Fuck. Did I mention my friend Chris is a doctor?"

"No you did not."

"Shit. Well, he's a doctor. Doctor Woggin. Sorry. Guess I *bungled* that joke." He took a gulp. "So, Billy, how'd you get into Oriental Antiquities?"

Billy sat his drink down and noticed he'd taken care of one-third of it in one jolly splash.

"I prematurely quit my job and needed some fast cash. My friend works at the museum with Jacob and put me in touch with him about delivering this stuff. I guess you know him? Jacob?"

"Only through third-party emails that I admittedly scanned. But my impression is that he's, uh, he's a *twerp*."

"*He is*. Wow. You could just read into it, the way he types?"

"I guess so. He just gave me that vibe. People give me vibes. It helps a lot in my line of work. Although … I didn't peg him for the type to own such a swank van."

"Well, some Vietnamese guy actually *owns* the van. But, either way, it's been a real curveball."

"Dude from 'Nam, huh? Tell me more about it." Larry munched on an ice cube. "The van, I mean. What's drivin' that baby like?" he asked with a full mouth.

"What's there to tell? Driving around in a van painted like Eddie Van Halen's guitar. Through Ohio, Indiana, Mizzou. Classic Rock Country, all of it. You know how many withered, funky dugs I've seen so far?"

Larry paused thoughtfully. "Six or seven," he ventured.

"Well, just two so far, really. But the honking has been absolutely incredible. Like I'm traveling in a V of geese." He made a demonstrative peace sign. "And I picked up some hitch-hikers, too." An excellent moment to take a drink and let the listener bask in the mystery. "*That*," eyebrow raised, "got interesting, as you might imagine."

"Hitchhikers'll have that effect."

"Young kids. Punk kids. Fresh off some protests in Pittsburgh."

"Right. The D-11s."

They finished their drinks and poured their glasses half-full. Billy felt woozier and wittier than ever. He chewed his remaining rind. Sour, boozy…a tangy buzz. The fly landed on his hair and Billy could care less. He took a sip and let the carbonation prance and flit across down his throat like ballroom dancers in floaty, thin-soled slippers.

A soft breeze blew in and circulated. The old distinguished man's napkin blew off the table.

"Oh my," he said, decorously pinching it up with his pinkie raised.

"You know, I got to admit, Larry: you're not who I thought I'd be handing this crap over to," Billy said with an honesty that signaled that he was already quite drunk.

"Yeah, I'm kind of a young gun in the game." He was focused on completely squeezing the juice from a lime wedge into his fizzing glass. "But let's be real here: I'm thirty-eight. That's not young. I've been doing this for well over ten, fifteen years now."

"And what is 'this' that you speak of?" Billy slurred.

"There's no real name for it. Flipping shit. I dunno. Buying low, selling high. Rednecks'll do it with cars, lawyers do it with houses. Buy it for a dime and sell it for a quarter."

Billy leaned forward. He was piqued. "I mean, that's cool and all, but…how do you *live* doing that? If I'm not being intruding." He meant to say "intrusive."

"Nah, man, nobody's intruding. Basically, I started off with books. Back in college, when I was getting grants and loans and everything else to keep me from real work, I'd go to thrift stores. I would buy these practically new paperbacks for five or ten cents and sell them to bookstores in town for paper *money*. Bookstores always need clean copies of *The Great Gatsby*, you know. So you see it, you pick it up, you make three or four bucks. And sometimes I'd find a nice, fat photography book or something that'd be, like, a buck but I knew it was worth maybe $60, used even. Same goes for textbooks (if the edition was current). So I could sell something like that and expect maybe thirty dollars—if the copy was clean, that is."

"I hate when people write in books. Notes cluttering up the margins, underlining pointless things. And highlighters... don't get me started. But, anyways, you were a book dealer?" Billy asked.

"No. Those guys are for real. I was more of what you'd call an *enthusiast*," he said with zip on the last syllable. "That is, until dumb luck sort of colluded with this hobby of mine. To make a long, mostly uninteresting story short: I'm working a summer job at this little bookstore along Highway 9, the Basket of Books, it was called, and this little old lady comes in with some of her little old lady shit and then there's this folio of William Blake stuff. You know Blake?"

"Sure. 'Tiger! Tiger! Burning bright, in the—'"

Larry interrupted Billy, not wanting to listen to a garbled recitation. "Yeah, that one. So, I notice this Blake stuff and I try and keep my cool. She's about as old as the book, man. 'It was father's,'" Larry said in a spot-on geriatric impersonation. "I ask her if she wants cash or credit, and she says 'Cash.' I tell her to browse around and that I'll let her know when I'm done. So she's busy looking at some bird-watching guides or something, and I'm, like, delicately inspecting this fucking *treasure*. I should've been wearing some white gloves because, man, it sure does *seem* like it's authentic." He grabbed his gin and tonic but just held on to the cold glass. "I'm working by myself in the store, the owner's not there. 'He doesn't *need* more money,' I told myself. Certainly not the way I thought I did at that time. Anyways, I offered the lady $100 cash for all the books, which she took, gladly, and I never saw her again."

"And you got the Blake?"

"Yes."

"For yourself?"

"Yes."

"And it was real?"

"This seems pretty real, doesn't it?" he said coolly while gesturing at the opulence surrounding them.

"I think so, yes."

"It is. It truly is. I mean, you hear about this crap all the time, right? Granny goes to a garage sale, buys a mirror and, boom: a copy of The Constitution is tucked in the frame. Mom gets a second-hand pawn-shop Stradivarius for her fourth-grader and the music teacher shits a brick Monday morning. But *it fucking happens*. Stuff's out there. It just helps if you know what you're looking at when it happens." Larry chuckled and finished off his drink.

"Wow. Did the boss find out?"

"Nah, I just told him I needed to focus on school. Which was a half-truth: I needed to; I wasn't *going* to; but I probably *should*'ve. I mean, I should've. Wouldn't've hurt," he said as he filled his glass up halfway.

"So…whadyoudowithit?" Billy needed some more water. "Wha' happen'd to the Blake?"

"Sold it to an Ivy-League museum for an Ivy-League-sized check. A ridiculous return on my investment."

"And you're still going of off that, or what?"

"Well…" he said in a rising, uncertain pitch, "yes and no. That was pretty much my seed money, so to speak. I tried hard to find that old lady and give her, you know, half, but…no luck. Maybe she died, I don't know. Either way: selling that Blake allowed me to do the same thing I was doing with the books, but just add a couple zeros on the end of it, you know? I wish I still had it, of course, but, really…it belongs in a museum, where it can be taken care of and appreciated, not above my toaster or on my shelf."

"My roommate cleans things at the museum. I mean, not like a janitor, but a restorer. He uses this tiny vac—" Billy leaned back and yawned uncontrollably. "Vacuum. Sorry. So you started buying nicer stuff at second-hand shops?"

"No, I mean: I started going to these freaky little swap-meet things. Estate sales. Go check out some guy's *barn* where there's some Clyfford Still paintings rumored to be stored. The random stuff you hear about when you get to know collectors. I never will find anything as good as that Blake again, really. Well." He crushed a piece of ice in his mouth. "*Probably* won't. But there's more'n enough stuff out here that makes its way through the cracks so a guy like me can get by. Money's not a problem." He produced a pack of cigarettes from his breast pocket. "And it really shouldn't be, Billy. Not unless you let it." Larry cupped a hand and lit with the other. He pushed the pack across the table.

"Oh, no thanks. I don't really smoke."

Larry went on. "So, now if I see a lamp somewhere for $100 that I knew was worth, say, $1000 (because I knew of a guy that was *really into* that particular light fixture and would pay that kind of exorbitant amount of money for it) then I could buy it and not lose sleep. Doesn't sound like much," he had a long, noisy slurp from his glass that he'd poured too full, "but $50, $100 was too rich for my blood in the beginning."

"Oh, I know how *that* goes," Billy said in eager agreement. "It's hard to find the right lamp. Do you ever *lose* money on something?"

Larry looked relaxed. His cigarette dangled from his finally-still hand for a brief languid second. His shades were on again. "Oh, sure, sure," he said, rushing the smoke back to his mouth. "A while back I traded, *traded*, an old Zenith tube radio and a rocking chair for an original Eero Saarinen Tulip Chair. You know Eero Saarinen, right?"

"Like, with a lot of vowels?"

"Yeah, he's a Finn."

"His name turns up in the crossword from time to time."

"Chair's still upholstered. A cat must've pissed on it, but that'll come out, easy. Rug Doctor it," he made a *vvvvvvmmmm* sound and pretended to move a steam cleaner over the table, "someone'll pay three or four grand, maybe more."

"So what went wrong? Sounds like a good trade."

The ice cubes were starting to melt. The two imbibed with less vim and vigor.

"Well, what happened was this guy I know got remarried and his second wife wanted a more throw-back look. '40s stuff, nostalgia. He had to get rid of this weirdo, plastic space-age shit that the first wife liked. He didn't care much either way about the wives or how they decorated. Dude was *loaded*. Serious cheese." Larry held an empty right hand out towards Billy and began wiggling his fingers. "He wore large jewels on these meaty fingers of his." He made a fist. "I figured 'Hell, I can pull a fast one on this guy, he's not gonna miss it, much less give a damn.'" He raised the fist up and then spread out his fingers, *voila*. Larry lowered his hand back to the table feather-gently. "Well, turns out Robert Oppenheimer owned that radio. I got it in Los Alamos. I might've guessed. But now it's in a museum somewhere." He did a Gallic shrug with his cigarette wisping smoke from the tip. "And that rocking chair, too—as if the Oppenheimer thing weren't enough—*that* was carved by some obscure swamp man that was six months away from dying and fucking *blow-*

ing up the folk art market last spring. But that's just the game, man. I guess that guy didn't get those jewels just sittin' around twiddlin' his fat thumbs." Larry put his hands behind his head and had a satisfied sniff of the clean desert air. "Money begets money."

"You still came out ahead, though, right?"

"Yup." He nodded slowly before taking his glasses off. "Although not as much as I could have if I'd been more diligent in my research and a bit less opportunistic."

"Excuse me for one second," Billy said graciously.

Max the waiter pointed Billy towards an elegant and refined door marked 'Gentlemen.' Inside was a single toilet and full-length, tiled urinal. He knelt down on the cool, clean checkerboard tile and quietly, respectfully vomited into the ornate porcelain toilet. He had to stand up in order to pull down the chain attached to the floating tank and banish his still-carbonated discharge. Billy thought his reflection still looked rather gentlemanly. He gave himself a cool sploshing from the tap for good measure.

Larry was standing up with sunglasses back on. He said nothing. They walked directly to the parking lot.

"You stickin' around town for a while?" he asked as they pulled out of the lot, stirring up pea gravel and dust.

Billy paused. He, for one, couldn't drive for another couple hours. Or it wouldn't be wise to do so, at least. "Um." That would mean getting on the road at five or six in the evening. "Not sure. Why? What's going on?"

"Nothin' that I *know* of." Larry did a penny-whistle slide with his lips. "Except, shit, you know what?" He grimaced and bongoed his hands against the steering wheel. "I invited people over tonight for dinner."

"That's cool, I can unload that stuff and be off shortly."

"What stuff? Oh, the rugs. What? You don't want to stay? No. C'mon, let's go get things for dinner." He peered over his left, sped ahead, and candy-caned the truck in the opposite direction. "You'll like the people coming over. Besides, you know what sounds good? On a hot day like this? Ceviche. Can't get that at a truck stop. Ah, wait, though. Damn. What time is it?" Billy was about to answer, but Larry looked at the hands on the dashboard clock. "Yeah, thought so. 2:30 practically. That stuff needs time to *marinate*. Well, hmm. We'll figure *something* out. Something will *call out to us*, Billy."

A gust of cold air whooshed people at the entrance to Honest Fare Market, stabilizing body temperatures for what was to be an optimal grocery shopping experience. Inside, some people scurried with the myopic focus of ants procuring food for a queen while others dallied.

An older, grumpier faction doddered along the unfinished hardwood, struggling to find preserves.

"They oughta be *here* by the fruit itself," a coot in a Panama hat griped. The brim sagged and the crown was pulled down tight over his bullet-shaped head. It looked like a pith helmet. "Has the world gone *loco*?" he wondered out loud in the local parlance.

"Probably over by peanut butter now," his shriveled co-shopper tartly muttered.

"I don't see the raisins here, neither."

Within a minute Billy had quit trying to keep up with Larry, who went through the store like he was on *Supermarket Sweep*. He sat at a booth near the front of the store and waited for his strange new friend.

There was a lot to observe at the Honest Fare Market. Two former lovers bumped into each other in the middle of the frozen novelties aisle. They redirected traffic around them like a boulder in a stream while forcing polite small talk and trying to get a good read on one another. Then Billy noticed a woman with a small, docile chihuahua that wore an orange vest emblazoned with a medic cross and the words SOCIAL ANXIETY/SERVICE DOG. *Does the dog have social anxiety?* Billy wondered. She was cradling it around the pasta aisle like a baby. She looked right at home while the dog shook uncontrollably.

Nearby:

"Can you find the *quinoa*, Arshile? Can you find the *quinoa* and put it in the *cart*?"

A tiny tot with a blonde rattail stopped and balanced himself on a miniature shopping cart. He took a few unsure steps towards the wall of boxed grains, stabilizing himself with his pudgy, dimpled arms spread out at his sides. His mothers watched and encouraged from above.

"*Keen*-wah," his tall, thin keeper repeated.

"Where's the quinoa, Arsh?" asked the shorter woman with a sleeve of tattoos running down her arm.

The boy wobbled around and put a stubby index finger in his mouth. He deliberated. Finally he grabbed a red box from the bottom shelf and dutifully returned it to his cart (spilling over with assorted animal-shaped treats and a few bottles of sparkling water nearly as big as him).

"Good job, Arshile! Way to go, buddy!" The tall woman bent down to high-five the little shopper. She stopped suddenly. "What do you think you're doing?" she demanded of the other mother, who was removing Arshile's box from the cart.

"He grabbed millet, babe," she said.

"Well, put it back," the tall one whispered severely. "We don't want it to be *confusing* when we praise him." She took the box from her partner's brightly inked hand and put it right back beside the Organic Gummy Bunnies. "Yay, Arshile! Yay! Good job!"

The boy had all his fingers, save his thumb, in his mouth now.

"Excuse me," a man with a cascade of white hair interrupted Billy's observation. "Might I be able to sit here?"

At first Billy took this as an unexpected come-on. But then he saw that all the other booths were full of people enjoying food from the store deli: pizza slices and paninis, the occasional eater of a single piece of produce.

"Of course. Sorry," Billy offered, getting up from the seat. "Just waitin' on a friend."

The man put down his cold grain salad and avocado-colored smoothie and did a thespian curtain call bow before sliding into the bench.

Billy stood up. He yawned. He felt acutely out-of-place. All at once he felt a chill. He lightly grazed his chest to make certain that his nipples weren't making small pointy impressions through his shirt. They were not. He was still drunk and in need of something salty to eat.

Larry stood behind his cart at the end of a rather snaky line that spilled into the vitamin aisle. Billy walked towards him with a bag of Gumbo Joe's Kickin' Chicken Cajun Kettle Bites in tow. The bag was stamped with the words 'SECRET RECIPE.' He stood next to Larry without saying anything. Billy quietly peered at Larry's cart, shallowly filled with one or two products from every section of the store.

"Hey, man," he greeted Billy without looking towards him. "This should just about do it. It's gonna be paella, by the way. I *think* I have some lobster stock at home, but—just in case—I went ahead and got some lobster."

"Better safe than sorry."

"Right? Make it myself. Easy. And better than the crap they put in a Tetra Pak. And mussels were on sale. You do mussels? You'd better. But, yeah, we got chicken thighs, Spanish *chorizo* and Portuguese *chourico* (there's a difference!), some *petite pois*, of course. Leeks. Lemons. These marinated fava beans are good, just for people to nosh on." There were six jars of them. "What else..." He took the bag Cajun Kettle Bites out from Billy's chilly hands. "Huh," he said, looking over Gumbo Joe. He tossed the bag in the cart.

"Right," Billy said, "easier to pay all together."

He reached for his wallet.

"No, don't," Larry mildly rebuked, as if his uncultured companion were about to raise a haunch and try to covertly pass gas in front of the queen.

"You sure, man?" Billy asked half-heartedly.

A look of utter dread clouded Larry's face. Billy watched nervously as Larry's eyes darted over their cart.

"Dude. I forgot about saffron. Run and grab it for me, spice aisle, go! Go! Three bottles' worth! It's a must, Billy, *a must!*," Larry shouted to him as he rushed off.

With a spaniel's obedience, Billy power-walked through the slow-moving masses, all the way to the opposite side of the market. Several shoppers were assiduously inspecting the wall of spices when he got there. Reading glasses were slid down low on many noses. Billy gambled that the spices were alphabetized and that only the finer, glass-bottled purveyors would sell a flavoring of such esteemed repute. He located it quickly.

"Fuck-a-duck ... twenty-six?!"

Concentration was shattered among a few focused label-readers.

He remembered the lobsters in the cart, though, and imagined Larry quipping something along the lines of, "You can never have too much of this stuff around." Billy's mood turned foul and broody as he marched back to the cart. How much richness could he stomach today?

Back at the cash register there was still a plastic gray baton separating the paella fixings from the order being rung up ahead. The conveyor belt jolted the goods some inches closer every few seconds.

"Right on, perfect, thanks," Larry said as Billy rested the tiny jars of amber-red threads down on a bag of fat bomba rice. They looked like crown jewels on a white velvet pillow.

Larry charmed and flattered the cashier, a short, cute girl whose big, dark eyes and intensely small and red lips lent her an exaggerated precociousness. Billy was ready to tag along and boldly invite her to dinner (again, he was still more than a little buzzed) , but then he heard her say "two-fifty-six-sixty-three" and instinctively slunked away.

The pair of outrageous paper bags slid around the bed of the rusty truck. Billy watched them in his enormous passenger-side mirror and felt a little revolted at the idea that each bag was worth $125, give or take. That was the equivalent of twenty-five hours' work at the AVI right there in each sack. The saffron bill alone would have taken him nearly two days of pointless letter-mailing and pep-talking to purchase. Each of those crocus strands equal to some minutes of his life spent doing something he did not want to be doing. Billy forgot that he no longer worked at the Institute and that he had not bought any of the ingredients in the bags. Incredibly, he did not even remember the $50,000 check with his name on it at home. He put a Kettle Bite in his mouth and sullenly chewed.

"Shit, I forgot beer," Larry announced in the middle of a daring left turn. An unlit cigarette hung between his lips. "That's okay. They're over-priced for liquor, anyways."

Billy waited in the cab while Larry ran into Hoot's, an institution for those in the know when it comes to cold drinks in Santa Fe. He kept an eye on the paper grocery bags (ever-weary of tailgate thieves) and soon saw Larry trudge towards him with a twelve-pack of Pacifico under each arm. The boxes were precariously placed beside a loose spare tire that was in the back of the truck. Larry turned around and went back into Hoot's only to reappear shortly with an azure eighteen-pack of Modelo Especial cans.

"This stuff doesn't go bad," he explained before turning the ignition. The truck backfired and sputtered but regained its composure. "Plus everybody here's an alcoholic."

They got back to the house at 4 o'clock and sampled a couple of bottles of barely-cool beer with lime wedges floating around inside. They tasted great. Everything was lovely. The mountains were sensational and the beer hit the spot. Billy's keel was evened. He eased back in a deck chair. The chips got his blood sugar right. He coolly decided *money: can't live with it, can't live without it*. It wasn't terribly original, but he nonetheless found solace in the bit of trite resignation. He tilted his Pacifico back and said "Damn straight" under his breath.

"What's that?" Larry asked.

"I said 'damn straight.'"

"Oh. Well, fuck yeah." They clinked their bottles together and drank some more. "Hey, man, I forgot to mention, but, just so you know, sometimes the altitude here can play tricks on you, in terms of drinking." Larry, dropping a spent cigarette into a now-empty bottle, advised that Billy might want to consider taking it slow.

There was plenty of paella that needed to get made—right after one more cigarette. Billy bummed one. They were menthols. They almost seemed good for your lungs, like breathing in Vap-o-Rub. The two sat in appreciative quiet while a fluffy cloud blocked out the afternoon sun.

They went inside after smoking. Two smaller rugs, a couple of prints, and a box marked 'Santa Fe' got unloaded and placed in an overflowing guest room beside a modern, squiddy chandelier while Larry made a phone call from his bedroom. His five minutes of work for the day neatly wrapped up, Billy went back on the porch to sop up some more scenery. He rolled his sleeves up and dreamed of having bronzed arms. Another cloud blotted out the sun and made the backyard dimmer. He sighed and sent a cloud of smoke out from his mouth. It was like those cigarettes were packed with tobacco and after-dinner mints.

"I need to go to Texas tomorrow." He snuffed out the butt into a clam-shaped ashtray. He was saying this to himself as much as to Larry, who was scouring the charcoal grill with a metal brush. "I need to be back in Philly by the weekend or this whole thing's gonna be a flop. I—"

"Hold on, I'm still listening, keep talking, do you need another beer?" Larry walked into the house with his grimy hands out in front of him.

"Sure," Billy yelled.

He couldn't keep talking without someone visibly there, though; he didn't feel like yelling his problems. What if some nosy neighbor heard him complaining? And then things became clear: complaints aren't problems. So many of his incessant and weedlike worries dissipated like the dark, rainless cloud that had just passed overhead. Billy suddenly saw how much limoncello he'd made from the sour citrus life had handed him of late. He knew the Van Halen van was parked out front in the enchanting New Mexico wonderland because he had piloted it all the way there. And at some point soon, he'd drive back to Philadelphia. A dotted line traced his path home and it was shaped like a reclining question mark. Water ran in the kitchen and then two bottles popped open. The next breath he took was the best one he could remember.

"Thanks, Larry." He took a robust pull and then watched it bubble up the long brown neck.

"God, you know." Larry shifted his attention to the Sangre de Cristos in the distance. "It's just such a beautiful day. It's so nice here."

"I was *just* thinking that. Is that why you chose to live here?"

"Well. It's why I chose to stay here. Let's put it that way."

Larry appeared lost in the warm pastel vista and neglected the grill. Beer made people sleepy. Billy wasn't sure how his host was going to pull off such a complex and demanding dish after daydrinking in earnest since lunchtime. But his host had shown a lot of spunk at the market. He had some kind of a reserve to tap into, a higher gear at his command.

"How about some music?" Larry asked on cue. "Maybe that'd help get things *percolating*."

By around 6 o'clock half of the guests had arrived. One early couple (Greta and Lyle) was a May-October sort of affair, with a steel-haired woman in a flowing black velvet shawl and white capris and a young man in dark Carhartts and a Judas Priest shirt. They were easygoing and politely interested in the current state of things in Philadelphia. While they chatted, Billy assumed Lyle was a handyman and Greta his benevolent employer. He found it peculiar to see the two of them holding hands and only fully understood the situation when he noticed the couple kissing later that night with plenty of tongue.

Early on the crowd discussed in hushed tones whether or not they thought Francis would show up. Everyone had heard that Mathilde had indeed left him.

"I invited Frankie, but, truth be told, he's not doing so great," a friend reported. "I don't know if he wants to be seen yet."

People expressed a desire to see and support Francis, but then Mathilde surprised the party minutes later in an orange sundress and people quickly reversed their pro-Francis stance. They now silently agreed that nobody wanted him there, just to avoid the discomfiting scene it would undoubtedly cause.

Larry raked the coals with a special instrument and issued witticisms and droll one-liners from the grill. He engaged the alienated and facilitated mingling.

A small man named Cameron showed up and drank three beers in under thirty minutes. He walked laps around the backyard while drinking a beer and then wandered into the kitchen. He came back out with a rocks glass half full of tequila.

"To the top of the bottom shelf," he toasted. He winced in pain after downing half his drink.

"Which one's that?" Billy asked.

"What one?"

"What are you drinking?"

"So Billy," Mathilde leaned over and began, "what brings you to Santa Fe?"

"I had to deliver some rugs to Larry. And a box of Chinese things."

"You're a delivery-boy, then?"

"Well, no. Actually, I'm a delivery-*man*," he said with a ribald wink that fell completely flat. "Of course, it's just a goofy one-time job. I worked at a school."

"Ah." She smiled diplomatically. "Both my parents are teachers."

"Oh yeah? That's great. What grade?"

"They're at Yale."

The party was twenty deep by 8:30. The house

was full of people and music from the front porch to the backyard. The social cogs were well-lubricated and people were happy and fun-loving within reason. Larry was in the zone, going between kitchen and grill, hopping past and zipping by his guests, birdlike and alert. All sorts of conversations were spilling over into one another. Cliques and circles drifted together tectonically. Physical Venn Diagrams were formed as certain elements of nearby discussions became disengaged and turned to one another.

A woman turned away from her friends. "Ugh, they're over there talking about *hunting*," she said with revulsion.

A man spun around and empathized, relaying to her his own disaffection: "Yeah, they're over here busy geeking out over that new werewolf biker show."

So then these two would talk about something of mutual interest and others would join in.

An hour after his arrival, Cameron was not black-out drunk yet. He bumbled around with a tumbler full of a nonspecific amber liquid. He placed a hand on Billy's shoulder—mostly for stability—and cut in on insightful topspin tips from a local tennis pro. He motioned for Billy to 'come along', swinging his head to the right.

"Sorry, Ricardo, one sec. I'll need to hear the rest of that." Billy looked around and found Cameron standing over by a large soft-green shrub. He walked over and waited for an explanation while Cameron drunkenly caressed the bush, stroking the soft branches as one might a cat's tail after a full-body pet. He put a hand out at Billy's face.

"Smell it."

He hesitantly sniffed. It was pleasant-smelling…earthy, and at the same time fresh. He rubbed the plant some, and then gave his palms a deep whiff.

"Russian sage. Like Duh…stai'vsky." He burped and chuckled. "Bro," he said with seriousness. "Did you know that this guy is a master gardener? *Larry?*" He made a baffled, incredulous face, scrunched his features up and shrugged. "He is, though. You smelt my hand. He got that plant *kicking ass.*"

Ten feet away Billy looked at Larry who shook his head in objection and stirred a massive wok of aromatic rice over the grill.

"That bush was here when I moved in, Cam."

"Well, you didn't *kill* it. I woulda kilt it," he added, *just-between-us-boys*-style.

Dinner was ready by about 9:30. A few of the guests were cranky and had been visibly drinking on an empty stomach. The food was a revelation, though, and Larry served it up in whatever his guests held out in front of him: an upturned frisbee, a small frying pan, a muffin tin.

"Just one cup for me," said a timid girl with a hefty Pyrex measuring cup.

"Ah, nonsense!" Larry said as he dumped a spoonful of fragrant rice before her. "You can handle a pint of paella, Amelia. You're practically wasting away!"

He didn't have service for more than a dozen, but nobody seemed to mind what they ate the lobster- and saffron-infused dish out of or with. In a true testament to how delicious dinner was and how greedily people ate, one could hear the wind gently blowing through the branches and leaves high above while throughout the house and backyard, diners chewed, savored, and swallowed. For five minutes the party turned as quiet as a cease-fire. It was good timing, too, as an exciting thunderstorm was passing over the mountains miles away.

The thunder reminded one guest, a swarthy man holding a glass of white wine peppered with dead fruit flies, of something his twin brother had done in third grade. "I was sick one day, a Monday, and Henry, my brother, told the class, the teacher, *everyone*, that I was dead. Struck by lightning over the weekend." This was supposed to be the punchline but nobody was laughing much. "He was just jealous because I got to stay home and play Nintendo." You could tell he'd never had this anecdote go so poorly.

It was getting dark and the outdoor lighting was insufficient. Still, people wanted to smoke and watch the light show over the Sangre de Cristos. A latecomer to the party, a thin strawberry blonde in tiny, tattered cutoffs and a sleeveless lime-green blouse sat down next to Billy with a coffee mug full of brightly-colored rice. She expertly set in on the paella with some chopsticks.

"Ha, would you look at this *adorable* mug?"

She showed Billy the mug. It was baroquely gold-foiled and featured a portrait of a blushing, seventeenth-century Dutch burgher. He had a smug, satisfied simper and the bountiful, upturned mustache of a coxcomb. She took another bite. The words 'THE LAUGHING CAVALIER' were revealed on the inner lip of the mug.

"It just keeps getting better!" she bubbled in personal delight.

"Not to mention the food in it."

Her face turned grave. "Yes, I know. Oh. My. God. So good." Then she arched her lips back up into a smile. "Hi, I'm Meadow, by the way."

Her hand was a little rough, but her fingers were long and elegant with fresh purple polish.

"I'm Billy." The day's copious alcohol intake and the man on the mug urged on something daring, dashing, and a little dumb. "*Enchantez* to meet you, Meadow." He fumbled the French and kissed her softly on a raw knuckle.

"Oh my!" she reacted. "You're quite the cavalier yourself."

"It takes one to know one. And *you* are quite handy with those chopsticks."

"Ah, that's so sweet of you," she said, touched. She looked at Billy for a wordless moment. "I was raised in this, well, let's just call it what it was: a *cult*. I spent some time in the Philippines, so-oo … not to brag, but: I got good with the chopsticks."

"Huh, you don't say? In the Philippines?"

"Yeah," she said through a mouthful of rice. "My mom and dad and some friends had this *crazy* idea that Ahura Mazda and Buddha and Christ were the same guy, just appearing in different cycles, and that he'd be back in the jungles outside Balanga sometime in the mid-'70s."

"I see," Billy said. "Did the group have a, uh, a name?"

"The People's *Free* Prophets," Meadow replied. "You might have heard of 'em, but we left before the nationals took it over and turned it into a junta."

"Riiight. The People's Free Prophets. Those twin teenage girls with the Uzis."

"Trina and Mina. Now, that was in the '90s." Her mouth was crammed with yellow rice and she had to take a swill of beer to wash it down. "*Mrmph*," she swallowed down her bite. "They claimed to be the incarnation that we'd been prophesying, just that the heavenly zygote got split, like Castor and Pollux, or Romulus and …" she moved her mouth far to the left and scrunched that side of her face in stern-but-cute deliberation.

"Remus," Billy said.

"Mmmm, right. Remus." Meadow raised her eyebrows suggestively and bit down on her chopsticks. Billy politely smiled. He didn't find the name "Remus" all that alluring. She continued. "Either way, Trina and Mina came well after we were there. I knew their mom, though, growing up. Cindy." She loaded another hefty wad of rice between her sticks and savored the flavor before an exaggerated Pelican gulp. "So it was a lot different when I was there, of course."

"Fascinating. Did you like it? Growing up that way?"

"Oh sure. I learned how to play guitar, how to use a machete, how to handle a snake bite. *All kinds* of useful things. People have a lot of preconceived notions about 'cults,' but by the time I came back to America, I knew my times tables through the thirteens."

Billy said he needed to go to the bathroom and went looking for Larry. Inside some music had started up. Not many people were dancing because it was a slightly older crowd indoors. The brown leather sectional was overflowing with friends holding drinks and interrupting one another until everybody erupted in hearty laughter together.

"Damn, that's funny…so it really *was* Allen Ginsburg's cock ring," said a reddened, beefy, bald man, "I'll sure-as-shit have to tell Gaston that one next time I'm in San Francisco."

Billy went all the way out front and found Larry standing by himself. He was just finishing a cigarette and began lighting another not long after Billy closed the screen door. A long string of fat, round bulbs crisscrossed above and draped them in yellow light. The main drag traffic rumbled and revved in the distance.

"So, Billy. What's next?" Smoke spewed out from Larry's nostrils like an angry bull. "And don't say something about delivering more rugs."

"Well, then, I don't know. That's what I was gonna say: deliver the other rugs." Billy felt his phone rattle against the car keys in his right pocket. "Sorry," he absentmindedly apologized while flipping his phone open. It was a message from Lucy. She wanted to know if he was busy right then. Looking at the tiny screen, Billy must've grimaced or looked worried, stressed.

"What's that about?"

"Ah…nothing." He took a cigarette. "An ex. She wants to talk."

"You need to talk, man? G'head." Larry began puffing faster.

"No, it's fine. I'll call her later or something."

There was a long quiet while they smoked. The stars were out and the van looked bad-ass under the serious moonlight. They respected its presence. Eventually Larry coughed and began talking again.

"Is that why you're running around? A girl? I mean, shit, don't get me wrong. I've got stamps in the back of my passport from followin' or gettin' away from some coozed-up thing or another."

Billy took a long, stoic drag. He felt like a cowboy with that additive-free, mentholated cigarette between his thumb and forefinger.

"Nah, I just was feeling a little too lonely last night when I got into town." He flicked the butt onto the patio brick. "Sorry." He knew better than to litter like that these days.

"You didn't, like, take pictures or anything, did you?"

"No. It's not that nice of a phone."

"Good. People keep getting into trouble, doing that. Anyways, so you miss her."

"Well, no, I didn't say that."

"Actually, I think you did." Larry rubbed his cigarette out against the edge of a nearby coffee canister. "But that's okay, man, I get it. I been there." He mechanically lit another and held the pack out for Billy. "You know, earlier, when I told you about the Blake prints and everything, I realized I was being kind of an asshole."

Billy snorted. "When you bought that pitcher

of gin-and-tonics that you shared with me?" he clarified with a cigarette stuck in the corner of his mouth, "is that when you were being an asshole?"

"Ha, yeah, I mean, that right there: I was showing off. Fuck," he ran a hand through his thinning hair and took two steps away. "I left out the real parts, man. How'd I get here?" He answered his own question right away. "I was delivering food for this Indian restaurant in New York." Larry's eyes widened. The whites were pink. "I was *maybe* twenty years old, *maybe*, and just having the worst time of it *ever*. Living in Brooklyn when you did *not* want to be in Brooklyn ... I was trying to be an actor."

"You didn't say you wanted to be an actor."

"I know. Like I said, I left out the real parts. And one night, out of the blue, I end up delivering food to *Willem Dafoe*." Larry clapped his hands together once. "And, you know, I've always been a big fan. A *big* fan. Obviously, I looked up to the guy. Still do. Anyways, he opened up the door and my jaw, you know, it dropped." Larry opened his mouth wide and flicked his ashes. "Of course, he could give a fuck about me—he just wants his saag paneer and his garlic naan. He doesn't want to be *gawked* at at his front door. So Willem Dafoe just hands me money, takes his food, and says, 'You look like shit, pal,' before he closes the door." He brought the cigarette up to his lips. Its tip glowed fiery orange and made Larry's face appear sallow. Smoke crept out of his mouth when he began to speak. "My jaw was still dropped, by the way. My mouth was completely agape, all the way back to Santosh."

"That sounds awful rude," Billy said. "Did he at

least give you a good tip?"

"*Yeah*, dude: a big fucking tip because I *did* look like shit and it took hearing it from my hero Willem Dafoe to get me to realize it, to get me to actually re-enroll in school (even if I didn't wind up getting any degree). He, of all people, got me working that shit job at the Basket of Books. I mean, the universe is so out-there, Billy. It hands you things and if you're smart enough and brave enough you try and make something of it."

"Sure." Billy was dizzy from the smoke and alcohol. Focusing on and understanding words, let alone a message, was no simple task. He was busy trying not to throw up for the second time today.

"Learn to *eat* that paella without just *devouring* paella," Larry proclaimed.

"Yeah, sorry," Billy said in an embarrassed voice. "It was just really good and I was hungry. I didn't mean to wolf it down like that."

"No, man…" Larry laughed to himself over this misinterpretation. "Basically, just enjoy things. Especially what you do. Then you don't sweat the rest. Just as long as you don't get hung up on money." He took a puff. "What'd Marx say?, he said, uh, he said—"

"Um… let's get rid of money?" Billy guessed.

"No, I'm talkin' Groucho. Something like, 'Money can't buy happiness but it can let you choose your own misery.'"

"Ahhh, yes, of course," Billy said. "Groucho."

"Or, no," Larry blurted out, "here's one: a friend of mine went to Russia when it was Soviet Union."

He said "Soviet Union" in a Yakov Smirnov voice. "He walked into a grocery store to buy a candy bar. He didn't know what kind he wanted, but he knew he was hankerin' something sweet. He went to the candy aisle." Larry took a deep pull. "There was only one thing there," he whispered, "just a bunch of boxes of the same chocolate bar." His smoke hung in the air. "No almonds, no peanuts, no *nougat*. Just *one* thing to choose. And he said he'd never felt freer in his life."

Billy rubbed the back of his neck. The story made him want dessert.

Larry was smoking like a chimney now. "Money. E'rrybody lets it ruin their own lives, whether they got it or they don't. And is there ever *enough*? Guy'll have fifty million dollars, lose half of it in the stock market and jump out of a window. Never mind the twenty-five cooling in savings like a pie on a window sill." The dry desert air thickened with their sweet smoke. "I know this is gonna rub you the wrong way, Billy—you being where you are in life right now—but money, cash, once you get a certain amount of it, it becomes another boring plaything. But God forbid you don't have it!" He scoffed. "And here *I* am, sounding like an even bigger douchebag than before."

"Hardly, Larry, hardly." Billy put his cigarette down and let it burn like temple incense. "If anything, I find this 'money's the root of all evil' sermon hard to swallow coming from *you* after all the ridiculous generosity you've shown me." His throat was dry. Had he had any water since breakfast at the

Larder? Did ice cubes count? "Jesus, man, I smell like trash. My fingernails have Flying J underneath them. I expected to dump off some Chinese shit at some rich jackass's place and be on my way *to fucking Texas* and instead I'm getting wined and dined all day and invited to hang out with friendly, with-it people. I —"

"Yeah, dinner tonight *was* good," Larry began. He'd put his sunglasses back on while Billy was talking. "And it cost too much. And when I was making it, listening to you and Cam and those guys and I kept thinking about being so hungry when I was living in California… thinking about being eighteen years old, stealing saltines and grape jelly packets from diners and how I ate that for dinner. And then, all of a sudden, I kinda wanted a fucking saltine! Instead of paella!" He snorted. "But I can't serve *saltines* at my own *home. In Santa fucking Fe.*" The lesson was becoming an unclear jumble of anger and sarcasm. This shared moment may have started off as guidance being passed from elder to younger, but now Billy felt compelled to say something supportive. Larry was a melancholic drunk when there wasn't a crowd.

"I liked the paella," Billy said, as sober-sounding as a judge. "All those people in there liked your paella. And now everybody's just stoned out of their minds on a good meal and having fun at your house, which is pretty cool."

On cue came a loud outburst of laughter and clapping.

"Thanks, Billy," Larry said with a crooked smile. "You're young and glandular still. I miss that.

I do. Going out there, man, making mistakes, taking chances. It's a thrill I don't get much anymore, which is okay. I'm not gonna force it, try and swim in cages with sharks or anything. I'm a grown-up and I used to be young. I remember it fondly, you know? But, Billy..." the glowing end of the cigarette was down near his knuckles. He took a long look at the party inside, the blurry shapes of his friends behind a thin yellow curtain. "Know that there's a feeling that comes with accomplishment...that you only get after fucking up some first." He put his cigarette out on the sole of his docksider. "I miss that." He reached into his pocket. "Anyways, here."

He handed Billy bills, folded many times over until it was about the width of a stick of gum.

"No, I couldn't, I actually have fifty— "

"Do anything other than put that in your pocket and I'll kick you square in the ass. Listen: go deliver that other shit the next couple days, don't get into an accident asleep at the wheel trying to hustle home, and use that little bit to do something different. Something you want to do but normally wouldn't."

"You just said you were done making mistakes and taking chances, Larry. I don't know what I want to do." He was holding the clean, new money in his palm like a delicate artifact.

"Okay. Then write a story for me. Nothing big: a short story. There's your advance. Or take some photographs. Consider it a commission. Whatever you end up doing, just make sure it fits in an envelope and mail it to me. Now let's go back in before people start getting restless. I'm supposed to be the host, after all." They started back inside before Larry stopped at the door. "Oh, hey. Do you need a place to stay tonight? Are you staying here?"

"I think I'm going over to Meadow's place."

"Well, that ought to be an interesting conclusion to your night right there," he said, patting Billy on the back.

The Van Halen van followed a dinged LeBaron through the interminable roads of a steep section of town. He stopped at a dumpy place that looked like the last unwanted square of days-old sheet cake. Billy got out of the van and stood unsure in the dark and rocky driveway. Meadow was on the phone inside the LeBaron. He thought about what he was getting into. Like the quirky girls in movies and television, she was sexually frank, speckled with freckles, and had bangs as stark and level as a good shelf. But she had an intensity about her that made him edgy. She knew how to wield a machete. She had eyes that could give you the heebie-jeebies: antique china doll eyes. Billy sensed the wrong sort of adventure, more risk than thrill. He kicked a rock and waited. The night had turned crisp.

"Sorry," she said, coming out of the car. "That was my old shrink. Boy, he's a mess."

It was twenty minutes after midnight. Meadow had a yappy Scottish terrier named Bogey ("as a rule, Bogey doesn't take to men") and a drunk roommate named Kyle asleep on the couch ("his dad was a television director, but Kyle just works at a video store"). Her room was messy, like a twelve-year-old boy's. There were socks and jeans abound—many near an overturned laundry basket. An old surf-rock electric guitar leaned against a wall, the high-E snapped and dangling. Overdue library books and assorted media piled up like cairns. She picked up a title, *America's Best Eulogies, 2012*, and read a remembrance that she was currently enamored with.

"One time I made my mom a pie, when I was twelve or thirteen years old. It was a surprise and she was taking a nap, as she often did … I'd never baked a thing before that pie and this was the last time I ever really made her feel true joy. It's alright, though. I still make a pie on occasion, for this old time's sake. And I hear today, for the first time since then, when I was twelve or thirteen, that my mother is happy." She snapped the book shut. "Isn't that just *breathtaking*? That was by Ivar Fluellen, by the way—the renowned Welsh documentarian. Have you seen *Gabardine Exile?*"

"Not yet. I thought that was supposed to be the *Best* American *Eulogies*."

"It is. His mom was American." She dropped the book where she stood. "Do you think you want kids? Wait a sec—have you read these poems by survivors of the Cambodian genocide?" She bent down and selected a thin volume from atop a stack. Meadow began reading aloud while sashaying over to her computer set up in the corner of the room.

"The dirt is deep/brown/red/and the rain clouds are so far away/that I think I may never see/ another plant grow."

"That was ... sad."

"But good, right?"

Several poker chips were strewn around the room. An empty Prosecco bottle was resting in Bogey's lumpy dog bed. A stack of old calendars waited to be utilized for a project next to the large exercise ball in front of her computer desk. Meadow bobbed around on it while cruising the net.

"One sec," she said in response to nothing.

Amid all of this Meadow's bed was made, though. The most in-your-face and by-the-books drill sergeant would have to stop and commend this bunk.

Billy commented on the unusual nature of the top blanket, red velvet gilded with minute beadwork and an assortment of mirrors and shells.

"Yeah, I got it in Mexico when I was, like, fourteen. My mom and granma and me took a vacation down to Cabo and, you know, they don't mind giving fourteen-year-olds shots down there. It's a party town. Well," she sat on the bed and patted the blanket appreciatively, "I got to feeling pretty sick at this cantina I'd wandered into and this Turkish man at the bar said he had some apple tea that would help my stomach. It was back on his boat, though. We were right by the marina, so I said, 'Sure, why not?' Then, next thing ya know, he asked for my hand and told me he had an island not far from there and a successful wheelchair factory back in Turkey. I had to tell him, 'No, I'm on vacation with my mom and granma.' Anyways, he sold blankets, too, on his boat. I think I paid $10 for it."

"Did you ever end up drinking his tea?"

"No."

"That's probably good."

The conversation with Larry not long ago gave Billy the feeling of being caught in a summer downpour and he felt soaked, so to speak, as well as worn out. He'd had more good booze and epiphanies today than he'd had during his entire time in Philadelphia. His mind being elsewhere and his eyes looking sleepy only lent him a "playing it cool" mien that made him irresistible, however. Meadow put on strange, discordant music and smuttily rambled on about her youthful indiscretions. The alcohol was wearing off and he involuntarily yawned as she began recounting a memorable bath she took with her roommate Stacy some years ago. Billy didn't want to be there anymore. She slipped her right hand into his jeans and kept talking. Truthfully, he felt not-so-fresh, three days removed from his last shower. She mashed and squeezed gently, pausing and retreating to take off her shirt.

"And *that* was the first time I ever really noticed how pronounced my labia were," she continued.

Billy felt like he was being molested by Roderick Usher. Bogey barked and jumped on the bed. While she put the dog back on his pad, the fact that he forgot to reply to Lucy's text message flashed by. If the universe was so interconnected, maybe he'd feel his phone buzz … now.

No vibration came.

He kicked his sneakers off, laid back, and waited with his head at an uncomfortable angle against the wall. He was sideways with his legs hanging off the bed. Meadow straddled and kissed him with antic fervor. Her tongue was quick and nervous, like a lizard's. Between kisses she said weird things in his ears, back of the bus sort of stuff. Billy nodded but couldn't smile. His ear canal felt too wet. He worried about getting an earache. He offered to cuddle before she took her bra off. Her nipples stuck straight out like fresh pencil erasers.

Meadow would try and get Billy going with her frenzied movements and lewd language, but then Bogey, who *had* to stay in the room, would stop his puzzled spectating and begin to menacingly growl and woof, dousing whatever puny spark there might've been.

It was close to 1:30 a.m. when he cleverly feigned sleep. But she stroked and toyed with him enough that Billy, sounding like he was dealing with a full sink of dishes following a party, finally offered his full services in the morning. The precious bit of rest he was after, however, was repeatedly interrupted by Meadow's night terrors. It was shaping up to be a long drive into Texas tomorrow.

12

"You're never going to call me again, are you?"

It was 7:31 a.m. and Billy was back in his jeans. One minute earlier his alarm went off. He pretended it was an important phone call and started to get dressed.

"I don't know. Maybe. I never thought I'd be in Santa Fe in the first place, anyways … so it just goes to show, you know …" He trailed off and began poking around in search of his other sock. His hangover was pronounced.

"Mmmm, don't go. You *owe* me, remember? You promised."

He went ahead and put his shoes on wearing only a left sock. Meadow writhed around and re-appropriated her groggy voice into that of a sex kitten. She sprawled out saucily as if her bed were a grand piano in a smoke-filled burlesque house. Her morning breath did not help her cause. He gave her a kiss on the forehead and left the room. Roommate Kyle was awake but still on the same spot on the couch, watching a bass fishing show. He had gotten a blanket at some point in the night.

"Morning," Billy said.

"Morning," Kyle said.

The southbound interstate was clear and cars moved straight and briskly towards Albuquerque. Once he felt a safe distance away from the night before, Billy gassed-up at a Pueblo service station and stocked up on orange sports drink. The drive ahead was long. Texas was big and not to be messed with it. Today had all the makings of a vision quest. A lot had been thrown at his mind and it was time to see what stuck. That meant no radio, no hitch-hikers, and no junk food. If he was going on a true vision quest there could be no food period. And no A/C. Excessive heat facilitated seeing things. The Van Halen van would roll on solitary and unstoppable through the open desert, a blistering and hours-long raga of a guitar solo. Billy would sift through yesterday's silt and find gold on his way to Marfa.

The first concession was made when Billy decided to listen to the radio and the local music kept him occupied and in good spirits until the signal dissipated. Then as the elevation dropped, the temperatures rose. If he was going to fast (save for electrolytes), he'd need to maintain a healthy temperature or he might pass out.

Once the mountains were out of sight it became a good time for introspection.

"Nothing to see here," Billy said.

He furrowed his brow. Nothing came to mind. He was too hung over to think clearly. A sign brightly announced the first commercial spaceport nearing completion just outside of Elephant Butte. A carload of young men had stopped by one of

the signs and were taking pictures with the last 'e'
covered by an oafishly-grinning head of one member. Then came postings for the world-famous hot
springs in Truth or Consequences, NM ("As seen in
Sunset Magazine"). Not long after that were several
hotels once occupied by Billy the Kid that lodgers
could chose from.

While fueling up later and still not in Texas, Billy
went to the bathroom just to wash his hands. They
smelled too much like Meadow. He realized that he'd
forgotten to see his friend in Albuquerque and give
him that rainstick. The rainstick was going to make
a big cross country journey, too. Then he called Lucy
and apologized for not getting back to her sooner.

"I was busy: I was in Santa Fe," he explained. "I
sent *you* a postcard."

"You did? How'd you get my address here?"
Lucy asked.

"Tell your mom to forward it to you."

"Oh. Okay."

"I have to go, though. I'm on a pay phone and
I'm out of quarters."

Lucy laughed. It was a pleasant sound Billy
hadn't heard in a long time.

"Why are you on a pay phone?"

"I dunno, I just thought it'd be kind of cool to
call you on a pay phone, my being at a gas station
in the desert. Sort of a Route 66 vibe, I guess. Also I
only had, like, one bar out here and I—"

Two beeps cut him off, followed by a familiar
operator's instructions to hang up, insert money,
and dial again.

Billy called Lucy back on his cell phone. Reception was poor so they had a brief but cordial conversation. She was selling seashells by the seashore, it was true. Devin had already moved back to New York. Billy was invited to visit on his way back. He'd call for directions in a few days when he got closer to Florida.

It was lunchtime in El Paso. Billy wondered if one might find better lunches in Juarez, but deemed that too risky.

Halfway through his mediocre carne asada torta he remembered his planned abstinence from food. *First things first*, he justified, *I need to get over this horseshit hangover*. Billy was occupied with making sense of Larry. His offhand free-handedness was one thing, but the $216 he'd forced on Billy (a relative stranger) was another. Angelic possibilities did not go unconsidered, although they were at once shot down. Billy chewed and pondered. Did he actually befriend a likable, thirty-eight-year-old man of affluence?

The thought gave him pause. It had always been assumed that anybody making more than they needed was inherently out-of-touch. Now Billy stood to take on more than he needed any day now. But he could be like Larry, right? Larry was still with it. Billy could spend freely on the right things. He too might someday personally know Igor in Tijuana.

Spitting out a hunk of gristle, Billy tried to focus on some of the guidance he received last night.

God, I was wasted, he recalled wistfully.

Instead of going over the details of what was discussed, Billy itemized everything he drank throughout the day and night. Larry surely exceeded him, guzzle-for-guzzle. As fragments of their discussion came back to him, Billy couldn't discern which words were genuine and which ones juiced. *En vino veritas,* but only a fool heeded a wino's counsel. Wino wasn't a fair label to hang on Larry, though. Maybe he was one of those folkloric drinkers. It wasn't like he was hiccuping or slurring words. But what *were* his words, again? Some things said struck Billy as being heartfelt directions, others the morose warnings of middle age.

Billy settled his check and sat in the van. He added up the blue lines on the map, the ones with driving times listed above. In front of the taqueria he'd just eaten at, a plump *borracho* laid himself out on a bench.

"That certainly doesn't look like Larry," Billy noted to himself as an employee came out and urged the man on lest the cops get involved. The drunk did not move save heavy breathing. "That looks more like me."

Clothes, Billy posited, *must really make the man.*

Clichés got to be clichés because they were true.

Billy decided to play it safe and leave before the cops came. He idled the van and quickly tallied the driving time up again. Marfa, the atlas said, was three hours away.

Two hours and fifteen minutes later, Billy reached a sign that said 'Marfa, TX pop. 1899.' Like the majority of what he'd seen today, this was a quiet and empty place. A few clean and geometric structures stood on the flatlands, as prominent as a beauty mark on an albino. 1900 souls seemed a rather generous figure.

The address he was to deliver to was not hard to find and, not surprisingly, was one of the isolated Tetris pieces made of glass, concrete, and unfinished wood. It was about 100 yards off the road from where the mailbox was. There was no driveway—you just drove up off the road, like you might at a flea market or fruit stand. The house looked new but the exterior already showed many signs of wear (cracks, stains, warping, etc.). Perhaps that was the point: something expensive to remind people of impermanence.

Complicating matters entirely, nobody was home. From what was visible through the glazed-over windows, the place looked empty. It had the appearance of a unit long stuck between renters. There was one bar's worth of reception out here. He had no number for the buyer in Marfa, anyways. Billy squatted down in the van's shade. He thought about what to do and made a decision five seconds later.

There were few clouds and no passing cars as he went about unloading two large boxes and a rug on what he guessed to be the back porch. But it could have been a front porch, depending on how you looked at it.

To whom it may concern: Billy wrote, *I attempted delivery, but nobody was home. Sorry I must leave this here for I am in an urgent hurry. Please call Jacob with your questions/comments/concerns.* He left no phone number on the note he scrawled on a napkin. Billy got back in the van, knowing he had at least another half-a-day's worth of Texas to drive through.

"Leaving Marfa behind" sounded like a country song. Billy turned on the radio on his way towards the freeway. No swingin' door road-house music came through, however. The radio was making for intermittent company and the ranchero and Tejano stations here made Billy pine for some of that New Mexico music he'd heard early this morning. What a musical aberration that FM station out of Santa Fe was! Everything in Texas was a tiresome, tuba-heavy waltz and the braying Spanish lamentations of heartache and loneliness were getting old.

Day turned into night very slowly over this particular portion of Texas endless.

Not many people were honking at the van anymore. This wasn't unforeseen, but Billy did feel dispirited some. He'd gotten used to the beeping and the Lone Star silence struck him as unfriendly. He watched his speed carefully on 20 East. Time passed as slow as the orange needle on the gas gauge. Eventually, Billy was taken in by the friendly Brontosaurus insignia of a Sinclair station and selected it over the bland facilities nearby. He was willing to pay one-and-nine-tenths cents more per-gallon for charm. Across the street from the fuel pumps was a rough-but-not-quite-rickety shack. Up front a hand-painted sign said 'BUTTS' in red, eighteen-inch letters. Billy was intrigued, to say the least. Neon glowed promisingly in the front window. The van looked so good in front of Butt's that he ran back across the street and bought a disposable camera at the gas station before it got much darker and the lighting changed.

It may have sounded bustling from the other side of the door, but nobody was inside of Butt's besides a stocky man with a horseshoe of blond hair and fleshy red lips. A rowdy song on the jukebox had fooled him. The man was watching the TV on mute. He leaned on the counter, not looking away from a closed-captioned courtroom procedural. He wore part-way shaded prescription lenses and a short-sleeved denim button-up. What hid below the bar remained a mystery. Billy sauntered to the counter and tried to catch up with the program.

The stern, crisply-dressed D.A. tossed an evidence bag on a table.

Lawyer:—A child's teddy bear, loaded with a kilo of raw, Colombian cocaine, sent by Mister Montez to Miss Cantucci;

Lawyer:—Objection, your honor!;

Judge:—Sustained!;

Jury: [whispers];

Judge: Order! [gavel banging] Order!;

Lawyer:—The exact same style of teddy bear seized at Fat Frank Lombardo's shipping facility. I ask you, the jury, what would the leader of the Lombardo

*crime syndicate want with 1,000s of adorable children's
toys other than shipment of controlled substances and
illegal contraband?*

The words were a few seconds behind. Once the
commercials came on, whose narratives were still a
source of distraction, the man behind the counter
shifted slightly towards his customer.

He slid a laminated sheet of paper towards Billy.

"Special today was carne adovada. We're closing in forty-five minutes."

- BUTT'S CHILI PARLOUR -
Texas Chili ... $5 (cheese +.50)
Texas Chili Burger ... $5 (cheese +.50)
Texas Chili Dog ... $4 (cheese +.50)
Texas Chili Fries ... $3.50 (cheese +.50)
Coke ... $1
Coffee ... $1
Pie ... seasonal

NO SUBSTITUTIONS
NO EXCEPTIONS
NO OUT-OF-TOWN CHECKS
NO CARDS

"I think I'll have that chili-burger," Billy said after a short deliberation.

"Good choice," the man said bluntly. "Jorge, *an-
dale! 'Riba!*" he shouted into the kitchen through a
small window. A screen door was heard slamming
shut in the back. "Chili burger, Jorge!"

"With cheese, too," Billy said.

"With *queso*, Jorge!"

Behind the bar and below a neon state flag was a terrarium with a desert scene and a live snake (fat and brown but no rattler). There was a large cross-stitch portrait of Lyndon Johnson framed in dark wood and a detailed charcoal pencil study of John Wayne as Rooster Cogburn on the left wall. They both looked contemplative, somber. Four tables lined the perimeter below their three watchful eyes. Each table had a single roll of paper towels at its center like an absorbent, white tower. Along with the six-stooled bar, this was all the seating. There was a jukebox, an actual old-timer with 45s, and by that a shuffle board table. Billy got up and inspected the jukebox. He scanned through the machine and eventually selected a song called "Tulsa Time."

Two dollars' worth of quarters sat on the bar in front of Billy's stool.

"Go on an' keep 'em coming," the man behind the bar instructed.

It was not easy to pick many songs, especially for a country and western novice, so Billy continued selecting the most compelling names and titles. By the time he'd returned to the bar, there was a red oval-shaped basket lined with a sheet of wax paper. Somewhere in there a cheeseburger lurked in a pool of Texas chili.

"Wow," was all he could say, plopping onto his stool.

"Ah, what in the hell?" the man yelled at the TV set. "Are you shittin' me?"

Lawyer:—You cannot be serious! Not guilty?! the television read as a redhead in a silver pantsuit stormed down the courthouse steps.

Lawyer:—How do you let Montez walk free? You're buying justice.

Lawyer:—It's called a plea bargain.

This defense lawyer was your typical big-money legal eagle, complete with slick hair and a pinky ring.

The bottom of the screen read *Welcome to America! [laughter]* while the defense and his client surely cackled together.

"Ah, that shit's dumber'n'hell anyways. How's that burger, son?"

"Mhumph," Billy replied with a steaming mouth of beef and spices.

"Glad to hear it."

He swallowed like a snake eating a bird's egg whole. "Could I have a Coke?"

"Which kind?"

"Coke."

The man behind the bar pulled out a blue can from a mini-fridge and placed it down near his customer.

"All's we got is R.C."

"Thanks." He gulped speedily and held down a belch. "I really like this place, man. It's damn near perfect," he complimented and then vented out a breezy, covert burp that sounded more like an exhausted sigh.

"Well, thank you, son." He turned the TV off. "Name's Butt Doyle." He put his hand out for a shake. He had a gaudy Josten's class ring on his index finger and downy, baby's hair covering his forearms. "And Jorge back there's the one that grills a mean burger. Course, the chili, well ..." and he suggestively lowered his glasses with the class ring finger, showing Billy his light blue eyes, "that's strickly a Doyle fam'ly secret."

"Well, Mr. Doyle—"

"Mr. Doyle was my daddy, please. Call me Butt."

"Butt, this is a pleasure. You, Javier, the chili, the jukebox, everything." The food had cooled into a delicious now or never. The spices square-danced all throughout Billy's mouth. He ate greedily and let the proprietor talk.

"Yessir, I s'pose you're wonderin' 'bout that chili."

Billy moved his head up and down as he consumed voraciously.

"Welp. The old man gimme the recipe."

Butt produced a 4x6 photo in a cheap gold frame from below the bar. Billy looked but did not touch. Every fingertip was daubed with earthy red drippings. He stopped chewing and bent a little closer to the frame. The man in the picture was standing beside a large wood pole. He was ornery and wore his safety helmet cocked to the side. His mouth was slightly slack, as if he'd just finished saying 'don't you take my pitcher, you sonuvabitch.'

"Wuddn't *his* recipe, a course. It was past down gen'ration to gen'ration, as these things are. I trace't it far back as some Cajun stock on my great-grandmother's side. The *Delamberts* outta Shreveport."

His French was impeccable and caught Billy off guard. "In a nutshell, though, Daddy was a cook-off man. Worked for the pow'r comp'ny. It was just about the only time he ever cook't, just so he could show off fur ever'body with his ribbons. Chili is a serious affair here, after all." He took his glasses off and wearily rubbed his temples. "He wore those bastards like a peacock would his feathers."

"You got the ribbons hung up somewhere 'round here?" Billy asked, looking across the rafters.

"No. They're out at Mount Carmel Cemetery, buried there with 'im."

Billy took a sip from his Royal Crown Cola. "It's an excellent recipe, Butt. Mr. Doyle was right to be proud. This might be the best *food* I've ever had, let alone chili." He began taking another drink but stopped with the can tilted at his lips. "And Javier's burger is damned good, too."

"Yeah, well, thanks, Billy. I 'preciate it. I knew from day one—I was practickly suckled on that there chili like a calf on teat—from day one, I knew that I had a *good product*." Butt lightly smashed his fist down. He lived for talking shop, clearly. "Daddy didn't *want* me going into makin' food (like a woman, he'd say). No siree. But, hell, it was *in my blood*. And you can't tell blood what to do. Even he knew that."

"So what'd he think? I mean, he must've been proud of seeing everything you got here?"

"Well, Billy..." he stopped to respect the sad strains of the slow song spilling out of the old jukebox. "That's the shit-end of the ol' corncob. Daddy past away some years ago, heart attack, rest his soul, and I was workin' for a cable comp'ny round here. Not a-tall happy with it. Over with Q-Zar, before they turned over to Q-Z-Western Cable Alliance. They're defunct now, a-course. Any-who, I was about to be promoted somewhat *significantly*, you might say, and I said, 'Nuh-huh.' I saw what that'd be like. Movin' my family to Fort Worth. Goin' to conventions all over the gotdamned place. Starin' at spreadsheets." Butt shook his head calmly. "That whole time I *knew*. This is what I always wanted to do. This here." He reached behind himself and gave the snake tank a light tap with his ring. "I took my savings, the li'l bit of money from Daddy's insurance policy, and I bought this spot. Used't have a part'ner, name of Dale *Cooder*, but he wanted more." He went into a whiny Dale Cooder voice. "Hire more people, Butt. Put more things on the menu. Kids like vi-duhya games, Butt. Where's our viduhya games at? We gotta get us some more tables, Butt. More tables mean more *bid*'niss." He stopped. "More locations. Franchises," he said in his normal Butt Doyle drawl. "More this, more that, more money, he'd say. I told him, 'Shit, go on an have fun without me.'"

Jorge came out from the kitchen and turned off the 'OPEN' sign in the front window. He was a tall, floating buzzcut, a buzzard-looking man right down to the pronounced nose and Adam's apple.

"Dale went on to start Chili Barn, which is fine. You might see 'em along the innerstate. Ain't got nothin' on that there meal you jes sat down to. Chili Barn chili tastes like a gotdamn baby's diaper, *a mon avis*. But, then agin, it must suit the tastes of some, as he's made hisself a small fortune."

"Yeah, well, nuts to him," Billy opined. He patted his gut. "This is up there, Butt. Like I said, one of the all-timers, in terms of dinner." He sopped up the last of his burnt umber puddles with a soggy piece of bun on the end of a fork and tried to swallow slow and deliberate, allowing the flavor to linger on.

Jorge sat down near Billy and lit a cigarette. He had half a bottle of Sol on the bar beside him.

"Hell, now that our business hours are up," Butt said, producing a partway-full fifth of Jim Beam from under the counter, "we may as well have a toast." He poured two generous belts of brown liquor into a pair of plastic pebbled Cambro tumblers normally used for water.

"There's three of us," Billy said.

"Jorge don't drink the good stuff," Butt said.

Jorge nodded once. "Good stuff don't make you sicker'n shit like dat shit dare does," he said.

Butt came out from behind the bar. He was bow-legged. And such thin legs, too! It looked as if his thin crescents struggled mightily to sustain such a full torso. He raised his cup high.

"To chili!" he shouted.

Jorge rolled his eyes and tilted back his Sol while the others swallowed bourbon and winced.

Billy started reaching for his wallet, but Butt Doyle said to hold it right there and that any stranger that stepped into his parlor and picked out a Doug Sahm tune on the juke didn't owe him a thing. Billy made another minute movement towards his left pocket.

"Son, you pull that wallet out and you're gonna get a size ten snake skin Tony Lama right square in the ass."

"You know," Billy said with a smile, "that's the second time I heard that threat of late."

Billy's phone buzzed while he sat and enjoyed Butt Doyle's chili and stories. His phone was in the van. Kurt was trying to get ahold of his friend. Again and again, he'd called. There were six missed calls on Billy's phone when he got back inside the van.

"Hello?" Kurt said faintly.

"Kurt. What's up, man. I see you—"

"Jacob got busted."

"What? Wait, whawhawhawhawhaddyamean 'busted'?"

"Okay, so yesterday at work, I see Jacob sometime after lunch, walking around the building, doing his hot-shot thing, and then later, when I'm on my break, I see him getting loaded into a cop car back behind the museum. In the back lot where you can look at the Water Works— "

"What'd he get arrested for?"

"Well, that's the thing," Kurt exhaled and coughed away from the phone. His voice was now noticeably weaker. "People at work say they can't talk about it for HR reasons or whatever but they're just losing their minds trying to cover it all up before it goes public. Not that anyone cares about the museum that much. So all I know is the gossip I hear."

"Tell me the gossip, Kurt. This could get *real* quick."

"I know! That's why I—"

"I'm talkin' *drive down to Mexico* real, Kurt. I'm in Texas. I can be there by sunrise."

This thought secretly charged Billy.

"I know! I know, dude. *I know*," he whispered the last part. "Okay, so, I heard that a) it's something to do with drugs or b) something to do with selling illegal shit. Cuz, you know, there's, like, laws against selling priceless things and cultural treasures. There's also laws against selling drugs, as we all know. These are both pure speculation, though. Just people guessing based on what sort of asshole they think of him as. Some are saying drugs, others think he's into some Carmen San Diego shit." Kurt stopped and crunched loudly on something.

"Are you eating some crackers or something, dude?" Billy demanded.

The snacking stopped. "Pretzels."

"Kurt," he said like a disappointed parent, "can you be serious here for a second?"

"Just because I'm eating pretzels doesn't mean I'm not serious, dude." He popped another one in his mouth to prove a point. "I'm tryna help you out here."

Billy took a deep breath. "You're right. I'm sorry I snapped at you like that. Just tell me what you think is going on."

"I understand, man. Shit's stressful. But *you* need to see from my perspective…For instance, how *weird* this is. Jacob's kind of a boss of mine that got arrested. At work. At the fucking museum. I'm trying to wrap *my* head around it still myself. But, personally...I think it's drugs, because it was just the Philly police that came and got him and not, you know, INTERPOL or something."

There was a long conflation of groaning and exhalation.

"Okay. Okay. Let's go through this together."

"All right," Kurt consented.

"So, the goods—God, it *does* sound like contraband, doesn't it?—the *things* I delivered. Before I left PA, my Spidey Sense wigged out and I checked in a box that was going to Santa Fe. Because I thought this might happen. *I fucking knew this would happen.* I—"

"Was there anything in it?"

"Little jade bottles, uh...some round ivory boxes. Everything was empty, though. I dropped that shit off, no problem, and the guy who got it seemed pretty clean."

Several thoughts burst into Billy's mind like a cloud of spooked birds taking off from a tree.

Larry seemed pretty clean...except for his constant chattering and over-excitability; obsessing over stereo equipment and audio fidelity; facility for boozing heavily and maintaining a generally upbeat, energetic disposition; his gaunt features; maniacally throwing money around and hosting lavish parties; the complaints that his life was in a rut, that he missed the chemical high of youth...

"Okay, and then what? Did you check the other boxes?"

"I mean, Larry, in Santa Fe, he was cool as hell, man, and super nice. He reminded me of you, you know, of guys like us. You don't think I dropped him off drugs, do you?"

"Hard to say, Billy. I didn't meet the guy," Kurt said. "If he reminds you of us, then, yeah, he probably dabbles in *some* drugs, right?"

"I know, but. Fuck. I checked his stuff out, like I said, and didn't see anything. Didn't see him *doing* anything. So, worst case," he reasoned (completely for himself), "Larry bought some historic valuables. Okay. He's a weird guy, but he's got money so it's no big deal. He's eccentric."

"What else?"

"Then today I dropped off a box or two and some rugs in Nowhere, West Texas and nobody was home."

"So that could've been anything."

"Yeah, I didn't look into that. Unloading it, they seemed like some ordinary, old Chinese textiles. Can you leave fingerprints behind on a rug?"

Kurt considered it. "Nah, man. Trace fibers, though. Stray hairs."

"Damn. We'll just have to risk it. I'm hours away from there. Hopefully some marauders ran off with 'em."

"There're marauders out there?" Kurt asked excitedly.

"I'm sure as hell hoping so. Then tomorrow I've got Mississippi, which is just rugs. No more boxes." He turned to the load in the back. "I'll take care of those, no problem."

They put their heads together a few minutes longer and came up with a plan, which was not much more than common sense: dump the rugs just about anywhere and drive home, wiping off the prints before parking the van near a subway station. Then come home and deposit the insurance check.

"Oh, by the way, you got another postcard from Lucy."

"What of?"

"A manatee. It says 'Chill Out.'"

"Hm. Timely. That's a good sign, though, dontcha think? What'd she say on the back?"

There was no hesitation this time. "Hold on, one sec." Then Kurt read: "Dear *BeeBee.*"

"A nickname. Continue."

"I never heard anyone call you BeeBee before."

"Well, no. That's more of a *pet* name, I guess."

Kurt paused. "Can *I* call you BeeBee?"

"... No, I don't like that, the way it sounds when a guy says it."

"Oh. Okay." He bit into a pretzel. "So, it says, "Dear BeeBee, Florida is nice (obvi) and people are buying my wares. I am on the beach almost all day. My skin is much tanner. I traded some shells with a clairvoyant who told me that my true love's name started with a 'W' and would turn up soon. Eerie, isn't it, William? Love, Lucy.'" He paused. "That's pretty sweet."

"Yeah, it is, isn't it? I just talked to her today. She left out the part about the psychic, though. Anyways, I'm probably a few days away. I'm in Texas, after all."

"How's Texas?"

"Fine. Big. Kinda dull. Another eight or so hours of it. Ate some good chili, though."

"Cool."

"Yeah. So, keep me posted about, um, the criminal activities. If there's any revelations."

"Of course, man." Kurt sounded remorseful. "Dude, I'm so sorry I got you into this mess, Billy."

"No, don't apologize, whatever you do. It's a fine sort of mess."

Driving east and deeper into the inky night, Billy analyzed the situation. He was cool and level-headed—perhaps too much so—and he kept his focus steely despite the odd chili-induced gurgling.

As it stood, Jacob did not have Billy's phone number or last name or place of residence. Kurt was the only link, and he was hardly a snitch. If anything, he'd want to take the frat boy dandy down.

It was unlikely, too, that Larry was receiving drugs. If he had been he probably would have offered Billy some. No, it seemed more plausible that Larry was buying some black market stuff, if that. And then who's to say that he even knew what he was buying was dirty? He'd call and ask, but he didn't have Larry's number somehow and only had the address.

Like he and Kurt concluded, the only other thing Billy needed to deal with presently was abandoning these two rugs going to Mississippi, which he would do as soon as he reached an adequately obscure dirt road or emergency truck pull-off. The latter presented itself around ten o'clock at night, not too many miles off of I-20, where the stars at night were big and bright.

Billy was deep in the heart of Texas. He could see the rugs outside without the aid of a flashlight.

He looked around over his shoulders many times and unfurled the first one. He knew he should just plonk the two of them down here and safely drive off, but that seemed too dull an ending. He rolled the first rug out with a push of the shoe. It was heavy and large enough to tie together a room the size of a tennis court. Its contents were clean. Just a flat old thing worth a lot of money. Billy took a picture with the disposable camera, thinking how the people in Marfa would like this statement. The flash made his head spin for a second.

He unloaded the smaller second rug and tossed it out on top of the first. It bounced once and went off into the dark a few feet further like an elaborately-patterned tidal wave. As it snapped all the way out, an object about the size of a regulation football popped out. After a brisk twirl, a frenzied double-check of the dusky panorama, Billy loped over towards the dark item near the corner of the rug. He left dusty shoeprints behind him. He got on his haunches and picked up a vacuum-sealed bag. It was warped and wrinkled. He held it to his nose but it had no smell to it. Billy lifted the thing up like a lunar offering but couldn't make out what it was. The cellophane shined brightly.

Back in the van, under the dome light, it was

clearly marijuana. It was a volume he was unaccustomed to and it looked to be quality stuff.

"Well, I'll be," Billy said.

Before he could decide what he'd be, which actions he'd take next, or even how to feel about his discovery, Billy saw two unsteady, dim lights in the rearview mirror. They were headed straight towards him, and quickly. He stuffed the contraband under the passenger seat and tripped out of the van, tangled up, ironically, by the safety belt. He spat dry, soft dust from his mouth and pulled himself up from the dirt and scrub brush.

The lights were closer. High, whining engines. Dirt bikes, by the sound of it.

He lunged towards the rugs and, from his knees, unsquarely laid them out on top of one another. He began frantically rolling them up together as one. His hands reached underneath them and the fine reddish dirt sifted through his fingers and got under his nails.

The headlights and the shadows were near enough to have a shape. They were low and square. They were all-terrain vehicles, two of them.

Billy took a deep breath and stood up. He lifted with his knees and not his back. He shoved one end of the rugs into the back of the van, then lifted and slid. He kicked the door shut. The light was brighter as the engines slowed. Billy looked one last time at the hazy figures. A tall one and a smaller one. He quickly turned his back to the ATVs and unzipped his pants.

The two vehicles decelerated when they saw

a man peeing near his van. In places such as this, relieving oneself in the out-of-doors was a man's right—and it needed to be respected with the utmost care. Billy hoped they would continue on their way, too busy to stop and chit-chat, but they came to a stop fifteen or so feet away and killed their engines as he shook and adjusted. The van's taillights shined like devil eyes. Billy pulled his fly up and cautiously turned around.

The shadows before him had rifles slung across both of their backs. Two silhouettes in boot cut jeans and hunting jackets dismounted. The ATVs were white, neon green, and neon blue. One man was older, six-foot-two and about 200 pounds worth of yeomanry. The younger one was half-a-foot shorter and fifty pounds lighter with more than a few years left to grow. They stood for a moment and spat to their right at the exact same time. Finally the taller one stuck the rifle butt into his hip. The gun barrel aimed right for Sirius.

"You need some help there, fella?" The man's face had a varnish of dark stubble and eyes so small and deep-set that they were only shadowy empty sockets from where Billy stood.

"No sir, I'm fine, just fine. Just hittin' the head, so to speak."

"Hey, Travis," he said behind him without turning from Billy. The pair of headlights beamed out for hundreds of empty yards. The kicked up dust billowed past the light and faded off into oblivion. "Wouldya look at that." He laughed a bit to himself. "You know who'd get a kick outta that?"

"No, sir," Travis said.

"Your Uncle Wyatt." He finally turned back to Travis. "He dragged me to see them back afore you were born. Brought his first wife, ol' what's her name. Darlene. You never met her. Shoot. That was the faggiest bunch I ever did see, with that little Barbie doll of a singer. You know who he looked like?"

"No, sir," Travis said.

"He 'bout favored your Grandma Beth, your mamma's mamma, with his little spandex tights and fruity shirts and that frizzy ol' blond hair." He cupped his hands six inches from each ear to illustrate how much hair he was talking about.

Travis chuckled.

"What in the hell was that sumbitch's name, Daryl Roy Lee or somethin'?"

"David Lee Roth," Billy ventured, trying to humanize himself before the gunmen.

"Yeah, Roth, that's the one. You figure him to be He-brew?" the man asked Billy.

"Maybe."

"Yup. And the guitar player, too," the man went on, "he was purty good, too. But he had a guitar done up the same way," he nudged his rifle towards the van and then looked at Billy. "Van Halen. *Runnin' with the devil*," he sang softly, almost under his breath. He shook his head like a daydreamer coming back to reality. "Ah, hell, I'm sorry, bud, we don't mean to scare ya or nothing. We ain't Mexican or drug banditos or nothin' like that. Just me and my boy out huntin' nutria. Varmints. Say 'hi,' Travis."

"Hi Travis," he sneered.

"Oh, okay," Billy exhaled. He patted the dust of the front of his shirt. Had he not come up with that bit of ingeniousness earlier, he would have surely pissed himself by now. "Hey, Travis, how's it going. Listen: I was just, hearing this funny noise in the back, and, well, I pulled off the road and, sure enough, next thing ya know: I gotta whiz."

They spat in the dirt again. "Uh-huh," the older one said. He leaned forward without moving his boots. "What're those, Chicago plates?"

"No, PA. I mean, Pennsylvania."

Billy tried to swallow what little spit there was in his dry mouth.

"Shee-it, that's a ways away now ain't it?" He reached a crooked finger in his lower lip and hooked out a wad of used chew. He flung it off into the night. "Well, then, we ain't ezzackly supposed to be out here shootin' these danged rats. You need a hand with anything?"

"No, sir, I think I got it, thanks."

"Alright then. You take care now. Go on and stay outta trouble."

"Will do. See you later, guys. Later, Travis."

They turned their motors on at the same time and Billy inched towards the driver's side door. He stopped to bend down and gauge his tire pressure while waiting for the sound of ATVs to fade away.

"Damn," Billy said from inside the van. He could smell the telltale pot beneath his seat. He started the engine. "I need a hotel tonight."

13

Billy loaded his Styrofoam plate up with a pair of perforated plain bagels, two servings of fancy cream cheese, a spatula of scrambled eggs, four glistening breakfast links, and, for auld lang syne, a Nutri-Taste Flapjax 'Sploder. There was no room left on the plate so Billy sprinkled red grapes and colorless cubes of honeydew on top of it all. He filled a cup with scalding coffee hot and added an entire individually-sealed ramekin of half-and-half. He didn't have time to let black coffee cool.

The AM clerk at the Dagwood Motor Inn of Kilgore, TX shook her head disapprovingly at this guest's flagrant gluttony. While others ate sensible portions, the breakfast sandwiches he constructed were towering. They tilted to the side. They were abominations. That boy was the spitting image of Wimpy. And the AM clerk never found Wimpy's high jinks the least bit amusing. She'd encountered actual people like that, folks that promised to pay you for Monday's hamburger on Tuesday, and she despised them.

She watched Billy closely, making certain that the miscreant didn't try and walk out of the Dagwood with his pockets full of complimentary donut holes and napkin-wrapped bacon strips. Billy paid her no mind, though. He'd read the foot-high fine print on the marquee out front:

FREE CONTINENTAL BREAKFAST WITH ROOM

No asterisk hung on the guarantee. Billy was going to get his money's worth. He'd already slept deeply on a lumpy bed and let the HBO play on all through the night. He'd already taken a long, steamy shower and used enough packets of shampoo and conditioner for two. Billy already rubbed the complete contents of a small, nameless bottle of lotion all over his body. And now he prepared to go back and top off with a bowl of generic bran flakes with raisins and 2% milk.

Billy was officially playing by his own rules and part of that meant not waiting thirty minutes before diving into the Dagwood's pool. So immediately following his hearty morning meal, Billy went back to his room and stripped down to his boxer-briefs. He slipped into his complimentary cotton-terry robe and walked out towards the heart of the Motor Inn.

Swimming hours were noon-to-dusk, seasonally. It was 9:45 a.m. and maybe not even the right season. The hair on Billy's legs stood at attention. Cars raced by on a busy two-lane that ran parallel with I-20, separated by a long chain-link boundary. A teal Miata shaped like a lady's shaver zipped by and jeeringly leaned on the horn.

In his dirty sneakers and robe, Billy coldly watched the car drive on. He squinted to get a better look at it. He made sure to note the plate number, as if he would someday exact revenge.

"Texas G7RP39," he said icily.

A chilly wind blew an old circular against his bare calf. He kicked about fruitlessly, undoing his cloth belt. Billy bent over and plucked the Autozone ad off his leg. He crumpled the paper into a ball, cinched his robe up, and trudged back into the lobby of the Dagwood. He had fifteen more minutes of breakfast bar privileges. He snagged two bananas and ate half a corn muffin before being asked to leave.

After the night at the Dagwood and two more stops for gas, Billy had $358 of Jacob money left and $145 remaining in Larry money. He kept these sums separate and in entirely different pockets. He wondered which account he'd dip into when he made his next move.

Billy bought a black Bic lighter with a cobra on it and then stood outside the convenience store in Jackson. He went to the pay phone and picked up the Yellow Pages. The book was in a durable casing and safely tethered to the phone by a two-foot length of steel-reinforced cable. People would still walk off with phone books if you gave them the opportunity.

It was easy enough to find 'C' and then 'Clothes.' But there were too many options (and of those, many seemed to cater exclusively to women). He flipped all the way to 'S', but none of the places offering suits seemed to fit what he was after. He wanted to find something with panache: all the establishments he saw listed under 'SUITS, MEN'S' had words like 'Depot' and 'Stable' in their name. He thought hard about it. Then he turned to the 'H's.

There was one haberdasher listed in the Jackson Directory and that was Alonzo's. Billy drove the van there forthwith. The building was dumpy, even by deep south standards. He worried it was out of business. Alonzo's was operating, though, and it reeked like mothballs inside. Natural light was blocked out by a translucent black UV-blocking film on the windows. The shop's mirrors were coated with residue that couldn't be cleaned off. The plastic casing around the fluorescents was at least thirty-five years old and buttery as a long-time smoker's teeth. Every reflection in the store looked like an old Polaroid.

Billy strolled through the aisles with a goal but sans plan, like when he'd searched for Easter Eggs years ago. His suit was in here somewhere. The cosmos had tucked away the right clothes for him inside of Alonzo's.

"Can I help yuh, young man?"

The salesman was on the other side of a rack of blazers. He was a portly man whose smooth, dark skin masked what must've been considerable age. His mustache was immaculately thin, straight, and gray. He came around to Billy's side. He had flowing khakis and a lavender cashmere V-neck sweater with a matching Kangol. He had small, rectangular shades. His shoes were of a lustrously-polished reptile skin and pointy as a pair of daggers. The guy looked cool, like a conga player in a late night talk show band. Billy right away trusted his sartorial acumen.

"Yeah, I'm looking for a suit. Something that says 'power.'"

"Suit that says *powuh*," the salesman echoed. "We got that. In a couple-uh varieties. So what *kind*a powuh you lookin' fuh?" The salesman already was dexterously running his hands through the hangers like a senior bureaucrat blazing through a cabinet of hanging folders. He pulled something out then wagged his head dissatisfied. "You mean ass-kickin' powuh? Get the baddest women powuh? Man-uh-gawd powuh? Cuz we got 'em all."

Billy weighed the options. "Sort of a combination of those first two," he said. "Something that's got toughness and finesse. Looks expensive but doesn't cost too much."

"Hunh. That's the numbuh one sellah right there." He cracked a smile. "Tell me: whattaya mean by 'too much'?" He began idly looking around at the walls.

"… Three-hundred," Billy said, not entirely remembering that, after the lighter, he had only $501 to stretch all the way to Philadelphia, PA.

"Sh-yooot, that kinda money? A young man like yuhself can dress *propuh*." He led the way. "Kick-a-ass, get the *baddest* of the bad women, *and* have a few dolluhs to spen' on her."

The first sampling of what the salesman offered was not at all what Billy envisioned. In fact, most of the suits he was shown *were* of a man-of-God cut. And not a trim, dark, functional metropolitan priest sort, but more of an ostentatious, double-breasted, silk pocket-square preacher variety.

The next options were not much different than the previous save the non-traditional lapels and collars. They all had a vaguely futuristic look that was at the same time right at home with an early '90s R&B group.

The two of them went through Alonzo's for

thirty minutes until all that was left was formal wear, cummerbunded prom getups and ensembles for jazzier groomsmen.

"What about over here?"

"Boy," the salesman rolled his tongue along the inside of his lower lip, "why in the hell you innuh hurry to buy uh tuxeduh or uh outfit like that? Eithuh you plannin' on getting' hitched befoe her daddy finds out or you a James Bond muthafuckuh." He smiled. Then a lightbulb practically blinked on over his cap. "'Cept now… hold onna minute… maybe… *maybe.*"

Billy was tired of driving aimlessly around Oxford. If he could avoid buying gas again today, he would. He didn't like being out and about in the Mississippi damp in his fresh garb. He had to be careful not to disturb the pins that held his cuffs back. Nearing his destination, Billy delicately pressed on gas and break with his stiff tobacco wing tip, making certain not to scuff his tony new shoes or undo his precarious thirty-four-inch inseam.

The suit Billy bought from Alonzo's at a steep discount had been special-ordered last May for a local high-school student's senior prom. The young man played varsity basketball and, at the last moment, left Jackson before the big formal to take a week-long West Coast swing, visiting several colleges that were offering him scholarships.

The then eighteen-year-old had the same-sized shoulders and waist as Billy, but was six-foot-nine.

"He's fillin' out, though, over at San Diego State," the salesman said. "An' he gon' need-ta bulk up *more* if he wantsta ball with them real men."

As long as those pins held it together, so would Billy. He looked sharp. Once he got it hemmed, the $277 he spent on the suit would be a memorable steal. This was an investment. Should someone die or get married, Billy was at last prepared to show up in style.

The neighborhood he drove into at 6:30 in the evening was green and well-shaded. It had been a bright and soft-clouded spring day. Billy hoped to execute his plan during an unsettling dusk and was somewhat satisfied that not much sun came through these oaks. It was a better option than killing time for another hour. He'd already seen Faulkner's house and his grave. Beyond that, Oxford was a college town, which always put him on edge.

The van rolled to a stop. Kurt called.

"Yo, Billy," he said. "Sorry I missed your call. Didn't check your message, man, 'cuz I got some news for *you*."

"What's that?" Billy unfastened his seat belt.

"Let me read to you from the *River Ward Times-Gazette*." Kurt cleared his throat. "Wait. Let me *first* start by saying that today, at work this morning, when you called, an announcement was made concerning Jacob."

"Go on."

"He was fired."

Billy waited and was *about to say* something profane in reaction to the obviousness of the statement but Kurt elaborated in time.

"Drugs. Narcotics distribution. Nothing to do with antiquities that fell off the truck. So you're off the hook for any UNESCO war crimes or anything."

"That's a bit of a relief, but I have some news of my own, pally."

"Shit," Kurt said. "Who goes first?"

"Uh…" Billy scratched his head. That motel shampoo and conditioner, in collusion with the humidity, was making his hair do things he'd never seen before. "G'head."

"K, then. As I was saying. As I was about to say. From the *River Ward Times-Gazette*, as reported by A.J. Primo. 'Prison for pot farmer.' That's the main headline in bold. Then below that in smaller italics it says, 'Kensington man arrested with quarter-ton of pot gets up to eight years.'"

"That's all you get for having 500 pounds of weed?"

"Welcome to Obama's America, bro."

Billy laughed for a second but then felt confused. "Wait. Jacob lived in Kensington? That doesn't seem—"

"Ah-ah-ah," Kurt said, likely wagging a finger on the other end of the line. "Allow me to continue." He read. "'The overwhelming aroma of laundry detergent and Febreeze spray coming out of a Kensington Avenue apartment last week was supposed to hide the smell of hundreds of fully-grown marijuana plants growing inside. It didn't work, though, as police officer Luke Dom*brow*ski noticed the recognizable odor while reporting to the scene of a burglary nearby. Now Kensington's Old *Pot*-Donald'—"

They each groaned.

"It's supposed to be a pun on Old McDonald," Kurt explained.

"Yeah, I know. That's *terrible*."

"Agreed." Kurt resumed. "Now Kensington's Old Pot-Donald, fifty-one-year-old…*Dack Kee-En En-Guy-Uhn* could be spending the next five to eight years behind bars.' Blah blah blah, it goes on, charged with risking catastrophe, outlets full of plugs, lamps and lights everywhere, father of four. Let's see. 350 big plants, 175 incubating ones, so on and so forth, dryer sheets, woah. 'One plant seized was over *five-and-a-half-feet tall!*'" Kurt laughed. "Far out."

"Right. Hey, Kurt: what was the guy's name?"

"*Dack Kee-En En-Guy-Uhn*," he repeated.

"Is that spelled all Vietnamese-like?"

"*Oh right*," Kurt said, "En-guy-uhn. I knew I'd seen that somewhere. That's the name of the grocery store in South Philly where I got those—"

"Fuck," Billy said. "Kurt! Kurt!"

"Yeah? Billy?"

"That's the motherfucker that owns this van, man! Dac Kien Nguyen, that's the fucking *name on the title*!" In desperate need of any degree of calm, he inhaled deeply. He perceived the skunky funk of the weed beneath his seat. "Fuck."

"No shit! No fucking way! See, what I wanted to tell you was…" Billy listened to the sound of paper being shuffled. Kurt read. "'In an attempt to lessen the severity of his charges, En-guy-uhn is purport-edly seeking a plea agreement with the district attorney. Sources say he is cooperative and willing to offer up names of those he wholesaled the narcotics to in the Delaware Valley.'" Billy heard Kurt put the paper down. "So, basically, dude, I don't think it's *coincidence* that this guy—"

"His name's on the title."

"Exactly. I don't think it's *coincidence* that—"

"I found a bunch of weed in one of the rugs last night."

Kurt paused.

"I mean. Sweet. But. Damn." He laughed. "Now what?"

"I dunno." It sounded honest. Billy closed his eyes and saw nothing. His mind was a blank. He opened them and looked into the rearview. "Hey," he began, "remember last week before I left, when we added up the mileage and stuff?"

"Unh-huh."

"Before we watched *The Running Man*?"

"I don't remember *that*, but I recall working out your gas and mileage, yeah."

"You fell asleep," Billy said, "but, more importantly, remember how we found out that Oxford, Mississippi was *exactly* halfway between Santa Fe and Philadelphia?"

Kurt took his time saying anything. "Yeah," he said unsurely, "that sounds familiar."

"I dunno," Billy said again, casual. "Just kinda crossed my mind again. I feel like I've already been way past halfway…but here I am, in Oxford, just the same. Anyways, I'll take care of this and be back." Billy patted down his hair with his free hand.

"Eventually." He smiled at himself in the mirror. "As long as I go the speed limit and use my turn signal, I'll be fine."

"Sure," Kurt said, sounding eased by his friend's confidence. "Fucking *Godspeed*, man."

"Thanks, Kurt." Billy pressed the little red button on the right side of his beat-up phone, ending the conversation. He closed his phone and his eyes and reclined the captain's seat back all the way. He put his hands behind his head and steadied himself with the knowledge that his name was minimally attached to anything. The cop that took a picture of the van in Kansas had even politely asked him to step out of the frame. He'd be alright. He still had options. The word Florida materialized in round-edged orange letters. $50,000 in the Sunshine State. He thought about retirement, never working another day in his life.

The lighting was perfect: the sky was a strange mix of dark colors like a large, slow-healing bruise. A portentous storm rode in from the West. Billy took deliberate, automaton steps up the walkway, mindful of the temporary hem-job. He stopped in front of the house and adjusted his lapels.

A man answered the knock at his door. His brown-black hair was curly and didn't provide much scalp coverage these days. He had the sensitive countenance of a poet and wore a distressed green rugby shirt with faded numbers above the breast. His face unmanned briefly in front of the stranger before shifting into genteel confusion.

"Yes, can I help you?" he asked in a librarian's voice.

"Yes, hello, may I please speak with Andrew Ebert?"

"*I'm* Andy."

"Mr. Ebert, I'm Agent Perkins with the Drug Enforcement Agency, Narcotics Unit. May I come in?"

All color was wrung from his face. "Certainly. Please. Right this way." He stepped aside and Billy strode into the foyer swiftly, like a shark. Andy slowly shut the door, taking time to notice the bizarre van parked across the street.

The living room would not be a suitable place for the interrogation—it appeared to be too comfortable, with ottomans and pillows and lamps offering warm lighting. Best to head into the kitchen. Billy marched ahead, sensing right where it would be.

The smell of toasted rye pervaded the room. It was a place full of windows and the countertops were of solid granite. The floor was clean and well swept, a rouge honeycomb of fine-glazed Mexican tile. A hanging plant floated manicured and healthy in a sunny corner. Billy saw the chromed toaster, two dark surfboards of bread poking out. He took note of the French butter bell crock beside a saucer. An oar-shaped butter knife rested on top of a folded-over paper towel. Ebert ran a tight ship full of nice things.

"Would you like a glass of water?"

"No thank you," Billy civilly declined. "Am I interrupting your snack-time?"

Andy turned back towards the toast. "Oh, that?"

He brushed it off with a curt shoulder-raise.

"Very well then," Billy said. "Please. Have a seat. I'd like to get down to business and not keep you much longer. If possible."

There were dark wood benches and a table built into a sort of nook that they slid into, across from one another. Andy nervously put his hands together on the table like Dürer's oft-tattooed set in prayer and uneasily began rubbing his palms together. Then he put them on his thighs for a moment before resting his hands flat and in plain sight on the table. Billy let him fidget. He deigned not to speak until three seconds of eye contact were sustained.

"Agent…"

On cue came a thunderous rumble. Andy looked out the window and then at the table top.

"Perkins," Billy said. Andy looked up at him. *One-Mississippi, two-Mississippi, three-Mississippi.* "Mr. Ebert, do you know Jacob…"

"Jacob… no. I mean, maybe. Jacob who?"

… "Uh, well. A *certain* Jacob…" He'd momentarily forgot his last name. "Jeffries! Jacob Jeffries, that's right. Name ring a bell?"

"I've heard a lot of names."

"That right?" Billy asked.

"Sure."

"So you're popular?" Billy guessed out loud. "You can't keep track of who's who, can't even recall the name Jacob Jefferies?"

"Well, no, I." Andy hesitated. He wavered. He waffled. He plainly made the wrong play, trying to act tough with Agent Perkins. "I'm a grad student," he quietly confessed. "American Studies."

"American Studies?" Billy moved his head up and down thoughtfully. "That's interesting. Vague," he sucked his cheeks in. "Sounds... *broad*. But I'm sure it's interesting, too."

An important part of Billy's plan was subtle, biting bits of belittlement, and it was working: Andy sat on the bench, plainly frightened into a state of immobility.

"But, see, based on the information we got on you, I woulda guessed maybe you were a student of *Eastern* History." He looked square at Andy. "You catch my drift?"

He shook his head fast and made a nervous, agitated sound.

"I figured a man so interested in *Chinese* rugs wouldn't be an American Studies major."

"What's that supposed to mean?"

"Cut the crap," Billy said. "We both know about the rugs, now admit it." He stopped short. He could feel himself slipping into an unconvincing, straight-to-video portrayal of Eliot Ness.

Andy looked down to his left and then back at stern, confident Billy.

"The rugs. Yes."

"Right. And now I'm here to talk about Jacob." He watched the hands across the table from him. They were clenched into puny fists drained of blood and pale. "You are aware, Mr. Ebert, that, inside of these rugs, there may or may not have been controlled substances? Illegal contraband?"

"Well, now that I—"

"Either way, Mr. Ebert, these rugs were addressed to you, being couriered to you."

"Right, but I—"

"Regardless, you're looking at accessory to drug trafficking. And if this is, indeed, the case—which we have good reason to suspect—and these controlled substances are, in fact, traced back to the Lombardo Crime Syndicate—which is under Federal investigation, then ..."

They stared at one another for a moment. Andy bit his lower lip. It looked like blood might come gushing out. He looked down at the floor and scratched his eyebrow.

"Can I, uh, see your badge?" he said when he raised his head back up.

"See my badge?"

Billy moved his head closer to Andy and widened his eyes. He stared Andy down like an owl tracking a field mouse. His heart sped up. Rain began to make contact with the roof and windows. Billy let the suspenseful drops drip. The torturous small patter seemed ready to break into deluge at any moment.

"Sure, Andy," he said affably.

Billy offered up a great unnerving grin and didn't change his expression until Andy did likewise. When he did make a barely perceptible movement towards smiling, Billy's mouth quickly went level.

"I left my badge in the car. You ready to take a ride with me? Then you can see my badge, my handcuffs, my, uh, radio scanner, the works. That whatchu want?"

Andy suddenly burst into tears and was soon childishly hyperventilating. "No! A-*huhhuh-huh*...Jake...a-*huhuhhuh*...Jake said...a-*huhuh-huh*...that—"

"Hold your horses," Billy cut him off. "Now listen. Get yourself together. Nut up, Andrew. Off the record, it's not you we're after. This is, frankly, some piddling shit. A few ounces of dope." He broke wind using his tongue. "Barry Obama *personally* told me enough with the small-time grab-ass. 'No more Mickey Mouse bullshit, Perkins.' His exact words."

Billy let the fact that Agent Perkins was tight with POTUS sink in. He smiled. *Friends in high places, bitch*, he telepathically told Andy.

The rain fell harder.

"It's Jacob we're after. He's dirty and you know it. Yeah, we busted him (and that retired V.C. he was pallin' around with—oh yeah, we got Nguyen). We nabbed Jacob on a trumped-up narco charge, but that's just to get him in our sights, so to speak." Billy paused for effect. "Frankly, 'tween you'n'me...this shit's *global*."

Andy blew his nose into a paper napkin. "Jake?"

"That's right. You're little friend Jake's been playing Indiana Jones and gotten his ass involved not just in drugs but in the black market. And the worst one, too: the oriental one." Billy pushed the bench out to stand up. The screech it made against the tile gave Andy a jolt. "A man can get into big trouble dealing with these folks, Mr. Ebbet."

"Ebert."

Billy stood and inconspicuously turned his right

cuff back in on itself some. "To wit: the goddamn United Nations has a file on Jeffries. They nearly extradited him in Venice, and that wasn't even for the drugs. We're talkin' rhino horns, dried tiger dicks, ancient talismans outlawed by church and state alike." Billy paced over to the window and stared pontifically into the backyard. He saw the swimming pool. "Your boy's dirty. And once you figure the narcotics into the equation..." He puffed his cheeks out and softly blew. "Well. Then you're looking at involvement with the Triads, the Yakuza. The Crazy 88s, even. There's no telling where this leads to or how high it goes."

"You mean," he honked again into a fresh napkin, "like, the guys with swords that wore suits and Zorro masks? From *Kill Bill*? They're real?"

"Here's what's real, Andy: play along and we'll cut you a deal. It's a pretty *sweet* deal, too. Play dummy with us and, well, I've only *heard about* Mississippi's penal system, but..." Billy pulled out a folded-over sheet of wide-ruled paper with an edge still tattered from the spiral ring binding. "A guy like you is considered a delicacy in these parts. You got a pen?"

There was a pen on the table, next to some sudoku that Billy interrupted.

"You write down everything you know. *Everything*. About Jacob, these rugs, the dope inside, and we let you go." He flipped out and revealed the empty palms of his hands in a gesture of magic disappearance. "You help us put him away—we forget this ever happened."

The sound of Andy's tapping foot sped up and

he reluctantly reached for the paper and pen. "You want me to snitch on my friend?"

"Your *friend*, Mr. Ebbet? Your *friend?!*"

"Ebert."

"Your friend that's gonna land you down in Parchment Farm? Do I need to remind you that you live in the only state in the union that still dresses its prisoners up in striped outfits? The kind with the little brimless caps? You wanna sit here and tell me that your *friend* that already tried to pin this shit *on you* is worth tryna save?"

"Wait, what?"

He laughed disdainfully at Andy's genuine surprise and hurt. "That clown made like Pagliacci and started singing *quick* once we busted him with the dope. Claimed *you* were the mastermind, which we knew to be false. It was all rather sad. Pathetic, really."

Billy inspected his cuticles while secretly watching Andy deliberate. He took a long breath and began to write furiously. Agent Perkins leaned back with his arms crossed and his eyebrows arched a bit.

"There ya go."

Andy was really writing. The rain was letting up.

"Just stick to the essentials. We don't need all the fussy details."

He stopped, nodded in consent, and resumed at an unchanged rate.

"Names, dates, anything useful…hey, you mind if I take you up on that water?"

"No," Andy responded dryly. "Glasses are to your right."

The glass Billy selected was heavy and probably imported from Scandinavia. The sound of the pen scratching on the paper was audible from the sink. He drank a glass of water, then another, watching Andy flip the sheet over and scribble some more.

"This is a nice kitchen," he mumbled unnoticed.

He found himself distracted, aimlessly opening drawers an inch or two. He looked at the pool once more. Tiny splashes disturbed the surface and created small waves. An inflatable gator floated around.

"Alright, I think I'm done."

He handed the paper over to Billy and nervously watched him pretend to read through it.

"Uh-huh ... okay ... *of course* ... interesting. Well, Mr. Ebbet—"

"Ebert."

"My mistake. My old partner was Detective Ebbet. Mr. *Ebert*, I thank you for your time. There's one last thing, though, that I need from you. It's of the utmost importance."

He swallowed. "Alright. What's that?"

"In order for this plan to go off without a hitch, the DEA needs for your *complete* and *utter* silence on all issues relating to this case. Do you understand?"

Andy nodded but made a face signaling anything but comprehension.

"That means you are to sever all ties with Mr. Jeffries and not discuss word one with his lawyers, which, given the hairy situation he's put you in, shouldn't be hard."

"Right."

"You so much as *answer* a phone call or text from him and the deal is off. And, believe me, we *will* know. This proffer was authorized by a secret FICA court hearing held in international waters on an officially-unrecognized Navy cruiser. You did not meet me. There is no Agent Perkins. And as far as you're concerned, there is no Jacob Jeffries. You did not write this."

Billy folded the paper in half and put it in his breast pocket. One of his needles poked him in the side of the hand. "Ow, goddammit," he said under his breath. He checked to see if Andy noticed this flub, but he had his head firmly in his hand. "I assure you," Billy went on, "that if you follow through on this promise, you *won't* be hearing from us again." He stepped towards Andy to put a reassuring hand on his shoulder. That wing tip heel sounded good against the tile. "We appreciate everything you've done in assisting us here today."

"That's it, you're just going to leave me alone and go after Jacob now?" His voice quavered. "You're just gonna forget about me, right? I don't have to go to court?"

Billy snorted. "It's called a plea bargain. Welcome to America." He gave off a few pompous and brassy *ha-has* and started for the door.

"Excuse me, but …" Andy gave his nose another blast into a napkin. "Can I still get those rugs? They're, uh, legal."

Billy stood and considered the question for a second. "Probably not. I'm no lawyer, but I don't think even the Ninth Circuit Court of Appeals out in San Fran would find in *your* favor. Not that you should be taking this matter to the law, as per our agreement. So no rugs, no drugs, and no jail for you, *capice*?" He bent down and poked one of his loose trouser cuffs into his shoe. "Sound fair, Mr. Ebert?"

Andy rubbed his nose and sniffed. "Okay," he croaked.

"Have a good day then, sir, and thank you for your cooperation."

And Billy left, laughing some more on his way out to the van.

14

Billy did the math at an Alabama rest stop and deduced that he'd roll into Philadelphia on fumes if he rolled into Philadelphia at all. He had $164 left in his pockets, $19.69 in checking, $0.00 in savings, and enough change in his cup-holder to get another half-gallon of gas or so. The smart play would be driving to visit Lucy, where he could hang fire and maybe even patch things up while waiting for his check to be mailed, deposited, processed, and converted into something tangible.

Lucy lived in Palm Coast, south of St. Augustine. She had a dazzling yet unpretentious beach house that was actually on the beach. It was of a style that they'd stopped making after the war—a cottage with three simple rooms and a nice gas range. The place had a magic to it. It was lucky. While the neighbors came and went, Lucy's house and its front-yard palm tree had survived decades of hurricanes. The fact that the house was the rare kind still made out of wood kept the rent down.

On their first Floridian day together, Billy and Lucy sat on her couch and listened to Bruce Springsteen's *Nebraska*. The music was a curious and incongruous choice for a sandy, sunny reunion. But she put it on and sat next to him on her salvaged maroon couch.

"The corduroy's kinda pilling," she said, picking

at the arm. "But I needed a couch and the sign said 'Free'!" She turned to Billy and smiled proudly.

"It was meant to be," Billy said, patting the backrest. A button popped off.

It was as if they'd never been apart, like they were still taking their coffee at The Experimental Liberal Arts College Sem II cafe after class. Billy told stories about working with streetwise kids and living with seven people. He said both experiences had greatly matured him. Then he segued into driving out West and how he ended up in Palm Coast which forced him to back-track into exploring what he evasively described as his "upcoming endowment." While Lucy talked about seashells, she let Billy stroke her exposed arm and his finger was like a feather. And when he began to kiss her up and down that arm, his lips were like feathers, too. Catching up was easy.

For the better part of four days, Lucy sold no seashells and stayed busy with Billy. The two of them went at it like jackrabbits, like it was going out of style. They made up for lost time and went for each other's bodies madly, repeatedly, relentlessly. Together they pantingly tried to absolve trespasses and purify one another in much the same way a dusty rug is cleaned.

At the end of the first night together, Lucy halfway confessed. "Devin never… *you know*." Her face was coy and flush. "We never did much, basically," Lucy said while they were laying in bed naked together.

"Yeah, well," Billy's voice tailed off. He swirled his middle finger around her belly button. "That girl Angela I told you about … we never did much, either. Like, we …" Lucy giggled. He quit twiddling his finger. "I couldn't bring myself to do anything. I missed you too much."

And for the next hundred hours they kept returning to physically loving one another, like listening on repeat to a song whose wordless sha-la-la chorus becomes so entrenched in your head that it seems like the only music you'd ever want to hear again. They'd repose beautiful and languorous wherever they happened to finish (a bed, the bathroom floor, the back porch facing the Atlantic) and they wouldn't say a thing afterwards. Billy tended to be the first to eventually get up and make something to eat.

His appetite was insatiable and Florida was proving bountiful.

A week into his stay at Palm Coast, the insurance check arrived. He and Lucy stared on opposite sides of the yellow Formica table in the kitchen and gazed reverently at the slip of paper between them.

"Pay to the order of William George," he read. "$50,000." He was spellbound.

"Oh, Billy," she said in a passionate *take-me-now* voice. "I'm so excited for you!"

"For *us*," he corrected.

Three days later, he was officially as wealthy as he might ever be and easily saw that, for the rest of his life, he'd simply keep a clean cottage, teach himself to cook elaborately, and romance Lucy. Somehow interest would do its magic and keep everything in this delicate ecosystem in perfect harmony. Save the odd natural disaster, nothing could make him want to leave the life he'd lucked into.

This, as they say, was the life.

Chinese rugs covered the worn floorboards next to their bed and in the living room. Every night the two of them got stoned on the top-shelf pot he'd brought and went for a dip in the warm saltwater. They each had a couple of designer bathing suits to choose from. The Rolls Royce of vaporizers sat on the coffee table and the specialized replacement bags were en route from Holland. That week Billy rode his first jet ski and ate his first conch fritter. He lived a life of absolute leisure and even bought a snorkel.

This sort of Rousseauian noble savagery went on for five weeks, until one day in May the news came: Lucy's great-grandmother had died of old age. She was hysterical. Billy privately thought it a hiccup in the scheme of things, a minor bump in their freshly-paved autobahn. He did his best to calm her, all the same. He knew her favorite comfort food to be chicken noodle soup and the night he bought her plane tickets back to New York he also surprised her with a bowl of restorative broth laden with thigh meat and egg noodles. He hoped that after the right meal she'd be in the mood for his affectionate touch once more.

Lucy lay in bed, torpidly tossing and turning on the new 1,000-thread count sheets. Billy brought the bowl in and placed it down on the nightstand. He tried to cradle her head on his lap but she refused. He face was puffy. He returned to the kitchen to get her salt and pepper.

"It's not right." She ambushed him as soon as he walked back in the room. "I wanted the kind in a can, the kind with long, stringy noodles, like my mom used to make. This is too chunky and thick and, and, *fancy*, it's too—" and she cut herself short and said sorry and ate the rest silently save some slurping, souping sounds.

After dinner they took an air mattress out onto the beach to look at stars together. The air was salty and the lights above were dim, dull, and most just barely visible—but, on the whole, it was a nice evening to go and gape at the universe (even if it was ill-lit). The waves lapped in that slow sempiternal rhythm while they lay there, comfortably obliged by the sixty-eight-degree dark surrounding them. They held hands on the mattress and stared up wordlessly, wondering what the other was thinking. Lucy nuzzled Billy on the neck. It wasn't long before they were at it again.

But this time was very different. Spooning with their shorts around their knees and his chest against her soft back was transcendental and soon enough not sex at all. In a breath Lucy asked for a baby and it all felt stronger, wilder. Crazier, for sure, but in a surging and good sort of way. Billy was omnipotent: he could make (and afford to bring) life into the world. It felt like fait accompli a minute or two later and they stayed as tangled as two possibly could be. Then, improbably, they did the whole thing over again identically, as if only to be certain.

Nobody talked afterwards. They woke up bare-assed on the beach before dawn while an old man shuffled twenty feet away with his metal detector scanning the sands.

Lucy went to the funeral and told Billy all about it afterwards over the phone. The service was dignified and she felt more at peace about losing her beloved great-grandmother.

"You know," she said, "I talked to Grandpa Alphonse and he really helped me to realize that ninety-eight years is a *long* time."

Her mom needed some more support, though, and Lucy said she was going to stay and console for a few days longer.

A week longer.

Billy mailed a check for the next month's Florida rent and paid Florida utilities. He'd sent Kurt $800 a while ago and said he'd be back eventually, just watch his stuff in the meantime. Without Lucy around, Billy knew nobody in Florida. He didn't want to try and make Florida friends. He smoked so much of the van stash that being straight was trippier than anything drugs could provide. Drinking got to where it didn't make him tired—it only made him sick. The weather was hot now. And being an older efficiency near the beach, the cottage only had a ceiling fan in the living room. It slowly circulated air and wobbled hazardously from the insubstantial popcorn ceiling. Billy took to sleeping on the couch even though it hurt his back, neck, and shoulders.

He called Lucy every day. She answered less frequently. More was going on in her life, (she was in New York City, after all), but when they talked, (sometimes for an hour or more), it was mostly chatter and weather and what they'd eaten up to that point in the day. Explanations and announcements never came up. After two-plus weeks since he'd seen her last, Billy finally demanded to know when she was coming back.

"I'm still not sure."

They played a variation on chicken for ten voiceless seconds. Billy lost.

"What about having a baby?"

"No, I don't think so. I don't think I can."

There was nothing final about what Lucy said but the very perceptible hint of sadness in her voice was the sound of the first string breaking. Granted, days and nights up to then had had a hesitant feeling, an about-to-fall feeling… but after talking to Lucy, Billy teetered alone on the couch all night, fearing the drop.

And when *she* called *him* the next day, early, the first thing Lucy said was that there was another whom she'd met, a man who had a serious, terminal problem with his lymph nodes. This man was her *soulmate*. Their time together was limited. She cared deeply about Billy but couldn't possibly leave her newfound love now, not even for an instant. She hoped Billy still wanted to be her friend.

It was a more precipitous drop than he'd imagined.

For the rest of the day every door swung open

the wrong way and every knob racked him in the balls. Every ray of sun burnt his pallid skin. Every seagull had his big head in its crosshairs.

Eighteen hours after Lucy's last phone call, he woke up on the floor of the cottage wearing nothing but a pair of $50 briefs and some unbuttoned jean shorts. Out of one open eye Billy saw a whiskey bottle three-fifths empty on the coffee table. Below the table the couture beach togs were sopping up some spill. Billy was still most definitely drunk. He'd perhaps been unconscious for an hour or two. It was early enough in the morning that he didn't find himself sweating. He was thankful for that and for still being buzzed.

Billy took the bottle to the beach and swigged half of what was left in it down. He plunged the wax-topped fifth into the sand and walked towards the ocean. The water was warmer than the air. He picked up part of a crab shell and flung it backhandedly into the water. A wave brought it right back to him. Billy burped. He groaned. He sat down in the surf and cried a second. He abruptly stopped. He burped again. Billy waited and hoped for the bubbly foam to tickle some small pleasure into the day. It didn't do much besides push the chunk of dead crab further up on him. He frisbeed the chipped carapace far to the left.

The water was not warm enough, after all. Sitting in it, Billy tried in vain to pee. He felt an ensuing rush of lucidity brought on by the strain and the whiskey. It gave him sudden, dumb ideas. Send an embarrassment of flowers. Hire a mariachi to croon beneath her window. Lease that empty spot in the strip mall down the way and open up a shell shop back here in Palm Coast. Billy laid flat on the wet, compacted sand and decided he'd finance a shell boutique. The water rushed over him and filled his nose with an unpleasant, burning brininess. He sat back up, coughing and sounding like a tubercular. From there, getting on his feet was no easy matter. He swayed back towards the house, plunging his heels deep into the sand for support. Halfway back, Billy realized that he forgot the bottle back there.

"There's more where that came from," he said.

Ultimately, the only thing to do was to sink down Florida like a smooth stone skipped into the sea and enjoy the motion of it all. Billy drank a mug of tap water and ate a piece of white bread. He stood and blankly stared for a minute before declaring himself sober. He left the cottage. The doors were unlocked and most of his recently-acquired possessions were left behind—he only packed the rugs, the pot, and the backpack of clothes he'd brought with him. He got in the Van Halen van and *drove*.

Florida loved the van, but Billy could give two shits. Billy had tunnel vision rolling down the coastal highways and paid even the most relentless breasts no mind. He didn't look over at the dune buggies or the T-tops, the muscle cars or the hulking hoggs and their teardrop sidecars. Their honks all went unnoticed. He was blind and deaf with grief.

A day later he lied about his experience as a short-order cook in the city of Cocoa and was given forty bucks and told never to come back following a disastrous lunch rush. He next met with a man selling a schooner and expressed deep interest, but conceded that he didn't know how to operate the vessel. Billy was denied an opportunity to swim with the dolphins because he wore cutoffs.

"Cain't letchew in with that fringe there, sir," the keeper said.

"But you guys took my money."

The dolphin splashed in the tank.

"*I* didn't take your money, sir." The keeper looked to be about seventeen. "The sign up front spuh-sifickly says 'no cutoffs,' 'no denim,' 'no fringe,' and 'no refunds.'"

"Do you have some loaner trunks or something?" Billy asked.

The dolphin popped out of the water and cackled.

Hoping to catch some winks, Billy parked the van in a lot outside a public beach in Melbourne but then he thought of the many episodes of *Cops* he'd seen where scraggly types not unlike himself got into trouble sleeping where they shouldn't. The maglights shining in his face. The easy questions he'd answer with outrageous, easy-to-disprove lies. There was a giant bag of drugs in the van that even *he* couldn't locate with certainty. (Last he saw it, it was under that pillow case back there, but ever since he made that U-turn at Cape Canaveral, the drugs had rolled out of sight.) Billy knew it was wisest to continue moving, lest his problems catch up with him.

He stayed the night at the Space Shuttle Inn and won $100 randomly betting on jai-alai at the adjoining Lift-Off Lounge.

Finding a new hotel hidey-hole every night got old quick. Two days of driving along the furthest strip of the state had obliquely led him south. The words "Key West" had been a last-ditch listed on the road signs for many miles. If nothing else looked good, that was the end of the line. And suddenly he was there. What those words signified, he did not know. Keys opened things. West was where the sun set. Key could also mean important. The West was a wild place.

Billy found a spot to park the van and sleep his first night in town. He tore a tiny strip of paper off the bottom of a photocopy tacked up to the corkboard at the front of a liquor store and called Kevin. He never met Kevin in person but ended up moving into his old room later that afternoon.

"I'll try'n' let Faye know to expect you when she gets off work."

"Great," Billy said. "How do I get in?"

"There's a spare key in the abalone shell out front," Kevin replied.

Sometime between midnight and sunrise Billy woke up. He thought someone was trying to strangle him. It took a second to understand that a woman was trying to put a Jell-O shot into his mouth. Once he grasped this, Billy began to struggle in protest. It was much like when an owner tries to force medicine on a pet.

"What the fuck," he spat. "Faye." He rolled over onto his stomach. "Why?"

The past nine months had turned into a real sit-
uational comedy down in Key West. Suffice to say it
was not the soaring seascape that gave poets ideas of
order. Beneath the surface, life there was not even as
up-tempo and major-keyed as a Jimmy Buffett tune.

"Jesus," he said, turning on his side. The lights
came on. Billy squinted and wiped jiggling red debris off his mouth. He looked around his bed. Jell-O
was everywhere, instantaneously staining the thin
white blanket covering him. "Turn those off... I
thought I locked that door."

"It *was* locked!" Faye giggled as she flipped the
switch back down.

What happened to Billy leading up to this particular episode was entirely predictable and mostly
inconsequential. He stopped feeling like his heart
was ripped out after five or six days in the Keys, but
decided that the healing process need not preclude
having a good time. He planned on preserving the
momentum of his shenanigans in the Van Halen van
(which he sold to a cover band, signing *D. Nguyen*
on the title papers). His day-to-day became a sordid
spin-off of that one-week adventure. Billy went into
character. He told himself (and sometimes others)
that he was on the run. He often introduced himself
as George Billy. If anyone asked about his past, he
was sure to remark that "some things happened in
Philly." He began wearing sunglasses everywhere, all
the time.

But his was far from a life of low-grade intrigue
and excitement. He developed a summer-break sleep
cycle and woke up each day around 1. He quit an-

swering phone calls from his friends. He quit checking messages. He got involved with one of Faye's
friends but he hardly felt like a playboy when Dr.
Fernandez swabbed his urethra at the walk-in clinic.
He was clean (relatively), lesson learned. The pain-
ful sensation he experienced during urination was
probably related to what the pale doctor flatteringly
described as "other questionable lifestyle choices."
He ordered rare T-bones to-go from the Hard Rock
Cafe; there was no cutlery at home so he took to eating them with his hands. Billy got a gut drinking
the good stuff that summer. He shit his shorts at the
beach after too much the night before and before that
and before that.

All of which led to the cherry Jell-O shot being
plunged into Billy's unsuspecting gullet late one night.

"How'd you get the door unlocked?" Billy
asked. He pivoted onto his side and saw Garcia
backlit in the doorway with a screwdriver. He raised
his glass of clear rum, silently offering Billy a cheers.

Garcia considered himself Faye's boyfriend. He
had little self-esteem and a receding hairline but
also wore a thin platinum chain and drove a newer
Dodge Charger. He still owed the bank a good deal
on the car—more than it was ever worth.

"Faye, I need to get some sleep. I'm really tired."

"Fuck that! Key West, baby! Woo! Woo!"

Faye put the plastic pill cup of boozy desert between her smashed together breasts and bent down
to Billy's mouth.

"No, Faye, that's all right, I—"

She angled down acutely until his face was

smothered in her ample bosom. Billy acquiesced. He didn't want to get gelatin and vodka in his eyes. Swallowing it down, he was ashamed by the lewd sound it made being sucked up. Garcia sipped and narrowed his eyes.

"Let's put another round in the chamber, bay-bee," Faye said. She was wearing a pink tube top with spaghetti straps and a pair of skimpy heather gray gym shorts with the word 'SUGAR' glitteringly stamped on the back.

Garcia spoke softly to himself or wheezed gutturally, one couldn't tell. From the corner of his eye, Billy saw that he finished off his drink. Garcia remained in the doorway, adjusting his belt.

"C'mon Faye," Garcia whispered while she stuffed the Jell-O in her bust.

"What?" she snapped back at him. "You tired of seeing that?" She took the plastic ramekin out from its nesting place and suggestively lowered it down towards her crotch. "You wanna see him take a shot down here?"

"Okay Faye," Billy groaned, "really now. That's a bit much, even for you."

Faye hopped off Billy and began bouncing on his mattress. "C'mon *you!* Get up, Billy! Wake. Up." She pulled the pillow off from over his face. "You can sleep when you're dead, tired-y pants!" Garcia turned the light on in the room but then went out for a smoke. Faye toppled over onto the bed. "I'm bored, c'mon." She stretched her leg to the switch and turned the lights out with her brightly-painted toe. Faye bit Billy's ear lobe.

He swatted her away.

"Can I please rest, please?" He rolled over and put his face into the pillow. "I promise we'll have fun tomorrow, I promise," he muffled.

Tired from the Jell-O incident, Billy still managed to wake up and leave before his roommate stirred. He left early for a drug store and bought a child's red plastic pail-and-shovel combo-set, a pack of Pall Mall unfiltereds, and a lighter with a generic stockcar on it. He went to the beach and chain-smoked a pack of harsh cigarettes while making a sandcastle that turned out to be more of a decaying medieval fortress. He took a picture with the last shot left from a disposable camera he'd bought in Texas and dropped it back off at the drug store's photo department.

Billy wandered from bar to bar, drinking drinks with tiny umbrellas before settling on a karaoke place where he sang long and rambling numbers. Some had vengeful sentiments and others were a bit more conciliatory. None of them were crowd-pleasers, but it was just him, the bartender, and the person running the karaoke machine. Everybody had a five in a hurricane glass next to them.

Time flew by to the tune of ninety minutes later and Billy went back to the drug store and picked up his photos.

He took the photos home and was about to study them in the living room when he felt and heard his stomach growl. It was a low-register frequency accompanied by a sound that a large, sick animal might employ to scare off eager buzzards. Billy wandered through the aisles of a nearby strip-mall convenience store looking for a cure-all. While the cashier, an Indian man with a neatly-trimmed beard, rang up his orange sports drink and miniature chocolate-frosted donuts, an out-of-control motorcycle burst through the large front window of the store, missing Billy by at most two feet. Glass was everywhere like shining blue grout between bags of knocked-over chips and still-capped two liter bottles full of bubbling soda. An alarm was ringing. A wire rack of maps fell off the counter and made a hollow clang. The motorcycle lay on its side near a refrigerated case of $7 milk, leaving behind it a clear path amid the junk food melee. The bike was a big, heavy Goldwing with built-in saddlebags and a small American flag still poking out of the rear. The back wheel continued spinning slowly and the driver, an older man not wearing a helmet, looked quite dead and bloody beside a knocked-over ATM. Twenties spilled out all around the lifeless body.

Billy checked to make sure that the cashier was okay and the two of them waited around for the cops. Somehow sirens were already approaching in the distance, though nobody had called. The Indian tried in vain to keep spectators at a distance from his blown-out storefront while Billy, in mild shock, held court in the parking lot and explained to inquisitive onlookers what little he knew about what just happened. Strangers urged both of them to sit down and more than a few offered their cigarettes.

After paramedics gurneyed the body out of the store, a wide-brimmed state trooper took down Billy's account of the incident.

"Jesus Christ, son, you don't even look scratched. You feel alright?"

"Yeah, I'm a little freaked out, but I'm okay. Everything missed me."

"You otta feel like one lucky son-of-a-gun."

"Uh-huh," Billy nervously laughed.

Once the paramedics shined a small flashlight into Billy's eyes and declared him "fine" and free to leave the scene, he walked over to Dampy, the store owner, and tried to pay for his drink and donuts (which he was still holding onto with his sweaty hands). Dampy was speaking frantically into his cellphone in his native tongue with words like "motorcycle" and "ambulance" popping in from time to time.

"Mebbe he have heart-attack," Dampy said to Billy right when he ended his conversation. "Mebbe he drunk." He looked fatigued. "I dunno … whaddaday." Dampy noticed the orange bottle. "No, go ahead, take, take," he said. "I cannot deal with dis right now. In-shurance will cubber dat."

Hundreds of sea birds circled the piers while tourists posed for pictures next to lacquered marlins. An old blues man chugged away at the same progression in E, killing time and wearing his thick pick down to a nub. Billy sat sequestered on a wood bench in front of a defunct ice cream parlor. He blended in seamlessly with the signs offering new flavors and two-scoops-for-the-price-of-one. He re-evaluated the parable of the Soviet candy bar that Larry had told him. His eyes followed a solitary sail-boat across the sparkling sea's horizon. The far-off tri-angle got smaller and smaller until he lost sight of it.

"Go on, little ship," Billy murmured.

Before he stolidly perched on the edge of America, Billy left the scene of the motorcycle crash and went into a nearby public library. He signed a clipboard for thirty minutes of computer access and read 100 haikus until his turn came around. Billy logged on and compared the price of various one-way tickets to Costa Rica. Then Guatemala. He looked into the exchange rate on the Quetzal and then found a deal on flights to Managua. He read reviews of Nicaragua. Billy visited the U.S. State Department travel website and wrote down an ab-breviated checklist for obtaining a passport using a stubby golf pencil. Someone tapped his shoulder before he got to step three.

"Hey. I got compooter seeks." The man was pale with a pencil-thin mustache and a fresh high-and-tight.

Billy observed the man for a moment, nodded, and motioned to finish his list. "Okay, I—"

"Hey." The man grabbed Billy's shoulder. He squeezed. "Eez two fit-teen. Eez *my* time." Just be-neath his words and squeezing: rage. Despite his neatly manicured hair, he had an unsavory air about him. "Dare's rules, main. Dare's a order," he said coldly.

And so Billy left the library and came to the pier.

A man selling shaved ice passed by him, ringing a string of jingle bells and pushing his festive three-wheeled cart around with all the enjoyment of a pack animal. Billy unfolded the slip of paper he'd written on. The soft lead had already smudged and faded. He didn't really want to spend another six to eight weeks here waiting for a passport. He didn't want his photograph taken. Cloud shadows slid over the placid waters and made silver-green shapes over the aquamarine. Billy itched like a snake ready to shed its skin.

Faye's Jeep Cherokee was not in the driveway, so Billy went inside. He fetched his laptop from the top of the closet where he hid it when not at home. He pulled the machine out of the lilac pillowcase that had been part of a $300 sheet set he'd ruined while eating Chinese food in bed. He bought specialized oxy-powered powders and tough-on-stains sprays. The mythic General Tso had crafted a stubborn and cochineal sauce, however, and Billy not-too-regretfully threw the sheets away save one pillowcase.

The laptop issued an explosion of light and, two seconds later, a majestic burst of sound like long, banderoled trumpets heralding the king's arrival. Billy sat cross-legged on the carpet and waited for his background and icons came up. He patiently watched as the wireless device was being searched for. This always took longer than he could stand. Once the four bars beside the time and date quit flashing and stayed solid green, Billy went online and found a cheap one-way to San Juan. Before he bought it, he checked on his checking account for the first time in a long time. And after laying down on his unmade bed for a while, he went back to the computer and began booking a bus ride to Philadelphia.

15

In his farewell to Florida, Billy had an enormous yard sale. Most of what he got rid of he did not remember buying. In a way, it felt like breaking even... although he knew *that* was hardly true. Plenty of what he sold was from Europe and, therefore, expensive: a Belgian waffle-maker *from* Belgium; Italian jet cufflinks in a matching sable box; an unused straight razor and boar's hair bristle shave brush hand-crafted in Great Britain (not England— *Great Britain*). Few people in the Conch Republic wanted such clean, sleek things—even at discounts steep by yard sale standards. Perusers wanted velvet Elvises and coconut statuary. The first thing he sold was the rainstick. But even unreasonable offers were not refused. The patch of sand and crab grass in front of Faye Darlin's place was a buyer's market.

The coup of the day occurred when a magistrate of the local court bought a pair of Oriental rugs for $60.

"Nice rugs. They'll look pretty durn good in the cabin of my catamaran," he said after getting Billy to go lower than the $50 each he had been asking. "I'll have to crop 'em down to fit, of course."

Having $400 pocket money was a good enough thing; but cramming the heretofore messy life he'd made for himself into a single bag was nothing short of a great unfettering. Billy stowed his belongings below, in an elongated luggage catacomb between the bus's wheel wells. He took his seat and took two of the going-away pills Faye had presented him with.

"For the road," she'd said a little sadly last night.

"Down the hatch," Billy said in his seat.

He put his head against the window. Florida was a sunny place. He'd miss all that warmth and leisure. Then the pills hit. Billy began a thirty-eight-hour-and-ten-minute-long dream. Initially, the dream was nice. Blues and greens whipped by kaleidoscopically and Billy was blanketed in sunbeams. The bus stopped and, even though his legs had turned into two long gummy worms, Billy got up and transferred in Miami. This bus was supposed to take him to Richmond.

Richmond also turned out to be the Vietnam vet that Billy sat next to on the new bus. He had skin with the color and texture of a spaghetti squash. The whites of his eyes were on the yolky side, too. His hands were busy and expressive, with blocky fingers and thick nails. His face was swathed with the dark stubble of a hobo clown and his hair was stringy and yellow-grey like that around the muzzle of a shaggy sheepdog. Richmond was tired of Miami and its bullshit. He was going to give the VA hospital in Baltimore a shot.

"An' after *that*," he said with a twinkle in his eye, "I'm goin' straight to Sturgis."

He talked and talked to Billy, who kept his right ear against the glass and his eyes on Richmond.

"Ya-know-what-I'm-sayin when I say Miami is bullshit, now don'tcha?" he asked.

Billy tried to speak but he was having one of

those dreams where you are voiceless. He blinked his left eye at Richmond.

"I'm sayin' Miami is bullshit 'cuz the whole place is fulla shit. The VA: bullshit. The car wash: bullshit. Hell, the rodeo there: it's bullshit." Richmond fruitlessly tried to hack up something from the back of his throat like a cat stuck with a hairball. "The only thing they got goin' is goddamn, goddamn, ol' what's his nuts—Dan Marino." Richmond fell into deep contemplation for a minute. "An' Marino, he was too bullshit to winna ring," he concluded before being wracked with another tussive flurry.

Richmond fell asleep and Billy dryly swallowed two more pills. They slowly dissolved in the back of his throat. The taste in his mouth was awful until he passed out and stopped tasting. During the next long, indiscernible period of time, Billy did not dream. When he finally came to, his vial of pills was gone and Richmond had been changed into a scraggly hag with an empty birdcage on her lap. Some kind of hex had made Richmond into an old witch.

So it was no longer a dream, then: it was a nightmare.

Billy shut his eyes tight and wished it all away.

The bus driver poked Billy in the ribs with an eighteen-inch carbon rod. He purchased the tool for just such an occasion and liked to use it liberally whenever he could.

"Alright, bud. Wakey wakey. Philly-delphia. Your stop. Time to go."

Billy held his side and rolled over. His eyelids were stitched together with a sticky mucous. He sneezed.

"Okay," the bus driver said disgusted. "Come on. That's enough out of you." He prodded Billy for good measure. "Gitcher ass in gear, gitcher bag, and git the hell offa my bus, bummy."

It was February in Philadelphia.

Standing in front of a line of people waiting to board the bus he'd just exited, Billy rummaged through his bag. Of course he didn't have a sweater. He'd just left Florida. He was still wearing boat shoes and no socks.

With a beach towel wrapped around each exposed arm, Billy tried to speed-walk to any store that sold clothes. But the city was covered with a gray, wintery slime. The sidewalks were slick. His slip-ons had no traction to speak of and his feet (despite the cold of his exposed ankles) felt like baked potatoes wrapped tight in foil. So he took short, choppy steps, slipping occasionally but never quite falling down.

A coffee shop came into focus before any clothing store and Billy went inside. Coffee was always there for you when you needed help. He pushed the door open and felt as if he'd interrupted a dozen serious conversations. In one corner a couple seemed to be breaking up while at another table a first date *had* been going well until he burst in and stunk the place up. Everyone else had been conducting very important business on laptops prior to Billy's intrusion. They all stared and turned their heads deliberately as he approached the counter.

The barista had on clothes like a jawbreaker's layers of colorful sugar. He had a black dress shirt and a loosely-Windsored white tie. Over that was a small red tee he wore like a tight-fitting smock. His oxford's cuffs were rolled up to his elbows, but his forearms were not exposed and instead further covered with a futuristic white thermal undershirt. Accessory-wise, he wore a black straw fedora, multiple bracelets and bangles, a pair of studded belts, and had a septum piercing that dangled like a silver door knocker. He looked at shivering Billy like he was scoping out a carnival freak (although, in his defense, the man nearing the counter had arms swaddled in beach towels).

"Cold enough?" Billy asked jocularly.

The barista shrugged.

"I just got off the bus from Florida, in case ya couldn't tell."

He cast his eyes away from the tedious weirdo and wiped off the espresso maker.

"Can I get a coffee?"

It was standing room only in the cafe, so Billy loitered near the tub full of saucers and mugs waiting to be bussed. He sipped coffee and picked the goo from the corners of his eyes. Nobody was leaving. He coughed loudly and hoarsely into his hand hoping for some pathos or, failing that, a germophobe. Nary an eye was raised (much less a laptop closed).

Management here probably had a far-reaching and well-worded policy, so Billy slipped on some socks in record time. He was surprised by this show of speed and cunning. He must not have been feeling those pills anymore, though he *was* feeling like he'd been painfully contorted for an extended period of time that he could not account for. He smacked his gums and tried to brush the film off his teeth with his fingertip.

Just then, the entrance opened and a frigid blast socked Billy squarely in the chest. It actually made his teeth chatter. This didn't just happen in cartoons, apparently. He moved a few feet to the left, closer to the garbage can, but he was still in the line of fire: a cold gush of air got him every time the door was opened. The hot coffee and the cold air expedited his re-acclamation, though. Billy recognized City Hall when he left the cafe.

Billy meandered through Center City and towards the bronze beacon of William Penn. The skyscrapers made long shadows where ice could not melt. They funneled and concentrated chilly winds into arctic jet streams. The smell of hot dogs and exhaust mingled with the solidified gutter juices he passed. Soon Billy crossed a street vendor selling magazines, lottery tickets, phone cases, sunglasses, and hooded sweatshirts. He bought two identical size 'L' hoodies that were red with a white outline of the iconic 'LOVE' statue only a few blocks away.

"Are you sure these are large?" Billy asked the hawker.

"Check the tag, man. What's it look like it says?" The salesman did not care for this customer's neediness. "Actin' like I don't know how to read or somethin'," he said under his breath.

Billy inspected the tag.

"Do you have any mediums?"

But he had already taken the sweater out of the plastic wrap. Billy tried to fold it back into its original shape and packaging but gave up. He'd basically bought it. "Sizes these days, you know … people are just getting bigger, I guess."

The merchant was himself a large man and wanted to know Billy meant by that.

"You want anything else?" he asked after his customer said nothing in response to his question.

"A soft pretzel and a Powerball ticket," Billy said.

"Thirty-six dollars," the man muttered while the ticket noisily printed out behind him.

Billy folded up his beach towels and left them in a bus stop shelter. Now swimming in his two layers of local color, Billy blended right in. He tried to move with purpose, but his shoulders ached mightily from the bus ride and the barely-padded straps that cut right into his tender deltoids did little to help matters. Viscous, pellucid ooze meanwhile trickled steadily out of his nasal passages. Billy snorted and blew hot breath on his hands, balled up into puny fists inside his flowing sleeves. He was sick, tired, and cold. He kept his eyes on the ground and took painstakingly short steps whenever the pavement appeared darkly-glazed. He looked up when he reached intersections and waited for the white man to signal that it was safe to cross.

City Hall was a towering optical illusion. It was not as close by as it appeared. The path that led to it was not straight—many sidewalks were under construction and closed to pedestrian traffic, people ahead of him moved slowly and unpredictably. When he reached Suburban Station, Billy was plainly freezing his ass off. The last thing he saw before descending was a caramel-colored middle-aged woman with a spiky sea-foam green visor and matching toga. She had on opaque shades and a radiant smile. She picked and strummed air-guitar on a torch-shaped sign that said 'LET FREEDOM RING TAX SVC., LLC.—JUST ASK ME!'

"Hey," a man in a black velour track suit said, approaching her, "they still giving out cash for clunkers?"

"Yeah, baby!" Lady Liberty replied energetically, "all kinds uh cash gettin' *handed* out!"

"Damn, ainchu cold, though?" the man asked.

"Hell yeah," she said. "Ainchu? Where's *your* coat?"

"Help get me that refund—then we can talk new coat."

Billy went down into City Hall Station. He purchased tokens from a machine and passed through a turnstile. His pockets jangled with loose change. Heading down the steps, the temperature dropped further. The air smelled like ammoniac with touches of axle grease. The ground was streaked with brown muck. Yellow cautionary signs stood sorrily in the middle of scattered puddles. One was flattened out and hidden underneath a turbid pool. Forty-gallon plastic trash bins overflowed with meltwater that leaked through 15th Street. In between the screeching trolleys, the trickle of water resounded. Water passed through the ceiling above in steady streams and down into great buckets below. The platform sounded like a lively men's room. The station was like William Penn's chamber pot.

The wait was not long and the El pulled up in front of Billy.

"Market-Frankford Train to Frankford Transportation Center—all stops," a cordial voice announced. "Doors are opening," it said, though only one door opened.

A woman at the helm of a stroller stood shielded behind the closed partition. The train was packed tight and nobody got off. Billy took a deep breath, knowing that his bulging backpack was going to make him wildly unpopular. He stepped in and was right away punched in the nose by a tangy scent.

"You know me!" a woman's voice clamored while he looked for a piece of railing to hold on to. "Some of you have seen me before!" Riders grumbled. "Hey! Look at me! Hey!" she cried. She waited until she had everyone's attention. "I do not look like you! I do not look like any of you! I am not *of* this place."

"Doors are closing," the polite voice said over the intercom.

Billy couldn't yet see the source of the commotion, but, based on her sound, she too was packed in the aisle with little room to move.

"I have been sent here to warn you!"

"Shut the fuck up," an unseen voice at the front of the car said matter-of-factly. "It's too crowded for your crazy ass."

"No!" she countered. "How dare you doubt the Lord!"

"Doors are closing," the voice repeated.

"Some of you doubt. And you may laugh, some of you. And you will know that I am not a joke! Soon enough! Can't you see?! *I do not look like you!*"

"Quit holdin' tha doors…dumbasses," the worn-out voice of the conductor said over the intercom.

The train lurched forward and Billy finally had a small zone to call his own. He grasped a bar and planted his feet on the rubberized floor. He pulled his outer hood over his head. Now he felt hot: the heat blazing on the train, the bodies huddled and jostling close together, the summery perfume of perspiration. It was all strangely welcome after the cold he'd waded through.

"Have you ever seen anyone that looks like me?" the woman proselytizing pleaded. "Have you?!"

Billy could now see her. She wore an enormous Syracuse Orangemen jacket and was light-skinned enough that her acne seemed to glow like embers on her angry face. Her features were pinched towards the middle. She had beady eyes. Her hair was buzzed short and dyed platinum blonde. Small, BB-sized piercings stuck into the dimples of her cheeks. In short, she did not look like anyone Billy had personally seen before, in real-life or in various media.

Next to the manic sermonizer, a gangly teenager with a snapback and headphones munched on hot chips with a nonchalant, barely awake look. He mouthed the words to his song in-between chews.

"I do not look like you because I am not *of* this world! I am God and I have been sent here to warn you!" she announced.

"Thirteenth street station," the polite voice said.

Two older Chinese women carrying their groceries boarded the train. Like Billy, they were wearing boat shoes with white tube socks. They stopped their conversation for a moment to take note of the howling nearby then went right back to speaking in their rubbery diphthongs once they found a niche for themselves. One of them took a small cabbage out of her bag and handed it to the other.

"I am trying to help you all—with a warning!" the woman bawled, "a warning to *get it together!*"

Next to the stroller, Dad talked to Mom under his breath. "You know," he said, "this lady's really starting to get me upset."

"Yeah," Mom agreed, "the bitch's crazy and needs to shut up. Scarin' our baby with her freaky Jesus talk." She smiled warmly at the stroller. "Aren't you scared of the crazy lady?" she cooed to her small, still-wrinkly baby, "ain't you confused by all her nonsense?"

The baby happily wriggled around in the stroller.

"That just ain't the way you spread the gospel, dang it," Dad said. He was clean-cut with a fresh fade. He was either flushed with pent-up anger or blushing after tagging on that 'dang it.' He pushed his small reading glasses up to the bridge of his nose. "You know what she is, Pamela? She's a *false prophet* is what she is."

Mom had a decidedly less grandiloquent take on things.

The oration, meanwhile, was as fiery as ever. A debate had sprung up between lector and passenger.

"You need to chill your dirty self out," said the woman sitting in the flip-down handicap-accessible seat. She was checking herself in her phone, patting the side of her hair down and puckering her glossy lips. "You all hype and shit."

"I am God sent here to warn you that the end is near!" the unworldly woman screamed with great passion. "And it is nearer than you think! And you'll know when it comes, too—"

"See, thaz what I mean: you all hype over some shit nobody wanna hear about." She remained seated with attention fixed on her phone.

"Next stop: 8th street station," the polite voice said, "Broad Ridge Spur ... Patco High Speed Line." Whatever it said next was drowned out by the sounds of the train. Before the recording finished, the El slowed to a halt. The door opened. "8th street station." A stout, grandfatherly man shuffled on and tried to make sense of things. He was befuddled. Where was he to stand? What's going on in here?

"Those of you that laugh: that's fine. We'll see who's laughing when it all goes down like I said it will! It'll be no laughing matter then! And still, you know me!," she began anew, "I do not look anything like you!"

The old man leaned over to Billy. "I'm getting' off at 5th Street—and a good thing, too," he added chummily.

Dad, meanwhile, had worked himself up and was issuing rejoinders for every point hollered on the other side of the train. "She's *not* Jesus," he said loud enough for the circle of riders immediately surrounding him to hear. "She's not Jesus, everybody." He reassured those listening: "If she *was* Jesus, we'd all be in heaven. The train would be up in heaven," he pointed at the roof of the train, "if what she said was true. Jesus won't come down *here* and take us *up*. It says so in the Bible. What she's saying doesn't make sense."

His wife rolled her eyes. The baby liked that. Mom leaned in towards her baby and made an even sillier face that delighted the infant.

"Fifth Street Station."

Grandpa got off the train offering plenty of good-humored guffaws and "'scuse me"s and offering his empathetic smile to those that cared to notice. Gramps was replaced by an affectionate couple of ruddy Irish stock (a shamrock tattoo on her dimple-knuckled hand confirming this). They felt each other up over their loose-fitting garments and frenched until the missus pulled her head back, revolted.

"Smells like a fuckin' *foot* up in here," she said.

He sniffed.

"Yeah, it does." He kissed her on the nose. "Yo, somebody take their shoe off or somethin'?" he queried loudly, clearly unaware of the situation he'd stepped into.

No one said anything about taking their shoe off. Everybody was more or less focused on the woman still fervently exhorting the train to prepare for endtimes.

"I've been sent here to tell you that you all treat each other *so bad*," she asserted with very real pain in her voice. "You all don't *take care* of one another like you should! I been sent here—"

"Shut the fuck up!" a voice implored.

"You're not Jesus!" Dad feebly shouted, pushing his glasses back up.

"Yes I am!" the woman screeched back. "I am *higher* than you will ever know or realize!"

Billy waited, stunned that nobody on board was making use of such juicy, tantalizing fodder. It was right there on a tee.

"Second Street Station," the polite voice said over the intercom.

A few sharp-dressed folks stepped off and no one got on. A man running full-speed in hopes of squeezing in slammed his shoulder into the door of the El like a hockey player checked into the glass. He yelled something at the train as it lurched forward.

Billy had some elbow room, but the car was still quite full as the whistle blew. They resurfaced from underground. Billy looked longingly at the traffic on the interstate and nearly slipped on an empty Arizona Ice Tea bottle that had rolled underneath him. He caught his balance and clutched the bar in front of him.

"I am Jesus, okay?! Just look at me! I—"

"Jesus didn't smell like a *foot*, lady," the Irish guy interrupted. Commuters laughed heartily. His lady-friend got on her socks-and-slides tip-toes and kissed him on the cheek.

"You mock me?! You mock the Lord?! Just as they did before, Father!" she raised one hand high and screamed at the top of the El.

"That settles it," Dad said. He had half a bottle of water in his hand.

"Where you goin', Jerome?" Mom asked, shaking her head in disbelief.

Jerome made his way past two girls in Catholic school jumpers as the train pulled into Spring Garden. "If you *are* God," he said in a stage voice, "then turn this into wine."

The ranting woman was seated now. All Billy could see over the crowd was the crown of peroxided hair. She looked towards Jerome and couldn't say anything fast enough.

"There you go," said the lady in the handicap-accessible seat. "There you go, okay, see? Man just *proved* you wasn't God, so go on 'head and shut it up."

People clapped at the shrewd trap. Jerome bumped the ball and the lady in the handicap-accessible seat spiked it.

Jerome waited for the huzzah to die down. "You cannot turn this water into wine, because only Jesus himself can do that! And you are not Jesus; you are a *false prophet.*"

"No!" the woman yelled back, "No! Don't you know that thou aren't supposed to tempt the Lord?!" She shook her head. "Thou shalt not tempt the Lord with alcohol," she said halfheartedly.

Jerome ignored her.

"No, you're talkin', you're talkin' …" the word was there on the tip of his tongue. Billy watched him deliberate. "You're talkin' *bullcrap* is what you're talkin.' You're sittin' here bullcrappin' everybody."

"*Bullcrappin*?" someone echoed mockingly.

"That's not how you talk about Jesus!" Jerome yelled. "*This* is how you testify."

"Preach!" a voice sarcastically yelled.

Jerome turned around and pulled out a receipt from his back pocket. He handed it to one of the schoolgirls filming things on her phone. "'Here you go, madam,'" he said with an enunciated, Sidney Poitier timbre, "'my name is Jerome Edwards and I want to share some information with you about our Lord and Savior, Jesus Christ. I thank you for your time, have a blessed day.' You see?" He looked around the car for support. "No, see, Jesus won't come down *here* to Earth! For we are *dirt*! … And he is *spirit*." A novel argument came into his mind. "I could kill you because *you're not Jesus*." People got quiet. "I mean, I don't *want* to kill you; I'm just sayin' that you can't *kill* Jesus because he is invincible and you are a person whose life *could* be taken, you see?"

The woman had completely stopped her preaching and sat still in her seat.

"Girard Station," the voice said over the intercom. A group of young men and women got off the train, an amoebic mass of pea coats and skinny-jeaned flagellum. At the head of the pack, two dudes sported identical 'wait 'til I tell the gang about *this!*' expressions on their bemused faces. This story would earn them *beaucoup* cred.

Jerome shifted his weight and made like he

was going to go back to his family. The train was finally quiet. He paused and turned back towards the bleach-haired woman staring out the window at the snowy row homes and shuttered factories flying by.

"You're a *false prophet!*" he reasserted with a dramatic finger-point.

"A'ight, yo," said a Puerto Rican guy in an Arctic Explorer coat. "You won, man. She quiet. Look. You won, thaz good."

Jerome stood and blinked. "Well, sir, I, uh, I respectfully apologize, sir." Jerome put a hand over his breast and then offered it out towards the front of the car. "I didn't mean to bother anybody with *my* testimony, I just—"

"You ain't gotta go an' *grind* on her like that," he said, admonishing Jerome, gesturing him back towards his spot on the train.

"He ain't *grindin'* nobody," Mom added as Dad worked his way back along the congested aisle. "Y'all should be thankful he stepped up like he did."

"Yeah, but she quiet now." The Puerto Rican man shrugged his shoulders and adjusted the fake coyote fur lining his hood. "I ain't got a prollem wit chu. All I'm sayin' is that she sittin' there quiet an' shit, *you* got to say your piece, so let's jus' leave it at that."

"Damn, Papi," said the woman on the handicap-accessible seat, "you ain't gotta be shoutin' all loud right over my head."

The train decelerated and rumbled noisily. Billy barely heard the intercom announce "Berks Station." Mom was offering her two cents to the woman on the handicap-accessible seat. Billy narrowly got out the single opening door.

The loft was empty and in the same loose order as Billy remembered it. A few new bikes hung from the A-frame. It was damp, cold, unlit, and quiet inside. Not a creature stirred. Walking in felt eerie, like creeping into a hermit's cave. Even after the lights flickered on, the enormous room remained clammy and still.

Billy went to put his bag in his room. He swung the door open and was surprised to find that all of his things had all been replaced. Even his resourceful garbage furniture was gone. The space was thoroughly Ikea'd.

He called Kurt and got no response. Julian did not pick up his phone. Those were the only two numbers he had of the six people he'd been living with. Billy sat on the couch that had, improbably, not yet disintegrated. He waited. He did two circuits of local television. Nothing on was good enough to kill his time. He threw caution to the wind and took a piss with the bathroom door wide open. He emptied the clothes in his bag and started a load of laundry. While the agitator churned in the background, Billy went over to the large window and watched the Ben Franklin Bridge. It was dusky and the Delaware rolled dark and glimmering like obsidian. Along the blue span red lights headed in one direction and white ones in another.

Billy got his computer and returned to the

couch. The password for the internet wasn't one of those cute, irreverent words you'd easily remember; it was a long string of letters and numbers that someone years ago had written and taped to the bottom of the router. Billy went into the kitchen. His shoes squeaked on the floor. He left mucky foot prints all wherever he'd been walking.

"Whoops," he said.

The fifth pen selected from the utility drawer had trace amounts of ink in it. Billy scrawled the password down on a Mexican take-out menu. His paper blotted up some of the moisture on the countertop. He wiped the menu against his pant leg and snooped around the kitchen some. Billy looked at the electric bill posting. He didn't see his name, naturally—but didn't see Kurt's or Julian's, either.

Keys stirred at the entrance. Billy felt his heart race. He heard the door swing open and listened to footsteps clomp closer and closer. He took a deep breath and watched Zeke, the building maintenance man, round the corner. He was loose-jointed and relaxed as ever. His eyelids drooped and he whistled an indolent three-note tune.

"Hey, Zeke," Billy said.

"Oh, Christ-a-mighty," Zeke said, startled. "What in the hell you doin' here?"

Billy smiled. He'd forgotten Zeke. He almost missed the folksy banter they shared—Zeke high up on a ladder patching up the rafters, Billy slouched and high on the couch. *How's the weather up there, Zeke? Say, what you got on the teevee down there, main man?*...

"I *just* got back from Florida today. I was down there—"

"Yah, 'sterminator said nobody should be in here fo' *four* hours while the bug bomb does its work." Zeke looked at his wristwatch. "Tol' me that at a quater-ta-four an' it's five to six now." He covered his mouth with his hand. "That's why you don' see them roaches all scattered dead everywhere yet. Means you prolly shouldn't be in here yet, neither." The washing machine buzzed and signaled that the load was finished. "You need to get somethin' uh yours go on and do it now," he muffled. "This en-viruhment ain't safe jes' yet."

Billy slid his foot over the wet kitchen linoleum. It made a long dirty streak. He filled his bag with wet clothes and fetched his computer. He walked out into the hall. Zeke came out behind him seconds later.

"Forgot my crescent wrench in there earlier today," he said, "otherwise, I wouldn't-a come in there." He shut the door and locked the dead bolt.

"I've been away," Billy explained. "I didn't know they were spraying the place again." He coughed.

Zeke checked his watch once more. "Yah, I'd say you're safe to go back 'round … 7:30 or so." He stopped at the door to 602 and took out his massive dungeon master's key ring. "8 o'clock'd be on the safe side."

"Okay. Good seeing ya, Zeke," Billy said, "glad you turned up and got me out of there."

He nodded without looking up and continued flipping through keys.

Billy waited alone at a booth at the Sidecar. He grabbed yesterday's *Inquirer* off a table near him and stuffed it into his bag, hoping that it might absorb some of his clothes' moisture. The paper crinkled loudly. The bar was quiet. It was the sedate period of outside dusk when barflies jawed with blue collar guys just sipping away the fleeting hour between work and home. Billy savored the first cheap domestic he'd had in many months. It tasted terrible and familiar.

Hector offered him a shot when he'd ordered it, on the house.

"Hadn't seen you in a while," he said. "And I already started pouring it."

Billy was honestly touched by the gesture. He reneged on his vow to abstain from hard liquor for a while and raised his tiny glass to Hector.

Biding time from his booth, Billy took the beer down slow. Kurt texted him that he was on his way from dance rehearsal. Billy had many questions to ask and had months of his own life to account for, but now all he could wonder was *when did Kurt start rehearsing dance?*

Though he'd always condemned 'that guy,' Billy found himself alone at the bar with his computer open. These were exceptional times, though, and circumstances extenuated themselves in a big way. Billy needed to research side-effects of noxious fume inhalation. He maybe needed to find a lawyer that knew how to strike fear into a slum lord. Billy had business to oversee—sometimes real emails landed in his 'spam' folder.

Billy also had a job to search for. The tough part was: Billy didn't especially *feel* like having a job. The only work in the online classifieds that appealed to him were scams, postings with too many exclamation points and unrealistic pay promised for easy work from home. He copied down information for an up-and-coming travel magazine seeking experienced writers. The last line of the want-ad read "Loafers need not apply." Billy mulled about whether or not he loafed too much until his concentration was disrupted by laughter bursting in through the back patio. Billy narrowed his eyes towards the source.

Sandwiched between two like-dressed, chortling minion-types, Billy glared at the leader. He had the fullest beard of the three. His trucker cap was the only one that was actually old. His nose was aquiline and important. He had lily-fair skin. He spoke the loudest and he talked the most. Billy listened.

"And then she starts sayin' that she's *Jesus*, right? Like, she really believes she's Jesus and she's here to warn us about the apocalypse!"

He let his friends snigger at the absurdity of the scenario before going on.

"Meanwhile: train's *packed*... and this lady has straight-up *pooped* herself." He pinched his nostrils as his friends dissolved into hoots and howls of laughter. "I mean, she literally, *literally*, has pooped her pants." He took a drink while his friends wiped away their jolly tears. "And while she's screaming about how the world's gonna blow up and we're all gonna die, this huge, gigantic guy gets up and says, 'If you don't shut the fuck up, ho … I'm going to kill you.'"

The audience hushed. *Then what happened?* their four widened eyes begged.

"I mean, I didn't get to see how it played out, cuz, you know, the El pulled up to my stop right then, but even if it hadn't, I'dda *booked it*, yo."

That wasn't how it happened, Billy thought to himself with a snotty look on his face. He was outraged by the aggrandizement (though he acknowledged there was also the remote possibility that this guy had been on a different train and witnessed a similar episode). *And who's he think he is saying 'yo'?*

Billy stewed over the stranger misappropriating slang and getting the details all wrong and before long started to wonder if that wasn't what Billy George sounded like a few months ago, holding court at the bar and sharing exaggerated stories about the Academic Vision Institute and the things he witnessed traveling to and from work. He didn't get too far with this thought before Kurt sidled up to his periphery.

"Billy! Dude!" he greeted his friend.

"Kurt!" Billy exclaimed, getting up quickly and banging his knee against the table.

They hugged and patted one another's shoulders then stood back and sized each other up.

"You look good, man," Billy said.

"You look … different," Kurt said. "You really got a new, um, *style* since I saw you last."

"Yeah," Billy said, taking his outer hood off.

"Things got kinda cold in a hurry."

It wasn't quite the good, old days again when they sat together at the table. Billy's mind was elsewhere. He stayed quiet and let Kurt go get himself a beer. When Kurt returned to his seat, he was distant and not wanting to get down to brass tacks right away. They sat and each took two small drinks before speaking.

"So." Kurt had nothing to add.

"Yeah." Billy tilted his can back. "Pretty much."

"How was Florida?"

Billy shrugged. "You know."

"Uh-huh," Kurt said. "Well…"

"Waitasec, hold that thought," Billy said. He dug down into his backpack and produced a packet of photos. "Wanna see pictures from my trip?"

"Sure," Kurt said.

Billy took the glossy stack out of the envelope.

"I haven't had a chance to go through these yet, either." He flopped the first picture down like a blackjack dealer skimming a card off the top of the deck. "Texas," he said.

They looked through the pile together. The lighting in the Sidecar was perfectly dim. The sequence of images told Billy's story far better than he could. The photos jogged Billy's memory, gave him cause to laugh or wince or sigh.

"If you're ever in the middle of the Lone Star State, just mention that you know Butt Doyle." Billy lightly tapped the photo.

Kurt nodded solemnly. "Butt Doyle."

"It's a name that means something."

They peered at the chili parlor and at a sun-bleached sign advertising boot repairs. Billy described the events surrounding the dusty deserted rug. He had nothing at all to add to the snapshot of a scrappy three-legged dog taken somewhere between Texas and Mississippi.

"That's Faulkner's grave, though," he said as he laid the next picture down. "The grass was trampled and the headstone was littered with mini-bar whiskies."

Then came an abrupt turn, a sequence of strange and lingering shots.

"Lucy," Billy said.

"Oh, so *that's* Lucy," Kurt whispered.

The pictures were voyeuristic and erotically-tinged and liberated but still shy of even the softest-core. In one image she was wet and shiny in a black bathing suit, laying some cobia on the grill. Billy explained that they had watched from the shore when the fisherman caught it and he was glad to give no small amount of money for that particular fish. This picture took him back and it actually felt good. He could taste the fresh sea and feel that months-old sun warm him over again. He cocked his mouth to the side, pursed and holding back untold words that caromed through his mind.

The last photos got laid out on the table one at a time like the rest. Each of these had their own shameful vignette that Billy had consigned to oblivion. He gave Kurt all the details he could manage. Billy shook his head and carefully studied Faye raunchily posing. She was still out there, having a good time. And so was the rest of spread-eagled Key West that he'd captured with his disposable: open-topped Jeep Cherokees unbridled and daiquiris in tall, alien-shaped guzzlers.

Finally there was his sand castle.

"Woah, man," Kurt said with mild astonishment. "The last couple months have been a real, uh ... work of art for you."

"You can say that again, amigo." Billy finished his beer. "I think I'm done here, Kurt."

"You need another beer?" Kurt moved to get up.

"No, I mean *here*. This bar, the Loft. I think I need to settle somewhere and start doing my own thing in my own time, you dig?"

"Whew, well, then." Kurt sat back down. He picked up a coaster and tapped it against the tabletop. "I was worried you'd be upset, but ..." He dropped the coaster flat. "I'm glad you said that, 'cuz I kind of moved you out of 609 while you were away."

Billy blew his nose into a cocktail napkin.

"What does that mean?" he asked, glancing down into the napkin before folding it in half.

Kurt's eyes roamed the room. "Well, basically, the story goes that ..."

And for fifteen minutes Kurt relayed uninterrupted a convoluted and Byzantine account of the decline of 609. The lease was up for renewal at the start of the year and residents were notified in late October. Kurt gave a summary of its perplexing language, including the intricate calculation and ultimate cost of the security deposit. He detailed the lateral movements Loft denizens made that Autumn and into the Winter months. Billy's eyes turned misty when he heard of Julian's absconding. He scoffed at Dylan's decision to return to Vermont to fix up his family's cabin in the dead of winter. Jenna left for Europe claiming she'd gotten time-sensitive endowment money, but carelessly-posted photos online revealed her to be tagging along in a nanny capacity with an employer-family. But for every soul that left, three more interviewed to replace it. In the span of three months, turnover at the Loft was on par with Old Testament knowing and begetting as Kurt went over each of the strange new names and faces brought into the mix.

"Matt's still there, though?" Billy asked.

"Matt's still there." Kurt snickered before turning serious. "I know you sent, like, money to pay your rent for, like, a year and keep your stuff there, but…" he hunched his shoulders and made a pained face. "No sense in staying, like you said. Right, Billy? I mean, Matt being the only guy you still know there and all…"

"Yeah, definitely. Most definitely." He clanked his beer can down like an aluminum gavel. "So I'm homeless." Billy clicked his teeth. "I'm homeless in this crazy ol' city with $800 to my name."

"You know you can totally crash with me and Wendy until—"

"You're living with *Wendy*?" Billy asked.

"Yeah, man."

They high-fived.

Wendy was a catch. All the guys liked Wendy.

"Good for you, Kurt. You two got a dryer?"

"Oh yeah."

"Perfect."

"And I still have all the leftover money you sent for rent," Kurt said. "So I can totally reimburse you, like, tomorrow. And your stuff is stored at my studio, so—"

"How much money, exactly, *did* I send you?"

Kurt thought about it. "You sent three grand, I think, in December. So there's probably at least twenty-five, twenty-six hundred left."

Billy blew air out the side of his mouth. "Hell, you said three *thousand* dollars?"

Kurt nodded.

"Shoot, there's no telling where three grand'll take me now."

"That's the spirit," Kurt said encouragingly. He stood up. "C'mon. You deserve another drink. This one's on me, so don't even try 'n' fight it."

Billy smiled as his friend walked towards the bar. The television was on mute and the jukebox was jamming some Floyd. They were doing the lottery drawing on the television. Billy couldn't hear it, but he'd seen this enough times to know: the clean-cut man holding the microphone was going over the rules and regulations, encouraging viewers at home to play responsibly or call an 800 number if they or a loved one had a problem. Billy pulled out the ticket he bought from the street vendor and smoothed it against the table. He left it there, mesmerized by the whirling white orbs sucked up, one by one. They passed along a clear tube and eventually bumped into place.

Kurt put the beers down and picked up the ticket. He paid close attention as the host walked towards a second machine stocked with red balls.

After much rotation, the machine drew. A red ball marked '27' came to a stop all by itself.

"Alright, dude," Kurt said excitedly. "You got the Powerball!" He flipped the ticket over and sorted through the small print. "If you match the Powerball you get ... four bucks!"

"Well then," Billy said, sounding rather pleased with himself, "I suppose that means the next round's on me."

Some guys have all the luck.

Wintfred Huskey models his writing game after baseball pitcher Jamie Moyer, relying on cantankerousness and persistence over charisma and proficiency. His writing has appeared in the *Oxford American*, *The Rust Belt Rising Almanac*, and *The Asteroid Belt Almanac*. He lives in Philadelphia.

Thank you to the early supporters of this novel:

Erik Amos
Michael Arrigo
Shaun Baer
Adrianna Borgia
Dan Brewer
Lanae Caulfield
Brittany Cardwell
Mark Clendaniel
Kate Evasic
Debra Finnegan-Suler
Michael Frederick
Owen Gibbs
Lesley Gold
Douglas Gordon
Wes Huskey
David Ilem
Rosa Kozub
Tim Lambert
Kate Logan
Allegra Love
Rob Nichols
Daniel Slavin
Asia Suler
Brian Walter
James Weissinger
Daniel Werwath
Brandon Wirtz